PRAI

"Bowen is adept at writing mysteries filled with intriguing clues, satisfying solutions, expertly captured historical settings, and a little romance."
—*Library Journal* (starred review)

"Rhys Bowen is a gift to all who love great writing, rich and complex characters and a plot that grabs from first words."
—Louise Penny, #1 *New York Times* bestselling author of the Chief Inspector Gamache novels

"Thoroughly entertaining."
—*Publishers Weekly*

"A truly delightful read."
—*Kirkus Reviews*

"Keep[s] readers deeply involved until the end."
—*Portland Book Review*

"Entertainment mixed with intellectual intrigue and realistic setting[s] for which Bowen has earned awards and loyal fans."
—*New York Journal of Books*

"[A] master of her genre."
—*Library Journal*

"An author with a distinctive flair for originality and an entertaining narrative storytelling style that will hold the reader's rapt attention from beginning to end."
—*Midwest Book Review*

"Bowen's vivid storytelling style holds readers enrapt. [She] perfectly develops both narratives with absorbing details about several characters and different geographical environments."

—Historical Novel Society

"Bowen's story sweeps up the reader on a nonstop rollercoaster ride of action, espionage, heartbreaking sacrifice, revenge, and reunions both joyful and painful."

—*Book Trib*

MRS. ENDICOTT'S *Splendid* ADVENTURE

MOLLY MURPHY MYSTERIES

With Clare Broyles

In Sunshine or in Shadow

Silent as the Grave

ROYAL SPYNESS MYSTERIES

MRS. ENDICOTT'S *Splendid* ADVENTURE

A Novel

RHYS BOWEN

LAKE UNION
PUBLISHING

Text copyright © 2025 by Janet Quin-Harkin, writing as Rhys Bowen
All rights reserved.

Published by Lake Union Publishing, Seattle

www.apub.com

Amazon, the Amazon logo, and Lake Union Publishing are trademarks of Amazon.com, Inc., or its affiliates.

EU product safety contact:
Amazon Media EU S. à r.l.
38, avenue John F. Kennedy, L-1855 Luxembourg
amazonpublishing-gpsr@amazon.com

ISBN-13: 9781662527180 (hardcover)
ISBN-13: 9781662527197 (paperback)
ISBN-13: 9781662527173 (digital)

Cover design by Jarrod Taylor
Cover image: © k_samurkas, © sarahgerrity / Getty

Printed in the United States of America

First edition

I'd like to dedicate this book to Danielle Marshall, my former editor at Lake Union, with thanks for all her support and her friendship, wishing her great success and happiness in her new venture.

As usual I'd like to thank the entire team at Lake Union as well as my fabulous agents Meg Ruley and Christina Hogrebe. You all make my job such a joy.

CHAPTER 1

Surrey, England, 1938

The bombshell was dropped over breakfast, normally a time of silence apart from the rustling of the *Times*, a complaint about the timing of the boiled egg or an occasional outburst when Mr Endicott read something with which he did not agree.

"That pumped-up little popinjay Mussolini has marched into Abyssinia, of all places. What on earth for? No natural resources that I've heard of. No good will come of it, you mark my words."

At the other end of the long mahogany table, Mrs Endicott spread honey on a thin slice of toast. She always found it hard to eat until her husband had departed to catch the eight fifteen to London. But on this particular morning Mr Endicott put down his newspaper with a defiant grunt and stared straight at her.

"What's wrong, Lionel?" she asked. "Did I not cook the egg to your satisfaction? I'm sure I gave it three and a half minutes exactly."

"Ellie, we must talk," he said. "I've been trying to find the right time to say this, but there never seems to be a right time." He gave that little cough in his throat, something he did before making a pronouncement. "Well, here goes, then. Ellie, I want a divorce."

Ellie Endicott stared at him, her mouth open. The request was so unexpected that she could find no words. In fact, she wondered if she had heard right.

"Well, say something," he said impatiently.

Ellie stared at him, trying to take in what he had just said. "I don't know what to say." She fought to sound calm. "I'm speechless, Lionel. I had no idea you were unhappy. Have I not been a good wife to you? I have certainly tried to make your life run smoothly. I boil your eggs for exactly the correct amount of time. I've made sure your blasted shirts come back from the laundry starched just enough so you don't get a rash on your neck. I've entertained all your boring business associates . . ."

Lionel Endicott held up his hand. "Please do not blame yourself for this, Ellie my dear," he said hastily. "Nobody could fault the way you have taken care of this house. It runs like clockwork. No, this has nothing to do with you. In fact . . . you see . . . the point is that I've met someone else. Someone I want to marry."

"You want to marry someone else?" She stared incredulously at his round face, his sagging jowls, his thinning hair that he attempted to comb over. Who would want Lionel? The thought passed swiftly through her head.

Lionel had gone very red. "I do. Her name is Michelle."

"French? But you hate the French."

"No, she's as English as you or I. Just a fanciful name. And a beautiful girl. Smart, pleasant . . ."

"'Girl,' you said?" Ellie was attempting to outstare him now. "You're going to marry a girl? Lionel, may I remind you that you are fifty-five years old."

His face was still red. "Well, not exactly a girl. Late twenties. Well educated. Went to a university, you know. Works in our overseas banking division."

When his wife said nothing, he shifted nervously. "Come on, old thing. You can't say that our life has been one of high romance, can you? We've grown comfortable with each other. You're like an old stuffed armchair . . ."

"I most certainly am not," she replied. "I work hard to keep myself trim and fit. I walk into the village every day to do the shopping."

"I meant figuratively. Something I've grown accustomed to. Comforting."

"But not exciting."

"No," he said. "Not exciting."

Behind them the clock chimed the hour.

"You'd better go," she said. "You'll miss your train."

"I'm not taking the train today. I'm meeting with my solicitor after work. Get the ball rolling. I'll take the Bentley. You don't need it, I take it?"

"Would it matter if I did?" she demanded, anger overtaking her shock. "Your needs have always come first."

His expression softened. "Look here, old thing. I don't want to make this hard on you. I know it's a bit of a shock, but all good things must come to an end, as they say. I'll make it as smooth as possible for you. No unpleasantness. I'll admit to being the guilty party, of course. I'll make sure you're given a good allowance. You won't have to worry about money."

"You're just going to leave me and move out?" She toyed with the words, as if trying to digest them.

"What?" He looked startled at this. "Oh no, dear. I'll stay put. This is a large house, far too big for one person. And I'd still need to entertain, for my business, of course."

"And where am I supposed to go?"

He cleared his throat, then went on, as if he had prepared the speech. "I thought you might want to move up to London. My portfolio contains a nice little flat in Knightsbridge—not too far from Harrods. It's only one bedroom, but you won't be entertaining or anything, will you? It should suit you nicely—easy to walk to the shops."

He attempted an encouraging smile. She continued a cold stare.

"I hate London," she said.

"Then we'll find you a nice little cottage down here. So that you can keep up your activities with the church. I think I saw one for sale in that row near the station."

3

Ellie stared at him incredulously. "You want me to move to a workman's cottage? In a row near the station? And you carry on here as if nothing has happened? You must think very little of me, Lionel." She took a deep breath. "If we're going to divorce, I want the house."

"What?" The word shot out like an explosion, then he collected himself. "Don't be ridiculous, Ellie. Why would you want a great big house to yourself? It's not as if you have many friends here. All the people we entertain are my friends, my business associates and clients."

"Precisely," she said. "Maybe it's time I started making my own friends. Besides, I like this house. I know it well. I've decorated it, made it what it is. And I'm comfortable here."

"Be reasonable, old thing." His voice was soft, but she noticed he was crumpling the edges of the *Times* with his fingers. *He hates creased newspapers,* she thought.

"I am trying to be reasonable, Lionel." She heard her voice rising, even though she was trying to stay calm. "It's not easy when my husband of thirty years announces that he wants a divorce. But I can assure you I am not going to keel over and play dead. I am going to fight for what I want. I may contest the divorce. Have you thought of that? It will get into the newspapers. Prominent London banker dumps faithful wife for floozy. Is that what the *Daily Mirror* might say? Hardly good for your image, is it? I think Mr Murchison might not be well pleased with that sort of publicity about one of his VPs."

She noticed he was now swallowing hard, his Adam's apple going up and down. "Dash it all, Ellie, I'm trying to be reasonable. How could you afford to run the house alone? Pay for the gardener and all the things that need doing from time to time? And you'd need a car to get anywhere. And think of the heating bill."

"Very well, then," she said, considering this. "Perhaps I don't want to be stuck in a boring little village, especially where everyone knows me. The last thing I want is pity. Oh poor Ellie. Her husband left her, you know. Perhaps this is the time for me to spread my wings.

We'll have the house valued, and all our other possessions, too. You can pay me half."

Lionel's face had turned that angry red again—more plum than beetroot now. He was coming close to one of his explosions, she could see. "But all of this was bought with my money." He spat out the words. "Money I earned working damned hard. Keeping you in a damned nice lifestyle."

"Entertaining your clients and business associates? Raising two boys in whom you showed no interest? Making sure you had clean shirts?" Ellie stood up, her linen napkin falling to the floor unnoticed. "Exactly how much do you owe me in back wages if we tot that up? Oh, believe me, Lionel, I have earned half this house and more. Now, are you going to see reason, or do I have to find my own solicitor and fight this in the courts?"

With that, she stalked out of the room. Her heart was beating so loudly that she was sure it must be echoing from the oak-panelled walls of the front hall. She went through to the kitchen, let the door swing shut behind her and stood, holding on to the pine table for support. Why had she been so blind? Why had she never suspected for an instant that he had been unfaithful to her? She realized with utter clarity that on those occasions he had said, apologetically, that he had another of those boring evening meetings with the shareholders and it had gone on so damned late that he'd better spend the night at his club, he was, in fact, spending the night at a little flat in Knightsbridge with Monique, or Marlene, or whatever she was called. She was pretty sure it was that same love nest he now wanted to foist off on his discarded wife. All very neat and tidy. Lionel liked everything neat and tidy. One woman moves out of flat and into house, other moves out of house and into flat. There. All taken care of. She could just see the wheels in his brain ticking over.

And she had thrown a spanner into these works. The submissive spaniel had suddenly jumped up and bitten him. He would not be liking it at all. And she allowed herself a small smile.

CHAPTER 2

Ellie waited in the kitchen until she heard the front door slam and then the crunch of car tires on the gravel driveway before she poured herself a cup of tea, pulled out a chair from the kitchen table and sank on to it. She looked around the kitchen, *her* kitchen for the past twenty years. Her gaze swept over her striped Cornishware bowls, the faithful pots and pans hanging on the rack, the cheerful gingham curtains and geranium in the window with the view of the manicured garden beyond with its lovely rose arbour. And now she was supposed to walk away from all this, move to some poky little place as a pathetic and lonely older woman, content with her crochet and good works at the local church?

"Over my dead body," she said out loud.

"What did you say?" said a voice behind her, making her jump and spin around.

"Sorry. Didn't mean to startle you." Her cleaning lady, Mavis Moss, stood in the doorway, her hair tied up in a kerchief and with a broom in her hand. A small woman, all skin and bones with sharp features, she had always reminded Ellie of a Cockney sparrow, with her beaky nose and her little dark eyes that darted nervously.

"Oh Mavis. I'm sorry." Ellie put her hand instinctively to her heart. "I had no idea. I didn't hear you come in. Is it really nine o'clock already?"

Mavis propped up the broom and came over to her. "What's up, Mrs E.? You look as if you've seen a ghost."

"I am the ghost," Ellie said. "The ghost is me, apparently."

Mavis went to scratch her head, then realized the kerchief got in the way. She put a tentative hand on Ellie's shoulder. "Is there something I can do? Make you a cup of tea?"

"I've already had two," Ellie said.

"So his high-and-mightiness took the Bentley today, I see." Mavis was already filling the kettle and then putting it on the stove. Her answer to everything was a cup of tea. "I thought you was planning to do some shopping in Guildford?"

Ellie shrugged. "I don't think I feel like shopping at the moment."

"Taken poorly?" Mavis asked. "I told you that sauce with the chicken was too rich."

"It's not that," Ellie said. "My husband has just told me he wants a divorce." She said the words as if she still couldn't believe what she was saying.

"Blimey." Mavis stared incredulously. "You could knock me down with a feather. Who would have thought that in a million years? What's he want, the bachelor life again? Open-topped sports cars and letting his hair grow long?"

Ellie shook her head. "He wants to get married again."

"Some girl must be desperate," Mavis replied, now warming the pot before putting in three heaped spoons of tea leaves from the caddy. "He ain't no oil painting, is he?"

"He seems rather smitten," Ellie said.

The kettle shrieked and then there was a silence as Mavis turned off the gas and poured the boiling water into the teapot.

"And what do you plan to do about it?" Mavis put her hands on her hips defiantly.

"I told him I wanted the house," Ellie said.

Mavis let out a whoop of laughter. "Good for you! What did he say to that? I bet he blew his top."

"He did, rather." Ellie allowed herself a smile. "I could hardly believe it myself that I'd said it. I just opened my mouth, and it came out."

"And do you want the house? A bit big for one person, isn't it?"

"You're right. I only said it because I was so jolly angry and upset. I'm not sure I'd want everyone around here feeling sorry for me. But I'm not going to let him walk all over me either. I've given him the best years of my life, Mavis. If he wants to be free of this marriage, he's going to pay for it."

"That's it. You tell him, Mrs E." She poured two cups of tea. "Anyway, maybe it's a spur-of-the-moment thing. Maybe he'll change his mind."

"I don't think so. He's gone to see his solicitor today."

"Well then," Mavis said. "You'd better go and see yours, hadn't you?"

"I don't have a solicitor, Mavis. Mr Endicott handled all those kinds of things."

"Well, you'd ruddy well better find one sharpish, hadn't you?" Mavis said. "There's always old Mr Furniston in the village. Another lady I do for thinks highly of him, even though he's half retired these days. And his wife is ever so nice, isn't she? Bakes lovely things for the Women's Institute."

"I don't know . . . ," Ellie began.

"You could do worse. Better to be prepared when his la-de-da-ship comes back with papers he wants you to sign."

"I suppose you're right, Mavis." She gave a big sigh. "Golly. I'm going to hate this. Leaving all that I love behind. My lovely house. My garden. It's not fair, after all I've done."

Mavis nodded. "You've put up with a lot for that man. Like a spoiled toddler, he is. Tantrums if he can't get his own way. Between you and me, I don't know why you've put up with him so long, Mrs E. If you want me two pennies' worth, you're better off without him. It's about time you got to live your own life, have a bit of fun."

She plonked a cup of tea down in front of Ellie, who looked up with an incredulous smile on her lips. "A bit of fun? I'm fifty years old, Mavis. A little old for fun, wouldn't you say?"

"Not at all. Life's what you make it. That's what I say."

"I don't suppose your life is actually a bed of roses, is it?"

A wary look came over Mavis's face. "Well, that's as maybe. Some of us poor working-class stiffs are just stuck with the lot we're given. But you'll have money. And you're posh. That's the difference. You can go anywhere and be accepted. I'd move to the seaside if it were me. Nice little bungalow. Meet a retired colonel . . ."

Ellie shook her head. "Oh no. You're not suggesting I get married again? Once bitten, twice shy, I think. I don't think I could face another Lionel and learning how he likes his shirts starched."

"They're not all like your hubby, you know. I bet there's some nice ones out there—kind, considerate, funny, adventurous . . ."

"You really think there are men like that?"

"Bound to be?"

"And also interested in women as opposed to other men?"

Mavis had to chuckle. "Who knows. But it's worth a try, ain't it? I know I'd be off if I had the chance."

"Would you really?" Ellie looked up at her.

"You don't think it's been a laugh a minute with Reggie Moss, do you? Never notices I exist unless he wants one thing"—she gave a knowing little nod—"or something's been done wrong, or maybe to help himself to my earnings to go with his mates down the pub. So maybe you're right. Maybe they're all the same. But I can tell you this, Mrs E.: you're better off without that one."

～

Up in her bedroom Ellie sat at her dressing table, her hand shaky as she attempted to put on some lipstick. Her face, unnaturally pale today, stared back at her. She hadn't let herself go, had she? Her face was still unlined, no grey yet showing in her ash-brown hair. She had not gone in for marcel waves like most women but instead still wore her hair up in a knot, and it accentuated her good cheekbones. And she'd kept her figure. She was careful with the sweets and puddings, and she walked every day. And yet she wasn't good enough to keep her husband's interest, apparently.

She looked away from her stricken face. The view from the bay window on to the lawns was perfect. The manicured grass, the herbaceous borders with their riot of colour, the rose arbour beyond— they were all so lovely, so elegant. And she was supposed to give all this up, walk away, live in a poky cottage, or in that flat she was now sure had kept his mistress? Anger welled up, and she felt tears brimming in her eyes.

She could refuse to divorce him, of course. The thought came to her. If she didn't agree, then it would be too bad. No divorce. He'd be stuck. But then so would she. Did she really want that? Lionel could be vindictive; she had seen that in his business dealings. He could make sure she was so miserable that she moved out. He could bring his mistress to live here, under this roof. And she found herself mulling over what Mavis had said: Would she really be better off without him?

She didn't love him. She was sure of that. Had she once? She tried to remember. She had met him at a cricket club dance. He had come down to the village with another clerk from the bank in London, both of them fresh from qualifying as accountants and excited for prospects in the big city. He had seemed witty and urbane and amusing. She realized later that he had drunk rather a lot and that had lowered his inhibitions, because he was rarely amusing afterward, but she had been desperate at the time to escape from the confines of village life. Her father was the vicar, the sort that loves to spout about sin and hellfire, and her mother was the frustrated daughter of landed gentry. She had married Ellie's father fully expecting him to be a bishop or at least dean but found herself trapped in a village backwater, taking out her frustration in finding everything wrong with her daughter. Ellie had finished school with very good marks and could have gone on to university. But according to her father, more schooling was a waste for a young girl who would only get married. And so she was trapped. Not enough money or status to be presented at court as a debutante. In those days girls didn't move up to London and share flats. In Edwardian England very few of them ever considered working outside the home, unless it was as a teacher or governess if you were middle class but desperate, or a servant if you weren't.

Lionel had seemed like a good catch: he had come from a humble background himself. His father owned a greengrocer's shop. But Lionel had studied for his accountancy exams and been hired by a major bank. He was ambitious and he needed a wife with class to make the right impression on business associates. And so they married. They first lived in a humble house in Clapham, then, as he got promotion after promotion, to a nicer house in Wimbledon and finally to this detached gentleman's residence in the Stockbroker Belt in Surrey. Thanks to Lionel's bank, they had come through the crash of '29 and the Great Depression unscathed.

The requisite children had arrived: two boys, one after the other. Lionel had insisted they be sent off to boarding school as was required of their station in life. Ellie had enjoyed raising them and missed them horribly after they were gone but had had no say in this. Lionel had made it quite clear. It was what the sons of the upper class did. Surely she of all people knew that. She really hadn't seen much of them since they left school and went into their respective professions. Richard had gone into the army, and Colin was now working for a bank in Hong Kong. Both far from home. She received the occasional letter, but all those years of boarding school had left them with no strong family ties. As yet there were no marriages, no grandchildren.

And so there was nobody, she realized suddenly, as she stared back at herself in the mirror again. Nobody close enough to care about her. No best friend putting an arm around her and saying, "Come and live with me until you sort this horrible business out." Lionel had been right. The people they entertained had all been his friends. She had nowhere to go, or everywhere to go.

"I've lived his life," she said to her reflection. Serious eyes that had once been dark blue but had now faded to an indeterminate grey stared back at her. How long was it since the sparkle and hope had faded from those eyes? "His life," she repeated. Oh, there were women in the village she had coffee with, worked with as a volunteer at church. Nice enough women, but nobody she could describe as a real friend—the sort of person she could run to now and let out all her anger. The closest to that was Mavis. Mavis had cleaned for her for the past ten years, always cheerful, willing and with no illusions about the character of Mr Endicott.

I'll miss Mavis, she thought. Then she thought about what Mavis had said. She should get her own solicitor. That would shake Lionel. She finished putting on the lipstick, grabbed her hat and came downstairs.

"I'm doing what you told me, Mavis," she said, passing her mopping the marble tiles in the front hallway. "I'm going to that solicitor."

"That's right, Mrs E.," Mavis said. "You show that no-good husband of yours that you're not going to keel over and play dead. You're going to fight him tooth and nail."

"Golly, you make me sound like a wild animal." Ellie had to smile.

Mavis chuckled. "You show your claws, love," she said. "You've let him walk all over you for far too long."

"I suppose you're right." Ellie stared at the pattern of stained glass on the front door, now sparkling in a rainbow on the freshly mopped marble. "He made the money and dished it out as he saw fit. He controlled everything, including me, and held the balance of power. I see that now. If he wasn't happy, and his life didn't run smoothly, then he wouldn't do well in business, and we wouldn't have this lovely lifestyle. He always let me feel that."

"So now's your chance, love," Mavis said. "You open that door and go and live whatever life you want. Only make sure he pays you enough so you can enjoy it."

Ellie looked back and gave her a beaming smile. "I will, Mavis. I bloody well will."

CHAPTER 3

When Lionel arrived home that evening, he had the satisfied look on his face that normally meant a successfully concluded business deal.

"How was your day?" he asked, as he always did. He sat down in his favourite armchair, took off his highly polished shoes and reached for his slippers. A confused look came over his face.

"What happened to my slippers?" he asked.

"In your dressing room, I expect," she said. "That was where you left them."

"But you always . . . ," he began.

"Always used to . . . when I was still your wife," she said. "Now I suggest you train Monique to have your slippers and sherry ready for you."

"It's Michelle," he said.

"I bet it's not." She gave a little chuckle. "I bet her real name is Brenda or Beryl or something equally common and boring, and she's become Michelle to snag herself a rich gentleman."

His face flushed again. "She's not like that at all. I told you, she's a highly educated girl with a bright future. Most amusing. Good-looking."

"Then why does she want you, Lionel—apart from your money?"

"We get along well. We're highly compatible," he said. "We laugh at the same things."

"You never laugh here," she said.

"No. You and I have never laughed much," he agreed. "That should tell us something, shouldn't it?"

"You're right. We have put up with each other for too long. Maybe it's time to make a fresh start."

She saw the relief in his face. "I'm so glad you've come to thinking that way. Better all around, eh, old thing? So . . . I did go and see my solicitor, and he's come up with some sensible suggestions." He reached for his briefcase, opened it and took out a sheaf of paper. Then he put on his glasses before examining the papers and looking up.

"He says it makes no sense to give you a lump sum to buy a little place of your own at this moment, until you decide where you'd like to settle. He suggests a nice monthly allowance, so you can check out various places."

"I agree," she said.

He grinned. A flash of triumph in his eyes. "I knew you'd be sensible. You've always been sensible, Ellie. Well done." He cleared his throat, an annoying habit he had, Ellie thought. He did it when he was nervous about what he was going to say next.

"So he suggests that thirty pounds a month will let you rent somewhere out of London with enough money for food and an occasional cinema. Now, how does that sound?"

"How much do you make a year, Lionel?" she asked sweetly. "Two thousand pounds, I believe you told me when you got your last raise. Now, I will be generous and won't demand half, but I want sixty pounds a month. What's more, I want the love nest in London as an investment, so I can sell it when I find where I want to settle."

His face had now gone white. "Quite out of the question, Ellie. My offer was a sound one."

"Not according to my solicitor, Lionel."

He sat up straight in his chair. "What do you mean? What solicitor?"

"The one whose services I retained today. A most wise and sound older gentleman, I found. Most sympathetic. He said it would be quite within my rights to demand half of everything, given the amount of time I've devoted to you. But I'm prepared to be magnanimous and not greedy. I have never asked for more than I actually need, have I? So sixty pounds plus the amount from the flat should be sufficient . . ."

His face had taken on that beetroot tinge again. "Out of the question."

"Fine." She had been perched on the arm of the sofa. Now she stood up. "In that case, no divorce. You and Martine can live together in the love nest, unmarried."

"But you don't understand . . . ," he blustered.

"I do understand, Lionel. Believe me, I understand you very well." She held his gaze. "You've always wanted your own way since day one, haven't you? Everything has to be convenient for you. And I don't see why you're making such a fuss about my allowance. Surely this Michelle makes a good salary, too. You'll be adding her money—and you won't need the love nest any longer."

"Well, uh, you see . . ." He was stumbling now. "She might not be working much longer. I mean, as my wife it wouldn't be right . . ."

"Oh, I do see now." A knowing smile spread across Ellie's face. "You've got her pregnant, Lionel. How reckless of you. So now you want to marry swiftly enough to make it all legitimate. Or is she the one demanding that you do the right thing and marry her? She'll make a fuss if you don't? Bring down your career? I wonder what she'd say if she found out I'd refused to divorce you?"

"But you have to, don't you see? You can't let the poor girl—"

"The poor girl who was fornicating with my husband behind my back?" Ellie cut him off in midsentence. "No, Lionel, I'm afraid I don't have much sympathy for the poor girl. But don't worry. I wouldn't want to keep you from your future happiness and the joys of fatherhood. I just want my fair share, that's all. Sixty pounds a month and the flat."

"Fifty," he said sharply. "No more than fifty, Ellie. My final word."

"Very well," she said, lowering her head in submission. "If you absolutely insist. I suppose it will have to be fifty pounds a month . . .

and the flat, of course. You can just make that over to my name. I'll rent it out until I need to sell it."

He got up. "Agreed, then. I'll have Smithers put it in writing tomorrow." He went to shake hands, then backed off. He looked around, realizing he was standing in his stockinged feet. "Now I suppose I'll have to go and find my blasted slippers."

As soon as he left the room, Ellie put her hand to her mouth to stifle a nervous laugh. Old Mr Furniston, the solicitor, had told her, "Ask for more than you really want. Give him some wiggle room. Pretend it's Baghdad market and make him bargain. Then he'll feel satisfied that he's got the better of you, and you'll get the right amount." He had suggested fifty pounds would be adequate as long as she had the lump sum in the bank from the sale of the London flat. And she'd done it. She'd outsmarted Lionel. Now all she had to think about was where she wanted to go and what she wanted to do.

~

Ellie woke the next morning, feeling the strange coldness of the bed beside her. Lionel had moved to the guest room until things were settled. It was only right, he said. Ellie quite agreed. There was no way she would share a bed with him again. She got up and decided she would make his breakfast, as a gesture of goodwill. The sight of him hobbling in his socks up the stairs to find his slippers was victory enough for now. She was actually feeling quite cheerful by the time he had gone off in the Bentley and Mavis arrived.

"Well, you're looking a lot more chipper, that's for sure," Mavis said as she came in through the back door to find Ellie watering the plants on the kitchen windowsill.

"I did what you told me and saw the solicitor. He gave me wonderful advice. I took it and got what I wanted," she said. "You should have seen Lionel's face when I demanded and bargained." She put a hand on Mavis's bony shoulder. "I was proud of myself, Mavis. I was in the driver's seat for once. It felt marvellous."

"So what now? You'll be moving out soon?"

Ellie refilled her teacup and carried it over to the table. "I expect I will. I lay awake last night trying to think where I'd want to go."

"You wouldn't want to go back home, would you? Your mum and dad aren't still alive, are they?"

"Mercifully no," Ellie replied. "And if they were, that would be the last place I'd run to. They both enjoyed being negative and critical. And I have no more close family. So I'm not sure where I'll go. I don't like London or big cities."

"What about the seaside?"

Ellie nodded. "You suggested that yesterday, and it might be nice. Although my recent experience of seaside holidays is always the same. We go to a big hotel in Bournemouth or Torquay or Eastbourne, and we take a walk along the promenade, then we have coffee on the glassed-in veranda while Lionel reads the paper or does the crossword. Utterly boring. My idea of the seaside is . . ." She paused.

"Yes?"

A wistful smile came over her face. "When I was eighteen, my great-aunt Louisa took me to the Continent. She was Mummy's aunt, and she'd led a colourful life with various lovers. A sort of black sheep of the family, I understand now." She looked up. "Oh Mavis, we had such fun. We went to Rome and Venice and Florence and Vienna and the French Riviera. Gosh, it was wonderful. We ate fish stew with lots of garlic, and she taught me about wines. And those colours—that deep-blue sea and the pastel buildings and the mountains. It took my breath away."

"But you never went back since?"

"Aunt Louisa had a heart attack and died the next year," she said. "And then I married Lionel, and he hates 'abroad,' as he puts it. A lot of bloody foreigners wanting money, and dirt and fleas and garlic. That's how he sees it."

"You could go back," Mavis said. "Give yourself a nice long holiday before you decide where you want to live."

"Back to France?" She toyed with the word, letting it conjure up images—palm trees and cold drinks on a terrace overlooking a blue sea.

"Yeah. Why not? Only yourself to please now, ain't there? About time you did something nice for yourself."

"I suppose I could." Ellie stared at her, her eyes bright with excitement now. "I really could, couldn't I?"

"You could take one of them tours."

"No." She shook her head. "Not a tour. I think I'd like to find a little pension or something and stay put for a while. Just being, you know. Not having to do anything or go anywhere or make anyone's blasted boiled eggs or fetch slippers. Just learning to be me and finding out what I want."

Mavis nodded. "Good idea," she said. "But how are you going to manage with the lingo? Do you parley-voos a bit?"

"More than a bit," Ellie said. "Of course I'm rusty right now, but my mother was of the old school who thought French was the language of diplomacy and that well-bred ladies throughout the world should converse in French. Although I had little chance of marrying a foreign count, she drilled me mercilessly until I was fluent at an early age. So I'm sure it would come back to me quickly if I wanted."

"How will you get there?" Mavis asked.

"There are plenty of trains. Golden Arrow to Paris and then a train south."

"What, on your own? With them all speaking a foreign language and all them foreign men around? I've heard what they're like. Are you sure that's wise?" Mavis was staring in wonder, having never been further than a day trip to Brighton herself. "They pinch bottoms, don't they?"

Ellie laughed. "It's been years since I've had my bottom pinched. I think I'm a little too old for that. But I might even enjoy it." She gave Mavis a wicked grin. "I'm sure I'd be fine."

"So it's France you'd go to, not Italy or any of them other heathen places?"

Ellie considered. "I did like Italy, too, but I loved that Riviera coast. It felt like the most magical place on earth. So I think I'd start off there. Maybe travel more later if I wanted to. But it would make sense to go somewhere where I could communicate when I got my bearings . . . got my feet wet, so to speak."

"Well, good luck to you. That's what I say, Mrs E."

"How funny," Ellie said, her face now serious again. "I won't be Mrs E. for much longer, will I?"

"I must say I'm going to miss you," Mavis said. "Not just the money from the job, but coming here every day and having you to chat to. You've always been a good sort to me. Never treated me like a servant like some of them ladies do."

Ellie stared at the other woman's gaunt face, her sharp features, her bony body, and realized how much she had taken for granted hearing her cheerful greeting every morning. It came to her with a jolt that Mavis would be losing a lot of work when she went. "I'm so sorry, Mavis. I realize this will be making things difficult for you. How will you manage for money? I'll try to make it up to you."

"Oh, don't worry about me, Mrs E.," Mavis said. "I've got more ladies asking me to do for them than I have time. And the vicar, he wants me to take care of the church, so I'll be fine."

"I do hope so," Ellie said. "I feel badly about this. You've been a good friend. I've really appreciated you, Mavis," she said. "I will miss you, too."

Suddenly Mavis laughed and gave her a playful shove. "Go on. Look at us, all mournful like a couple of ninnies. You're about to have the time of your life. We should be celebrating."

"You're right," Ellie said. "Tell you what—I'll go and see if the fishmonger has any crab today. We'll have a crab salad and wine with it for lunch. And I'll pick up a sinful pastry at the baker's."

"Well, blow me down," Mavis said, looking pleased. "That's what I call a good send-off." She paused. "So when do you think you'll want to leave?"

"As soon as possible," Ellie said. "I can't think of anything worse than staying in a house where I'm not wanted. He might even bring his floozy down to measure up for curtains in the nursery. I couldn't stand that."

"Oh, so that's how it is." Mavis gave a knowing little nod. "Got her in the family way and now thinks he's doing the right thing. Well, he'll soon learn. Let's see how he handles a squawking baby in the middle of the night."

"He'll do exactly as he did with my children—pretend he can't hear and go back to sleep," Ellie said.

~~

Over the next days Ellie and Lionel were awkwardly polite to each other. She cooked his boiled eggs as a gesture of goodwill and sent his shirts to the laundry as she always had. They drifted past each other, trying not to make eye contact. Two ships passing in the night. He was often out in the evenings (with Michelle, she surmised) and Ellie enjoyed cooking what she wanted to for dinner—sometimes only an omelette or even beans on toast instead of the meat and two veg Lionel expected every evening—and listening to the wireless alone. She was pleasurably surprised at this. *It will be all right,* she thought. *I'll manage by myself.*

Eventually Lionel produced papers for her to sign. They all seemed in order. He was admitting guilt. She was leaving the marriage without a stain on her character. She was provided for financially. The monthly allowance and then the deed to the flat with the proceeds from the eventual sale, just as she had requested. She was going to sign, when she reminded herself that she was not going to be the compliant little woman.

"Thank you, Lionel. I'll take these to my solicitor, so that he can check them," she said.

She watched the familiar red flush rising on his cheeks. "Of course everything is in order," he said. "Just sign the damned things." Then, as he saw her placid expression, staring at him, he corrected himself. "Of course. If it makes you feel better. But you'll find everything's very fair and aboveboard. I have no wish to cheat you in any way, Ellie dear."

Ellie did show them to her solicitor, who could find no fault. "The flat in London will be a nice little investment for you," he commented as he returned them. So the next day they went to Lionel's solicitor's office and she signed. How simple it was to negate thirty years in one flourish of a signature. When they returned home, Lionel poured them both a large cognac.

"I assume there are various items around the house that you'd like to have for sentimental reasons, when you set up a place of your own," he said. He was being generous because he felt he had won, got the better of her in the deal.

Ellie looked around her. It was an elegant sitting room with a Persian carpet in the middle of a polished floor, French doors opening on to the back terrace. A flower arrangement on a low table, a grand piano in the corner. Most of the furnishings had been her choice. Being the son of a humble shopkeeper, he had relied on her good taste. They'd been secondhand to start with—clever finds in antique shops that fit their meagre budget—but over the years she had replaced them when they could afford better. But did she really care about any of them? Her gaze went to the piano. There had been a time when she had played a lot. She had been part of a quartet until the violinist died and the others drifted away. She had played for village theatrical productions, but recently the joy of playing seemed to have gone. Besides, she didn't think she'd be renting the type of house with room for a grand piano.

Then the little writing desk caught her eye. It had been one of her best finds in an antique shop. "I might want the writing desk," she said.

"Didn't you say it was Queen Anne?" She heard the slight tension in his voice. Queen Anne and therefore valuable. Worth money. It was all about money for Lionel.

"I believe so. But it's a small piece. It would fit nicely in a cottage eventually." She paused. "Of course I won't take anything at the moment. Not until I've settled."

"So where do you think you'll go now?"

"The seaside, I thought."

"Oh, what a good idea." He sounded extra hearty. In his mind he was picturing her in a boarding house in Bournemouth or Worthing, a couple of streets back, where it was cheaper, taking healthy walks along the seafront, listening to the band, eating grey boiled beef and overdone cabbage for dinner. "Have you decided where?"

"The Riviera."

"Oh, you mean Torquay? You love Torquay, don't you?"

"I mean the French Riviera."

"France?" He stared incredulously. "You'd want to go abroad? To France?"

"I just said so."

"But you don't like travelling abroad."

"No, Lionel. You don't like travelling abroad. I loved it when I was a girl."

"But you never went again."

"No. When we were first married, we couldn't afford it, and after that you became rather set in your ways. Always the same resorts."

"I suppose you're right. You could have said . . ."

She gave him a pitying smile. "As if I ever got what I wanted. You'd have given me every reason in the world why we were going to Eastbourne instead of Nice."

His face had flushed again. "But you can't travel all that way by yourself. How will you get there? Or will you take a coach tour?"

"There are trains. And porters, too, so I understand. I'll manage perfectly, I'm sure. I do speak excellent French, or I used to. Remember my mother insisted on conversing in French from the moment I could talk. I'll start brushing up again."

There was a long pause. The clock in the front hall struck eight. "How long do you think you'll be gone?" he asked. There was a tone of uncertainty, almost wistfulness in his voice.

"Now what possible interest could that be to you? Maybe a month, a year, whatever I feel like. I am now fancy-free, Lionel. No longer your wife. Free to do exactly what I choose. But don't worry. I will let you know when I'm leaving." She sensed him staring after her as she left the room.

CHAPTER 4

Now that she could leave when she wanted to, she hesitated. It had been one thing to announce to the world that she was going to France for a while, but complications arose. There was the flat in London to take care of—leaving the renting in the hands of an estate agent. Her passport to update. And she had acquired stuff over the years—not only clothes but toiletries, her silver-backed brushes, favourite books, sheet music, photograph albums. Clearly she couldn't take them all to the South of France. She went through her clothes, deciding which she would no longer need. No need for furs in that climate. Or her evening gowns. Or even smart tailored suits. She laid them on the bed, staring at them. Would she ever use them again? When would she go to the sort of formal dinner where they'd wear strapless evening attire? And yet she was reluctant to sell them or give them away.

In the end she had Mavis help her pack them in tissue and store them in garment bags, laying them in trunks in the attic. Because, as Mavis put it, you never know. "You might meet a millionaire on the Riviera and find yourself living in a stately 'ome."

Mavis was an eternal optimist, in spite of a miserable life growing up in a slum and then living with her lout of a husband.

Eventually Ellie had her most suitable clothing assembled for the trip, hanging clean and pressed in the wardrobe, with the trunk open and ready to be packed on the bedroom floor. She examined the items critically. She remembered the Riviera as being impossibly chic. She owned nothing that could loosely be described as fashionable. Her wardrobe was suitable for village life with the odd dinner party thrown in: sensible tweed skirts and jumpers for winter, cotton dresses for summer and one or two long silk gowns for when they entertained. Not a single backless pyjama or any of the other things that people wore in Nice, according to women's magazines. And too late to have any made now.

"I'll just have to make do," she said. "I'll be the frumpy middle-aged widow, certainly not the gay divorcee. I'll blend into the scenery, and everyone will look on me with pity or leave me alone."

The one item she had decided to take from the household was the photograph album from when the boys were young. She looked at their bright, cheeky grins as they played on the beach, or climbed over rocks, and felt a pang of regret. When did they stop being fun-loving, adventurous little boys and turn into dull, serious young men? Men who were polite to their mother and pecked her dutifully on the cheek.

She was ready to go. She should book a ticket on the Golden Arrow to Paris. But now she hesitated. The news from Europe was not good. A crisis was looming over the Sudetenland, part of Czechoslovakia that was German-speaking and that Hitler was trying to claim. Prime Minister Neville Chamberlain had recalled his ambassador and was planning to go to Berlin himself to make Hitler see sense. And yet that all seemed very remote from the South of France, didn't it?

But still she hesitated. She had never really been alone in her life, moving straight from her parents' house to marriage with Lionel. That trip to Europe had been booked by Aunt Louisa. She had merely followed along, confident that trains and hotels would show up at the right time. Alone in her bedroom at night, she doubted for the first time. Was she insane to think she could go to the Riviera by herself? She stared at her worried face in the mirror.

"You are alone," she said to herself. "You have nobody now, so it's about time you learned how to survive." The trip to France would be a good test. If she could cross the Channel and travel alone, then she would be ready to do anything. She had to smile at this thought. It wasn't the Sahara or the Himalayas—she knew women a century ago had conquered those exotic places alone. But it was "abroad" and thus different—a challenge. And she was not going to back down now and lose face in front of Lionel. She could tell he was rather impressed with this new, confident Ellie. She would go through with it at all costs.

There were a few last-minute responsibilities she had to take care of. She had to wait for her passport to arrive. She wrote to both of her sons.

> My dear Colin/Richard,
> You will no doubt have heard by now from your father that he is divorcing me and plans to marry someone called Michelle. He expected me to melt away without much protest and live the rest of my life in a tiny cottage somewhere. However, I have surprised him by deciding to go to the South of France. I'm not sure how long I'll be gone, whether it will be a short holiday or a long stay. You'll be able to reach me through my bank should an emergency arise. I send you my love and hope that you stay healthy and happy.
> Your loving mother.

She checked with the bank and obtained letters of credit and traveller's cheques. And, being the responsible sort, she had to let people in the village know that she was leaving. She couldn't just leave the church altar guild and the Women's Institute in the lurch. It was simple enough to telephone Mrs Saunders, explaining that she'd be going away and thus would not be helping with refreshments at the next meeting of the WI. Mrs Saunders was sympathetic. Yes, she'd heard something of a rumour that Ellie would be going. Mavis had told someone. She was most sorry to hear it. Ellie had always been such a reliable helper.

Miss Smith-Humphries was not going to be so easy. An old-school spinster, she ran the altar guild with a rod of iron, inspecting each altar cloth, each flower arrangement, as if she were a general inspecting her troops. And she did not believe in telephones. That meant that Ellie could either send her a letter, or she could visit in person. She knew it would have to be the visit and was not looking forward to it.

Miss Smith-Humphries lived in a cottage on the village green. A statuesque woman, although she was now elderly, she held herself very upright with a permanent expression of distaste on her face. Her white hair in rigid curls. Rather like Queen Mary in many ways. She was the sort of formidable person who has a hand in all aspects of the smooth running of a community: parish council, Girl Guides, beautification committee and altar guild. Even grown men were afraid of her steely gaze. Ellie took a deep breath before she went up the front path between immaculate flowerbeds. There were the last roses of summer still framing the front door, and their sweet scent hung in the air as she knocked.

"Mrs Endicott!" The haughty, unlined face nodded graciously. "We heard that you would be leaving us. A great pity. A great pity indeed. Do come in."

Ellie was relieved that, thanks to Mavis, the world seemed to know her situation. Miss Smith-Humphries invited her to sit in an armchair by the bay window and went to get tea.

"I'm sorry to be deserting you," Ellie said. "But as you've heard, I'm leaving the area."

"We are all shocked and sorry to hear it." The old lady gave her a sympathetic nod. "You have been a stalwart member of our community for years. Most valuable to our little life here."

"Thank you." Ellie felt tears prickling at the back of her eyes. She hadn't realized that she had been appreciated, that she had mattered here. She looked around the small living room with its knick-knacks, old prints on the walls, a bookcase full of interesting volumes, its vases of flowers, the crocheted throw rug over the back of the sofa. It was a room stuffed with memories. *This will be me in the future,* she thought.

Miss Smith-Humphries brought out a tray with tea things and chocolate biscuits on it. The tray had a white cloth with lace edges and the teacups were Spode. The teapot was silver. She poured and handed Ellie a cup before she said, "May one ask where you are going now? You have family somewhere?"

"Unfortunately no," Ellie said. "My sons are both bachelors, one in the army and the other with a bank in Hong Kong. My parents are dead. I was an only child, and so I have no close family. I'm actually going abroad for a while."

"Abroad? My, that's adventurous. Where?"

Ellie took a sip of the tea. She stared out at the village green. Two little boys were kicking a ball while their mother watched, bringing back fond memories of her own sons. They had been such happy, carefree little boys until Lionel had insisted on sending them off to boarding school. An old man was walking his dog. On the far side the pub sign swung in the breeze. The Five Bells. All so lovely and safe and normal. She took a deep breath.

"The South of France."

Miss Smith-Humphries gave a little gasp—of pleasure, it transpired. "How lovely. I visited the Riviera as a young woman, and I found it enchanting. Nice, Cannes, Antibes . . . Which resort do you favour?"

"I'm not sure," Ellie said. "I loved Nice as a young girl. But I'm not sure where I'll end up. I plan to go until I find the right spot to stay for a while."

"You plan to stay for a while, then? Not just a holiday?"

Ellie put down her cup. "I think so. I want to be far away when my replacement moves into the house."

"I can assure you she will not be welcome here," Miss Smith-Humphries said angrily. "You are most treasured in this community. We do not approve of the way your husband is behaving."

"Neither do I," Ellie said, "but there's not much I can do about it."

"I hope he made a decent settlement on you."

"He did," Ellie said. "I think I can live quite satisfactorily, but not extravagantly."

Miss Smith-Humphries nodded approval. She took a drink of her own tea.

"I envy you," she said, putting down her cup. "A new start. New experiences. What an opportunity for you."

"I'm so glad you see it like that," Ellie said. "I've been a bit apprehensive about going all that way on my own, but you're right. It is an opportunity for me to see what I'm made of." She finished her tea and put the cup back on the tray. "I should not take any more of your time."

She made for the front door, exchanged final pleasantries and left. Outside she let out a sigh of relief. That had gone better than expected. At least Miss Smith-Humphries did not think it was beyond her capabilities to go off to the South of France by herself. It was about time she went home, packed her bags and set off.

~~

Mavis had left for the day, and Ellie was alone in the bedroom, wondering how many pairs of shoes one needed on the Riviera, when there was a knock at the front door. A decisive knock. Not the postman. He had already been. Ellie went downstairs, opened the door to see Miss Smith-Humphries standing there, pink cheeked and looking rather breathless.

"Miss Smith-Humphries, is something wrong? Did I leave something behind this morning?"

"Not at all." She put her hand to her heart. "Might I come in and have a word?"

"Of course. Please do. Would you like a glass of water? A cup of tea?"

"Water, please. I'm afraid I walked a little too fast." Her hand was on her heart.

She was shown into the sitting room and settled on the sofa. Ellie brought her the water, and she took a long drink before she spoke.

"You're going to think it frightful cheek of me," she said.

Ellie waited, wondering what was coming next.

"After you'd gone I started doing some serious thinking. I started remembering . . . how wonderful it was there. The blue sea. The scent of the flowers. The bougainvillea spilling over walls. And the food . . . Everything tasted so fresh." Her face had completely transformed as she spoke, and she looked like a younger, softer version of herself.

"Yes." Ellie nodded emphatically. "You're so right. All those things."

"So I wondered . . ." Again a long hesitation. "Whether I could come with you. Oh, I know it's awful cheek," she went on, the words just spilling out now, "and you can be as rude as you like. But my doctor tells me I don't have long to live, and I got this great urge to go to somewhere beautiful again, to a place I once loved." When Ellie said nothing, she continued. "I wouldn't be a burden, I promise. I'm not without funds. I'd pay my way, of course. And if I needed a nurse or assistant, I'd hire one. No, I guarantee you would not find me a burden."

Her look was expectant, hopeful.

"I don't know what to say," Ellie said. She also hesitated, trying to digest this request. "This is so unexpected. But yes. Actually . . . I'd welcome the company. And if, as you say, you don't have long in this world, I'd be delighted that you'd be able to experience a place that had given you joy."

"So kind." The woman actually took out a handkerchief and dabbed at her eyes. "So very kind of you. You don't know how much this means to me. When would you be leaving? I'd need a few days to get my things in order, see my bank manager, that sort of thing."

"You have a passport, do you?"

"Oh yes. I've always kept a passport up to date, just in case, you know. When I was young, I travelled a lot with my father, the brigadier, and afterwards, too."

"Then we'll leave when you are ready. I've made no bookings. We'll be fancy-free and open to any place that speaks to us."

"How utterly splendid," the old woman said. "I can't wait. A few days, that's all I'll need. I'll have to look at my French dictionary. It's

33

been years since I've had to use my languages. I'll be rusty. Thank heavens my last cat died in the winter. So nothing to keep me here. Nothing to tie me down at all. Fancy-free, exactly as you say."

As Ellie shut the door behind the departing Miss Smith-Humphries, she stood, frozen, in the cool darkness of the front hall. *What have I just done?* she asked herself. *Agreed to travel with a difficult, critical older woman. She will share my compartment on the train. She might want to share my room at a hotel. Perhaps her health will deteriorate rapidly, and I'll have to look after her.* And she was going to die. Ellie had never had to handle a death. It was all she could do not to open the door again and yell after Miss Smith-Humphries that she had changed her mind and it wouldn't work after all. But compassion overtook all other emotions. The woman didn't have long to live. One good thing that Ellie could do was to make sure that her last days were pleasurable and that she didn't die alone. She hoped someone would do the same for her.

CHAPTER 5

That evening Lionel came home with a worried frown on his face.

"Ellie, we must talk," he said as she put a bowl of nuts beside the sherry.

"Michelle doesn't want to marry you after all?"

He flushed. "No, nothing like that. She is really anxious to see the house, decide what changes she wants to make. And she won't do that until you've gone."

"At least she has some feelings of propriety," Ellie said. "But don't worry, I'm all ready to go. I'm just waiting for the nod from my travelling companion."

"Your what?" His jaw dropped open.

"I'm travelling with a friend. So much nicer, don't you think?"

"A female friend?"

Oh, how tempted she was to reveal that it was actually a Frenchman called Marcel. But she had never been a good liar. "Naturally. A woman of good character and impeccable background. Her father was a brigadier, Lionel. She was presented at court. You don't have to worry."

"I wasn't worrying. Of course it's splendid that you're travelling with a friend. It's the destination that worries me. Ellie, I don't think you should be going to France at this moment."

"Why on earth not?" Since he hadn't poured himself a sherry, she poured her own and took a sip.

"You must know that the situation in Europe is not looking good, I'm afraid. That blighter Hitler has designs on conquest, you mark my words."

"Yes, but surely his aim is to reclaim territories that used to be German—Poland and Czechoslovakia. Eastern Europe, not France."

"That will be only the beginning, I'm afraid. He may well draw us into another war."

Ellie looked up, horrified. "Surely not after the carnage of the last one. Neither side would think it was a good idea to go to war again."

"You'd think not, wouldn't you? But he's not a rational being, if you want my opinion. He's a new Napoleon. Highly dangerous. We've already got Franco and that idiot Mussolini. Hitler doesn't want to be seen as less than them, I can assure you. He's been busy amassing weapons, and any day now he'll annex Czechoslovakia, then it will be Poland, then God help the rest of us."

"You really think we could find ourselves in another Great War?"

"You'd hope not, wouldn't you? But as I just said, Hitler is not rational, in my opinion. And he's got the whole population brainwashed into thinking he's some kind of god figure who is going to make the Aryans rule the world. An empire to last a thousand years—that's what he's saying."

She felt a chill gnawing at her stomach but attempted to sound light. "Then England would be in as much danger as the South of France, I'd imagine."

"We have the Channel as a barrier."

"And they have aeroplanes. I don't think the Channel is going to protect England any longer."

Lionel slapped the arm of his chair. "I'm just thankful I'll be too old this time. After what I went through in the last lot."

"You were in the pay corps, Lionel. You didn't see a trench for four years."

He bristled at this. "I wasn't that far from the front at times. I lost good friends. I got the war medal."

Ellie tried not to smile. Everyone got the war medal, she wanted to say. Then the smile faded. "But the boys," she said. "Richard's already in the army. And Colin . . . he's safely far away right now, but."

"But look how Japan is sabre-rattling and has similar imperial designs on the Far East. Look what they are already doing in China. Colin will not be safe in Hong Kong. Anyway, I expect his bank will send him home if there is a threat of war." He paused, looking up at her now. "Our bank is already moving assets from vulnerable countries."

"Gosh," she said.

"I don't want to alarm you too much, my dear," he said, "but I do think you should reconsider your plan to travel. Go somewhere pleasant in England. Go to Devon or Cornwall."

Ellie shook her head. "I'm not going to France permanently, Lionel. Just a long holiday probably, and I don't think that Mr Hitler intends to start a war within the next couple of months."

"Let us hope not," he agreed. "At least Mr Chamberlain is all for appeasement. He's heading there himself, but I just wanted to make you aware of the situation. We had a meeting today, and I can tell you that the bank's president is taking this whole thing very seriously indeed."

"Then I'd better go and have my holiday without delay, hadn't I? And return to the comparative safety of an English village."

"Quite right," he said. He put out a hand and covered hers. "I do still feel responsible for you, Ellie. I'm very fond of you in my own way, and you've been a good wife to me."

"Not good enough, apparently," she said. She pulled her hand away and left the room.

∼∽

"Is that the lot, then?" Mavis was helping her to get the last items into a trunk. It was a blustery autumn day, and rain was peppering the window.

"I hope so," Ellie replied. "There's not another inch of space. I couldn't even take more hair clips. Gosh, I hope there really are porters everywhere. I have to make my way to Paris before I take the train to the Riviera."

"You ain't backing out now, I hope," Mavis said. "You don't want to let him feel that he's got the better of you."

Ellie pushed a strand of hair back from her face. "No, I won't back out. I'm just trying to face the realities of the journey."

Mavis leaned over to try and close the lid of the trunk. Ellie went to help, then stopped and stared. "What did you do to your arm?"

"Oh, that?" Mavis went red. "I bumped into something."

Ellie could recall other occasions when Mavis had accidently hurt herself. Bumped into something, brushed against the stove and burned her arm. Before, in the true British way of minding one's own business, she had said nothing, but today she couldn't help herself. "He did that to you. Your husband. Didn't he?"

Mavis turned away. "He'd had a drop too much again, and I hadn't kept his dinner hot enough for him."

"He hit you."

"No. He shoved me into the stove," Mavis said.

"Let me take a look at it." Ellie took her arm.

"It's just a bruise," Mavis said, backing away. "I'll live."

"This time, yes. But what about next time? It always escalates, Mavis. When he finds he can get away with it once or twice, it gets worse."

"He don't mean it," Mavis said. "It's just when he's had a drop too much."

Ellie put her hands on Mavis's shoulders, turning the other woman to face her. "Do you love him?"

"Love?" Mavis gave a bitter laugh. "I can't say I ever did. He was a soldier in the war, quite good-looking in his way in those days, and he was going off to the trenches and I was keen to get away from home—I was eldest of six kids in our house and not enough food. I didn't know he'd turn out to be a worse bully than my old dad." She gave a big sigh.

"It might have been all right if kids had come along, only they didn't. He blamed me for that, of course. Called me a barren cow. I once said it might be his fault, but I got a black eye for saying that."

"Mavis, you've got to leave him," Ellie said. Her grip on Mavis's shoulders tightened.

"Leave him?" Mavis frowned. "And where do you think I'd go, eh? I don't have no nice fat bank account. I couldn't even afford to rent a room somewhere new. I'm trapped, that's what I am."

"Why don't you come with me?" Ellie said impulsively.

Mavis stood staring, facing Ellie. "What, abroad? To the Continent? You must be joking."

"No, you'd love it. It's so beautiful, and the food is so good, and it's warm. I'll pay your way. It will give you time to think about what you want to do next, just as I'm doing."

Mavis stared out of the window. A big gust of wind rattled the frame and blew leaves from the apple tree. "I suppose you will need help with your things . . . ," she said hesitantly. "Someone to do for you over there . . ."

"No, don't think you'd come as a servant, Mavis. Come as a friend. You've always been a true friend to me."

"I ain't coming if I can't be useful," she said, but her voice cracked with emotion. Ellie could see tears in her eyes. "I'm going to do my share."

"Then you'll come?"

Again Mavis hesitated. Ellie could see she was torn between the desire to escape and the worry about what her husband would say.

"He ain't going to like me going away," she said. "He's used to being waited on hand and foot."

"Then it will be good for him," Ellie said.

"Yes, but you don't know what he's like if . . ."

Ellie understood what was going through Mavis's mind. She was worried he wouldn't let her go—make sure she didn't go. "Maybe you shouldn't tell him in advance, Mavis. Leave him a note to say you've been called away suddenly."

"I can't do that," Mavis said. "There would hell to pay when I came back."

"Mavis, do you really want to come back?" Ellie reached out and put her hand on Mavis's arm. "Are you happy with him?"

"Of course I'm not bloody happy, but . . . I did promise for better or worse, didn't I?"

"And so did I. And look where it's got me," Ellie said. "Out on my ear. Nowhere to go after thirty years. And my husband never laid a hand on me. Yours is liable to do you serious injury one day."

Mavis nodded, digesting this.

"Now's a good time to make the break, Mavis," Ellie continued. "Don't tell him ahead of time, but leave him a note to say you are accompanying me to the Continent. And then, if you decide you are better off without him, you write to him again and say that you're not coming back. That way you never have to face him."

"But what do I do when you come home? How do I survive on me own with no money?"

"You stay with me until we figure something out. I promise I'd never leave you stranded. You could find a job as a live-in housekeeper for a while or stay with me until you've enough new jobs to pay for a little cottage of your own. You could even go back to school, learn typing or some other skill. Either way we'd make it work."

There was a long silence.

"It's certainly tempting, missus," Mavis said at last.

"Then say yes. It's your perfect chance to escape, to lead a life *you* want." She put a tentative arm around Mavis's shoulder, leading her across the room. "I'm not doing this because I want company or I want someone to help me. I'm doing this because I'm genuinely fond of you, and I'm frightened that you're going to wind up in the morgue one day after he loses his temper. Your one chance, Mavis. What do you say?"

There was a long pause, then Mavis gave a sigh.

"All right. Why not? What have I got to lose?" She broke off. "Here, hold on. I don't have no passport."

Ellie sighed. "That is a problem."

"No, it ain't," Mavis said, her face suddenly lighting up. "Remember Major Radison at the Grange? I used to clean for them. They went abroad once, and her maid got to go with them as a servant, so she didn't need no passport of her own. She was written in as part of the group."

"That's splendid," Ellie said. "We'll go up to London today and get you added to my passport."

"London? Today?" Even the thought of that made Mavis uncertain.

"Yes. We want to get on with things, don't we? So take off your apron and let's get going. We'll take the Bentley."

As they drove off in the car, Ellie gave Mavis a delighted grin. "This is splendid. We have our own little tour group."

"What do you mean 'group'?"

"Now there are three of us . . ."

"Three?"

"Oh, I didn't tell you. Miss Smith-Humphries is joining us."

Mavis recoiled. "Her? Oh no. Stop the car. Turn around. I ain't coming if she's part of it. She's a critical old cow. Told me I didn't polish the church brass properly."

"She's dying, Mavis. She wants one last trip to a place she loved. We can't deny her that, can we?"

"I suppose not," Mavis said grudgingly.

"If you had to choose between Miss Smith-Humphries and a trip to the Continent and being left at home with your husband, which one would it be?"

Mavis gave a nervous little chuckle. "All right, then. But listen, I know I'll be on the passport as your servant, but you make it clear to her I ain't her bloody servant. And I'm not taking no nonsense from her."

"I will." Ellie had to laugh, too. "What a motley crew we'll be. The Three Musketeers—all for one and one for all. I don't know how we're going to manage getting three of us and our luggage on and off trains and . . ." She stared out of the windscreen, watching the wipers sweep away raindrops, as the thought slowly formed itself in her head. "We could take the Bentley," she said.

Mavis put her hand up to her mouth and let out a shriek. "What? Take your hubby's car? He'd have a fit. He'd go bananas."

"Well, why not?" Ellie said. "He was complaining the other day that it was ancient now and he should look into getting a new car. And he said I could have my share of our possessions. I'll leave him a note saying that I am taking the Bentley in lieu of any other items that would rightfully be mine."

"He won't like it, Mrs E.," Mavis said.

"He'll just have to lump it," Ellie replied. She and Mavis exchanged a delighted grin.

CHAPTER 6

Mavis's name was added to the passport without a problem. People acquired new servants all the time. Encouraged by the way everything was falling into place, they stopped off at Barkers, around the corner from the little flat Ellie now owned, and she bought a summer dress for Mavis and a pair of navy linen trousers for herself. Lionel did not approve of women in trousers, so it made the purchase all the sweeter.

Ellie didn't tell Lionel she planned to leave the next day, nor that she planned to take his Bentley. They ate dinner together—lamb chops, his favourite, followed by baked apples.

"Is Michelle a good cook?" she asked when he had complimented her on the dinner.

"I've actually no idea," he replied. "We haven't eaten that many meals together. But I expect she'll learn quickly. She has a splendid brain. Sharp as a tack. You're leaving your cookery books for now, I take it. She'll study them and be cooking in no time at all."

She looked at him, almost fondly. *Oh Lionel,* she thought, *you are in for such a shock.* Of course she said nothing. She bade him a polite good night and went up to her room. Sitting at her dressing table, going through the familiar routine of cold cream on the face and placing the hairnet over her hair, she noticed how old she looked. Old and strained and tired.

"What you need is fresh air and sunshine, my girl," she said firmly to her reflection. "You are doing the right thing."

"God, I hope so," she answered herself. Then she realized there was something she had not yet done, had put off, kept putting off because it seemed so final. She removed her wedding ring, struggling to pull it off. It came free and she stared at it, lying smooth and gold in her palm. *Thirty years,* she thought. Then she opened the small jewellery case she was taking with her and popped it inside.

In the night she lay awake worried that he'd decide to take the car in the morning. Or that he'd have a fit when he found she had taken it—alert the police, get her stopped at Dover and brought back in disgrace. She told herself he couldn't do that. He wouldn't do that. She had written a note that made her position quite clear:

> Dear Lionel,
> You will notice that I have taken the Bentley. I took your concerns to heart about me taking trains on the Continent, so the car seems so much easier. And you did offer me my share of our possessions. So consider the Bentley my share of everything that we owned together. You may keep all the furnishings, including the two paintings in the sitting room that came from my family and I understand may be quite valuable. Also the Queen Anne desk. And you did say you wanted to get a newer model car—now you can.
> I hope you have a good life.
> Yours sincerely, your former wife,
> Eleanor Harkington (formerly Endicott)

~~

Now that she was actually going to do the deed she fought back fear. Could she really do this? She had never really driven much further than Guildford, only five miles away. Even an expedition to London was a big adventure and required every ounce of her bravery. But taking the car across to France, where they drove on the wrong side of the road—was she out of her mind to think she could do it? And travelling with two women she hardly knew. How was that going to work? Miss Smith-Humphries would order Mavis around. There would be tension, which Ellie hated.

"Why did I say yes?" she asked herself over and over. "Why on earth didn't I do as Mavis suggested and take a nice safe tour?" Let someone else make the bookings and arrange the hotels and food and see that everything went smoothly. This was insanity. She sat up in bed, ready to tell the other women that she had changed her mind. She would not be going after all. But then she remembered . . . Miss Smith-Humphries wanted to revisit a happy memory before she died. Mavis wanted to escape an abusive husband. How could she deny them their own share of happiness?

And she realized something else—this was the turning point in her life. If she didn't take charge of her own destiny now, she'd become the pathetic, abandoned woman who kept cats and devoted her life to good works. She was absolutely not going to let that happen. Besides, those images of the Riviera were now all too vivid in her memory. All she had to do was to get there.

~~

Fortunately Lionel did not want to take the Bentley. Breakfast went without a hitch; he took his bowler hat from the rack in the hall. "I'll be off, then," he said. "Goodbye, Ellie."

He went to kiss her on the cheek, as he had done in their previous life, then remembered, gave an embarrassed cough and went out of the door. It was almost as if he had sensed it might be for the last time.

The moment he had gone, Ellie placed the note she had written on the table in the sitting room, beside his sherry decanter. Then she brought her hatbox and small suitcase downstairs. Mavis arrived with a small suitcase of her own.

"Well, I've been and gone and done it," she said. "I left him a note like you said. I hope we're across the Channel by the time he reads it, or else . . ."

"We will be," Ellie said. She looked at Mavis's small suitcase. "Do we have to pick up your big bag from your house?"

"What bag? This is it, love. I don't have many clothes, and most of them are only good for scrubbing floors." She headed for the staircase. "Is your trunk up there? Come on, then, let's get it down and get going before I decide I need my head examined and change my mind."

~~

It was just after nine when they pulled up outside Miss Smith-Humphries's cottage. The old lady was waiting for them. She came out dressed in a black tailored suit with a fox-head fur draped around her shoulders and a jaunty little black pillbox hat on her head. As she approached the Bentley, her face broke into a smile. "Oh, you've brought your maid with you. So sensible. I was wondering how we'd manage the luggage. Mine's in the front hallway, my dear. Be careful with it, won't you? It is rather heavy." This was directed to Mavis with a wave of the hand.

Ellie saw Mavis about to open her mouth and stepped in hastily.

"Mavis is coming with us as a friend, Miss Smith-Humphries. As my guest, not as my maid."

"Oh." Miss Smith-Humphries froze, staring at the car. Ellie could see she was deciding whether to come with them or not.

"That's rather irregular, isn't it?" she said.

"Not at all. Mavis has been my faithful helper for many years, and she needs a good holiday. I'm treating her to one. Now, would you like us to bring out your bags for you?"

"Don't worry, Mrs E., I'll get them." Mavis emerged from the back seat, went up the path and into the front hall. Miss Smith-Humphries made eye contact with Ellie. "But what does her husband think of this?"

"Mavis is much better off without her husband." Ellie mouthed the words as Mavis emerged with a large pigskin suitcase in one hand and a Morocco leather train case in the other.

"Oh, so that's it, is it?" She gave Ellie a knowing look. "One has heard, of course . . ." And she left the rest of the sentence unfinished.

They managed to squeeze her suitcase into the trunk. Mavis took the back seat, with a hatbox and train case beside her. Miss Smith-Humphries was seated in the front.

"And off we go!" Ellie said.

"You did settle things with your husband about taking his motor car, I hope," Miss Smith-Humphries said as they left the village behind and green countryside stretched out on either side of them. It was a pleasant autumn day with slanting sunlight making the turning leaves glow amber. The smell of bonfire smoke hung in the air.

"Not exactly," Ellie said. "But I did leave him a note, making my position clear. Besides, we'll be across the Channel and past Paris by the time he gets home. I don't think he'd know how to track me down in France." And she laughed. She had laughed a lot recently, she realized. It felt strange after years of not smiling much. Almost as if her face was being reborn.

I am being reborn, she thought. She came to the junction of the main road and headed south, to the coast and the car ferry to France. They drove the Bentley on to the noon ferry to Calais. As they stood on the deck, the stiff breeze in their faces, watching the white cliffs move away in the wake, Ellie stared in wonder. It was actually happening. She had escaped. She was free. She felt triumph surge up inside her. But at the same moment, Mavis gave a wail.

"I can't believe I've been and gone and done it," Mavis said. The receding coastline had suddenly made it real to her. "Now I can't never go back, can I? He'll kill me for running off like this."

"That's precisely why you can't go back to him, Mavis," Miss Smith-Humphries said. "If you'd stayed, he might have eventually killed you. When we've all had a good rest we'll help you decide what you want

47

to do and where you want to be. But in the meantime this cold wind isn't good for us. I suggest we all go down to the saloon and have a decent meal."

And so they did. As they boarded Mavis had expressed her dismay about being on the sea but barely noticed they were moving and ate a hearty meal. The crossing could not have been smoother. Their arrival in France could not have been smoother, either. The customs and immigration men looked at the Bentley, the distinguished lady driving it and glanced into the back seat.

"My aunt and my maid," Ellie said in her good French.

"Welcome to France, my lady," the man said, barely glancing at her passport as he handed it back to her. "Have a good holiday."

The women exchanged a giggle as they drove away. It almost felt like being naughty schoolgirls getting away with a prank. They stopped first at the bureau de change, where Ellie and Miss Smith-Humphries exchanged money. They then filled up with petrol, bought a map and set off.

"It don't look much different from back home," Mavis commented. She had been staring out of the car windows as they crossed a dockside area and then drove through the town of Calais.

"What did you expect, people with two heads?" Miss Smith-Humphries said in her usual cutting fashion.

"No, but I thought, you know, I'd heard about abroad and how the people were different from us, so I thought . . ."

"This is a dockside town, Mavis," Miss Smith-Humphries said. "Lots of commerce. Once we're in the depths of the countryside, I expect you'll notice the difference."

They left the port behind and found themselves in the French countryside. The afternoon was warm for late September. The grains had been harvested and piled into small haystacks to dry as they drove past fields. The road was lined with poplar trees, giving pleasant shade. They drove through a village: cream-coloured houses with brown and green shutters, a shop with vegetables in baskets outside and a café with old men sitting at a table, smoking and nursing glasses of wine.

"Look at that. Drinking wine and it's not yet three o'clock," Mavis exclaimed.

Miss Smith-Humphries gave a sigh of pleasure. "How delightful it all is. I remember it so well. This is going to do me good; I know it is."

Ellie was just thinking that it was doing her good, too. All the tensions of the past weeks were already slipping away. In two or three days' time, they'd be on the Côte d'Azur.

Having consulted the map and questioned the petrol station attendant, they took the road that skirted Paris to the north. There would be a faster road leading out of Paris, but then she'd have to navigate the city, and she wasn't prepared to do that. After a while the road veered around to the south, and the flat grain fields of the coast gave way to rolling hills, their slopes covered with vines. The road had been fairly empty thus far, for which Ellie was grateful, as she had worried that driving on the wrong side could be a challenge. But as they moved into the region of Burgundy they saw plenty of activity. Women working in the fields wore colourful kerchiefs around their heads. Some of them wore aprons over full skirts.

"Now they look different," Mavis said. "What are they growing in them fields?"

"This is a wine-growing region, Mavis," Miss Smith-Humphries said. "You've heard of Burgundy wine, haven't you? They are harvesting the grapes." As she was speaking, a tractor pulled out in front of them, towing a trailer piled high with dark-purple grapes, making Ellie apply the brakes rapidly, her heart beating fast. A little later they came to a small town. Half-timbered houses with red tiled roofs lined the narrow cobbled street. The Bentley bumped its way forward. There was a suspicious lack of activity, however. Nobody sat at the corner café, and the shops were shuttered.

"Where is everyone?" Miss Smith-Humphries voiced Ellie's concern.

"I don't know. It's not siesta time, is it? And they don't go in for siesta this far north. Could it be early closing day? It's almost as if—" Ellie broke off speaking and stopped the car.

"Oh no," she said. There seemed to be some kind of barricade ahead of them. "It looks as if the road is closed."

Miss Smith-Humphries had assigned herself the role of navigator. She studied the map. "It would be most inconvenient to go back. There doesn't seem to be an easy way around this village."

Ellie was thinking more of trying to reverse back up this narrow street. She wound down the window, hoping to find someone to ask for directions. They were immediately aware of the sounds behind that roadblock. People shouting, a baby crying.

"Is it a revolution going on, do you think?" Mavis asked, gripping the seat in front of her. "Are we going to be murdered?"

"Don't be silly, Mavis. France is a civilized country," Miss Smith-Humphries said, but she too sounded alarmed.

"I think we'd better . . . ," Ellie began, but before she could put the car into reverse two men appeared. They saw the motor car and came towards it. Mavis gave a little whimper.

"Mille pardons, mesdames," one man said. A thousand pardons. "You wish to pass. We will remove it instantly." He stared at them with interest, noting the English car. "You are from England?"

"Yes, we are," Ellie answered, also in French. "We are driving south to the Riviera."

"Ah, how nice. A good way to spend the winter, I think."

The other man called something to him. He turned back, then addressed the women again. "We are celebrating. The harvest is in. It's the Feast of Saint Michael. My friend says you should join us for a glass of wine."

"How very kind," Ellie replied, "but I'm afraid we need to keep going. We must find a hotel before it gets dark."

"But you can stay here, in our town," the man said.

"Yes. Here is good." The other man had joined him now, and several more were coming around the barricade. "See—just a small way along that street. Auberge de la Reine. Very good. Very clean. And then you come and join us, eh?"

"It will be dark soon," Miss Smith-Humphries muttered, having understood the French. "It might be wise to stay here."

"Come." The first man motioned to the others. Two of the men picked up what had been the barricade but now turned out to be a trestle table on its side and moved it away. They beckoned the car through. Ellie edged forward as the men accompanied her, shouting to each other.

"What do they want?" Mavis asked. "Are they taking us somewhere?"

"It's all right, Mavis, they are friendly," Miss Smith-Humphries said. "They are inviting us to have a glass of wine with them. It's a feast day."

"But you're never going to go drinking with them men, are you, missus?" Mavis sounded alarmed.

The street opened into a central square, lined with ornately half-timbered houses, each with a sloping tiled roof. At the far end of the square was an impressive grey stone church. More tables had been set up, covered in red-and-white-checked tablecloths, and women were busy putting out bowls of food. Families were already seated at some of the tables. Most of the women were in some kind of local costume with flowing red skirts, white blouses and bright scarves tucked in at the waist. They wore white lace caps on their heads. So did the small children. Some of the men, Ellie noted, wore wooden shoes. It was all so delightfully different, so foreign.

Lionel would hate this. The thought passed through her head and made her smile.

"Look, there are plenty of women, too, and children. Whole families," she said, turning back to Mavis. "It's a festival. It would be rude not to join them for a few minutes."

"If the hotel proves to be suitable," Miss Smith-Humphries said. "I have no wish to catch fleas."

Several of the men took it upon themselves to escort the Bentley down the street to the auberge and demanded that the landlady give these visitors from England the best rooms for the night. They insisted on carrying the small suitcases upstairs. Miss Smith-Humphries was given a tiny room to herself, Mavis and Ellie a twin. It was simple in the extreme—two narrow beds, each with a comforter, a washbasin with a mirror over it and a crucifix over the beds, but it seemed clean, and the price was more than reasonable. As Ellie worked out the francs in her head, she was pleasantly surprised. Was all of France going to be as cheap as this? In which case they could live quite well.

Two of the men were still waiting, lounging against a wall, smoking thin black cigarettes, when they came down again. "Now it's time for a drink," one of them said. "Leave your vehicle. It will be quite safe."

"Are you sure?" Miss Smith-Humphries asked. "We have our large bags still in the boot."

"Pierre will guard it, do not worry," the man said. "And we are not thieves here. Everyone knows everyone else in this village. We respect the stranger. Do not worry."

They allowed themselves to be escorted back to the square, where lights had now been turned on and sparkled festively. Bunting fluttered from the church. One of the men called out something, and immediately room was made for them at one of the tables. Wine bottles were passed down, and glasses were poured for them. These were followed by plates of bread, cheeses, pâté, sausages, tomatoes, various salads and bowls of grapes.

"Is it all right to eat this, do you think?" Mavis whispered. "I'm famished, but."

"I'm sure it's quite all right, Mavis. Go ahead. Enjoy yourself." Ellie helped herself to a piece of bread and handed over the basket. She took a sip of the rich red wine, feeling its warmth instantly flowing through her. She sat as if in a trance, taking in the scene around her: the twinkling lights, the unfamiliar smells of grilling meats, onions and garlic, the sounds of music, the shouts of children, the laughter. And she felt a bubble of happiness rising within her, as if years of frost and loneliness were already starting to melt.

Everyone at the table wanted to know all about them—where they had come from, where their husbands were, how many children they had, where they were going. Ellie's head was spinning as she tried to answer them in her rusty French, but the villagers listened patiently and nodded as she spoke.

"You have our language. That is good," an old lady said, patting Ellie's hand.

They all expressed dismay that two of the women had no children and that none of them had a husband. "Madame Girard here, she is also a widow," the woman opposite Ellie said. The woman gave a sympathetic nod. *They think we're widows, which is good,* Ellie thought.

A band assembled in the square—a fiddle, an accordion and motley instruments. Music started playing, echoing out through the evening air. People got up to dance, holding hands in a circle, moving faster and faster until they broke apart laughing.

More wine and food were pressed upon them. They were told that the harvest had been a good one this year. God had been good to them.

The church clock was striking ten as they walked back to their inn, leaving the celebration still in full swing. Ellie was feeling the effects of the wine as well as the constant conversation in a foreign tongue, but she was also feeling a deep contentment that the decision she had made had been the right one. The risk had already paid off.

"Those people know how to have a good blowout, don't they, missus?" Mavis said. "You don't see them having a good time like that in England."

"No, Mavis, you don't. And I'm sure English people would not take strangers to their hearts the way these people did."

"I was quite touched," Miss Smith-Humphries said. "They treated us like long-lost kin. If the place we eventually stay is like this, it will be most interesting."

"If a little exhausting," Ellie added.

Miss Smith-Humphries smiled. "That is true, of course. One would not like this type of thing to happen every night, but I'm glad we experienced it as our introduction to France. It reminds us why we have such fond memories from our youth."

Up in their room Ellie listened to the distant sounds of laughter and singing. *So far from home,* she thought. Lionel would have found her note by now. Would he be fuming about the car, or would he actually be missing her? *He's no longer my husband,* she thought. *It doesn't matter what he feels or thinks.*

CHAPTER 7

The next morning they were greeted with a breakfast of fresh baguette and apricot jam as well as milky coffee. Simple but satisfying.

"I remember how good the bread tastes here," Miss Smith-Humphries said. "So how far do you think we will get today?"

"Let's look at the map when we get back to the motor car," Ellie said. "Not all the way to the coast, I'm pretty sure, but I hope we can stop beyond Lyon."

They loaded up the car again, finding it untouched as the men had promised, and the two women in the front seat studied the map.

"I suppose it depends how fast we can go," Ellie said. "If we have to go through many villages with narrow streets like this one, we will probably have to spend the night in Lyon."

"One forgets that France is a big country, doesn't one?" Miss Smith-Humphries said. "There are not many places in Britain that could not be reached in two days. The north of Scotland, maybe."

Ellie turned back to Mavis. "You're awfully quiet, Mavis. Are you not feeling well?"

"I'm all right, missus," Mavis said. "I'm just not used to drinking wine, and I think it's sinking in that I'm a long way from my home."

"That's true," Miss Smith-Humphries said, "but would you rather be there or here?"

Mavis looked out of the window. It was another glorious autumn day. "Well, if you put it that way—I never thought I'd get to see a bit of the world before I died, and now I am. So I'd ruddy well better make the most of it, hadn't I?"

"That's the ticket," Miss Smith-Humphries said. "Ready for adventure. And so am I."

They set off, driving due south now, through the towns of Châlons and Dijon. Ellie was coming to terms with driving on the right-hand side but drove extra carefully through busy streets. Once in the countryside again, they rolled down their windows and enjoyed the warm air in their faces. They approached the city of Lyon around four o'clock.

"I suppose we should find a hotel in the city," Miss Smith-Humphries said. "I doubt there will be any proper establishments on the other side of it until we get to Avignon. Last night's inn was clean enough, but that bed—the springs creaked loudly every time I turned over, and the facilities were sadly lacking."

"I agree, but I'm anxious to reach the coast tomorrow if we can," Ellie said. "Should we not take our chances again? No harm came to us from last night, and it was so cheap that it was almost embarrassing."

"We are in your hands, Mrs Endicott," Miss Smith-Humphries said, her voice cold enough to let Ellie know that she didn't approve. Ellie noted the frigidity now in the car.

"That's another thing," Ellie replied. "Since we've now embarked on this adventure together, I think we should start to be less formal with each other. Mavis's name we know. I am Eleanor but have always gone by Ellie. And your surname is a real mouthful, Miss Smith-Humphries. May we know your Christian name?" She turned to the older woman.

"I suppose so." Miss Smith-Humphries hesitated. "It's Theodora."

Mavis gave an unvoluntary splutter of amusement.

"I agree, Mavis, it is cumbersome," she said, "but in my youth it was shortened to Dora, and I like that much better."

"Dora," Ellie said. "I like that, too."

They came to the suburbs of the city, and ahead of them was the Rhône River, glinting in evening sunlight as it flowed south.

Luckily the main road south hugged the western bank and did not cross the river until well south of the city centre.

"It seems we have bypassed Lyon without meaning to," Ellie said. "I must say I'm grateful. I was rather dreading it. But it also means we've passed any hotels. Do you mind if we press on? It's still quite light."

"Whatever you think is best," Dora said. "I'm looking at the map, and I don't see any big towns before Valence. But maybe there will be a small hotel, or we can even get as far as Avignon for the night."

"Avignon!" Ellie let out a little sigh. Even the name sounded romantic. She started to hum "Sur le Pont d'Avignon." Dora joined her, and they began to sing it out loud.

Feeling cheerful now, they drove south with the river flowing beside them. Barges came down with the current, and steep hills rose on either side. The light began to fade.

"We really should keep our eyes open for a hotel now," Dora said. "I don't like the idea of negotiating this road in the dark."

Ellie looked at the dials in front of her. "Oh no. I'm afraid we should have filled up with petrol in Lyon," she said. "We haven't passed a garage for ages now."

"I hope you don't intend us to push," Dora said. "Oh well, we've got Mavis to do it for us."

"Here, just because . . ." Mavis sat up, leaning forward.

"Just a joke, Mavis. Meant to lighten the mood." Dora looked back at her and patted her hand.

"Oh, all right. Bob's your uncle." Mavis sank back into her seat.

Darkness fell. Headlights of occasional passing cars flashed in their faces and were gone. Their own headlights lit up the churning waters of the river, flowing beside them, as the road wound along the bank. It was flowing awfully fast. Ellie felt a knot in her stomach. Then they came around another bend and saw lights ahead.

"Thank God," Ellie said.

They drove into a small settlement. There were houses with lighted windows, a bakery, now closed, a bar with several men sitting outside and then a garage with two petrol pumps. Ellie came to a halt at one of them as an attendant came running out and started unscrewing the cap. "You wish it filled, madame?" he asked.

Ellie nodded. "Please."

"I think we should all use the facilities if they have them," Ellie said. "Why don't you go while I stay with the motor?"

She wound down the window and sat in the darkness, smelling the watery smell of the river mixed with the odours of petrol and the herby scent of French cigarettes. From one of the houses, a radio was blaring out a woman singing in a nasal voice. There was also the scent of frying onions, reminding Ellie that they hadn't eaten for some time. But there didn't seem to be a café in the village, just the bar, which didn't look too welcoming.

The attendant finished pumping. She handed him money, and he shuffled off towards the building at the back to deposit it. As Ellie looked around, her gaze moved to the lorry that had pulled up at the pump beside her. A man got out and headed off into the darkness, presumably obeying the call of nature. Ellie noticed a movement in the cab window and looked up. A young girl's face stared back at her—a face white with terror—and the girl mouthed something.

Without hesitating, Ellie got out and went over to the lorry. She opened the door.

"Are you all right?"

"Aidez-moi. Help me," the girl said in French. "He will be back soon."

"You don't wish to travel with him?" Ellie asked. "He is not your father?"

"No," the girl said. "I accepted a lift from him. But then he started saying what we would do when we find a hotel for the night. Awful things. And I couldn't run away because I have nowhere to run."

"Then come with us," Ellie said. "We'll take you safely where you need to go."

"Really? Oh, God bless you, madame." She was already beginning to climb down.

"Do you have your bags?"

"Only this small bag behind my seat." She reached for it and scrambled out as if she couldn't get away fast enough.

"Get into the back seat of my car." Ellie opened the back door. "It will be a bit cramped but better than the alternative. See if you can crouch down on the floor." As the girl climbed in, Ellie covered her with the travel rug, then placed a hatbox on top of her. "Don't move," she said.

At that moment, Dora and Mavis returned.

"You won't believe what we've just had to do," Mavis said as they approached. "The toilet was a hole in the ground. I'm not joking. Just two boards on either side of a hole. That was it. I didn't know what I was supposed to do. Nowhere to put me bum."

"I'm afraid it was terribly primitive," Dora said. "I don't know if you want to use it, Ellie."

"I won't use it now," Ellie said. "I want to be away from here as quickly as possible. Get in, please."

"Why, Ellie, what's wrong?" Dora asked.

"I'll explain later. We just need to drive on before a man comes back."

"Gracious. What on earth?" Dora said as she took her seat, and Ellie hurriedly closed the door behind her. She assisted Mavis in, then returned to the driver's seat. The car started, and they eased out towards the road. They had to wait for a passing car and were about to turn on to the road when they heard a shout. The man had returned to his lorry and found the passenger gone. He came over to them—a big, burly man in blue overalls. "Hey, you." He banged on the bonnet of the car. "Have you seen where the girl went?"

Ellie rolled down her window, staring at him angrily. "I'm sorry," she said in clipped English tones, "I'm afraid we do not speak French. But do not touch my motor car."

"Fille. Jeune fille." The man waved his hands, trying to indicate a girl.

Ellie shook her head. "I'm sorry we can't help you. Don't speak French." She spoke the words slowly and distinctly, shaking her head.

The man moved closer, peering into the back of the Bentley. He saw Dora in the front seat, Mavis with several cases piled on the seat beside her.

"I don't know what you want, but please go away." Ellie gave him her haughtiest stare. "Go away, or I will call the manager or the gendarmes." She shooed him like a chicken. He ran off, checking out where the girl could have gone. Ellie put her foot on the accelerator, and they drove into the darkness as fast as she dared.

"What on earth was that about?" Dora asked. "Did that man try to accost you when we were away? What an unpleasant individual."

Suddenly Mavis gave a scream. "Something touched me. There's something alive here."

"It's all right, Mavis," Ellie said. "We have a girl hiding in the back seat. She was being kidnapped by the driver of that lorry."

"Blimey," Mavis said.

"All is well, mademoiselle. You are safe. You can come out now," she said in French. "Help her up, Mavis," she continued in English. Mavis removed the hatbox and the rug, and the girl emerged, looking around her in wonder.

"Have you lost all reason?" Dora demanded. "Driving off with a strange girl in the car? You know nothing about her. She could have been with a relative or even a husband, and you could be the one who finds herself accused of kidnapping."

"She looked terrified, Dora. I saw her staring out of that window. She beckoned me over and begged me to help her before he came back. She said she'd accepted a lift from him, but now he was starting to talk about his awful plans for her when they went to a hotel together. I couldn't leave her there, could I?"

"I suppose not," Dora said. "But I do ask myself whether it is wise to get ourselves mixed up in something that is none of our business in a foreign country."

She turned back to the girl. "What is your name, ma fille?" she asked in her stilted, anglicized French.

"Yvette, madame," the girl replied in scarcely more than a whisper.

"Well, Yvette, why did you agree to travel with this man? Did you know him?"

"No, madame. I was just trying to head south, and he came along and offered me a ride. It was all right to start with. He bought me some food. But then it got dark, and he said we'd go to a hotel together and I could repay him for taking me. He asked if I was a virgin, and he said awful things."

"I'm so sorry, my dear," Ellie said. "So why did you need a ride? Are you running away from home?"

"I had to leave my home in a hurry, madame," Yvette said. "I was not wanted there. I thought I'd go south, where it was warm and pleasant, and maybe find work in one of the resorts on the Côte d'Azur."

"Should you not be in school?" Dora asked.

"I am seventeen, madame. I come from a farm. There was little opportunity to go to school when I had to help with the farm chores. My father was a strict man."

"Well, Yvette, you are safely with three English ladies, and we are driving to the Côte d'Azur, so you can ride with us. And when we arrive, you can decide what you want to do."

"You are too good, madame," Yvette said. "You are angels of mercy. God will reward you."

"Here," Mavis said, having sat silent as the conversation in French went on around her. "Will someone explain to me what the devil's going on?"

CHAPTER 8

Soon after, they came to another small settlement, but Ellie was loath to stop, even though she was now aware that she had not visited the lavatory like the other women. She'd just have to hold it.

"What if the man spots our car and comes to check on us again? Maybe somebody saw me helping Yvette." She stared straight ahead. "We must drive on until we come to a big enough place where we cannot be traced."

That proved to be the town of Valence, on the bank of the river. From what they could see in the darkness, it was a city of parks and elegant buildings.

"Ah, this looks more like it," Dora said, sitting up in her seat. "There's bound to be a decent hotel here. And a decent meal, too, one hopes."

Ellie left the riverbank, and they followed a wide boulevard towards the city centre.

"There." Dora pointed. "Hotel Bristol. That should do."

"It looks as if it's quite expensive." Ellie examined the grand edifice, brightly lit, with a courtyard and flags flying. "There are four of us."

"I'm sure they must have maids' rooms for Mavis and the girl," Dora said dismissively.

"Thanks a lot," Mavis muttered.

"Oh no, madame," Yvette exclaimed from the back seat. "I cannot stay here with you. I have no money for such luxury. I will sleep in your motor car and guard it for you until the morning."

"Certainly not," Ellie said. A small warning voice whispered that they should not be too trusting, however grateful the girl seemed. It would be too easy to rob them of their belongings or even drive away in their car. "You can stay in a small room beside mine for the night, unless you would prefer to leave us now. But tomorrow we will be on the Riviera if you have patience."

"Madame is an angel once again," Yvette said. "I will kiss your hand, madame."

"Not while I'm driving." Ellie had to laugh.

She suddenly felt overcome with exhaustion, not wanting to seek further, and the hotel did look inviting. They left the motor car outside and went into the foyer.

"But of course," the receptionist said, noting the Bentley parked outside. "I can arrange a room for mesdames with a small chamber off to the side for the maids."

"Thank you. Most satisfactory," Dora said before Ellie could reply. She turned to Mavis. "I hope you don't mind for one night. It will take a while before she stops thinking of you as a servant, but she'll come around when we reach the South."

Mavis gave a shrug. "I don't mind kipping in her maid's room, but I ain't shining her shoes. Not the way she talks to me."

And so it was arranged. Ellie would sleep with Yvette in her maid's quarters, and Dora would take a grand room overlooking the garden with Mavis. The car was driven into the garage. A bellboy carried up their overnight bags. The servant's room was quite adequate with a bed and washbasin. Ellie's room had a bathroom with an enormous clawfoot tub.

"Quite delightful," Dora said as they met downstairs. "French doors opening on to a balcony, and I can hear a fountain playing down below. I shall sleep well tonight."

"Mine ain't no worse than where I've lived most of me life," Mavis said. She moved closer to Ellie. "As long as she don't snore." She gave Dora a frown.

They did not feel like facing the grand dining room at the hotel, where guests were in evening attire. Instead they asked the clerk for a recommendation and ventured into the town. On a narrow backstreet they found the bistro and were warmly greeted. The set-price menu was consommé followed by duck breast and crème brûlée. A carafe of red wine was brought to the table, and they all ate heartily.

"What would my doctor say if he could see this?" Dora chuckled as she poured herself a second glass of wine. "I'm supposed to be on a bland diet of milk puddings and fish. Stupid man. I told him it's not my stomach that's going to give out, it's my heart, and my heart needs good, solid nourishment."

Ellie examined her. She had forgotten for a moment that the reason Dora was coming to France was that she did not have long to live. Ellie noticed now that her skin was quite transparent, the veins standing up blue on the backs of her hands, and that she had a frail look about her. She had always been so formidable that this realization came as a shock.

Yvette had sat silent through the meal, not daring to make eye contact with the others. Now she looked up and thanked Ellie again.

"You have saved my honour if not my life, madame," she said. "Who knows where I would be now—maybe floating lifeless in the Rhône. He was clearly a violent man."

"Yes, you had a lucky escape," Ellie said. "So tell us, why did you have to leave your home so suddenly?"

Yvette studied her coffee cup, toying with the spoon. "It's my father," she said. "He is a horrible man. Unkind, critical. My mother died when I was young, and my father treats me as a servant. He expects me to do all the housework and take care of the animals . . . and then . . ." She broke off, blinked, and took a deep breath. "He wanted me to marry the son of the man who owned the next farm over, so that our lands could be joined. Gaston was horrible—fat, ugly, rude. I refused. My father said he would force me. So I had to leave."

Ellie covered Yvette's hand with her own. "My dear girl, I'm so sorry. You are safe now. You travel with us to the South, and then you can find yourself a job and a place to live, and all will be well."

Yvette gave a weak smile. "Thank you, madame. You are too good."

Dora insisted on paying half the bill, and they walked back together to the hotel.

Ellie slept well that night, partly because of the wine, but also because she was exhausted. She awoke to narrow stripes of sunlight coming in through the closed blinds. When she opened them, the breeze that greeted her already had a hint of the South to it, perfumed and caressing. She felt her spirits rising. With any luck today, they'd be seeing the blue Mediterranean Sea, finding the perfect place to stay . . .

Mavis appeared, dressed and ready, now wearing a cotton frock. Like all her clothes, it hung off her bony frame, and Ellie realized it was the first time she had seen Mavis not wearing her apron.

"I reckon it's going to get ruddy hot, don't you, missus?" she asked. "If it's this warm already . . ."

"So how are you enjoying your adventure so far?" Ellie asked, smiling as Mavis began packing her things into the suitcase without being asked.

"Blimey, I never thought, in a million years, that I'd be seeing things like this," Mavis said. "You've opened my eyes, that's what you've done, and I'm grateful. I expect I'll miss home eventually, but right now I just want to take it all in."

"That's the spirit," Ellie said. "You need time to become a person in your own right, just like I do. We need to find out who we are."

"What about that French girl?" Mavis said. "She hasn't scarpered with your jewellery, has she?"

"She's in the bathroom," Ellie said. "Poor little thing."

"Well, I don't trust her," Mavis said.

"It's because she's foreign and doesn't speak English, Mavis. But don't worry. We'll get her settled in Marseille before we go on to find the perfect spot for ourselves. It's only another day you have to put up with her."

Mavis didn't reply but gave a little sniff.

After breakfast they stood as the hotel employee loaded their suitcases back into the Bentley. Dora drew Ellie aside, glancing at Yvette, who stood clutching a pathetically small cardboard suitcase, looking young and vulnerable.

"I really must insist that you stop rounding up strays, Mrs Endicott," Dora said. "For one thing, there is no more room in the motor car."

Ellie smiled. "But we're all strays, don't you see? I'm a stray. You're a stray. We've nowhere to go, and everywhere to go."

"I suppose you're right." Dora frowned. "Why are you so darned optimistic? Fate has dealt you a dirty hand, the same as it has for all of us. I'm being cheated out of time, Mavis out of a loving husband and enough money and Yvette out of a loving family. You've been cheated out of your nice, comfortable life and your lovely home and all the work you've put into it . . ."

"I am on my way to the South of France where who knows what adventures we'll have. What could I want more?" Ellie said. "And I have the whole world before me to do exactly what I want for the first time in my life. Do you realize, Dora, that I've spent my entire life trying to please other people: my parents, who never thought I was good enough, clever enough, pretty enough, holy enough, and then my husband, who took everything I did for granted, gave me no credit for any of his success and then tossed me aside without a second thought?"

She spread her hands wide. "It's all possible, Dora. I can't tell you how wonderfully free I feel. If my husband had had his way, I'd have been moved to a tiny flat in Knightsbridge, the flat where he had once kept his mistress, I suspect. I'd have mooched around Harrods once a week, looking at clothes and foodstuffs I could no longer afford, and then spent my evenings sitting alone, listening to the radio. Or I'd be living in a grim little cottage—he suggested the one by the railway line, you know—doing good deeds with you at church and getting whispers and looks of pity whenever I went out."

She exchanged a glance with Dora. "Instead we're going to find a lovely place overlooking the sea and eat octopus and drink lots of wine."

"Good gracious me." Dora shook her head.

They set off, the Bentley's nose pointed due south with the Rhône River flowing beside them. Boats going south moved swiftly with the current. Those going north struggled under full power. There were no bridges for a long while, meaning the people on both banks led quite different lives, Ellie surmised. Vineyards still covered the hillsides, their leaves starting to turn golden, and buildings were now solid stone rather than gracefully carved wood.

~~

They came to the medieval city of Avignon.

"There is a way around the city which would save us some time," Dora said, looking up from her map.

Ellie hesitated. "Have you ever seen Avignon?"

"I can't say that I have. All I know is the song, 'Sur le Pont.'"

"I think we should spare a few moments to see it," Ellie said. "The bridge and the Palace of the Popes. A lot of history."

"Ah, sur le pont d'Avignon," Yvette chimed in from the back seat, having understood these words. And she broke into the song with a high, sweet voice.

That settled it. Avignon had to be visited.

"Even if we have to spend the night in Marseille and go further along the coast tomorrow," Ellie said. "After all, the one thing we have is time."

They drove into the city centre through narrow streets, many of them cobbled. Ahead of them rose the formidable Palace of the Popes, looking more like a great fortress with its crenelated buttresses and fortified tower.

They went down to the riverbank to see the bridge.

"But it's only half there," Mavis exclaimed as they stared at the yellow stone span reaching out into the turbulent water, abruptly ending halfway across.

"Yes, I believe the power of the river kept knocking down the arches," Ellie said. "It was abandoned long ago."

"Don't they have nothing modern in France, then?" Mavis asked, eyeing it critically.

"I'm sure they do in Paris and in all the cities," Ellie said, "but it's the history that makes it so charming, isn't it?"

Mavis just grunted. After Avignon the landscape changed again. They were now coming into the landscape of the South—dry and dusty with the occasional hilltop village. The road had moved away from the river. They passed vineyards or fields of maize, the cobs already harvested, the stubble now dead and dying. There were olive trees surrounding solid stone farmhouses, donkeys carrying loads from the fields. On the hillsides grew umbrella pines, Italian cypress and herby shrubs whose scent filled the car—sage and rosemary and other smells that Ellie could not identify. She breathed in deeply, letting the scents remind her that she had escaped, that she was now far away and starting a new and different life. *I may never go back,* she thought, toying with the idea. What if she found a place she liked and stayed here forever?

CHAPTER 9

It was about four o'clock when they approached Marseille. The road wound down from rocky hills, and they got their first glimpse of the city, crowned by the basilica of Our Lady of the Guard, its gold statue shining from a hilltop.

"How lovely," Dora muttered as they first glimpsed it.

"Have you been here before?" Ellie asked.

"Never," Dora said.

"Neither have I," Ellie agreed. "We came to the Riviera from Italy the last time I was in France, years ago. A train from Genoa to Nice, and when we left we headed straight up to Paris." She looked around them as they drove. "I can't say I'm too enamoured yet. It looks a little run-down, doesn't it?"

As they came into the city centre, they found themselves on a wide boulevard lined with shops, including a couple of department stores, and what looked like municipal buildings.

"Ah, this looks a little better," Dora said. She consulted her map. "This main street is called La Canebière and leads directly to the port."

Ellie stared ahead and kept driving. It seemed important to her to get that first glimpse of the Mediterranean and to know they had arrived. When she looked into the rearview mirror, she saw Yvette, now sitting up and alert, staring out of the window with an alarmed look on her face.

As the street approached the port, it became busier and more run-down, lined with bars and smaller shops. They noticed sailors of various types, sizes and colours, strolling in bands, sitting at bars, talking, laughing. Two men in white sailor uniforms were chatting to a girl who lounged at the doorway to a building. As the Bentley passed, the girl nodded and they followed her inside.

"Oh my," Dora said. "It doesn't look too savoury around here. We certainly couldn't leave Yvette in a place like this."

Ellie agreed. "We don't seem to be coming to anything like Nice. I thought there might be a promenade with good hotels. Perhaps we should just push on." She turned back to Yvette. "We do not think this place would be suitable for you to stay here. Not with all these sailors."

"I agree, madame," Yvette said. "I have been feeling most apprehensive. I do not think I would feel safe here. If you don't mind, I would like to remain with you until we come to somewhere less dangerous."

Even as she said the words, there was a shout from the other side of the street. A man emerged from an alleyway, pursued by other men. He stumbled out into the street, almost colliding with their car. Backed up against the car that had come to a halt in the traffic, he wheeled and pulled out a knife. The men following him hesitated. A crowd gathered. Attempts were made to grab him. There were more shouts; a whistle sounded. Police arrived. Mavis gave a little cry of alarm. The traffic moved, and Ellie drove on as quickly as she could, looking for a place to turn around, which she could not do until they reached the port itself, its quayside lined with ships of all sizes, from fishing boats to small freighters to a couple of liners, their white decks gleaming in the setting sun. There were indeed hotels on the quayside but not the majestic ones Ellie remembered from Nice. Ellie's heart was still beating fast from the encounter with the knife-wielding man.

"I really don't think we'd want to stay here, do you?" She turned to Dora.

"I most certainly don't. Even if we're safe, it's too bustling and noisy for me. I'd like a place with peace and quiet. And beauty, too."

"I agree," Ellie said.

"I ain't half glad we're getting out of here," Mavis said as they drove back up the main thoroughfare. "I would have worried about getting murdered in me bed. I've never seen such unsavoury-looking types. And that one with the knife. Blimey. Me heart nearly jumped out of me chest when he ran towards us."

"Don't worry, Mavis," Dora said. "The towns on the Riviera are most civilized. What's more, there are plenty of English people there. Yvette should easily find a job as chambermaid at one of the big hotels in Nice or Antibes or Cannes."

Yvette looked enquiringly at the sound of her name. "Nice? Antibes?" she said. "You go there?" she asked Ellie in French.

"I expect so," Ellie said. "We haven't made up our minds yet. But they would be good places for you to find work. What sort of job do you think you'll want to do? What skills do you have?"

"I have no real skills, madame. I think I am not fit for anything other than being a maid," Yvette said. "The only problem is . . ."

She left the rest of the sentence hanging.

"Yes?" Ellie had come to a stop as a policeman held up traffic. Ellie turned back to look at Yvette, who had now blushed red.

"You are so good," she said. "I was going to say that I wanted a better future than backbreaking work on a farm, but I cannot lie to you any longer. You must know the truth. My father threw me out when he discovered I am pregnant. He told me I am no longer his daughter, and he told me never to come back."

The other two women didn't understand when Ellie gasped.

"What did she say?" Dora asked. "Neither my French nor my hearing are as good as they were. Why did she leave?"

"She says she found out she is going to have a baby."

"Pregnant?" Dora exclaimed. She switched to her painfully slow French. "But you're a mere child yourself. Who is the father of this infant? Why does he not do the right thing?"

"He is far away, madame," Yvette said. She swallowed back a sob. "He is in the army, and he was suddenly sent to North Africa before I knew that I was with child. I don't know where he's gone. He said he'd write to me as soon as he found out which country he'd be stationed in, but now I will never get the letter. He would marry me if he knew, I'm sure of it. He was so sweet and loving to me."

"You poor girl." Ellie reached back and patted her hand. "Don't worry. We'll try to help you. Maybe we can contact your sweetheart through the French army headquarters?"

"Maybe." Yvette did not sound too hopeful.

"How do you plan to support yourself with a child?" Dora asked. "Or even during the latter stages of pregnancy? You will not be able to work."

Yvette shook her head. Tears were now trickling down her cheeks. "I do not know, madame. All I know is that I have no home. No one I can turn to."

"You have no relatives who can help?" Dora asked.

"My mother died when I was an infant. My father has raised me alone. I had grandparents, but they have now passed away, too. There is my father's brother, but he is as bad as my father. I would not be welcome there."

Ellie cleared her throat. "Well, Yvette, ma petite, you are in safe hands now. We will take you with us, and when we reach our destination, we will decide what is best for you."

Yvette lifted a tear-stained face. "Really? Oh madame, I cannot thank you enough. You don't know what it's been like, not knowing what to do. I seriously thought of taking my life, drinking rat poison, even though I know that it would be a terrible sin, and I'd never go to heaven . . ." She wiped a tear from her cheek again.

The policeman blew his whistle again and motioned the traffic forward. As they drove off, Dora moved closer to Ellie. "I hope you know what you're doing," she muttered. "First you saddle us with a housemaid and now with a pregnant girl. Are we to be a Noah's ark for the lost souls of the world?"

Ellie looked at her, then she smiled. "If that's what it takes, then yes."

~~

They drove out of the city and took the road signposted to Toulon.

"We won't be able to get as far as the Riviera proper tonight," Ellie said.

"We should make it to Hyères or Toulon." Dora was back in her role as navigator. "I hear that Hyères is most agreeable. Didn't Queen Victoria stay there in her later years?"

"In that case, it must be good enough for us." Ellie laughed. "How far would you say it was?"

Dora studied her map. "Fifty miles maybe. But the road looks awfully winding."

"We should be able to do fifty miles before it gets dark," Ellie said.

Dora traced the road on the map with her finger. "There are small villages along the coast but nothing inland until we get to Toulon. And that's another naval town, isn't it? I'm sure I read that the French navy are headquartered there."

"Then definitely not Toulon. I don't think we could handle more knife fights." Ellie steered the car around a bend. The road was entering a wild and mountainous area, the hillsides covered in bushy scrub. It cut through a steep-sided valley, wound its way up to a crest, then down again. Ellie found herself gripping the wheel as she stared ahead. The valleys themselves were already bathed in gloom, and the sun only highlighted the cream-coloured rocky summits above them. It grew gradually darker.

"I hope it's not too far now," Ellie said. "We haven't passed a village in ages, and we'll need petrol soon."

"I thought of mentioning that before we left Marseille," Dora said, a note of smugness in her voice. Ellie swallowed back her annoyance.

As they climbed to the top of another ridge, she stared in alarm. "Is that smoke? Do you smell burning?"

A white mist was rising from the bonnet of the Bentley.

"I do see smoke, or is it steam?" Dora peered out of the windscreen.

"Is the engine on fire?" Mavis sat up in alarm, clutching Dora's seat. "Shouldn't we get out before it blows up?"

"I think it's steam," Ellie said. "It must be the radiator. I should have checked before we left. Oh damn and blast. How far to the nearest village, do you think, Dora?"

Dora peered down at the map. It was now quite dark and hard to see.

"I don't see anything on this road for a while. There are villages along the coast. Maybe we should head for the closest one. Take the next turnoff."

They proceeded slowly, the Bentley still showing its displeasure, hissing steam escaping. At the foot of the slope, a tiny road went off to their right. A small hand-painted sign read "Saint-Benet."

"It might just be a church or a monastery," Dora said. "I don't see it on the map."

"At least there would be someone who can help us." Ellie turned the car on to the road, little more than a track. It took them down another steep-sided valley, lined with thick pine forest. Olive trees grew beside the road. Vineyards climbed in terraces up the hillsides.

"At least there is cultivation," Dora said. "We're not in the middle of nowhere."

"I don't see any houses." Ellie peered hopefully through the windscreen.

The road snaked downward, seemingly forever, the tall hillsides blotting out the last of the setting sun. Ellie found she was holding her breath, waiting for the inevitable moment when the Bentley ground to a halt and they were stuck far from any help.

Then, at the moment the valley was about to be plunged into darkness, it widened out. There were small farms with stone farmhouses in the middle of cultivated fields, their shutters already closed for the night. Buildings appeared on either side of the road—a church with a square tower, a row of narrow houses. The street ended in a small harbour lined with pastel-coloured buildings. On either side of the village steep cliffs rose, the sandstone glowing blood-red in the last of the setting sun. Brightly painted fishing boats bobbed at the quay, and beyond stretched the Mediterranean, as wine-dark as Homer had described it. Lights already shone in some of the buildings and sparkled on the water. From somewhere came the sounds of an accordion playing, a baby crying, voices, laughter.

"Oh my." Ellie slowed the car, her mouth open, staring in wonder. She had never seen anywhere more perfect. The thought came to her that she didn't want to leave. As if confirming this, the Bentley gave a hiss and died.

CHAPTER 10

Ellie got out of the car, her hands stiff from gripping the steering wheel so tightly, and looked around. To the left of the harbour there was a bar or café with a group of men sitting at an outdoor table. At that moment she noticed a man stand up from the group at the bar and come towards her. He was a big man with unruly, dark curly hair, a hint of stubble at his chin and a scowl on his face. He was wearing an old open-necked shirt, revealing a hairy chest. There was a sense of menace in the purposeful way he strode towards them. Behind her she heard Mavis give a little gasp of alarm.

"Hey, what do you think you are doing? This is not a place to station your car. Move it at once," he roared in French, waving his arms as if shooing away pigeons. He took in the Bentley. "You think because you are English that you can park wherever you wish, eh?"

Ellie turned to face him. His eyes were flashing angrily, and his whole appearance was quite alarming. She took an involuntary step back. "I am sorry," she said, trying to form French sentences in her head. "We have had a small problem. We need a garage for the car."

She saw him realize that she was a woman, not a man. "There is no garage here, madame." He was still glaring at her but no longer roaring. "You must move your vehicle. The lorry comes to pick up the fish first thing in the morning and must station itself here."

He was now towering over her, at least six feet tall, and burly but not fat. Muscular. She couldn't tell how old he was. Maybe forties?

Fifties? His hair showed no signs of grey in the failing light, but his face was weathered from a life in the sun.

"Monsieur, I'm afraid the car will not move. There was smoke, steam. I don't know what's wrong, but now it has stopped. It will not go." She found she, too, was using her hands to speak. "Is there no garage nearby? No mechanic?"

She thought she saw a flicker of amusement in those dark eyes. "There is Louis," he said. "He does the repairs around here. Everything—boat engines, plumbing, probably automobiles. He will be able to tell you what is wrong. And maybe be able to acquire the parts you need." He gave a very Gallic shrug meaning "maybe yes, maybe no." When she didn't respond, assessing this, he went on: "We are not much in need of automobiles here. Monsieur Danton has one, he is the notaire. The doctor . . . And the priest has a small Citroën. But apart from that . . ."

Again he shrugged.

"So how do you get into the nearest town? Is there a bus?"

He smiled now, the smile completely changing his face. He was younger than she had thought. "Oh no, madame. No autobus. There is the postal van, a lorry that brings supplies once a week, and we sometimes take the boat into La Ciotat or even to Marseille. It's not too long a journey on a good day."

"Oh, I see." She looked around. The other men at the table were now watching with frank interest. "Could you direct me to this Louis? Would he still be working, do you think?"

Now he laughed. "Oh no, madame. Louis is sitting here, with us, drinking wine. He will attend to you in the morning. In the meantime, however, we must move your automobile." He shouted something to his friends. As they came across from the bar, Ellie asked, "Is there a hotel where we can spend the night?"

"I regret there is not, but there is the pension," he said. "Pension Victoria, named after your queen who used to come here to spend the winter, as you probably know."

"Here, to this place?"

He was still smiling, making him look less formidable. "No, not exactly here, but to Hyères, which is not too far away. And of course to Nice and Antibes."

"Where is this pension?" Ellie looked around but saw no large buildings amongst those lining the waterfront.

"The yellow house at the far end of the harbour—you see?"

The house didn't look any different from any of the other buildings around the harbour. A little larger, with faded green shutters. "And they will have space, do you think?"

"Madame, who comes here in October?" he asked. "It is not yet winter; it is no longer summer. They will have rooms for you."

"What's going on, Nico? What is her problem?" one of the men asked as they approached.

"The car doesn't go. We must move it," the first man said. He peered into the car. "Oh, you have brought your family with you. These ladies must get out before we move the car. We are strong men, but there are limits to what we can push."

Ellie leaned in. "You have to get out."

"Are we about to be murdered?" Mavis asked as men surrounded the car.

"I don't think so. They are trying to help. They are going to move the car off the road for tonight. There is a pension where we can sleep."

"I suppose we have no choice." Dora climbed out, moving stiffly after sitting for so long. "It's not a bad place to spend the night—rather attractive, in fact."

Yvette got out, too, moving hastily to stand near Ellie. "I do not like the look of these men, madame," she said. "I heard there are corsairs in the south. Pirates. Brigands."

"I'm sure we're safe enough, Yvette," Ellie said. As she spoke, one of the men slid into the driver's seat. The others pushed, and the car was steered off to the left, then manoeuvred next to the harbour wall.

"It will be safe there for tonight," the first man said. "Would you like us to escort you to the pension?"

"What about our luggage?" Ellie stared at the car. "I don't like to leave it overnight in the motor car."

"Who would take it?" Again the man looked amused. "We are the only people here. Outsiders do not come at this time of year. And we have no need of your possessions, I assure you. There is not much crime in our village. In this place nobody locks a door."

"But we will need our small valises," Ellie said. "And this lady is too frail to carry hers all that way."

The man turned back. "Jacquot. Aid these ladies. They will go to the pension. François, come."

Immediately another man picked up some of the bags while the big man took the rest. The third man insisted on taking Dora by the arm, although she tried to tell him she could manage without help. The big man strode out ahead of them, following the harbour wall around until they came to the last building, set against the cliffside. It had crumbling yellow paint and faded green shutters, but above the door was the sign "Pension Victoria."

The first man, whom Ellie had heard called Nico by the others, pushed open the door, and they found themselves in a small, spartan reception area with a counter at one end. The floor was tiled, and the only adornment was a side table containing some tired silk flowers and a poster advertising the Côte d'Azur on the wall.

"Hello. Madame? Anyone there? We have brought customers for you," he shouted in French, impatiently hitting the bell. After a while a woman appeared from a back room, hastily untying her apron as she came. She was a large woman with several chins and an impressive chest, her hair back in an old-fashioned bun. The small eyes that surveyed them were not friendly.

"Bonsoir, madame." Ellie stepped forward. "Our motor car has broken down. We are in need of rooms for the night. We are four ladies."

The woman picked up on Ellie's accent. "You are English?" she asked in that language.

"Yes." Ellie looked at her in surprise because the accent definitely had a tinge of cockney. "My name is Endicott."

"Well, blow me down," she said. "We don't get too many English. Not at this time of year, anyway. I'm Alice Adams. Me and the hubby run this place."

"What a surprise," Ellie said. "Have you been out here long?"

"Seventeen years, isn't it?" Mrs Adams did a quick mental calculation. "Yeah. Quite a long time now. Sometimes I'm surprised myself it's been so long." She gave a little chuckle.

"What made you come out here in the first place?" Ellie asked.

Mrs Adams leaned across the counter as if she were conveying a secret. "Mr Adams got gassed during the Great War. Horrible, it was. His lungs were shot. He couldn't go back to his job with the building company. In fact, the doctor told him he didn't have long to live. So I said to him, 'What you need is sunshine and good food.' He thought I was mad, bringing him out to France again, where he didn't exactly have the best memories. But I thought sunshine might help. And it did. We liked it, sold our little house, cashed in his life insurance policy and bought this place. We make just enough to keep our heads above water. But enough about me. What are you ladies doing? On a European tour, are you?"

"We're on an extended holiday," Ellie said. "We had intended to get as far as Hyères tonight, but the motor car had other ideas. We'll be here until the motor can be fixed. Only a few days. So you've rooms for us?"

"These are your maids?" Mrs Adams asked, eyeing Mavis and Yvette.

"Travelling companions," Ellie said.

"We've only got two singles," Mrs Adams said. "Who wants to share?"

"Mavis and Yvette can have the singles," Ellie said. "Miss Smith-Humphries will want a decent room. So shall I. We can both take doubles."

"Right you are. Facing the waterfront, I expect?" She nodded. "Right. That will be . . ." She paused. "Let's say two hundred francs."

Having stayed two nights in France, one at a superior hotel, Ellie knew immediately that they were being gouged. She turned back to the men, who were waiting patiently behind them, presumably not having understood this conversation.

"Is this a fair amount to pay at this time of year, do you think?" she asked in French, giving him the quote.

The big man called Nico gave a derisive laugh. "You think that these ladies are paying for the entire pension, do you, Alice?" He took a step forward, gesticulating in animated fashion as he spoke. "They do not wish to buy it. Only to rent rooms for one or two nights. And I happen to know that you charge thirty francs for a room. So considering the single rooms are not as nice, I think one hundred francs would be a fair price for four of them, don't you?"

Ellie was surprised that the woman clearly understood this rapid tirade, when she only just got the gist of it herself. His French was heavily accented.

"Where else would they go?" Mrs Adams asked, her own French surprisingly good.

"You take advantage of your countrywomen?" He made a tut-tutting sound.

"They can afford to pay, I'm sure. They are not dressed like paupers." She muttered the words, assuming that Ellie and the others could not understand if she spoke quickly.

Nico shrugged. "I expect we could find them rooms elsewhere. Henri sometimes rents out during the busy season over the bar, doesn't he? And Madame Blanchet, she has a spare room and could use the extra cash . . ."

Mavis looked across at Ellie. "What's going on?" she asked. "Ain't they got no rooms here?"

"They have rooms. We are just negotiating a price," Ellie said. "They want a little more than I was expecting to pay, having paid less for a first-class hotel last night."

"We were about to close up for the winter," Mrs Adams said, recoiling a little at Mavis's accent and perhaps realizing it wasn't going to be easy to get the better of a fellow East Ender. "Not much call at this time of year. So we'd have to go to the trouble of getting everything up and running again."

"Then you should count yourself bloody lucky that you've got some customers you didn't expect, right?" Mavis said. "If I were you, I'd be grateful."

Mrs Adams gave an exaggerated sigh. "Well, I suppose I could do you a favour, since you're fellow Englishwomen and had a bit of bad luck with your motor car. Let's agree on a hundred, then, if you're just staying a couple of nights."

"It includes breakfast, I assume?" Dora had been silent through the negotiation but spoke up now.

"Of course," Mrs Adams replied.

Ellie got the feeling it might not have included breakfast if Dora's tone had not been so forceful. She suddenly realized that they'd need to eat that evening.

"Do you serve dinner?" she asked. "We will need to eat."

"We serve meals when we have extra staff during the high season," Mrs Adams said, "but not without warning like this."

"I quite understand," Ellie said. "Is there somewhere we can get a bite to eat tonight?"

"I expect they can rustle up something to eat at the bar and bistro on the other side," Mrs Adams said. She repeated the gist of this in French to the men who were standing there.

"But of course. Henri will find something so that these ladies do not starve," Nico said, getting an affirming nod from one of the other men.

"Thank you. We will come when we have settled in our rooms," Ellie replied.

"Good. We will warn Henri. Then you ladies are satisfied? We leave you, then, and bid you bonsoir." He gave a polite little bow.

"Bonsoir, and thank you for your assistance," Ellie called after him in French.

"I'll get Mr Adams to help with your bags," Mrs Adams said, "if you'd just sign the register for me."

"Oh, no need for that," Ellie said. "Especially if he has a bad chest. He shouldn't be climbing stairs. We've only brought our overnight bags. The rest of the luggage is locked in the boot of the car."

"Right-oh, then. Here are your keys. Up the stairs and then turn right. You can decide who sleeps where. Bathroom and WC at the end of the hall. Hot water will be on in the morning for two hours. Breakfast at eight." With that gracious speech, she plonked the keys on to the counter.

Ellie signed the book for all of them, then took the keys, picked up her small valise and turned to the others. "Mavis, perhaps you can carry Miss Smith-Humphries's bag."

"I can manage," the old lady said haughtily.

"It's no trouble," Mavis said and gave her a smile. "Those stairs look steep."

Yvette had been standing silently through this whole exchange, and Ellie realized she didn't exactly know what was going to happen, since most of the discussion had been in English.

"Come, Yvette," Ellie said. "We have rooms for the night. You shall have a small room to yourself."

"Madame is too good," Yvette said. "How shall I repay you?"

"No need. I am glad we have been able to help you at a difficult moment."

She started up the stairs. The others followed. A narrow hallway was lit with one naked bulb so that the end of the hall was in deep shadow. Ellie checked numbers on the doors and opened the first one on the right, facing away from the seafront. "Ah. This is the small single. For you, Yvette."

"A room alone? For me? But no, madame. I don't need a room to myself. It is too much."

"It's all right. Put your bag inside. We will visit the toilet, and then we shall go to dinner at the bar."

"At the bar with those men?" Yvette looked nervous. "I did not like the big one. He is a corsair, I think. Dangerous."

"There is nowhere else to eat in this place, and besides, he was most helpful," Ellie replied. "I don't think any harm can come to us eating outside at a bar."

"What did she say?" Mavis asked.

"She thinks the big man is a pirate." Ellie had to smile.

Mavis was given the other single. The last two rooms along the hallway were identical, both with double beds, a small chest of drawers with a mirror above it, a giant wardrobe that took up most of one wall and over the bed a framed poster from French railways illustrating the Côte d'Azur. Simple in the extreme. The window was latched, and the shutters outside were already closed.

"I'll take the room nearest to the facilities if you don't mind," Dora said, going ahead into the end room. Ellie put down her bag beside the bed. The headboard and chest of drawers were mismatched and would have been at home in a second-hand shop. On the bed was a pink eiderdown. Beside the bed was a faded braided rug. But it seemed clean enough. She took off her jacket, then went through into the bathroom and splashed cold water on her face. Fifteen minutes later they walked together around the harbour to the bar. Lights now twinkled in the dark water, and the smell of salt and seaweed wafted towards them. On the other side of the harbour wall, the boats creaked and groaned at their moorings.

Ellie noticed that Yvette had stopped walking. "Is something wrong, Yvette?"

"Oh no, madame. I am just realizing that I am looking at the sea for the first time in my life. I have dreamed of this moment, and now it is real."

"Yes, it is real. We have made it this far," Dora said. "Let us hope we all enjoy our time here."

Yvette lingered a moment longer as the water lapped and slapped against the harbour wall, then followed them, still staring out. At the bar a table had been set up for them with a basket of bread and a flask of olive oil already in place. The men had returned to their own table and their wine glasses. Two of them were smoking the thin black cigarettes, and the strange herby smell wafted towards the women. An older man came out of the bar, bringing a carafe of red wine and glasses.

"Welcome, dear English ladies," he said. "I regret that I can only offer you the simplest of meals tonight. At this time of year I do not have help in the kitchen, so I can only offer you a soup."

"Thank you. That would be fine," Ellie said. She turned to translate for Mavis.

"I suppose that's better than nothing," Mavis said. She glanced across at the next table. "I don't know if I feel like eating much, not with those blokes watching us. I think I agree with Yvette this time. They do look like ruddy pirates."

"I'm sure they are fishermen, Mavis," Dora said. "Not pirates."

Ellie poured the wine, then took a sip. It was rich and strong but not unappetizing.

"This will make us sleep tonight," she said, laughing.

They had almost finished the bread when Henri appeared again, putting a big bowl on the table with four soup bowls. The smell of garlic and herbs rose from the steaming bowl. Ellie took the ladle and spooned hot soup into each of the bowls. It was a rich red colour, more like a stew, with plenty of bits and pieces floating in it. Mavis picked up her spoon, then gave a cry of alarm.

"What the devil is this?" She held it up for the others to see. "It looks like a dead spider. Do they eat spider soup here?"

Dora examined it. "It's squid, Mavis. Squid tentacles."

"What's that?" Mavis was still staring at it with a look of horror on her face.

"It's a sea creature. Like an octopus," Dora said, prodding her own bowl. "In fact, there is also octopus in the stew. This is obviously a bouillabaisse. A fish stew. I remember eating it when I stayed here years ago. Rather good, I remember."

Yvette's reaction was similar. She prodded her bowl uncertainly. "I have never seen such things," she said. "Do they try to poison us?"

"Nonsense. I'm sure it's quite delicious," Dora said and bravely put a piece of octopus into her mouth. It proved to be rather chewy, but she kept a smile on her face until she had swallowed it. Ellie tried the broth first. It was garlicky, with lots of onions and tomatoes. An unfamiliar taste, but she quite liked it. She also hesitated at the squid tentacles but bravely ate hers, enjoying the shrimp, mussels and pieces of fish more.

"I expect we'll have to get used to a different way of eating now we're here," she said.

"When we are at a proper hotel, I'm sure they will cater more to English taste," Dora said. "I am not a big fan of garlic and onions. My mother would never allow them. She said they make the breath smell, and a lady's breath should only ever smell of peppermint."

In spite of their reservations, they emptied the big bowl, using the last of the bread to wipe their plates. When they had finished, Henri produced a basket of figs and grapes along with more bread and a plate of cheeses. He also replaced the carafe of wine.

"You enjoyed your meal?" one of the men called from the next table.

"Thank you. It was good," Ellie replied.

"Henri, he is a good cook," the man said, nodding to Henri, who was now standing in the doorway with the bill in his hand. "He was once a chef at a big hotel in Nice, correct, Henri?"

"That is true," Henri said, "but I inherited this place, and it suits me better. When I have more time, I will cook for you ladies."

"I'm afraid we'll only be here until the vehicle is mended," Ellie said. "Then we will be going to one of the bigger resorts for the winter."

"Of course. Your husbands will be joining you?"

"We have no husbands, monsieur," Ellie said.

"Ah, they are widows," Ellie heard another of the men mutter. She decided not to correct him. Besides, she did not know the French word for divorce, and she assumed that in a Catholic country it would be frowned upon. She paid the bill, quite a modest amount, and stood up.

"Good night, gentlemen," she said, "and thank you for all your help."

"I will take a look at your motor car in the morning," an older man with a shock of grey hair called to them. Louis, obviously. "Do not worry yourselves. It will be made right."

Ellie felt content and a little tipsy as they walked back to the pension. She opened the windows and breathed in the soft night air with the tang of salt to it. As she lay down to sleep, she found that the tension she had been carrying for the past weeks had melted away. It didn't matter if the car had broken down or if it would take days to mend. It didn't matter that they hadn't reached their final destination and didn't even know where they were going. The worst was behind them. She had found her way through France. They were here at the Mediterranean, and everything was going to be all right.

CHAPTER 11

Ellie woke to find sunlight pouring into the room. She had opened the blinds before she went to bed, not wanting to shut out the sparkle of lights on the water and the smell of the sea. Outside she heard a noise that she first interpreted as babies crying, cats yowling. She lay trying to process this, looking around her in wonder. It took a moment to remember where she was. Then she realized that the noise was the mewing cries of seagulls. She had slept deeply and peacefully without waking all night. She got up, went across to the window. Outside, the tiny harbour was a hive of activity. A fishing boat had come in, and men were now unloading wooden trays of fish on to a lorry that was parked near to where her car had stopped the night before. Some of the men wore dark-blue jackets or overalls, cotton caps on their heads. One wore only a singlet above baggy trousers, revealing deeply tanned skin and impressive muscles. Seagulls wheeled and darted around them. Beyond the harbour the Mediterranean Sea sparkled in dazzling sunlight. As she breathed in deeply, her nose picked up the smells of brewing coffee and baking bread. She gave a sigh of content.

After a quick shower in water that never became hotter than lukewarm, Ellie put on the linen trousers she had dared herself to buy in London, along with a white blouse and navy blazer. A glance in the mirror told her that she looked smart, although she wasn't quite sure who she wanted to impress in a backwater like this. It wasn't Cannes or Antibes, where what you wore mattered. As she came out of her room, the door beside hers opened and Dora emerged. She was dressed exactly as Ellie had always known her, same dark suit with a white blouse and a gold brooch. She was not going to make allowances for the mild climate, clearly.

"Good morning. How did you sleep?" Ellie asked.

"Well enough," Dora replied, "although I don't think the rich food and wine agreed with my stomach. And you?"

"Surprisingly well. I think the wine helped. It's a pretty view, isn't it?"

"Yes. Very pretty," Dora agreed.

Hearing voices, Mavis opened her door. She, too, was dressed as she always was at home, in a flowery dress with a hand-knitted cardigan over it. "Oh, you're up," she said. "I wondered if I should wake you. I couldn't half do with a cup of tea. I've been awake for hours."

"The bed wasn't comfortable?" Dora asked.

Mavis gave an embarrassed shrug. "I ain't never slept in a room on my own, to tell you the truth," she said. "I shared a bed with my sisters until I moved in with Reg. And I was worried about bedbugs and fleas."

"Oh, I think the place is clean enough," Dora said. "Not the smartest of rooms but clean."

"And as I lay awake all night, I worried about what was going to happen to me when I went home. My hubby is going to knock the daylights out of me, isn't he?"

"Then don't go back to him," Ellie said.

"All right for you to say." Mavis's voice quivered. "But what am I going to do? I don't have no money, no house, no education—nothing. Where am I going to live? How am I going to support myself?"

"We'll face that when the time comes," Ellie said. "I gave you my word that I'd look after you, Mavis. But who knows, we might not want to go back."

"What, stay here? In a foreign country?" Mavis shot her an alarmed look.

"You may come to like it, Mavis," Ellie said. "I have to tell you that I'm feeling better already. I'm glad I made this decision, and I'm proud of us for getting this far. I like this place. I'm glad the car died here."

"No sign of Yvette yet," Dora said. "She must be sleeping in." She paused, her hand poised to knock at Yvette's door.

"Oh, let the poor girl sleep if she has to," Ellie said. "She may have been on the run for days and needs her rest."

"I would have thought growing up on a farm she'd be up with the dawn, milking the cows," Dora said.

"I've said it before and I say it now," Mavis said. "I don't trust that girl. There's something about her . . ."

"Let's be charitable, Mavis. She's pregnant, on her own and scared. We have to help her."

"So what do you propose to do with her once we reach our destination?" Dora asked. "They won't take her to work in a hotel if she's expecting a child."

"Let's wait and see, shall we?" Ellie asked. "At the moment let's enjoy this glorious sunny day, and I smell coffee brewing."

She headed for the stairs. The other women followed her. The dining room was to the right of the reception area and faced the harbour. Again it was simple, with small tables covered in checked gingham cloths. They took a seat in the window, watching the activity outside as the last of the catch was unloaded.

"Good morning, ladies." Mrs Adams came in, looking friendlier than last night. "I hope you slept well."

"We did, thank you," Ellie replied.

"You all like coffee?" she asked. "I can do tea if you'd rather. We have tea sent out from England on account of the English visitors liking a taste of home."

"I'd like tea, if it's not too much trouble," Mavis said.

Mrs Adams smiled at her. "From London, are you, ducks?"

"That's right. Born and bred in the East End just like you."

"We've both come a long way, then, ain't we?" Mrs Adams said. "I can see we'll have some good old chats once you've settled in." She nodded to Mavis. "That's the one thing I miss about living in this place. People to have a chat with. We get English guests during the season, but they are usually a snooty lot and don't want to talk with the likes of me." She smoothed down her apron. "Well, I can't stand here all day, can I? I'll have Mr A. bring your breakfast in."

"Well done, Mavis," Dora said as she departed. "You've tamed the dragon."

They looked up as a scrawny and unassuming little man came in, bearing a tray. He had a drooping moustache and eyes that turned down at the corners, giving him a perpetually sad look. Ellie's immediate thought was Jack Sprat and his wife—the enormous, overbearing woman and her tiny, henpecked husband.

"Here you go, ladies," he said and unloaded the contents of the tray. He had the gravelly voice of someone who coughed frequently. There was a basket of croissants and a sliced baguette with butter and apricot jam, along with plates, cups and cutlery. "Coffee and tea will be out in a jiff," he said. "I hope you enjoy your stay with us."

"Thank you," they muttered.

"Out from England, then, eh? What part?"

"Surrey," Ellie said. "Not far from Guildford."

"Oh, right. Surrey. I remember riding my old bike up the Hogs Back. You know that hill, right? Blimey, it was a hard slog. But it's lovely country, Surrey. So green."

"Do you miss it?" Dora asked.

"Sometimes. Yeah, I do."

Ellie nodded with understanding.

"I don't suppose you get many English visitors, do you?"

He finished unloading the tray and stood, hugging the tray to his front. "Oh, we get our share, during the season. We have regulars who come every January, February. Old ladies, retired colonels. Especially those people who've lived in India. They feel the cold back in England.

But we don't often get English guests this time of year," he added. "Planning to spend the winter, are you?"

"Somewhere on the Riviera," Ellie said. "We had car trouble yesterday, which is why we're here."

"Yeah, I suppose you want to go to one of them fancy places," he said. "Not much to do here, really, unless you like peace and quiet."

"So what do your other English guests do, during the season?" Dora asked.

"They make their own entertainment, really," he said. "The doctor's wife has musical evenings. They have play readings; there's whist and bridge, and quite a few of them are painters. Do any of you paint?"

They shook their heads.

"Lovely landscapes for painting here. If you hike around the Calanques."

"The what?" Mavis asked.

"The coastline between here and Marseille—all these little bays with steep sides. Lovely, they are, if you don't mind a good, stiff walk." He glanced out of the window. "We've got a resident painter here. Quite well known, he is. I expect you'll meet him if you stick around." He stared out of the window again, then turned back. "Of course, at quiet times like this, between seasons, there's not much going on." He leaned closer. "Between you, me and the gatepost, it gets bloody boring at times. Oh, don't get me wrong, the French people are nice enough here, and we sort of fit in now, but it's not the same as at home, is it? We don't laugh at the same things. They don't enjoy a pint down the pub, and they don't—"

"Abe, don't stand there gossiping all day," came the fierce voice from outside. "Go and fetch the ladies their coffee."

"It's clear who rules the roost in that household," Dora muttered as he shuffled off again.

～

Breakfast was quite satisfying. The bread was still warm from the oven, and the coffee was made with hot milk. Ellie found she had quite an appetite, different from when she used to eat just the one piece of toast at home. "Home." She toyed with the word. It was no longer home. She had no home. That was alarming but also freeing. She could go where she wanted, do what she wanted, and nobody was going to stop her.

"So the first order of the day should be to have the mechanic see to the car," Dora said as she put her napkin back on the table. "And to wake that girl. It's not healthy to lounge in bed all day. I hope we can soon be on our way and deposit her somewhere. She's a liability I don't personally want."

"I agree," Ellie said, "but I also worry about her. We can't just turn her loose in a strange town."

"I would imagine that somewhere as big as Nice would have charities that take in girls in difficult situations," Dora said.

Mr Adams came in again. "Enjoyed your breakfast?" he asked. "That's good. At least they make good bread here. The bakery's just across on the other side of the harbour. We get baguettes fresh twice a day. And the fish, of course. We get great fish. Oh, and would you like to see the newspapers? The lorry always brings us newspapers from Marseille when it comes. Sometimes even an English one."

He put down a couple of French newspapers on the table and loaded the dirty plates on to his tray.

"Fat lot of good these are." Mavis prodded them. *Paris-soir* and *Le Figaro*.

"Maybe you should start learning French, Mavis," Dora said. "If the Adamses can do it, so can you."

Mavis shot her a suspicious look. "What, me? Get me tongue around them words? I don't see that happening in a hurry."

"It would be a challenge while we are here," Dora said. "And just think, if you go back to England and want to get a job, having a second language would be an enormous benefit."

Mavis considered this. "Nasty-looking bunch there." She pointed at a grainy photograph on the front page. "What are they, anarchists? Communists?"

Ellie read the text.

"They are a gang of bank robbers, just been apprehended in Paris," she said.

"Blimey. If there are criminals like that everywhere, I don't know that I'll feel safe," Mavis said. "Look at them blokes with knives in Marseille."

"I doubt that organized crime will reach Saint-Benet," Dora said with a smile. "So maybe we should stay here."

Mavis was still staring. "I don't know. One of them blokes looks like that man who carried the bags. Swarthy type."

At that moment there was an intake of breath behind them. They turned to see Yvette standing there. "I am so sorry," she said. "I didn't mean to startle you. I have just seen the sea in the daylight. Look at it. So big. It seems to go on forever."

"Not forever, Yvette," Dora said. "If you swim far enough, you will arrive at the coast of Africa."

"Unless you bump into Corsica on the way," Ellie said with a smile. "And then Sardinia and perhaps Sicily. I'm not sure if they are all in a line."

Yvette looked puzzled. Then she said, "I am sorry. It seems I am too late for breakfast. I have never slept so late in my life."

"You must have needed the sleep," Ellie said, leading her over to the table. "Worry and fear can be exhausting. But sit down, and I will have Monsieur Adams bring you food and coffee." She pushed the newspapers towards Yvette. "And in the meantime, you can read these."

"Alas, madame, I do not know how to read well," Yvette said, pushing the newspapers away. "Only the most basic of words that we were taught in school."

"Then this would be a good time for you to improve your education," Ellie said. "You and Mavis shall have a lesson every day."

"What's that about me?" Mavis had not understood the conversation.

"I told Yvette that you and she will have a lesson in reading and writing French every day."

"Blimey. If I'd known it was going to be like school, I wouldn't have come," Mavis muttered.

CHAPTER 12

They left Yvette eating her breakfast and went out to see about the Bentley. There was a fresh breeze off the sea, reminding Ellie that even here in the South of France winter was approaching. But she breathed in deeply, savouring the saltiness and that hint of seaweed. It felt good to be alive, and she thought that she had not felt this way for ages. For years, maybe. When did she last feel such excitement and energy that she was ready to tackle anything? She couldn't even remember. Her life had been so regimented—boiled eggs, starched shirts, dinner parties where Lionel told the same jokes over and over. And now life was a mystery. She had no idea what tomorrow might bring, but she didn't care. She almost felt like skipping, but the austere presence of Dora, walking straight backed and stiff beside her, made her reel in her joie de vivre.

Ellie paused for a moment, taking in the layout of the town. The harbour was lined on three sides with narrow, pastel-painted houses, with red tiled roofs and contrasting shutters at their windows—a yellow house with green shutters, a pink one with brown. Some had tiny balconies with pots of flowers spilling over them, some of them with shops beneath living quarters. On the far side of the harbour there was one bigger building, separate from the row, a white villa, and beyond that a small park with palm trees and benches surrounding a sandy square of open ground that was presumably for the bowls game Ellie had witnessed all that time ago when she had travelled with her aunt.

Was it called pétanque? Behind the harbour a couple of rows of houses rose up the steep hillside. There was the one street leading out of town the way they had entered. But that was about it. A tiny hamlet of a place—certainly no glamour or luxury.

The boats had been unloaded, and the lorry had departed, leaving the quayside empty. The seagulls had cleaned up the last scraps of fish, but the odour still lingered.

"The first thing is to find this Louis, the mechanic," Dora said. "We should have asked Mrs Adams."

The bar where they had eaten last night was not yet open. The outside chairs were stacked upon the tables, and there was no sign of life. But several buildings down the quay, there was a shop with a sign outside advertising Gauloises cigarettes. They walked to it and found it to be a tabac—a newsagent and smoke shop. Inside Ellie saw that it was much more than just newspapers and cigarettes—it was a tiny general store with everything from toothpaste to knitting wool to tins of condensed milk. There was also a display of beach toys, buckets, spades, inflatable balls. *Rather hopeful at this time of year,* Ellie thought. She hadn't yet seen a beach but was happy to know there had to be one nearby and that children played here.

"Bonjour, mesdames," the elderly man behind the counter said.

Ellie bought a French women's magazine and some peppermints, then asked about Louis.

"He has a place of business next to the gendarmerie," the owner said. "You may find him there." The shrug and waving of the hands as he said this indicated that they may not. "The gendarmerie. Last house as you leave Saint-Benet," he continued. "Alphonse will no doubt be sitting outside on a sunny day." He smiled. "You are here on holiday? From England?"

They told him that they were. "Our little town is rather quiet," he said. "Not many winter visitors. We have no casino, no fancy hotels and nightclubs."

"We are not intending to stay long," Dora said. "Our car sustained a . . ." She did not know the word for breakdown. "Did not go any more," she added.

"Ah. I see. That is why you require Louis. He is a good man. He will help you if he can."

They bade him good day and set off again, heading out of the village the way they had come the night before. There were no more shops on their side of the street, but they passed two side alleys rising steeply in a series of steps up the cliffside. Lines of washing stretched between houses. Small children were playing, a woman was scrubbing her front step and two old men were standing together smoking. As they passed, each person looked up and bade them bonjour. A cat lay sunning itself in the middle of the street, confident that no traffic was likely. On the other side were several more shops, the bakery and one selling charcuterie, cheeses, and pâté, as well as trays of vegetables and fruit, a barber and one that seemed to have boating supplies. They came at last to a simple stone church, and behind it what had to be a school, as they heard children's voices chanting a times table. And facing it, a bigger building, rather more ornate than most of the houses, with a carved wooden balcony and a Victorian feel to it.

A lone policeman, who was presumably Alphonse, was indeed sitting outside, smoking and reading the newspaper as if he hadn't a care in the world. He greeted them without curiosity and pointed to a big shed, set back from the road.

"You'll find Louis there," he said.

They crossed a yard littered with bits and pieces of equipment, wood pallets and other kinds of junk. The sound of hammering came from inside the big shed. The door was open, and they went in. Ellie recognized the man with grizzled hair and a stubbled chin from the table last night. He raised a hand, still holding the hammer, in salute. "One moment, if you please, ladies," he said.

He gave a couple more taps, nodded in satisfaction, then turned back to them. "You come about your automobile, madame," he said.

"I will get to it today, I promise you, but first I have a chicken coop to attend to."

"Is not a motor car more important than chickens?" Dora asked in her stilted French.

"Not if you are a fox or a hawk," he said with a smile. "Besides, what is the hurry? The sun is shining. It is a perfect day. Enjoy it. If you were back in England, it would be rain and more rain." He put down the hammer and wiped off his hands on a blue cotton apron. "I was there once, after the Great War. In England, I mean. I did not enjoy it. Rain and more rain, and the people always looking so gloomy. Nobody laughed. Nobody sat and took time to enjoy a glass of wine with friends. Everybody in a hurry, shut away with their own little lives and their own little problems."

He's right, Ellie thought. *That's how it is in England.*

"If you leave the keys to your vehicle with me, I will take a look and see if it is something I can fix."

"And if it's not?" Ellie asked.

He shrugged, chuckled. "Then you will have to find a lorry to transport it back to Marseille. Or you leave it here and go on your way without it." He paused then added, "But I expect it can be mended so that you can hurry off to be with other English people and complain about the lack of tea and proper English pudding." He gave a big, hearty laugh.

Ellie handed him the key. He stuffed it into the pocket of his apron. "Off you go," he said. "Make the most of your day."

"He's right," Dora said as they walked away. "We should make the most of our day. Of every day. Especially for me. Every day is a precious gift, especially in a lovely place like this. I will endeavour to enjoy myself."

Ellie looked at her fondly. "So what would you like to do?"

Dora gave an almost naughty grin. "I should like to paddle in the sea. I expect it's too cold to swim at this time of year, but at least we could paddle."

"All right," Ellie said. "We can do that. We'll have to find the beach. There has to be one, or they wouldn't sell buckets and spades."

"So what was he going on about?" Mavis asked. "That man in there. He certainly laughed a lot."

"He was telling us not to worry but to enjoy the nice weather," Ellie said. "He said he'd been in England once and everyone was gloomy all the time."

"That's true enough," Mavis said. "Everyone always looks so bloody miserable."

They returned to the pension to find Yvette had retreated back to her room.

"We're going exploring. Do you want to come with us?" Ellie said. "We want to find the beach."

"Oh yes." Yvette's eyes lit up. "I've always wanted to see a beach, like on the posters with the glamorous ladies in their bathing suits."

"I don't think you're going to find any glamorous ladies on a beach here," Dora said.

"Maybe I should change back into a skirt if we intend to get our feet wet," Ellie said. "I don't want to risk spoiling these new trousers."

"And I should remove my stockings," Dora added. "What about you, Mavis?"

"Oh, I ain't going near no water," Mavis said. "I can't swim. I'd be scared I'd be knocked down by a big wave. That happened to me once at Brighton, you know. Me and Reg went on a day trip with his firm, and I was standing at the edge of the water, and this ruddy great wave knocked me over. And do you know what he did? He laughed. He didn't give me a hand or anything. He said I looked like a bloody beached whale."

"You're well rid of him, Mavis," Dora said. "Don't think about him again."

"I'm trying not to," Mavis said, "but he'll be there, won't he, when I get back? He'll give me hell to pay for leaving without telling him. I should never have come. It was stupid of me."

"We could help you get a divorce, if that's what you want," Ellie said.

"A divorce? Me?" Mavis looked scared. "Only rich people get divorces."

"No. I'm now a divorced woman, and I'm not rich," Ellie said.

"But it was your hubby what wanted it. I know Reg. He'll contest it just to be spiteful. He'll make up awful lies about me."

"Let's not talk about it on this lovely day," Dora said. "We'll change our clothes and go to find this beach."

A little later they set off, wearing sandals and showing bare legs. They crossed the harbour area, passed the bar and the white villa, then the little park where two men were now playing pétanque, the metal balls echoing with a clang as they made contact. Then they found a narrow path that hugged the foot of the cliff. It was shaded by pine trees, and they were enveloped in that wonderful piny smell. As they came around the headland, they saw a small bay ahead of them, a tiny half moon of white sand beneath steep craggy rocks.

"Oh, how perfect," Dora exclaimed. She hurried forward, almost breaking into a run. Ellie stared in wonder at this newly revealed Miss Smith-Humphries, trying to equate her to the stiff and critical spinster who had complained about the least crease in the altar cloth. They put towels down on a rock, then ventured tentatively to the edge of the sea. The bay was quite calm, with tiny wavelets rushing forward to break on the sand, then retreating again with a gentle hiss. Dora went boldly to the edge, didn't hesitate as she walked into the water, and stood there, an ecstatic smile on her face.

"Wonderful," she said. "Not even too cold. Next time I shall bring my bathing suit. I do still have one, you know, although the elastic may have gone by now."

"Shouldn't you be a bit careful, Dora?" Ellie said, feeling the unfamiliar warmth of sand under her bare feet. "Your heart. That cold water can't be good."

"Oh, but it is," Dora said. "And anyway what better way to go than to be swimming in the Mediterranean." She waded in deeper, holding up her skirt until the water was almost up to her knees. Ellie followed her into the water, finding it quite cold enough, and stood ankle deep as waves swept past her. Mavis and Yvette stayed up near the rocks.

"Try it, Mavis," Dora called out in English. "Come on, Yvette. You have to try new things."

"I have fear, madame," she said. "I have never been near such water before."

"It's quite safe, I promise you," Dora said. As she spoke a wave, bigger than the rest, came up behind her. She gasped as it soaked her to the thighs. Then she burst out laughing. "Well, that was a surprise. I'm glad this is only an old skirt." She beckoned to the two on the beach. "You do not need to come in far. Just get your toes wet. A first introduction."

"I think I'll wait," Mavis said. "Too many new things for my liking right now."

"And I am not sure. The shock might be bad for the baby," Yvette said.

"We'll have you in and swimming in no time at all," Dora said. She waded out, sat on a rock and dried her legs. "I used to love swimming when I was young. I remember swimming all the times when my father took us abroad. I begged to be sent to a school with a swimming bath, but that request wasn't granted. Who knows, I could have tackled the Channel."

Ellie came up to the rock and perched beside her. "What held you back? What turned you from that adventurous woman to Miss Smith-Humphries of Surrey?"

Dora was staring out, watching the waves. The water beyond the bay was a rich, deep blue. "You forget. I'm much older than you. When I came of age, there was only one option for a girl of my class, and that was to marry. I'm afraid I was rather too forthright in my opinions for many young men, and the ones that wanted me, I did not take to. My father died. I stayed as a companion to my mother until she, too, died, and then later I inherited enough money to buy my bungalow. The only place for me in society was doing charitable works."

"You've done a lot of good," Ellie said. "You should be proud."

"I shrank," Dora said. "I should have dreamed bigger. I accepted what society wanted me to be."

"I've done the same," Ellie said. "I've been the dutiful wife and mother, and look where that has got me. Cast aside like an old shoe."

"You're young. You can have great romances and remarry if you wish," Dora said.

Ellie had to laugh at this. "Great romances, at my age?"

"Why not? Continental men can be awfully attractive in middle age."

Ellie was still chuckling.

"And you, Mavis. Maybe you'll meet a nicer man," Dora said.

Mavis gave a shriek of laughter at this. "When I don't even speak the lingo?"

"English people come out here for the winter," Dora said.

"I think I'll enjoy my freedom, even if it's for a little while," Mavis said. "It will be the only time in my life that some man hasn't bossed me around and knocked me around."

They dried off their feet and walked back towards the village.

Lunch was a simple meal of bread, cheese and pâté, bought from the shop and eaten on a bench in the little park. After this they had a siesta in their rooms, tired from unaccustomed sun and sea. When they came down and found a conservatory at the back of the pension, they were delighted when Mr Adams offered to bring them tea.

"Most civilized," Dora muttered.

Ellie worried about the car, having not heard from Louis all day. What would they do if the car had to be towed into Marseille? Would any lorry even come out this far? How long might they be stuck here? She was loath to go out for a stroll in case they missed him, but Dora persuaded her to come and see the sunset that was painting the cliffs opposite a rich rosy pink. As they came out of the house, Louis was coming towards them. They waited, Ellie holding her breath.

"I have examined your vehicle," he said, delivering the words slowly and gravely. "And from what I can tell, it is the hose that connects to the radiator that is broken. I have telephoned from the gendarmerie to a garage I deal with in Marseille, telling them the make and model of your motor car. They did not know whether an English motor car might have a different-size hose from our French vehicles. But they will find out. If the size is the same, then all is well. A new hose will be sent out with the next visit from the postal van. If there is a problem, then maybe a hose must be procured from a place where they are used to English visitors and such vehicles—Antibes, or even Nice. Then it might take a few days before it arrives."

"Oh, that's good news," Ellie said. "At least it's something simple."

"As far as I can tell," he said, holding up a cautioning finger. "As I say, I am not a car mechanic. I work on the engines of boats all the time, and tractors, and I do not have the facility to put the vehicle up on a ramp and see underneath. It could, of course, be that your radiator is damaged. In that case, maybe I could patch it, or you might need a new radiator, which would have to be sent in from Marseille, or Nice."

He spread his hands in that gesture she had now seen several times in France. Maybe yes, maybe no. "But let us hope for the best, yes? Then you can be on your way to the place where your countrymen spend the winter and enjoy your afternoon teas and your English puddings."

"You are most kind," Ellie said. "I thank you for taking the time."

He gave a polite little bow. "I am most happy to be of service to such charming ladies," he said. "I only wish you decided to stay longer so that I could make your acquaintance. And maybe play chess with you on dark winter evenings."

"Oh, you're a chess player," Dora said, having understood the conversation. "I used to play with my father. He was good, always beat me."

"Then we shall play sometime, madame," he said. "I look forward to it."

"Well, that was an eye-opener, for sure," Dora commented as Louis walked in one direction and they made their way around the harbour to watch the sun sinking behind the Mediterranean. "A grubby mechanic, and yet he speaks most eloquently and plays chess. And the owner of the bar is a former chef at a hotel . . . I wonder what other surprises await us here?"

CHAPTER 13

Henri was prepared for them at the bar that night. He served a lentil soup followed by small fried fish and a salad of tomatoes, red peppers and crumbled white cheese.

"Oh, whitebait, how lovely," Dora said. "I used to be very fond of whitebait."

"You are in luck, mesdames," Henri said. "There was a good catch brought in today. The bigger fish go to the market in Marseille, but we keep the ones they can't sell. The anchovies are good, no?"

Mavis looked down suspiciously at the fish, still with their heads on and eyes staring up at her. "I've had fish and chips," she said, "but I ain't seen anything like this."

"They're delicious, Mavis," Dora said. "Try one."

The fish were cooked perfectly in a light coating, crunchy on the outside, moist in the middle. Mavis had to be reassured it was all right to eat the bones and they wouldn't get stuck in her throat and choke her. After this, Henri brought out small pots of crème brûlée and gave a shy smile when complimented.

"You are wasted here, Henri," Dora said. "You said you were a chef at a hotel in one of the resorts. Why did you leave?"

Henri shrugged. "This suits me better," he said. "I am my own chef here." The word "chef" meant "boss" in French. "At the hotel I had to obey the whims of the owners and the customers. Don't serve it with so much cream. Serve it with more cream. No garlic. More garlic. Here I can create a dish, and if they don't like it, tant pis. Too bad."

"But do you have enough to do, to make a living?" Dora persisted.

"Now it is quiet. In the season there is plenty to do. The English come in January, February. The French in the summer. Then I hire people to help me. Nico's mother comes to help cook."

"Nico?" Ellie asked, attentive now. "The big man with the deep voice?"

"That's the one."

"His parents live here?"

"His father is dead. He takes care of his mother. But she does not like to be idle. She rents out a couple of rooms at her house, and she helps me cook."

"And Nico fishes for a living?"

Henri shrugged. "Sometimes. When he feels like it. He does not need to work all the time like the rest of them."

"What does everyone do here?" Ellie asked. "Is there enough work?"

"When the visitors come, of course. There is enough work for everyone in Saint-Benet."

"And at the other times, what does everyone do?"

"The men fish," he said. "Or they go to work in Marseille or Toulon for a while."

They paid the bill and got up to leave.

"If you are here for a few days, I shall import supplies and cook you a proper meal."

"I can't tell how long we shall be here," Ellie said. "It depends how soon Louis can mend my broken car."

"He is a good man, Louis," Henri said. "He will do his best."

They parted company and went back to the pension. Ellie realized that Mavis and Yvette had been quite silent, Mavis because she didn't understand and Yvette because she was probably too shy to join in. Her eyes followed Yvette as she went up the stairs. What was going to happen to her? She'd have to give up the child if the father could not be located. And even if he was found, he could not leave his post with the army to come home and marry her. Perhaps he had not told her his location on purpose. Men were quite happy to deceive young girls, to promise them love to get them into bed. She shook her head. There was nothing she could do about it at the moment. At least Yvette was safe. When they got to a bigger place, Ellie would try to get her settled.

∿

They woke to another brilliantly sunny day, the water sparkling, the fishermen calling out to each other as they worked on their boats or put out to sea. They were in the middle of breakfast when they heard Mrs Adams speaking with someone.

"I'm sure they wouldn't want to see the likes of you," she said, her voice harsh.

Ellie assumed it was a beggar or other undesirable. But then she thought she heard what sounded like an English voice. Out of curiosity she stood up and went through to the foyer. A tall, fit-looking man was standing there. His grey hair was neatly parted, and he sported a thin Ronald Colman moustache. He was wearing a royal-blue open-necked shirt with a white silk cravat at the neck and white linen trousers. His tanned face broke into a smile when he saw her.

"A very good morning to you, dear lady," he said in a smooth, educated English voice. "We heard that English guests had arrived, so we thought it only courteous to come and greet you and welcome you to Saint-Benet."

"Thank you." Ellie returned his smile.

"I am Thomas Ramsey," he said. "Resident of this place."

"Ellie Endicott." Ellie shook the hand he had extended. She could see Mrs Adams still glaring and couldn't understand what there was not to like about the gentleman.

"I came to invite you to luncheon today, if you've nothing on your calendar."

"How very kind. Thank you," Ellie replied. "We shall be delighted. There are four of us. Is that all right?"

"The more the merrier," he said. "I'll expect you at twelve, then. It's the last house on the right up the street beside the tabac. Up against the hillside. Lovely view."

Then he gave another smile, a sort of half salute, and left. Mrs Adams was still scowling.

"I hope you know what you're doing," she said. "He's one of them, you know." She leaned closer, as if she were imparting a secret. "He lives with another man. Lived with him here for years, right out in the open, like."

"Well, I lived with a man for years," Ellie said. "I don't think it did me too much harm."

"That's not the same thing at all, is it?" Mrs Adams said angrily. "That's how God intended it. Not the unnatural way."

"I've no idea what God intended," Ellie said. "He seemed like a nice gentleman, and I'm only going to have lunch with him."

She relayed the information back to the others.

"What was there about him that made her so shirty?" Mavis asked.

"He lives with another man, Mavis," Ellie replied.

"So what's wrong with that?" Mavis asked. "It's nice to have company and to share the rent."

"I think there's more to it than that," Ellie said. "I think Mrs Adams meant they are a couple."

"A what?" Mavis gave an uncomprehending stare.

"You know. Living together. Like Noël Coward."

Recognition slowly dawned. "Oh? Oh, I get it now." She turned bright red.

Ellie had expected disapproval from Dora, but she merely shrugged. "It should prove interesting," she said.

Actually Ellie was surprised at her own easy acceptance. She tried to remember if she had ever actually met a homosexual. She knew all about Noël Coward—everyone did. He was famous enough to be adored and thus not judged. But she also knew that Oscar Wilde had gone to prison and had died soon afterward. Lionel had always been vocal in his disapproval of such things. He called them "bloody fairies."

But then, Lionel had disapproved of anyone who did not think and act the way he did. Thomas Ramsey seemed like a nice, polite man. She would be interested to have a chance to chat with him.

Just before noon they set off. Yvette had excused herself, saying the conversation would be in English and she would not understand. So they left her at the pension with some provisions for lunch.

"We'll have to make some sort of decision about that girl," Dora said as they walked away. "She can't stay with us indefinitely."

"What would you have me do, put her on the lorry and drop her off in Marseille?" Ellie replied testily. "Of course I'm concerned about her. I want to help her. When we're settled I will write to the French war ministry and try to locate her young man. At least then he can take responsibility for a child if he wants to. If not, then we'll have to think again. The world is not kind to unmarried mothers."

"She got herself into this position," Dora said with a sniff of disapproval.

"Young girls in love make foolish decisions. Young men find it easy to persuade them there is marriage in the future. I don't know how I might have acted at Yvette's age if I'd been seduced by a more experienced man. As it happened, Lionel was my first real boyfriend, and he wasn't the seducing type." She had to laugh at this.

Mavis took Dora's arm as they started to climb the steep cobbled street. Stray cats slunk into shadows. Laundry flapped from balconies. A baby cried, a dog barked. The houses on either side of them did not look too promising, but when they came to the top of the street, where it ended up against the cream-coloured rocks, there was another house, set apart, painted butter yellow with light-blue shutters. Before they could knock on the door, it opened, and Thomas Ramsey stood there.

"Dear ladies, welcome. Do come in," he said. He held out his hand to Dora.

"This is Miss Smith-Humphries, and Mavis Moss." Ellie made the introductions.

"Pleased to meet you," Mavis said, eyeing him gingerly.

"Please call me Mr Tommy," the man said. "That's what everyone calls me around here."

"As you can see we are only three," Ellie said as they stepped into a flagstone front hall. "The French girl who accompanied us doesn't speak English so stayed behind."

"She's your maid?"

"She's a young woman we rescued from a bad situation," Ellie said. "Now we have to decide what to do with her next."

"Well, anyway, welcome to our humble abode. Come on in and have a glass of wine." He went ahead down the hall and into a large room on their right. It proved to be a kitchen with blue and white tiles around an ancient stove and sink. A rack of copper pans hung above it, and to one side there was a string of onions and another of bright-red dried peppers. A large window was open, and a breeze stirred white net curtains. A window box was full of herbs. In front of the window there was a plain wooden table and ladder-backed chairs. The chairs had blue and yellow cushions on them. On the table were simple raffia mats and earthenware plates with a blue-and-yellow pattern. A carafe of rosé stood in the middle. On the walls were several bright and modern paintings of the harbour, the coast and ships. It was a simple room but had a welcoming feel to it. Ellie compared it mentally to her kitchen. It had been well appointed, efficient but certainly not welcoming. Nobody was allowed in her kitchen when she held dinner parties. It was a solitary haven where Lionel never ventured.

Mr Tommy turned at the sound of footsteps. "And let me introduce you to my friend Clive," he said. "Clive Webster—three lovely English ladies. What more could you want?"

The second man came into the room. He was younger, good-looking with finely sculpted cheekbones and dark-blond hair that flopped boyishly across his forehead. He wore a blue peasant shirt over baggy trousers, and his eyes darted nervously, as if he wasn't sure of the reception he'd get.

"How do you do, Mr Webster." It was Dora who extended a hand first. "It was so kind of you both to invite us."

Clive's face relaxed. He smiled, extending a slim and elegant hand. "Not at all. Our pleasure to meet fellow English people. One grows a little tired of having to speak French each and every day. I'll pour the wine, shall I, Tommy, while you put out the hors d'oeuvres." He indicated the table. "Do take a seat. Enjoy our view. We do."

As they approached the table, they saw that the window looked out over the whole harbour area with the cliffs, jutting one after the other down the coastline until they faded into the blue distance.

"It's lovely," Ellie said.

"We can see everything that goes on from up here," Mr Tommy said with a chuckle. "We can be really nosy."

"We'd probably make a good living at blackmail if we wanted to." Clive was pouring wine as they took their places. "This is a local rosé," he said. "The region is known for it."

Mr Tommy put small plates in front of them. They contained slices of a bright orange fruit with little mounds of white cheese.

"What are these?" Dora asked.

"Persimmons and goat cheese," Mr Tommy replied. "Our persimmon tree. The cheese is from our own goats."

"You keep goats?" Ellie asked.

"Two of them," Mr Tommy replied. "Ursula and Hortense. Clive named them because they look like two dowagers with their haughty expressions. Absolutely affronted at the thought of us touching their lady parts to milk them. They rule the roost outside, along with our chickens, while the cat dominates our inside space."

As if hearing its name, a white cat appeared, pausing to rub against Clive's leg. Clive bent to pick it up. "This is Minou," he said. "We rescued her. You've probably noticed all the stray cats around here. The local inhabitants are not exactly kind to their animals. We found her as a kitten when someone tried to drown her in the harbour." He planted a kiss on Minou's forehead, then placed her back on the floor. She walked a few steps away, then sat with her back to them and began washing herself.

"Standoffish," Mr Tommy said. "Affectionate when she feels like it."

They joined the women at the table, and Mr Tommy lifted a glass. "Cheers, then."

"Cheers, and thank you for inviting us," Ellie said.

"We weren't sure you'd come. We thought that the witch at the pension would have gone out of her way to make our home sound like the house of the devil. The irony is that she and her husband never set foot inside a church, while we attend every week. Father André is remarkably broad-minded in his version of Catholicism. He happily baptizes babies of unwed mothers and makes people like us feel welcome."

"So how long have you been here?" Dora asked.

Mr Tommy looked at Clive for confirmation. "Seventeen years, is it?"

"We came in twenty-two," Clive said. "So almost seventeen."

"Goodness. That's quite a while," Dora said. "What brought you here?"

"The question is rather what drove us away," Clive said.

Mr Tommy nodded. "Clive and I met during the Great War. I registered as a conscientious objector. I thought it was quite wrong to kill other human beings. So I was sent straight to the front as a medical orderly. My job was to go out on to the battlefield and retrieve the dying and the bodies."

"Naturally they picked the worst job possible to teach people like Tommy a lesson," Clive said with bitterness in his voice. "I was young and naïve enough to do my duty and enlist at eighteen, and I was sent straight to the front. Absolute hell. It's no wonder men's minds snapped. Anyway, I was one of the bodies that Tommy retrieved. Just about alive. Horribly wounded. He brought me to safety, and he came to check on me all the time while I hovered between life and death. When they were convinced I'd live, I was sent to a convalescent hospital. Tommy came to visit me once he was back home. Without his care and encouragement, I don't think I'd have made it."

He and Tommy exchanged a smile.

"Anyway, our relationship grew during that trying time." Tommy glanced across at Clive as he said this, as if assessing if he was saying too much. "I went back to my old job as a teacher at a private school, and when Clive was discharged from the convalescent home, I realized he wasn't ready to live alone, so I brought him to live with me. And all went well until a meddling female teacher found out about us and alerted the authorities. We learned they were coming to arrest us, so we made a rapid exit. Clive is a painter, so we came to the South, where the light is so marvellous. Found this place. Loved it. Sold my house in England, inherited a small amount from my parents and here we are."

They had finished the first course, and Tommy got up to clear away the dishes. Then he brought out a large pie from the oven and put it on a mat in the middle of the table. "Mushroom tart," he said. "It's the time of year for mushrooms. And don't worry, we gather them all the time. We're not going to poison you."

The pastry was light and flaky, the mushroom filling rich and almost meaty, and it was accompanied with a salad of mixed greens, including what Ellie assumed to be dandelions. Silence fell as the women ate.

"I'd love the recipe for this," Ellie said. "It's delicious."

"You like to cook?" Tommy asked.

"I do. At home we gave frequent dinner parties, so I had to do a lot of cooking."

"We?" Tommy asked. "You're a widow, then?"

"Divorced," Ellie said. "My husband suddenly decided he wanted to marry a younger woman, so I was cast aside."

"Stupid man," Tommy said. "He wants his head examined."

"It's probably the best thing that ever happened to me," Ellie said. "For the first time I feel free to make my own decisions, live my own

117

life. I have no idea where we'll be tomorrow, and I don't find that frightening at all."

"Good for you," Clive said. "What about you, then?" He turned to Mavis, who went red.

"I'm just having a bit of a holiday, I suppose," she said.

"Mavis used to help me with the housework," Ellie said. "She had a violent bully of a husband, so I persuaded her to come with us. It will give her time to decide what she wants to do next."

"And this lady is a relative?" Clive turned to Dora.

"Just a good friend who had a longing to see the South of France again," Ellie said for her. "So we escaped together, three of us on an adventure, only now we are four. We rescued a young French girl who finds herself pregnant and abandoned."

"You're as bad as us and our cats," Clive said, making them laugh.

"So you're a painter," Dora said, changing the subject. "Are these your work?" She pointed at the walls.

Clive nodded. "What do you think?"

"So fresh. So vibrant," Dora said. "I always regret that I never learned to paint. I think I would have enjoyed it."

"It's never too late, dear lady," Clive said. "If you stay on here, I'll be happy to give you some lessons. I do for the English winter visitors, you know."

"Oh, how kind." Dora looked quite pink with excitement. "Alas, we are only staying until the motor car is mended."

"If we did want to stay longer," Ellie said hesitantly, "is there anywhere one could rent?"

"Various people rent out rooms during the season," Tommy said, looking at Clive. "But all pretty basic and nowhere where you could cook for yourself. Nowhere you'd want to stay long-term."

"There's always the villa," Clive said with a wicked smile on his face.

"Villa?" Ellie was instantly alert.

"The Villa Gloriosa," Clive repeated, still smiling.

"There's a villa for rent?" Ellie asked excitedly.

"He's just joking," Tommy said. "There is a villa on the cliffs just above the village, but it's abandoned, deserted. It hasn't been occupied for maybe thirty years."

"Who owns it, then?" Ellie asked.

"I believe it was a famous opera singer. She was the mistress of a Parisian duke, who gave her the villa as a present. But she lost interest in coming here, or she lost the duke as a patron. Anyway, she stopped coming, and then we heard that she had died. So presumably she has a next of kin somewhere who still owns it but doesn't want to live in it. It's in bad shape, anyway. The locals think it's haunted."

"How interesting," Ellie said. "I'd love to see it. Who would know how we'd get in touch with the current owners?"

"I believe Monsieur Danton, the local notaire, keeps an eye on it, pays the taxes and things like that. He'd know, anyway. But I think it would be quite sad. We saw it once, long ago. Already falling into ruin then, unlike the other villa nearby," Tommy said.

"Other villa?"

"Very grand. Alas, not for rent," Clive said. "Owned by a reclusive viscount. He spends half his year in Paris, then retreats here when it gets too hot or too cold. Not exactly the most friendly of chaps, or so we've found. Très snobbish."

"But his villa is magnificent," Tommy added. "More like a château. Perfectly manicured grounds, a swimming pool. Just divine." He got up again. "Would you like coffee? And macarons?"

"Oh yes, please," Dora said before Ellie could answer.

Clive cleared plates away while Tommy brewed coffee. The macarons were heavenly, so light they melted in the mouth.

"Did you bake these?" Ellie asked.

"I'm afraid I can't take credit." He gave an embarrassed little shrug. "Madame Blanchet at the boulangerie bakes them. She has a great flair for pastries, so her shop is really a pâtisserie, too."

"We did see pastries in the window when we went to buy bread yesterday," Ellie said. "That's good to know. I'm afraid I have a sweet tooth."

"So what exactly do you do here?" Dora asked with her usual forthrightness. "Do you have a job?"

"This and that," Tommy said. "I help out teaching at the school. I help Henri at the bar when it gets really busy. Clive paints."

"Then how do you survive?" she asked. "You must have private money, one supposes."

"I wish that were true," Tommy said. "Actually Clive's paintings are quite popular. Whenever we need a little extra, he sells another painting. And we are practically self-sufficient here with our goats and chickens. Our needs are few, apart from the occasional trip to Marseille and a shopping spree."

Ellie felt they were becoming too intrusive. "I think we should be going," she said. "We don't want to outstay our welcome."

"You'd always be welcome here," Tommy said. "As I said, we get few English guests, and one does miss the homeland in certain ways. Next time you can tell us all about what life is like there now. What is in the shops on Oxford Street."

"I'm afraid none of us is actually a woman about town with the latest wardrobe," Dora said. "Like you, we manage to get by."

"Before you go, would you like to see our goats?" Clive asked, standing up. They followed him out of a back door. On a small flat patch against the hillside there was a pen with the goats in it, a chicken run beside it and a raised vegetable garden. The last tomatoes were turning red on dying plants.

"Oh blimey. Aren't they big and fierce-looking?" Mavis exclaimed. "Look at them horns. Do you really milk them?"

"We do," Clive said. "Of course I have to sing to them while I do the milking. They like the sound of my voice." He grinned. Ellie couldn't tell if he was pulling their legs. He seemed to enjoy a good joke.

"One thing we would like is actually more land," Tommy said, "but we do love this little house, and there is nowhere else to expand our garden."

The guests were escorted round to the front of the house. The cat appeared, sensing they were leaving and probably glad that her masters' attention could now be fully on her again.

"Come and see us any time," Tommy said. "We love unexpected visitors."

～

"What interesting men," Dora commented as they made their way down the hill. "And how sensible of them to live here. Can you imagine what a scandal there would have been if they'd lived in our village? Gossip all the time. And I did like his paintings."

Ellie studied Dora as she went ahead, holding on to Mavis's arm. It was as if Dora had already shed the strict and haughty exterior of her previous life. Maybe it had been a shield, Ellie thought. *Maybe we all build up walls around us as a defense, so we can't be hurt.*

CHAPTER 14

As they reached the harbourside, they noticed that the Bentley was no longer there.

"Let's hope that Louis has had it towed away," Ellie said. "Otherwise someone has made off with it and all our belongings."

"I think that's unlikely," Dora said. "In this place there is always someone watching."

"And who would want old women's not very fashionable clothing?" Mavis added.

They were laughing as they went back into the hotel. It seemed that Yvette had gone up for a nap. They retreated to the conservatory and asked Mr Adams for some tea. They were still drinking it when Ellie was summoned to the foyer and found Louis waiting for her.

"I have news, madame," he said. "The good news is that a hose can be procured for your vehicle. The bad news is that there is a leak in your radiator. A crack at the bottom. If you wish, I can try to repair this, but I can't guarantee that it will work or last long. The alternative is that we can send away for a new radiator, and I will install it for you."

"Which do you advise?" Ellie asked.

Louis gave that delightfully Gallic shrug. "It depends what you plan to do. If your aim is to drive around the Côte d'Azur, up and down mountains, then I would say you should order the new radiator to be on the safe side. Next time you break down, you may not find a

Saint-Benet close by. If, however, you decide to stay here for a while, then why do you need a motor car that runs perfectly?"

Ellie did mental calculations. It would certainly be cheaper to stay at the pension than at a more glamorous hotel in one of the resorts. It was cheap to eat in the village. Therefore the money saved while they waited for a new radiator to arrive could be spent on the replacement. But the patch might work just as well. Also, she had to admit, she was not ready to leave this place yet. And she had a desire to see the haunted villa.

"Very well," she said. "I suggest you try to patch the radiator. And if that does not work well, then we will send off for a new one."

He nodded as if he thought this was a wise decision.

"We will need our suitcases from the motor car if you are to work on it at your workplace," Ellie said.

"Already taken care of, madame," he replied. "You will find your baggage in your rooms."

So he already suspected that they would want to stay longer. Ellie went back to the others and reported what Louis had said. "And he's had our bags delivered to our rooms," she finished.

"So you are willing to risk driving on with a patched radiator?" Dora asked.

"If we go any further, we'll reach Toulon, or another of the big towns, where they will have proper car mechanics and radiators," Ellie said. "And I don't know about you, but I'm not ready to go anywhere yet. I like this place. It seems like a sort of refuge where I can come to terms with what has happened and what is going to happen. Also, I have this strange desire to see the villa."

"The place what's supposed to be haunted?" Mavis looked horrified. "You're not thinking of renting it yourself and staying there?"

"I'd just like to see it," Ellie said. "It may sound silly, but when they mentioned a villa I found myself thinking that I'd been waiting for it, as if it was all planned."

Dora looked at her suspiciously. "I suppose it can't hurt to see it," she said. "I must admit that I'm a little curious about it myself. Built for a duke's mistress, then abandoned . . . It sounds very romantic."

"Right," Ellie said. "Tomorrow we'll go and visit the notaire to see if he can arrange for us to see it."

By five o'clock, Yvette had finally risen from her nap. "I don't know what is the matter with me," she said, "but all I want to do is to sleep and sleep."

"I understand," Ellie replied. "You have had a bad shock. When you sleep, you don't have to think about it."

"You are right, madame," Yvette said. "I am so worried all the time. How can I think about the future? What will happen to me? What will happen to my child?"

"It will not be easy for you, I fear, but we will try to help you, Yvette," Ellie said. "You are amongst friends now. We will try to work out what is best."

"You are my guardian angel, I am sure," Yvette said and flung her arms around Ellie. Ellie stood there, feeling awkward with the unwanted embrace. She didn't remember anyone ever hugging her fiercely like this. Certainly not Lionel, certainly not her parents. Her grandmother maybe?

That evening they set off across to Henri's bar on the other side of the harbour. Clouds were gathering out to sea, which tonight presented an inky blackness. A chilly wind was blowing, making waves slap against the harbour wall and the fishing boats creak and groan at their moorings.

"Goodness, I wish I'd brought my fur coat after all," Dora said, wrapping her scarf around her throat.

Henri was waiting outside the bar to greet them. "Dear mesdames, welcome. Tonight I think you will want to sit inside as the nights are now getting colder." He led them through the open doors to where a table with a white cloth and silverware had been set up by a fireplace in which a log fire was burning. "Winter is on its way, is it not?"

"It's certainly cold out there," Dora said.

"You will be delighted with what I have prepared for you this evening," he said. "I have made the poulet Basquaise, the chicken in a rich sauce of the Basque people. And to begin the meal, a terrine."

Ellie wasn't sure what a terrine was, but she smiled politely as they took their seats. The first course was produced. The terrine was a thick slice of what looked like various chopped meats surrounded by aspic. It was served with thin slices of toasted bread and decorated with a sprig of rosemary. There were definitely herbs in the dish. Ellie tried to make out the flavours. Rosemary? Thyme? She realized she had no idea that something so simple could be so full of amazing flavour sensations. She had always liked to cook and prided herself on her cooking, but the dishes had always been simple ones: a piece of meat, vegetables and potatoes, roast beef, pork chops, liver and bacon, stews. She did make shepherd's pie with leftovers, or occasional steak and kidney pies, but they were flavoured with salt and pepper at best. Nothing like this attack on the taste buds. *I'm going to learn how to do this,* she thought.

She noticed the others were also scraping their plates clean.

"I don't know what that was supposed to be," Mavis said. "I didn't like the look of it to start with, but it didn't half taste good."

"It pleased you, mesdames?" Henri asked, whisking the plates away.

"It was wonderful," Ellie said. "If we stay here, perhaps you will teach me how to make such a dish."

"It would be my pleasure to give you instruction," he said. "But wait until you taste the poulet."

Chicken was regarded as a luxury item at home, and Ellie roasted one on special occasions, but chicken had never smelled like this dish put before them: the rich, red sauce clearly had tomatoes in it, but so much more. The chicken fell off the bone.

"I don't think I've enjoyed food so much for years," Dora said when they had finished. "When one cooks for oneself, it is hard to get enthusiastic about food. It was usually the most convenient thing that didn't require me to make saucepans dirty—a lamb chop, a piece of poached fish, or even scrambled egg or toasted cheese. Now I find I have quite an appetite."

"Maybe this was all you needed to make you well again," Mavis said.

Dora looked at her almost fondly. "Oh no, my dear. It's my heart, you see. It's gradually slowing down until it stops."

"Then we'll get it sped up again," Mavis said.

Dora smiled. "If only you could. I was becoming weary of life until now. It didn't seem to matter that the stupid heart would just stop one day. But now . . . I don't think I'm ready to go after all."

There was no dessert tonight as Henri said that the main course was rich enough and he thought that fruit and cheese were more appropriate. Nobody argued with that. When he brought their coffees, there was the sound of male voices outside and some of the men came in.

"It's cold enough to freeze your balls off," one was saying, then stopped short when he saw that ladies were present. "Mille pardons, mesdames," he muttered.

Ellie noticed that the big pirate, Nico, was amongst them, tonight wearing a navy woollen coat with the collar turned up. "Ah, the English ladies. So you are stuck with us, eh? You found your luggage, I hope," he said. "We helped Louis move your automobile. He has told you what was wrong, yes?"

Ellie nodded.

"You are lucky you made it here with no water in your radiator," he said. "And now it will take time to fix. You will have to stay here, I think. That pleases you?"

"Yes," Ellie said. "We are happy to stay a little longer. This place is most agreeable."

"More agreeable than those big towns," one of the other men said. "There it is all about rich people showing off their wealth. What shall I wear today?" and he mimicked a woman tossing back her hair.

"What is more, the food is better," a third man added. "Henri here knows how to cook. In those big hotels, they think the English don't appreciate fine food. Although if you stay longer, do not let that Madame Adams cook for you. You will be poisoned in minutes."

The other men laughed.

"So, will you take a drink with us?" Nico asked. "A cognac to finish the meal?"

"Oh, I don't think—" Ellie began but Dora cut her off with "Thank you, why not?"

He snapped his fingers, and Henri produced small glasses of cognac while the men sat at the next table. The men introduced themselves: François, Jacquot, Luc, Nicolas.

"We do not stand on ceremony here," François said. "You probably think it shocking that we introduce ourselves by our first names, but I think it easier than last names you probably can't pronounce. Besides, you will move on and never see us again."

"Eleanor, Theodora, Mavis, Yvette," Ellie replied, feeling awkward with such familiarity.

The other women acknowledged this with a half-hearted bob and a muttered bonsoir.

"You all know French?" François asked.

"I do, although it is mostly of the schoolgirl variety," Dora replied. "Yvette is French. This lady does not. We will have to translate for her, unless you gentlemen speak some English?"

"Not me," François said. "Nico does."

Nico shrugged. "It is long time now," he said in English. "I do not practice and forget much."

"So how is it at the pension?" Luc asked them. He was younger with a cheeky grin. "Is it up to your standards?"

"It's certainly simple," Ellie said. "But it's clean. It will do for now." She was going to add something about the villa but stopped, suddenly shy about sharing too much.

They took their leave soon afterward.

"You see, Yvette? They are not such brigands and corsairs when you get to know them," Dora said as they walked home. Yvette merely shrugged.

CHAPTER 15

The next morning they were woken by wind rattling the shutters. When Ellie opened hers, she felt rain in her face and saw an angry dark sea. So winter had come to the Côte d'Azur. This made her realize that staying in this small town might not be so desirable after all. If they were stuck all day in the pension, what exactly would they do? There were no cinemas, tea rooms or other delights to amuse them. The so-called lounge was a rather dreary room with a couple of ancient leather sofas and a bookcase containing some board games and a few novels. Ellie suspected they'd soon get sick of each other's company. But she was still determined to see the villa before the radiator was mended. So after breakfast she paid a call on Monsieur Danton, the notaire. The rain had intensified, so she left the others in the warmth of the hotel lounge and wished she had brought her stout English raincoat as she made her way down the village street. Monsieur Danton had an impressive office in the same building as the police station, and Ellie realized that in a village this size he was the equivalent of a mayor, handling permits and fines and everybody's business.

Monsieur Danton was a little man, immaculately dressed with a high starched collar and dark suit. His thinning grey hair was parted in the middle, and he sported a thin moustache. He wore wire spectacles and had a perpetually surprised expression. This became even more pronounced when Ellie explained her mission.

"My dear madame," he said, "this so-called villa is not what you think. It is not suitable to be occupied at this stage. It is a tumbledown ruin, untouched for many years."

"Would it be too much trouble to enquire of the owners if we could at least see it?" she asked. "I find its history quite romantic. You do have an address for the current owner, do you?"

"I certainly do," he replied. "But as to whether the owner will want you to see it? Who can say?"

Ellie left, not feeling too hopeful. They passed the rest of the day in reading or playing cards. Mr Adams managed some ham sandwiches for lunch, and in the evening they bundled up and hurried across the harbour to Henri. He apologized that the van with supplies had not arrived, due to a mudslide, but he would make them omelettes. These proved to be amazingly light and stuffed with tiny shrimp and herbs. With them were layered potatoes in a creamy sauce and a spinach salad.

"Who knew that ordinary old eggs could taste so nice," Mavis summed up for all of them.

After an apple tart and coffee, they retreated to the pension, just in time, as another round of storms came in, buffeting the shutters. "If it's going to be like this all winter, it hardly makes sense to stay here," Dora said testily. "We'd do just as well in Bournemouth."

"We're not going home already, are we?" Mavis asked in alarm.

"Of course not," Ellie said. "We're not going to let one little rainstorm drive us away."

After they went to bed, Ellie slept fitfully. What was she doing here? she asked herself. Was it really the right place for her? Where was a right place for her? She belonged nowhere. But she felt responsible for Dora and Mavis and Yvette. What was to become of them?

At last she fell asleep and awoke to blue skies, seagulls wheeling overhead and fishermen already busy bailing water from their drenched boats.

"So what do you want to do today?" Dora asked. "See if the radiator is fixed and we can move on?"

"I'd like to find out if Monsieur Danton has managed to contact the owner of the villa," Ellie replied.

"That damned villa. You've become obsessed with it, haven't you?" Dora replied.

"Maybe just a little." Ellie managed a smile. "But it can't hurt to take a look, can it? We go and visit old houses and castles in England. This is the same sort of thing. Historic value."

"Hmph" was all that Dora replied. Ellie noted that she was not in a good mood today and suspected she might be in pain. The rain certainly would have made arthritis flare up in an older person.

"Do you want to come with me to see Monsieur Danton?" she asked.

"I'll come," Mavis said. "This place ain't exactly cheerful, if you know what I mean."

"I should like to meet this man who seems to rule the roost here," Dora said. "Yvette, do you wish to come with us?" she asked in French.

Yvette shrugged. "This town is boring," she said. "There are no good shops. No cinema."

"I hardly think there were many good shops near your farm," Dora replied archly.

Yvette nodded as if this was true. "I will come," she said. "At least I can look at the pastries in the window of the boulangerie."

They set out. Women were busy hanging out laundry after the wet day, righting outside furniture and plants that had blown over during the storm. There was a line at the baker's. The owner of the other food shop was putting out baskets of apples and peppers. Before they could reach Monsieur Danton's place of business, they saw him walking towards them. His officious manner of walking echoed his dress and personality.

"Ah, the very person I was coming to see," he said, beaming. "I have good news, mesdames. The owner, he says that I may escort you to see the villa. But he warns that you will not find it agreeable, and please be careful as it could be dangerous."

"Oh, we'll be very careful," Ellie said. "Thank you so much. When might be convenient for you?"

"Why, now," he said. "This is why I was coming to find you. Let us take advantage of the fine weather. At this time of year, one never knows."

"Thank you," Ellie replied. "It is most kind of you to give up your time to do this."

"Not at all." He was now gracious and all smiles. "If you'll follow me, we have a steep way ahead of us."

Behind the row of buildings along the waterfront ran a narrow lane. Bougainvillea spilled over an ancient wall that butted on to the cream-coloured limestone cliff. In the middle of that wall they came to a flight of steps going up the cliffside. Monsieur Danton turned back to them. "I hope you are in fine form, ladies," he said and started upward. The steps were uneven, steep and worn in places, making the going a challenge, but they were shaded with scrubby oaks and pine trees and the rich, piny smell was around them. At the top they paused, all breathing heavily. Another flight of steps rose before them.

"Is this the only way to the villa?" Ellie asked.

"No, madame," he said. "There is a driveway leading up to the villa from outside the village. You can approach it in a motor car from there, and there is a garage and the formal entrance. But this is the quick way up."

"Are you sure you can do this, Dora?" Ellie looked at her in concern. "Isn't it bad for your heart? Mavis could take you down."

"Absolutely not. I'm as keen to see this villa as you are," Dora said. "Besides, it will give this old and failing heart a good workout." And before anyone could answer her, she started up the second flight of stone steps. They emerged on to a path that wound its way around the cliff, until it was lost amongst the pines. As they went to follow it, Monsieur Danton said, "No, no, madame. That is the path that leads to the Calanques. This way if you please, ladies. Follow me." And he started up a third set of steps, this one mercifully short and ending in a high wall covered in some kind of creeper. In the middle of the wall was a tall iron gate. Monsieur Danton took a key from his pocket and inserted it into the lock. There was a click, and the gate opened with a protesting squeak.

"Please proceed with great care," he said, standing to one side and assisting each of them up a final steep step into a garden. Ellie entered but then stood transfixed as she looked around her. It felt as if she were in the book *The Secret Garden*, or rather in the magic realm of Sleeping Beauty, fallen asleep for a hundred years. In front of them what had once been a lawn was now a dying mass of dried grass and weeds. The ubiquitous bougainvillea tumbled over the walls, in a riot of reds and oranges. At the far end of the lawn was an orchard of fruit trees: a pomegranate still bravely producing its brilliant red fruit after so many years of neglect, what might have been a persimmon and several citrus.

Ellie turned the other direction and saw the villa itself. Before it was a gravel forecourt in which stood a stone fountain, now long dry. And behind this was the Villa Gloriosa. Now no longer glorious. Ellie had expected a ruin but found she was looking at a perfect villa with a red tiled roof. The house was painted pink with pale-blue shutters. It took Ellie a moment to notice that the paint was now peeling and some of the shutters were hanging at crazy angles. Tiles had fallen from the roof. There had been some sort of veranda or trellised arbour along the entire back of the house, but this was completely overrun by what looked like wisteria, although the leaves were now dying and lying in a yellow carpet. Another vine with dark red and brown leaves—grapes this time?—climbed up the far side of the veranda and competed with the wisteria in a mad tangle.

"This way." Monsieur Danton interrupted her reverie. He began to walk towards the house. The path was lined with an avenue of palm trees, now casting a neat row of shadows across the gravel. Ellie followed him around the side of the villa to an impressive pair of oak double doors carved with a pattern of vines. Monsieur Danton produced another key and was about to lead them inside when Ellie looked past him, to her left, and gasped.

"Wait." She broke into a run.

"Careful, madame. Watch your step," he called, but she didn't care if the flagstones were cracked and uneven. She ran past the house and came out to a terrace overlooking the sea. It was edged by an ornamental stone balustrade topped with carved pineapples, some of which were now missing, but Ellie didn't notice this. She crossed the terrace and stood with the whole panorama unfolding before her. Directly below her Saint-Benet lay nestled in its little hollow, the village mainly in shadow, the cliffs on the far side glowing in the sun. Beyond were more promontories, more cliffs, fading into blue distance. On the horizon was a chain of rocky islands. As she watched, a boat with a red sail glided out from the harbour into a Mediterranean that went from shades of pure turquoise to deep, rich blue.

"Oh," she said out loud. "This is heaven."

CHAPTER 16

"Madame, do you not wish to see inside?" Monsieur Danton's crisp voice brought Ellie back to reality.

Reluctantly she turned away from the view. "Oh yes, of course. Thank you." She returned to the others and went to step in through the open door.

"Are you sure you wish to proceed with this?" He peered in as if he expected an attack. "Maybe just look from here. It could be dangerous. Who knows if the ceilings are about to come down? Nobody has touched this place for years, you know."

"I'll be careful," Ellie said. "It seems a shame not to look around when we've come all this way."

"Very well, if you insist." He gave a curt nod. He stepped aside to let her enter but did not follow. Ellie looked back at the other women and saw the hesitancy on their faces. "I'll take a look first, if you like," she said. "Just to make sure it's safe."

Then she took a deep breath and stepped over the threshold into a marble entrance hall. An impressive white marble staircase curved up to a second floor. There was a green marble side table on which stood a huge vase containing some very old and faded silk flowers; otherwise the foyer was devoid of decoration. Ellie stood staring in surprise. She had expected devastation—crumbling ceilings, great cobwebs—but the place merely felt as if it was asleep. Monsieur Danton showed no desire to come into the villa, so she ventured into the room on her right through an open door. The green velvet curtains were closed, bathing the room in eerie darkness that felt like being in an aquarium. She looked for a light switch, then laughed at her own absurdity. Of course there would be no electricity turned on. As she took a step into the room, she recoiled almost immediately as something tall and thin loomed up beside her, draped in white. She remembered the inhabitants of Saint-Benet claiming that the villa was haunted, but then she realized that every object in the room was covered in a dustsheet, and this had to be . . . She pulled off the cover, releasing impressive amounts of dust in the process, and found it to be a curio cabinet peopled with porcelain figures.

Feeling braver, she crossed the room and pulled open those tall curtains. The green velvet crumbled at her touch. French doors opened to the gravel forecourt and the garden beyond. Sunlight flooded into the room, making dust motes dance. She looked around her. The long oblong that took up the centre of the room had to be a huge dining table. She lifted one corner of the dustsheet cautiously, not wanting to breathe in more dust. It revealed a white painted wooden table, gilded, and the chairs that surrounded it were also decorated with gold with silk seat covers, now partially nibbled away by mice or moths or both. So this had been the dining room. A door at the far end led to a kitchen. As she entered it, the feeling of Sleeping Beauty's castle returned. The kitchen looked as if it had been in use, not packed up to be forgotten. There was a pan on the old-fashioned wood stove, scales on the pine table, a tea caddy, a milk jug—all looking as if they expected the owners to return.

Ellie came back out to the foyer and opened a door leading to the back of the house. These were the rooms with the lovely view over the water. The first was a pleasant sitting room with a couple of sofas hidden under their dustsheets, a porcelain stove and some wicker rocking chairs. The walls were painted in a fresco of palm trees and beaches, echoing the real-life view. And next to it was a smaller room that made her heart beat faster again. That shape under the sheet in the window had to be a grand piano. This had been a music room! Of course it had. Its occupant had been a famous opera singer.

"Oh, how lovely," she muttered, and immediately she pictured herself sitting at that piano, looking out at the blue sea as she played. But as she stood there, she experienced the sadness that she had been sensing since she entered the house. The famous opera singer had made this place beautiful and then left, never to return. Why? She had not died until later if accounts were correct. If the duke had gifted her with this villa, why did she not come back, even after their relationship broke up? It had been hers, because they had been told that her next of kin now owned it. What had driven her away and made her leave all her lovely things under dustsheets?

"It's not very big, is it?" Dora's voice made her jump, realizing that she had been unaware of anyone else as she explored the house. "Suitable for one person. I'd expected grander."

"I think it's perfect," Ellie said. "I can't believe how well it's been preserved. Almost as if it's asleep."

"I'd say the mice have done their share of damage," Dora said. "And look at the stains on the wallpaper where the rain has come in."

But Ellie had seen none of these faults. "Shall we take a look upstairs?" she said and headed towards the staircase.

"Proceed with great caution, madame," Monsieur Danton called, still peering in from the doorway. "Who knows if the floors are still stable."

But Ellie hardly heard. She went up the stairs, her hand feeling the cold smoothness of the marble banister. Upstairs doors opened on to a small square landing. As she stood there, she heard a noise that made the hairs on her neck stand on end. "Ooooh. Oooooh." Just the sort of noise one would expect a ghost to make.

"Rubbish," she said, but she opened the first door cautiously. There was a flapping sound. Something white brushed past her face. She let out a scream, her heart thumping, and retreated hastily from the room, until she saw that roof tiles must have fallen off in one corner. The

137

ceiling had come down there, and pigeons had found their way in. There were copious droppings on the floor and on a single bed frame with quilts and pillows piled at one end.

As she went to close the door again, another figure was standing behind her. As a second scream was about to escape, she saw that it was only Dora.

"Oh goodness, you startled me," she said.

"I heard you scream, so I came up to check on you."

"You shouldn't have come up these stairs," Ellie said. "I'm sorry. I opened that door, and something flew in my face."

"Heavens. What was it?"

"Only pigeons." Ellie grinned. "The roof has a hole in it, and they got in. It's rather a mess in there, I'm afraid."

"Perhaps we should retreat again without looking any further," Dora said. "Who knows what we might find?"

"Oh no. I have to see," Ellie said. "You go on down. I don't want you in any danger."

"Nonsense. If you're going to look, so am I," Dora said.

They opened the door to the second bedroom at the front. It was large and contained a double bed, its eiderdown folded on it, a wardrobe and dressing table.

"This is a nice room," Dora said. "I wonder if it was hers?"

"More likely his. It has a masculine feel to it, don't you think?"

"They slept in separate rooms? Hardly likely." Dora snorted.

Ellie closed the door again, and they moved over to the bedrooms facing the sea. As she opened a door, she heard Dora give a little gasp.

"Oh, what a perfect view."

The cream-coloured silk drapes were tied back, and the whole coastline spread out below them. "I should die happy if that was the last thing I saw," Dora said. "This must have been her room. Look at the bed."

It was a huge brass bed piled high with quilts. There was also an enormous wardrobe. Ellie opened this, still cautious, and saw it was full of women's clothes . . . long silk gowns, light wool two-piece suits, all from the early days of the century.

"She didn't take her clothes with her," Dora said. "So either the opera singer was wealthy enough that she didn't need to take her clothing with her, or something prevented her from returning."

"There are lovely things here," Ellie agreed, fingering a brocade ballgown. "It is a puzzle."

The last rooms on the floor were a bathroom complete with an enormous clawfoot tub and a rather fearsome-looking contraption to heat water, and next door was a WC, its walls also painted with an elegant beach scene.

"Madame, is all well up there?" Monsieur Danton called. "I heard you call out."

"It was only pigeons." Ellie walked back at the top of the stairs. "I was startled."

"You see, the place is decaying. Wild creatures have gained entry," Monsieur Danton said. "Please come down before something befalls you."

"But that's not true." Ellie came down the stairs slowly, making sure Dora was behind her. "Most of it is not too bad. Oh, I can see where the rain has come in through a window, and the paint and paper are peeling, but overall it's survived remarkably well." She came down the stairs carefully to see the other women watching her from the bottom.

"We heard you cry out," Mavis said. "We thought you'd seen the ghost."

"I thought so, too, for a moment," Ellie admitted, laughing now, "but pigeons had found a way in. One of them flapped past me."

"You have now seen enough?" Monsieur Danton asked, his eyes darting for the way out.

"I think so," Ellie said. She followed him out. "So, monsieur, what do you think the owner might say if we wanted to rent this for a while?"

Monsieur Danton gaped at her. "Rent this place? Madame, you cannot be serious. You have seen with your own eyes. It will fall on your heads."

"No, I think it's quite sound. Most of it, anyway," Ellie said. "Could you at least ask the owner?"

Monsieur Danton shook his head. Dora had only just understood the conversation in French.

"Rent it?" Dora froze on the bottom step, staring at Ellie. "Are you out of your mind? Oh, it was interesting enough to see, as a curiosity, but the place is falling down. There's a hole in the roof. Pigeons flapping around. We couldn't live here. How could we ever make it habitable again?"

"But I think we could," Ellie said. She lingered, staring back up the curve of those marble stairs. "It's mostly cosmetic—taking down old wallpaper, repainting—and we could have someone in to patch the leaks, mend the shutters."

"That would cost a great deal of money, I expect," Dora said.

"Not as much as staying in Nice or Antibes," Ellie replied. "Look, Dora, I can quite understand that you don't want to do this. Maybe it's just a silly fancy of mine, a fantasy if you like. But the moment I heard about this place, I knew I had to visit it. And the moment I stepped inside, I felt it calling me to make it whole again. Something sad happened here, and I think I should make it right, somehow."

Dora was staring at her as if she had never seen her before. "This can't be the same Mrs Endicott who was in charge of the jam sale at the Women's Institute," she said. "Always so sensible and reasonable."

"Maybe that was because I had to be," Ellie said. "All my life I've been sensible and reasonable. I've done the right thing, tried to please everybody, when nobody ever tried to find out what I wanted. I had dreams once, just like you did, Dora. Those dreams were always stifled until now." She put a hand on the older woman's shoulder. "Come on. What have we got to lose? We have no plans, no destination. We could stay on at the pension until some of the rooms at the villa are properly habitable again. Oh, and I wouldn't expect you to do any hard work. I don't mind funding it myself if you don't agree, but couldn't we at least give it a try?"

Dora glanced at the others. "I think you're quite mad," she said. "Talk sense to her, Mavis."

Mavis was staring, trying to make sense of a conversation that had gone on in two languages. "You want to rent this place? Stay here, you mean, and fix it up? But that's going to take months, isn't it? It's not like a bit of whitewash would make it all right again."

"You're right. I expect it will take quite a while."

"So you want to be away from England for . . . months? I hadn't realized. I thought it was just a holiday, really. You know, how people take trips to the Continent to get some sunshine?"

"I hadn't realized myself how long I meant to be away," Ellie said.

"But that means I can never go home again," Mavis said, a bleak look on her face. "If I went on holiday with you, he might understand, but if I was away for months, I don't know what he'd do."

"Mavis, I thought we'd talked about this," Dora said. "You really don't want to go back to him, do you? In your heart you're glad to be free of him?"

"Yeah, I suppose I am. But I'm still scared, Miss Smith-Humphries. I'm scared he'd come after me when I get home. Make me pay for leaving him."

"You have us, Mavis," Ellie said. "We'll look after you, I promise. And if you're away for a few months, you can write and tell him you're never coming back. And you're filing for divorce."

"God strewth," Mavis said. "That makes it sound so final. I don't know if I could do that."

"But it's what you want, isn't it? You can't tell me that you'd go back to him."

Mavis paused, looking around her. "I like it here," she said. "I like this place and the people, even if I can't understand them. Better than cleaning houses and being knocked about by a drunken husband. So

I suppose you're right. I'm willing to give it a go. I ain't afraid of a bit of hard work. And Yvette here, I bet she's used to working hard on her farm. I reckon we could scrub and paint and that sort of thing if your heart is set on this, Mrs E."

"I can see I'm outnumbered," Dora said huffily.

"Oh no, Dora," Ellie said gently. "If you are completely against it, then we'll forget all about it. We'll get the motor car fixed and be on our way to Hyères or Saint-Tropez. Wherever you want."

"You don't even know that the owners will agree to our taking it over," Dora said. "And if they do, then I propose that you tell them we pay no rent until the house is fully restored. We are doing them a great favour. They will end up with a viable property, so it's in their best interests."

"So you're willing to give it a try?" Ellie asked.

Dora gave a little sigh. "I also must be quite mad, but I suppose so."

Ellie gave her an impulsive hug. "It's going to be fun," she said.

~~

"How long do you think it will be before you might hear back from the owners?" Ellie asked Monsieur Danton as they made their way down the steps again. He had waited patiently, not fully understanding, while this dialogue had gone on.

He shrugged. "Who can say? I will have no problem in contacting the owner through his representative, but he may want to think this over. He has shown no interest in the villa until now, but he may be reluctant to let anybody else use it. One never knows."

"He? So it's a man, is it?" Dora asked.

"The one who represents the interests of the inheritors is the notaire. I will put your proposition to him, and then we wait."

"If we did want to do this, are there any men around here who would be willing to do the heavy work, do you think?"

"The fishermen are always glad to pick up extra work during the stormy winter months," Monsieur Danton said. "And of course Louis. He is the man who can mend anything. He will help you, I'm sure. And Madame Gauchet's son, Bruno. He is, how do you say it . . . simple. He has the mentality of a small child. But he is strong and willing and eager to please. If you show him how to do something and speak to him patiently, then he will work most diligently at any task. And the extra money would certainly help his mother, who is a widow."

They continued down the next flight of steps. "So tell me," Ellie said. "Have you lived in this place all your life?"

"For most of it," he said. "I had to do military service in the Great War, and of course I went away to study law. I thought I might live in the big city, but in the end my mother was frail and alone, and I came home."

"So did you ever know the opera singer? The one who owned the villa?"

"Jeannette Hétreau? I believe I spotted her once when I was a young boy, passing in her big motor car. But she was very private. You can see how the villa is built. Completely cut off from the rest of us. She could enter up that driveway without anyone seeing her, and she brought her own servants. She did have produce and groceries delivered, but the servants took care of that. So no, she never mixed with ordinary people like us. Although sometimes . . ." He paused, considering. "Sometimes we would hear the music. Someone would play the piano, and she would sing. That sound, floating out over the waters . . . it was enchanting. Magical."

"And you have no idea why she abandoned this place?"

"No idea at all. We never knew when she came and went. But apparently one day she just didn't come any more. I was a small child in the early days of the century when I heard she had not returned. But it was much later when we read that she had died. During the Great War, I believe, although I'm not sure how and why she died."

"But then you were contacted by her next of kin?"

"Their lawyers, of course, and we were asked to take care of taxes for the building."

"But not to keep it up? That's strange, isn't it?"

"I thought so. But the new owner expressed no interest in ever wanting to use it. There may have been a clause in the will that he couldn't sell it. I don't know."

They reached the bottom of the steps and came out into the alleyway. Monsieur Danton gave a nodding bow. "I shall take my leave of you, dear mesdames, and relay your request at the earliest moment."

"Thank you so much," Ellie said. "And thank you for taking the time to visit the villa with us. You have made us very excited. You will tell the owners that, won't you? That we are keen to restore the villa to its former glory. Villa Gloriosa can live again."

"I will tell them," Monsieur Danton said. He turned and walked away, leaving them standing with bougainvillea spilling over the wall around them.

CHAPTER 17

"Well, that was an adventure." Dora paused, still catching her breath. "We did say we wanted adventures, didn't we? At least it won't be boring or humdrum."

Yvette took Ellie's arm. "What about me, madame? Do I understand that you plan to stay in this place? You want to rent this villa?"

"That's right," Ellie said.

"Where am I to go? What am I to do?"

Ellie had almost forgotten about Yvette. She always made herself so inconspicuous, hanging back in the shadows. She had not even come into the villa to look at it, Ellie realized. She had been so captivated with her own excitement that she hadn't realized its implications.

"Oh Yvette," she said. "Yes, of course. Of course we'll have to make arrangements for you. What would you want to do? When my motor car is mended, I can take you back to Marseille and maybe you could find a job there, or maybe I could drive you to one of the Riviera resorts." She saw the panic in Yvette's eyes. "Or . . ." She paused, glancing at Dora and Mavis before she went on. "You could stay here with us until the baby comes. Help us fix up the villa and make it beautiful again?" She stopped, hesitated, realizing that she hadn't consulted the other two about this. "If the other ladies are in agreement, of course?" she added. She repeated what had been said in English for Mavis.

"Where else would the girl go at this stage?" Dora said. "And a pair of strong arms might be helpful, although in her condition she shouldn't do too much. But she can help with the garden and the kitchen. We can train her to be a maid so that she has job prospects for after the child is born."

"Right." Ellie beamed, glad that Dora was willing to consider this. "And what about you, Mavis? What do you feel about all this?"

"I suppose the poor girl's got to go somewhere," Mavis said. "It probably ain't her fault that she's in the family way. I can show her how to do housework properly and maybe even teach her some cooking."

"Wonderful. So it's all settled." She turned back to Yvette, who had been standing, her eyes moving from one speaker to the next, not understanding a word. "Yvette," she said. "If you wish, you may stay here with us. We will provide for you. Your food and a place to live. You will help us as much as you are able until the baby comes. What do you think of this idea?"

She saw relief on the girl's face. "I am happy to hear this," she said. "I was worried about where I could find a job until the baby comes. So I thank you. I am most grateful to you. You have been my angel, madame."

"That's good," Ellie said. "And we will help you, too. We will try and contact the army to learn where your sweetheart is posted, and we can write to him for you. Maybe he'll be happy to learn he is to be a father, and all will be well for you."

Yvette did not look as relieved as Ellie thought she should. "Maybe," she said. "But I can try to get in touch with him myself, madame."

"You said you couldn't read and write," Dora said, frowning.

"Enough to compose a simple letter, madame. We all had to learn that much," Yvette said. "And I'd even like to learn English if you ladies will help me."

"Splendid," Ellie said. "We will have English classes, and you will help Mavis learn French. It will be a time of growing and learning for all of us."

~~

They passed the rest of the day going for a walk around the cliffs, spending more time on the little beach, although Dora exclaimed to her regret that the last storm had made the temperature of the sea a little too cold, even for her. "It may warm up again, if we get sunny days," she said, "although in October I doubt it." She stood at the water's edge. "I must acquire some new clothing, suitable for our lifestyle here. Sensible trousers and cotton skirts, I think. When the motor car is mended, I suggest we take a trip into Marseille."

"We are assuming the owners will agree to this crazy scheme," Ellie said. "If not, I don't think we'd want to spend the winter in the pension."

"That's true," Dora agreed. "Not exactly the most warm and welcoming of places."

"I wonder how long it will take to make the villa liveable again?" Ellie said.

"I suppose it depends how many willing hands we can enlist," Dora said, "And how much structural damage there is."

"Oh dear, I don't want to get my hopes up too much," Ellie said, "but after this it will feel a letdown to rent an ordinary little house or flat in another seaside town. At least this gives me a sense of purpose . . . the sort of challenge I haven't had since I furnished our first house when we married." She smiled at the memory. "Lionel had come from a humble background and had lived in furnished rooms. He didn't have much idea about good furniture and how to decorate. So I did it all. I went to second-hand furniture shops and local auctions and found some nice pieces. I chose wallpaper. My parents gave us things they no longer wanted, and when they died

I inherited good antiques from them. I loved the look of my sitting room . . ."

She broke off, staring out at the waves breaking on the shore. An image of that serene room with its bowls of flowers and grand piano swam into her head.

"And that fool didn't appreciate what you'd done for him," Dora said. "Raised him to the middle class, that's what you did. Taught him how to act with our sort of people, I expect."

"Oh, he'd learned a thing or two at his accountancy training and the bank when I met him," Ellie said. "But just not the niceties of social life." She gave a little sigh. "I hope Michelle knows how to give dinner parties, not only how to cook and keep everything hot to be served at the right moment but how to be the gracious hostess at the same time, making it look effortless."

"I expect they'll hire a cook," Dora said. "She'll get through his money quite quickly."

"I expect she will." Ellie had to laugh. "I should feel sorry for him, but I don't."

"Of course not," Mavis said. "He was the one what let you down. He treated you badly. And you're getting the last laugh on him. Look at you—happy as a sandboy."

Ellie looked down at her bare feet, now covered in sand. "That's an apt image, Mavis. Yes, I am truly happy at the moment."

They repeated the order of the previous day. When they returned, sun-kissed and sandy from the beach, they were met with a disapproving glare from Mrs Adams.

"I don't want sand brought into my house," she said.

"Of course not," Dora said. "Where would you like us to rinse off our legs, then?"

"I'll bring a bucket outside for you," Mrs Adams said.

"I'm surprised you don't have a tap," Dora said. "After all, I expect most of your guests go to the beach from time to time, especially if they have children."

Mrs Adams didn't reply to this, and Ellie got the feeling that she was just looking for a way to be critical.

"So how long do you think you'll be staying, then?" she asked. "When is the motor car supposed to be ready?"

"When Louis has time to finish it," Ellie said, "but we may be staying on longer."

She watched the woman's face change, her brain quickly working that she might have guests for the off-season.

"Well, in that case," she said, "we can probably find you better rooms. More comfortable. With heating."

"And why weren't we offered those before?" Dora asked.

"They are reserved for our long-term guests," Mrs Adams said smoothly. "And they weren't made up. We keep a few rooms ready just in case, but they are simple to take care of for us. But now you might be staying on, I'd be happy to show you . . . They are in the annex at the back. Nice and private. There's even a little parlour between two of the rooms."

"We might be needing them," Ellie said. "We are waiting for news." She didn't say any more, leaving Mrs Adams curious but not about to pry.

They enjoyed an afternoon rest, tea in the conservatory and dinner chez Henri—this time a rabbit casserole. Ellie found it hard to sleep, her emotions stretched as tight as violin strings. She wanted the villa so much. She truly believed that it was a sign from above, or maybe from the opera singer, that she should live there and make it beautiful again. She lay looking up at the ceiling and wondered if it would be acceptable to pray about such a thing. She had gone to church every Sunday, had been a devoted member of the churchwomen's guild in charge of flowers and the annual fete. She had said the prayers and sung the hymns, but she wondered now how much she believed. There had been her father, the vicar, who loved to preach about the wages of sin being death, not about a God who loved everybody and wanted them to be happy. Ellie wanted to believe this herself.

"If you're up there and actually can hear us," she said into the darkness, "I really would like the chance to live in that villa. Can you make it happen? I've been good all my life, I think. I've never tried to hurt anybody, and I've done my duty, so if you could work just this one little miracle, I'd be most grateful."

Then a sudden thought came to her: *Does one have to pray in French when in France?* This made her laugh, and the tension was broken. Whatever was going to happen, it was good.

~

Ellie didn't know how long it would take to get a response from the new owners of the villa. She couldn't understand why anyone would not want it restored, or why they had not wanted to live in it themselves. Maybe they lived in another country, they had moved to America or somewhere halfway around the world, in which case it would take weeks to get a reply. But shortly after breakfast, Monsieur Danton arrived.

"There's the notaire come to see you," Mrs Adams announced. She lingered, hoping to hear what the notaire might want with a group of Englishwomen.

"Thank you, Mrs Adams," Ellie said. "Please show him in here."

Monsieur Danton entered. Ellie couldn't read from his face whether it was good news or bad.

"I presented your offer to the guardian of the estate," he said, speaking so slowly and formally that Ellie wanted to shake him. "He was intrigued. I would have expected him to say no, knowing his feelings about the villa, but to my surprise he seemed quite amused that you would take this on. He says you have three months in which you pay no rent, but after that you agree to rent it for one year at a price to be decided based on the current value of the house."

He saw Ellie about to object to this but went on, "He did state that the rent should be a reasonable one and not what one would expect in Antibes or Saint-Tropez. He understands that you are widows, alone without the protection of a man. He was, if I may say so, remarkably reasonable considering my former dealings with him."

"So when can we start?"

"I have brought the keys with me," he said. "And the owner wishes you bonne chance. And I believe he actually laughed."

"I see. He expects us to fail," Ellie said. "We'll get it to a certain level but won't be able to complete the project, and then he'll get a house he can finish by paying his workmen."

"I can assure you he has shown no interest in finishing the villa until now," Monsieur Danton said. "I just believe the prospect amuses him. Perhaps he is bored, and he needs something to pique his interest."

He reached into his briefcase and brought out the bunch of keys, which he solemnly handed over to Ellie. "I also wish you bonne chance, madame," he said. "I think you will need it."

CHAPTER 18

Mrs Adams had been lurking just out of sight, eavesdropping. As soon as Monsieur Danton had gone and the women were sharing their excitement, she came back in.

"What's this about renting a house, then? Where is this house? I didn't know there was a house to rent in Saint-Benet."

"It's the villa, Mrs Adams," Ellie said. "The Villa Gloriosa."

The woman's mouth dropped open. "But that place is a ruin. Nobody's lived in it for donkey's years. They even say it's haunted."

"It will be a challenge, Mrs Adams. I need a project, and this is a good one. Besides, it doesn't look nearly as bad as you think. I don't suppose you ever met the opera singer, did you?"

Mrs Adams shook her head. "By the time we arrived, after the war, she hadn't been here for years. She might already have died, and if she was still alive, I don't think she was famous and in demand any more. Probably too old to attract the men. Her heyday was the belle époque, you know. That was the time when rich noblemen set up their mistresses in flats in Paris and all that kind of immoral carrying-on. The things I've heard about what went on at that time . . . enough to make your hair curl. I said to Mr Adams once I'm glad we're respectable people. So when would you plan to move into that place?"

"Obviously not for a while. If you don't mind, we'll stay on here until we've made some of the rooms at the villa liveable. I can't tell how long that will take."

She could see Mrs Adams totting up the money.

"Well, of course you're lucky about the time of year. We don't have the real influx of visitors until after Christmas. So I should be able to keep the rooms for you."

"That's good of you," Ellie said, half meaning to be sarcastic, but the woman nodded. "I'm happy to help out a former Englishwoman in distress," she said. "Have you recently lost your husband, then?"

"Very recently," Ellie said and did not expand on this. "That's why I have to be busy and start a new life."

"Well, good for you, that's what I say. Some women would stay home and shut themselves away, wrapped in their misery. But not you."

～～

By the time they went out for their walk, it seemed that half the village knew their plans. They decided to pay a call on Louis to see if the Bentley might be ready and to ask him for his help with the villa. They had only gone halfway down the street when they heard a loud "Yoo-hoo?"

Mr Tommy was running after them. "I've just heard the news," he said. "I can't believe it. Are you really going to rent the haunted villa? Clive only said it as a joke, you know. We weren't serious. It's supposed to be an awful ruin."

"We are serious," Ellie said. "We've seen it, and we love it, and we're going to bring it back to life."

"I've never seen it properly myself," Tommy said. "Only once, when Clive and I were first here, we went up the drive and climbed a tree to see over the wall. But there were so many trees in our way that all we saw was glimpses of a pink house, completely taken over by a wisteria vine."

"Yes, that's right," Ellie said. "Of course at this time of year the leaves have fallen, so we could see the structure of the veranda beyond. But we've been inside the house, and it really just looks as if it's been asleep for a long time."

"Like Sleeping Beauty?" he asked. "A magic enchantment?"

"That was exactly what I felt. I somehow knew I was supposed to wake it up again. I'm sure that sounds silly and sentimental."

"Not at all," he said. "I'm a great believer in intuition. Maybe you were destined to come to this place—your car breaking down at the right moment, and then the villa." He clapped his hands with joy, like a small child. "How utterly exciting. You must let us help you. You couldn't find anyone who knows more about painting than Clive. He can help you choose colours. Shall you be getting new furniture? Is the villa empty?"

"No. That's the strange thing. All the furniture is in place. Under dustsheets. Some of it has damage from mice or moths or something, and of course we didn't look at it all, but I think most of it can be resurrected."

"Then I'm your man for that," he said. "I've upholstered many a chair in my life. And made cushions. We have a sewing machine you're welcome to use."

"How splendid," Dora said, joining in the conversation. "I'm no good at sewing myself, except for mending things, but I expect that Mrs Endicott is."

"And me," Mavis said. "I've done a good bit of sewing in my life, ain't I, Mrs E.?"

"You have, Mavis. You made my last lot of curtains."

"Then we'll go on a lovely shopping spree into Marseille or Toulon and buy lots of delicious fabrics," Mr Tommy said. "I can hardly wait."

"First I'm afraid it's a lot of hard work cleaning and stripping old wallpaper and patching leaks," Ellie said. "We're on our way to see Louis to find out what he could help us with and who else might be useful. I was told there is a so-called simple boy whom we could employ."

"Bruno? Oh, he'd love to help you. Not exactly a boy any more. Maybe late twenties, but still with a child's mind and a sweet nature, too. And strong. Perfect for you."

He insisted on accompanying them to Louis's workshop. The man looked up as they came in.

"Ah, the ladies, ever impatient for their motor car. It will be ready any moment, madame, I promise you."

"We came about something different," Ellie said. "We have decided to rent the Villa Gloriosa."

Louis frowned. "The old villa? The ruin?"

Ellie nodded. "It's not a ruin. It just needs fixing up. We wondered if you might be the man to help us. The roof needs repairing. The windows need resealing. Lots of repainting to be done, and goodness knows whether the stove and the water heating still work. Would you have time to do any of those?"

Louis was staring at her as if he was summing her up. "You are sure about this? It is not a foolish dream that can never be accomplished? You will perhaps walk away when you find it is too much?"

"I don't think so," Ellie said. "If we found that the roof was about to collapse or that there were termites in all the wood, then perhaps we would have to agree that it was too much for us. But at first glance it seems sound enough, only in need of care."

He was nodding as she spoke. "I could take a look, I suppose," he said. "See what parts of it I could help with. But you'd have to understand if there is an emergency in the village, if a tractor suddenly breaks down or a water pipe bursts, then I would have to attend to that."

"I quite understand." Ellie also nodded now. "But you'll come and take a look?"

"When would this be?"

"We have the keys. I thought we'd go up there tomorrow morning."

"Then I'll have time to finish this radiator first," Louis said. "Although now it is not so urgent, since you will not be going away."

∿

The next morning Louis, Mr Tommy and Clive accompanied them up to the villa.

"I don't see myself going up and down these steps every day," Louis said. "I'm not as young as I used to be. And I certainly weigh a lot more. But since my house is just outside the village, I can come up the driveway on my motorbike and that way bring my tools with me."

Ellie stood outside the tall metal gate and put the key in the lock. It turned. The gate swung open, and she gave a little gasp as she stepped inside. *My new home.* The words rang in her head.

"Oh my," Tommy said again. "Look at that, Clive. You should paint it now before anything is done to it."

Clive smiled. "It is charming. I had no idea. Quite charming. I'll bring my paints up tomorrow."

"I hope you're going to have time to help with the sort of painting we need," Dora said. "Walls and furniture."

"I don't actually see myself as a labourer," Clive said, "but I will advise you on colours."

"Those shutters will need replacing for a start," Louis said, having managed to understand some of the English. "I think I've got some shutters somewhere in my workshop. I will search them out for you."

Ellie opened the front door, and they followed her inside, looking around the marble foyer with interest.

"Lovely. Quite lovely," Clive said. "Whoever designed this had great taste. Look at the sweep of that staircase. You could come gliding down that in a ballgown."

Ellie laughed. "I don't see that happening. I doubt there are too many balls in Saint-Benet."

"You'll need to see about reconnecting the electricity for a start," Tommy said. "And the water. I wonder if you're on a well up here or if it comes up from the village? And how is the place heated?" Ellie showed him the porcelain stoves. "They will need a good deal of wood in the winter. Where is the boiler? Are there no radiators? Maybe we can arrange to put a couple in for you."

As he spoke Ellie was having second thoughts. She had been so caught up with the romanticism that she hadn't considered the realities. Nothing worked. Everything was old beyond belief. How would they find wood and a well, light stoves? She stopped as she heard Mavis's voice.

"Yeah, I've used one like this," she said. "It looks sound enough." And Ellie found her standing with Louis as they examined the kitchen stove.

Louis seemed to have understood her because he nodded. "It needs cleaning out," he said. "This lady will do a good job."

"He says you'll do a good job, Mavis," Dora said. "I think he's got eyes on you."

"Don't be silly," Mavis laughed and blushed.

By the end of the morning Louis had checked out the boiler, the bathroom geyser and the roof. He told them he could get everything back in working order and even put in a radiator based on the present boiler, but he wasn't going to tackle the roof. He had a fear of heights, he said. They'd have to call in someone else for that. But he thought he knew someone . . .

Meanwhile Tommy and Clive had been examining walls and furniture with Dora and made lots of notes about what was needed.

"If we listen to them, we'll be bankrupt in a week," Dora muttered to Ellie as they made their way down again. "That Clive fellow might have a good eye for colour, but he has extravagant tastes. Silk wallpaper indeed. Just because it was once silk, we're not going to replace it. I see nothing wrong with plain white walls, do you?"

Ellie smiled. "With a view like that through the windows, I don't think the walls matter much."

A shriek from the dining room made her go running. Clive was standing there, pointing. "A mouse," he said. "A mouse just ran across the floor, right in front of me."

"We know there have been mice," Ellie said. "We've seen the damage they have caused. We'll bring up traps from the village."

"What you need is a cat," Clive said. "There are certainly plenty of those in need of a good home. I'll keep my eye out for a nice kitten."

Ellie went through to the music room, taking the dust cover from the grand piano. She ran her hand over the smooth surface, feeling a shiver of joy. A piano, like the one she had left behind. She sat on the bench, opened the lid and tentatively touched some notes, then some chords, then did a run up the octaves. It clearly needed tuning, but the notes seemed to be all there.

"Oh, there you are." Dora came in. "I thought I heard music. Is it still playable?"

"After a tuning," Ellie said. "Do you play?"

Dora shook her head. "I never learned, but I have always enjoyed listening to someone else play."

Ellie closed the lid again. "I shall so enjoy sitting here, with this lovely view, playing and thinking of the opera singer, sitting here before me."

Dora shook her head. "You never struck me as a romantic before now," she said. "I think this trip has awakened a new side of you."

Ellie looked up, smiling. "Maybe," she said. "And a new side of you, too."

"Perhaps," Dora agreed.

~~

Progress was slow to start with. Dustsheets were removed, rooms swept, windows washed, furniture assessed. Louis worked on the kitchen stove and boiler while Mavis scrubbed shelves, table, pantry. Mr Tommy produced Bruno, a big, lumbering lad, who smiled shyly and said he liked to work. He immediately was put to stripping wallpaper beside Ellie and Yvette while Dora checked and wiped down furniture.

"I don't like him," Yvette complained. "He's creepy. He stares at me."

"He's more like a small boy than a man, Yvette. Don't worry."

"He is big and strong for a small boy," she said, glancing over her shoulder at where Bruno was working. "I would not want to be alone with him."

Ellie studied the girl. Yvette must have had bad experiences in her life, she thought. She was fearful of men. Ellie herself found Bruno quite lovable. When you praised him, he'd give the most beaming smile, and it didn't matter what you asked him to do—he'd nod his head and off he'd go, not stopping until it was done. He also had the endearing habit of humming or singing to himself as he worked, mostly hymns but sometimes popular songs, too, of which he clearly didn't understand the words, since some were risqué. His speech was slow and ponderous, and sometimes he was a little hard to understand. When Ellie or Dora misunderstood and got it wrong, he would laugh and say he was supposed to be the stupid one.

Louis produced two men who came to repair the roof and replace the missing tiles, the damaged shutters and the leaking ceiling. They worked happily on the roof, swiftly putting on new tiles, but they seemed uneasy to be working inside the house.

"It's because of the ghost," Louis said. "They think the place is haunted."

"Do you?" Ellie asked.

He shrugged. "I'd like to see a ghost take me on," he said. "I reckon I've got enough solid flesh to win any fight against a spectre, don't you?"

There was a tense moment when they tried to turn on the water. Louis was sceptical that the villa would be connected to the water mains that supplied the village. He went hunting and discovered there was a well outside. After much grunting and quite a lot of swearing, he got the well cleaned out and the pump working again and declared the water was good.

It was an exciting moment when they first lit the stove. The delightful smell of burning wood came from the kitchen.

"Now if only we had tea things here, I'd make us all a cuppa," Mavis said. She had been working tirelessly, taking on the hard jobs and remaining cheerful.

"We'll bring up tea and milk next time we come," Ellie said. This did not prove to be easy. French people do not drink English tea. In the small tabac, there were herb teas, rose hip tea and chamomile tea, but no black tea at all.

"You may find it where the English people stay," the shopkeeper said. "In Hyères, perhaps."

Ellie asked Mrs Adams and was given the name of a shop in Marseille where she usually managed to find hers. "Also I have parcels sent out from England," she said. "You want to ask your family at home to send you out what you need."

"Unfortunately I've no family at home," Ellie said. "My sons are abroad. My parents are dead. So it better be the shop in Marseille. We have to go there anyway to get all the supplies we need. I've been making a list, and Tommy's been adding to it." She turned to Dora. "Goodness, I hope it's not all too expensive. I might have to telegraph my bank and ask for some kind of advance."

"Don't worry, my dear," Dora said. "I told you I have funds, and I'm quite happy to use them. I've had nothing to spend money on for a long time. Let's go into Marseille and enjoy ourselves. I shall be looking for some sensible clothing, and you should, too. And you need a bathing suit!"

When Tommy heard about the expedition, he insisted on coming with them.

"You'll need Clive's good eye if you're choosing fabrics and paint," Tommy said.

"I'm not sure we'll all fit in the car."

But then Yvette said she did not want to come with them. "You do not need me," she said. "I have no money and no interest in your plans for the villa."

Ellie frowned as she walked away. She was glad they'd have enough room to take everyone, but what young girl would not want to look at shops in the big city? Unless her pregnancy was making her feel unwell all the time. Ellie remembered her own sickness and felt sympathy for Yvette. She was essentially alone in the world. She didn't know what would happen next. No wonder she was withdrawn and scared. She had nobody to tell how she was feeling. Ellie resolved to do her best to help Yvette find her beloved and see her happily reunited with him.

So the five of them crammed into the Bentley, and they set off, Ellie holding her breath that the Bentley had been well and truly mended. It purred along beautifully, negotiating the windy mountainous road, and they reached Marseille quickly. Luckily Tommy and Clive knew the layout of the city and directed them through complicated suburbs, and they parked on a busy shopping street near the old port and Galleries Lafayette department store. Mavis went off to the kitchen department. Ellie had to restrain Tommy and Clive from buying expensive fabrics, but they settled on good material for curtains and reupholstering. She gave in to Clive's desire for bright cushions after he insisted on buying the fabric as a present. There were new bed linens and towels to buy. Luckily some of the linens they had found in the linen closet were miraculously still good, but the eiderdowns were beyond saving, as the mice had enjoyed them over the years. Tommy arranged for the shop to deliver the large items that wouldn't fit in the car.

Meanwhile Dora had been shopping for clothing. Ellie joined her and was persuaded to get simple skirts, trousers and sandals, as well as that bathing suit.

"How ridiculous, when you think of it," Dora said, with what sounded like a giggle. "Buying clothes at my age and in my condition. So frivolous of me. I certainly won't ever have the chance to get good use from them."

Ellie turned to stare at her. Sometimes she forgot that Dora had only been given a short time to live. And here she now was, making a joke about it. Impulsively she took Dora's hand. "Let's hope they were all wrong and you wear those clothes out," she said.

Then it was on to a hardware store for paint—white for the interior, blue for shutters, pink for the exterior walls. Ellie was glad of Clive's good eye. She would have had no idea which shade of blue to use. They stowed their packages in the boot of the car, then had lunch at a little café—a delightful grilled cheese, called croque monsieur, and a sparkling water. Then Tommy and Clive went off to do a bit of shopping of their own. Dora said she was tired and would sit on a bench outside a church. Mavis volunteered to stay with her, not liking the look of some of the sailors who passed them on the street. Ellie went off alone, asking directions to the public library. There she found the address of the War Department for Yvette, then, on a whim, she asked a librarian to search the archives for information on the villa's mysterious owner, Jeannette Hétreau.

After quite a long wait, the librarian returned. "Not very much, madame," she said. "You should write to Paris, maybe. I'm sure they will have more." There were several articles on Jeannette performing, once in Marseille, once in Nice. Her lovely voice as Violetta in *La Traviata*. But not a single mention of her living in Saint-Benet. So it seemed she had kept it a secret, a private love nest for her and the duke.

The last call was to the grocery where the Adamses shopped. There they found their English tea, as well as tins of baked beans, favourite biscuits and chocolate bars. They were in a triumphant mood as they drove home, everyone with packages on their laps and the car boot fully laden. Tommy started singing, and they joined in all the old music hall songs they could remember. Ellie saw for Tommy and Clive it was a time of great nostalgia, a reminder of the life they once knew and had given up. She'd probably feel the same way if she stayed long enough, she thought. This made her consider . . . How long did she intend to stay away? Just for the winter? For a year? And if less, then why all this effort and expense on the villa?

Until I'm ready to go home, she decided. In the library there had been English newspapers. She had read them while she waited for the librarian. The news of Hitler and the possibility of war looked more like a real threat. Mr Chamberlain had been to Munich and had returned declaring "peace in our time." So perhaps Hitler had been appeased and would be content to occupy Czechoslovakia. And she could go on happily living in Saint-Benet.

CHAPTER 19

Move-in day came in November, just as the weather turned really wet and blustery. Bruno had been put to work collecting dead wood from the gardens for the various stoves. Luckily there was plenty of it, and it was now stacked under the veranda, ready for use. Louis had also managed to find a radiator, which he connected to the boiler, and so the living room would be warm. The walls had been painted a pristine white apart from the mural on the sitting room wall that Ellie couldn't bear to part with. Enough furniture had been restored that they had places to sit and eat. The rest, that needed more work, had been shut away in the dining room, which they were not yet using. Instead they ate in the warmth of the big kitchen, around the pine table. Mavis had mastered the stove beautifully, and the larder was stocked with basics.

They had discussed what to do with the opera singer's clothes that she had left in various wardrobes and drawers. Ellie paid a visit to Monsieur Danton and asked him if the owner would like the clothing delivered to him. The answer was that he had no need of the clothing, and they could do what they liked with it. This gave the ladies a happy afternoon of going through the items, seeing if any of them could still be used and might fit them. Unfortunately the opera singer was petite and slim, and the clothes were horribly dated. But they did rescue some silk undergarments, wrapped between sheets of tissue, a fur stole, a jacket or two. Mavis took some of the long dresses, saying she could use the fabric to make herself summer dresses and a maternity outfit for

Yvette, who was now beginning to burst out of her own clothes. The rest they packed into a trunk. In a drawer in Ellie's bedroom, she found scarves, cosmetics and a tortoiseshell box of costume jewellery. She opened it, sifting through brooches and hair combs and came upon a locket containing two photos. She presumed that one was Jeannette and the other the duke. He was handsome, older, with dark hair streaked with grey at the sides, but staring arrogantly at the camera. Clearly a man of substance. The opera singer was looking winsome. There was something about her. Ellie carried it over to the window to see better. What was it? Then she realized. Jeannette looked a little like Ellie herself as a young woman. Again she had the same strange feeling as when she first entered the villa—that she was somehow meant to be here.

"Rubbish," she said and was putting the items back in the drawer when she came across another photo, this one not in a frame and lying between tissue paper and silk undies. It was of a baby with dark curls and big eyes fringed with long lashes, staring solemnly at the camera. So, she wondered, did Jeannette have a child, or was this the child of a relative? Was this child now the elusive owner of the villa who lived in faraway Paris and had no interest in it? Perhaps he or she had inherited more impressive properties from the duke, and this small villa was not worth thinking about. She wondered if she'd ever find out.

～

They ate a first meal, a simple stew, and toasted each other with wine.

"To our new home," Dora said. "May it bring us health and happiness."

"It don't seem real," Mavis said. "Imagine me here, in this lovely place, with you ladies. How did I get to be so blessed?"

Ellie looked from one face to the next. How happy they looked, except Yvette, who hadn't understood and sat silently, spooning soup into her mouth. Ellie had passed along the address for army headquarters. "Would you like me to write for you?" she said. "If you give me your young man's name, I will see what I can do."

"No need, madame," Yvette said, taking the address from her. "I will do it myself. But I do not know if it will do any good. If he is now stationed in Africa, they will not let him come home before his tour of duty is over. Perhaps he has no interest in a child." She turned away.

"Let's hope for the best, shall we?" Ellie put a tentative arm around her.

Yvette was still looking away and said nothing.

~~

That first night Ellie stood at the window of her new room, looking out over the gardens. The stormy weather of earlier in the day had passed, and the grounds were bathed in moonlight. She had generously given Dora the best bedroom that faced the sea and taken the second-best one. She had remembered Dora's face as they had first toured the bedrooms. Dora had stared out of the big windows. "Oh, what a perfect view," she had sighed. "I should die happy if that was the last thing I saw."

And so Ellie had claimed she'd rather sleep at the front of the house, facing the gardens. "I think the noise of the waves might keep me awake," she said. "I'm a light sleeper." And seeing how happy Dora was, she knew she'd made a good sacrifice. Who knew how many more months Dora had left? She still seemed well and quite energetic. Maybe the doctors had got it wrong, and this trip could turn out to be a miracle cure. She found herself hoping this was true. She had become fond of the old lady.

Moonlight danced as palm trees rattled and trees swayed in the breeze at the far end of the garden. Then she stiffened. Was that someone moving between the trees? As she peered into the darkness, she thought she saw a figure, moving swiftly. It vanished into shadow, and she lost sight of it. She shook her head. She must have been mistaken. The moonlight had been playing tricks. The gates were no longer locked as Bruno or Louis came and went, but who would want to be in the garden at night? There was nothing worth stealing, and besides the figure was moving away, not towards, the villa. Suggestions of the ghost did cross her mind, but she put them aside. Ghosts only lingered where they had lived in life, didn't they? And the opera singer had died far away from here. But what of the duke? Hadn't he tired of her and moved on to another mistress? So he wouldn't have died here, either. And they took their servants with them. So no ghost. Only a trick of the moonlight.

There were no curtains up yet as Mavis hadn't had time to make them, so Ellie felt a little uncomfortable as she moved away from the window. Was it possible the figure had been a peeping Tom, come to spy on the ladies? It could have been one of the local lads, coming up on a dare, or something more sinister. Bruno came into her head. Yvette had described him as creepy. He seemed to Ellie completely harmless, but would he get a thrill from watching ladies take their clothes off? She'd have to make sure she did not undress with the light on and warn the others just in case. And help Mavis make those curtains as quickly as possible. She climbed into bed, feeling the cold strangeness of new sheets and no longer feeling at ease. They were, after all, four women, far from home. Perhaps there were brigands and corsairs, as Yvette had suggested. She lay for a while looking at the moon. Then she put worrying thoughts aside and told herself not to be silly. They had done it. They were here, and it was going to be perfect.

"My new life," she said. If Lionel could see her now, would he even recognize the old Ellie?

~~

"You know what I think," Mavis said the next morning when they came down to tea and fresh bread. "I think we should have a party to celebrate."

"A party?" Ellie asked. "And where did the bread come from?"

"Louis brought up a loaf when he arrived," Mavis said.

"That was very good of him," Ellie replied. "So he's here already."

"That's right. He's brought the hardware for the shutters and the windows."

Ellie wondered how Mavis, speaking no French, seemed to know this.

"We've already spent a lot of money to get this place up and running," Ellie said. "We don't have unlimited funds, Mavis."

"But people have done a lot for us," Mavis said. "Louis has put in many more hours than he's charged us for. He's found us the new shutters and the radiator, and look at Mr Tommy and Clive. They've been up here all the time and haven't wanted a penny."

"That's true," Ellie said. "And we don't have to pay any rent for another month or so. So we are living free, essentially. What do you think, Dora?" she asked as the older woman came in. "Do you think we should have a party?"

Dora nodded. "I think a party is a lovely idea. It doesn't have to be too fancy, does it? Wine is so cheap here, and bread and cold meats, cheese and olives. Just a thank you gesture to those who have helped us."

"Right you are, then," Mavis said. "You choose a date, and I'll get to work. It had better be all finger food because we don't have enough plates to feed the multitude."

"Multitude?" Ellie said. "I thought this was a little thank you to those who have helped us."

"Mavis is right," Dora said. "I suspect that once word gets out, the whole village will want to come up and see what we've done."

"Get Yvette to help you, Mavis," Ellie said. "You're doing too much already."

"Her?" Mavis rolled her eyes. "She's about as much use as a bull in a dairy. She pretends to be helping, then she slips away. And I'll tell you something else . . . she smokes. She don't let us see, but my Reggie smoked, and I can smell it on her clothes."

"I don't think we can hold that against her, Mavis," Dora said. "She is expecting, after all. She may feel nauseous and worried, and smoking may calm her nerves."

Mavis grunted as if she didn't agree. "There's something not right about that girl," she said. It wasn't the first time she had expressed such a thought. Mavis was no fool, but was she just prejudiced because the girl was foreign and she didn't understand her?

～～

When they announced the date for the party, they found that providing the feast would not be as hard as they had imagined. Tommy and Clive said they would bring the wine. Henri offered to bring a terrine and smoked fish. When Ellie went to pay him, he shook his head. "You have kept my little restaurant going at a time when there are usually no tourists," he said. "And you are such enchanting ladies. It is my pleasure."

They ordered bread and pastries from the boulangerie, olives, cheese and cold meats from the charcuterie.

"Now we just have to see who comes," Dora said. "We may have a lot of food left over."

But everyone came. Louis, Tommy and Clive, Bruno and his mother, the priest, Monsieur Danton. Ellie was a little surprised that the Adamses came. Mrs Adams had ignored them since they moved out, hardly greeting them when they passed in the street, but clearly curiosity got the better of her, and Ellie noticed her snooping into every corner. "You got yourself a nice place here," she said. "If I'd known it was as nice as this, I'd have snapped it up myself. We heard it was a ruin."

"But it was," Ellie said. "We've worked damned hard to repair and restore everything."

"With lots of help," Mrs Adams said. "Everyone in the village falling over backwards to help you."

And Ellie realized she was jealous. She felt threatened. Ellie wanted to tell her she didn't need to but couldn't find the words.

Henri shut his bar, and two of the fishermen who had chatted with them came: François and Jacquot, but not the big man, Nico. Ellie suspected he did not approve of the English ladies and the amount of attention they got from Henri and the other men. He was a strange one, she decided. She remembered how rude he had been when they first met, but then he'd negotiated with Mrs Adams to get them a better rate at the pension. Since then he had been pleasant enough when they encountered him at the bar, but more aloof than the other men. Anyway, he had chosen not to come.

Father André, the priest, introduced himself and offered to bless the house for them. He knew that they were not of the faith, he said, but Anglicans, after all, were just misguided Catholics. They had the same doctrine, the same form of service, but they just had forgotten about the pope. Ellie had been rather alarmed about meeting a priest. The Catholic Church in England was viewed with much scepticism and even fear. But Father André had a twinkle in his eye and had brought a bottle of blackcurrant brandy made by a local monastery.

"I hope to see you at Mass one day," he said. "We may make good Catholics of you yet."

The doctor and his wife also came. She was quite distinguished-looking and fashionable; he was hearty and older than her. They brought the women a bottle of champagne and invited the ladies to the next musical soirée. Everyone brought some sort of gift—cheeses, wine, cognac, tomato plants and a lemon tree for the garden, candles for when the electricity went out in the next storm. Tommy and Clive had a special gift in a basket: a small orange striped kitten.

"Here is your mouser," Tommy said.

Ellie picked him up and felt his purring as he lay quietly in her hands. She realized she'd always wanted a cat, but Lionel didn't like them.

"How charming," Dora said. "I've been missing my cat. And now we have our own little tiger."

And so Tiger he was named.

Everyone stayed rather late. There was lots of toasting and wishes of good luck. Lots of laughter. Ellie stood watching, feeling her heart so full it might burst. All those years in her village at home and she had never felt this warmth or joy. She realized that she hadn't felt much at all for years. She had loved being a mother and looking after her little sons. When they went away to school, there was no one to hug or care for, just Lionel and his damned three-and-a-half-minute eggs. Always worrying that she was failing him, not pleasing him, and never stopping for a moment to think that nobody was concerned about pleasing her.

CHAPTER 20

The next night Ellie undressed in darkness. Before she got into bed, she went over to the window and looked out. It was another clear, moonlit night. There was no breeze, and the garden lay still and peaceful. She looked forward to getting to work on the grounds, bringing back the lawn and the flowerbeds, growing vegetables. Then she froze. The figure was there. He'd come back. Definitely a man. This time he was coming out of the trees at the far end of the garden and walking towards the house. Hastily she put on her robe and slippers. Enough was enough. She was going to make sure this stopped now. They had a right to privacy, and intruders were not welcome. Not thinking of danger, she went downstairs and let herself out of the front door. The light from the foyer streamed out as she stepped into the cold air of the night.

He was coming up the path beside the overgrown lawn, wearing some kind of dark jumper and baggy trousers. A seaman's cap was on his head. She stepped out in front of him. He came forward, head down, not seeing her. She was about to hail him when he looked up, gasped and froze. She expected him to turn tail and run away. Instead he stood staring at her, shocked.

"What do you think you are doing here?" she shouted. "This is private property."

Then he said, "Oh, it's you, English madame. You startled me."

"I startled you? I looked out of my window to see a strange man crossing my garden. I was the one who was startled. Did you not know that this place is occupied, that we are living here now?"

"Oh yes, I heard." He came slowly towards her. A shiver of fear shot through her. This had not been wise. If he was intent on mischief, she was now alone. She should have brought some kind of weapon to defend herself. Then she saw his white teeth. He was smiling. Or was that laughing?

As he came closer, she saw that it was Nico.

"If you've come for the party, you are a day too late," she said, standing her ground and eyeing him defiantly.

"I am not one who enjoys parties," he said. "But I heard it was a great success."

"What are you doing here, then?" she demanded. "This is private property. Did you think you could come to spy on us? You find it amusing to stare at English ladies?"

He was still smiling. "I have no intention of spying on anyone, madame," he said. "And if I wanted to ogle undressed women, I would choose ones younger and with the right sort of curves." He paused. "I came to retrieve some fishing gear, that is all. I store things in the shed at the back of the garden, and I use the steps from the terrace to go down the cliff to the water, where I sometimes moor my boat. You have seen the little dock down there?"

"No," she said. "I hadn't noticed the steps." She paused, thinking of what he had said. "You store things in the shed? Here? Who gave you permission to do that?" She still sounded haughty.

"The owner. He knows."

"The owner?" She tried to outstare him. "You know the owner?"

"I do," he said. "A good fellow. He has no problem with my crossing this property, and neither should you."

She felt he was bluffing. Of course he didn't know the owner. He had probably been helping himself to items from the shed and the gardens for ages, and now these women were in his way. She remembered

Yvette saying that he looked like a corsair, a brigand. Perhaps it was the other way around. He didn't take items—he used the shed to store contraband, bringing it from his boat, coming up the steps to the villa, out of sight of the village.

She folded her arms. "Well, that was before the property was let," she said. "Now we live here, and we do not want intruders, especially at night. If you have to retrieve your fishing gear, please ask to do so during the day."

"Such an officious woman," he said. "What were you back in England? A schoolteacher? The mayor of your town? Let me tell you, madame, here you will find that we don't go in for rules much. If I am about to take my boat out and I find that one of my nets is no good, I am certainly not going to wait until morning to retrieve another one, when the best fishing is on a still night like this."

"I don't see you carrying a net," she said.

"That was merely an example," he said. "Tonight it is the simple matter of a battery for my torch and some fishhooks."

He put his hand into a pocket and produced some. "So I suggest you go back to bed, tuck yourself in and forget I was ever here." When she didn't move, he added, "Come. I will escort you back to your front door. You should be glad that you have a strong man to keep an eye on your grounds so that you can sleep safely."

He went to put a hand on her arm. "I can find my own way perfectly well, thank you," she said, shaking off his hand. She heard him chuckling behind her as she strode back to the house. Back in her room, she found that she was trembling. She took off her dressing gown and slid between the sheets. How stupid she had been to go out into the night alone, in her nightclothes. She was lucky he had only been interested in fishing gear, although she still didn't quite believe that this was what he came for. She made up her mind to have a word with Monsieur Danton to see if Nico really had an agreement with the owner or was lying to her.

When she woke, it was to bright sunlight streaming in through her windows, and her fears of the night had melted away. The villa had been empty for years. What was to stop local people from borrowing the shed, helping themselves to fruit, using the steps as a shortcut to the seashore? She had to remember that she was a newcomer, maybe not even here for very long, and she had to get along with the local people, not antagonize them.

After she had washed and dressed, she went downstairs to find Mavis already busy in the kitchen.

"Oh, you're up early," Ellie said. "I thought we might have eggs for breakfast for a change. I've had enough of bread and jam, haven't you?"

"You won't believe what I found on the kitchen table this morning," Mavis said. "Look at this!" And she pointed to a platter on which lay two large fish. "I'd swear they weren't there last night. You didn't bring them in, did you? Bruno's not here yet, and Louis isn't coming today."

"I think I know where they came from," Ellie said. "The fisherman called Nico."

"The big one with the frown and the deep voice?"

"That's him." Ellie stared down at the fish and pictured Nico. "I caught him coming across our garden last night, and I'm afraid I gave him a piece of my mind about trespassing. He said the owners let him keep his tackle in the shed and he took our steps as a quick way down to his boat. I think this may have been a kind of peace offering so that I don't tell Monsieur Danton about him. They are really beautiful, aren't they?"

Mavis nodded, then reached down to grab the kitten. "Not for you, you little monster. We'll have to train some good behaviour into you quickly, I can see." She put the cat down and moved the fish to the centre of the table. "I'm not sure what they are or how to cook them, but I'll give it a try. Pity Louis isn't coming today. He'd know."

Ellie stared at her. "How do you manage it, Mavis? You don't speak French, and yet you seem to be able to communicate with Louis."

Mavis blushed. "Well, he speaks a bit of English. In the war he had to do reconnaissance for English troops, and he picked up a bit. And I don't know. We just seem to understand each other. There's a lot of arm waving and acting, but we get the gist usually." She chuckled. "It's about time I started those French lessons, now we're in the house and we've got things up and running."

"Good idea," Ellie said. "We'll start today, although I do want to get those curtains made as soon as possible. I'm now concerned about what can be seen through our windows with strange men wandering around in the dark."

Mavis nodded. "I know. I have started on them, but it's a big job. I really need that table in the dining room to cut things out, and for the sewing machine."

"We'll clear space for you in there," Ellie said. "We can stack the chairs and see which bits and bobs we can get rid of. But first let's have some breakfast."

"Bob's your uncle," Mavis said. "Tea's already made. I'll fry some eggs, shall I?"

"You don't have to do everything, Mavis. You're not the cook or the servant. I don't want you to think that you are. You're one of four friends."

"That's a maybe," Mavis said, "but one of the so-called friends don't do much, and poor old Miss Smith-Humphries gets tired really easily, so it's just you and me, and Bruno and Louis when he comes. And I don't mind the work, honestly. I like to keep busy."

Dora arrived as they were sitting down to breakfast.

"How lovely. Eggs. I've been missing a proper breakfast," she said. "I don't suppose anyone around here sells bacon, do they?"

"I haven't seen any," Ellie said, "but we have ham left from the party."

"That would go quite well," Dora said. "And where did we get those magnificent fish?"

"A present from one of the fishermen," Ellie said quickly before Mavis could mention the nightly intrusion. She didn't want Dora worried. "We have to find out how to cook them."

"There's certainly too much for one meal," Dora observed. "Perhaps you should ask Henri how he makes his fish stew. That would last us for several days."

"I'll do that," Ellie said, "but first I want to get the dining room set up so that Mavis can sew the curtains. I feel vulnerable when anyone can see in."

Dora laughed. "I think we're suitably far away from any prying eyes up here, don't you?"

Ellie looked at Mavis. Don't say anything, her look said.

CHAPTER 21

They settled into a routine. Bruno, who seemed to have adopted them and considered himself part of the family, came up in the mornings, bringing a baguette. Tiger, the kitten, was naughty but delightful, chasing anything that moved before collapsing exhausted on to a lap where he lay purring. Mavis sewed at the long table, while Ellie or Dora instructed her in French. Ellie was rather impressed how easily she picked it up. Mavis clearly had a good brain but had been forced to accept her role in life. *How many people are held back because of lack of education?* she thought. *What could I have done if I'd been allowed to go to university? I, too, was forced into my role—docile, loving wife and mother, making sure the house ran smoothly for the breadwinner. And now . . .* She paused, smiling to herself. *Who knows what is next?*

～

One morning she came upon Dora, sitting on the terrace, staring out to sea. At first she thought Dora was lost in contemplation but then noticed one hand was on her wrist. She was taking her pulse.

"Are you in pain?" she asked, going over to sit beside her.

Dora looked up, startled at being interrupted from her reverie. "Oh no. No pain. It's my heart, you see. Congestive heart failure. It's funny, but for a while I'd forgotten that I was supposed to be dead by now. All the excitement of coming here, finding this place. I'd really forgotten.

And it was only now that I noticed how quickly I became out of breath and how weak my pulse had become."

"Should we take you to a doctor?" Ellie asked in concern.

Dora shook her head. "Oh no, my dear. Doctors can't do anything. One day it will just stop beating, and that will be that. It shouldn't be a messy death for you."

Ellie looked at her with tenderness. "Are you afraid to die?"

"Afraid?" Dora shook her head fiercely. "No, I'm not afraid. Only annoyed."

"Annoyed?" Ellie had to smile.

"Yes, at all the things I never managed to do. I never climbed the Himalayas. I never rode with the Bedouins across the desert. I never wrote a novel or found a drug that might cure cancer. I leave no legacy, no proof that I was ever here."

"I'm sure you were missed in the village," Ellie said kindly.

"Missed, yes. But not beloved. That fussy old woman. That bossy old woman. That's the height of my achievement in life, I suppose. Properly ironed altar cloths and found perfect flowers for the church. They'll miss the flowers, but not me."

"I'll miss you," Ellie said. "Let's just see if we can keep you around a little longer, eh? Buck you up with some good food."

Dora smiled at her. "You've been a good friend, Ellie. One of the only true friends I've had. I'll be sorry to leave this place." She turned away, staring out to sea again. Today the Mediterranean sparkled under a cloudless sky. A sleek yacht passed, far out to sea. The breeze was scented with blossom.

It was a while before she spoke again. "I've had such a small life. So much of it wasted with trivialities: those perfectly ironed altar cloths. As if they mattered. I'm sure they didn't to God." She stopped talking, staring out at the view again. "So many things I wanted to do. I told you my father was in the army, didn't I? He was often away for long periods, but I grew up in a splendid big house in Hampshire. Acres of grounds with trees to be climbed."

"Trees to be climbed?" Ellie said, giving Dora an amused look.
"Oh yes. I was the best one at climbing trees. I had four brothers;
I was the only girl, but I did everything with them. I was even allowed
to share their tutor, and he told me I had a good brain for a female. But
nobody suggested that I might want to go off to Oxford like two of my
brothers. One by one they went. Army, colonial service to Kenya, tin
mining in Malaysia, and I was left at home. I was supposed to make a
good match. That was my job. What they meant was someone to take
me off my parents' hands."

"But you never fell in love, found the right man?"

"Not one that wanted me," she said. "Looking back on it, I suppose
I was too blunt and forthright for a woman. I've always spoken my
mind and never hidden my intellect. Men like a pretty but dull wife.
Not too smart. In no way a challenge to them."

I wonder how Lionel is handling clever Michelle who went to university.
The thought flashed through Ellie's head.

"So you remained at home?"

"There were not many jobs for a woman in those days," Dora said.
"At least not for a woman of my social level. I wasn't about to be a
companion. But then I read about typewriting machines having been
invented. I sent off for one and taught myself, secretly in my room, then
I got a job in the city. My mother was horrified. Going up on the train
with all those men? What was I thinking? But I was good at it. And I
loved it, in spite of the fact that the young men I worked with thought
that, as a female, it was my job to bring them coffee and generally wait
on them. I set them straight on that, of course."

She looked up at Ellie, who nodded encouragement.

"Eventually I became personal assistant to the company director.
Mr Ambrose. Such an interesting man. Powerful but not arrogant. He
appreciated my good brain and never talked down to me. And then . . ."

There was a long pause.

"And then we drew closer. Too close. I became his mistress." She
looked up and laughed. "I see you are shocked. I was a little shocked

myself. But we had some good years together. I knew my place. I realized our time together was precious and this would be the closest to happiness I'd ever come."

Ellie had to laugh. "And there I was thinking you were the consummate spinster, you sly old thing."

"I had some good years. I travelled with him—here to the Riviera once, and to Paris, of course. Then one day he had a heart attack and died," she said. "He left me a bequest in his will. *To my devoted secretary who has given me years of unfailing loyalty and service.* Quite a nice sum. I decided I didn't want to work for anyone else, so I moved to the village and bought my cottage. My parents had died around the same time, so I inherited enough money to live quite comfortably. And with my organizational skills, I soon found that I had taken over the running of almost everything."

"I'd say you've had a pretty good life," Ellie said. "You made our village run smoothly. At least there was once a man who appreciated you, maybe even loved you."

"I suspect he did," Dora said. "He told me I was the only person he could ever talk to. He loved me for my brain more than my body, I fear." She laughed again.

Ellie stood up. "Well, it's not too late to make your mark."

"I'm not planning to ride a camel across the desert now, I can assure you."

"You could try that novel. I know you're a shrewd observer of the human condition."

"But probably not a good writer. I can write a succinct letter, but." She hesitated. "I have been trying my hand at some poetry. Oh, I suspect it's utter drivel, but I wanted to capture the feeling of this place somehow, and I can't paint."

"Would you like to show me?" Ellie asked.

"Certainly not. As I say, utter drivel. You can read them when I've gone. Not before."

Ellie went back into the coolness of the house and stood thinking. She, too, had led a small life. Nothing to be remembered by. No deserts crossed. No mountains climbed. And nobody to weep for her when she died. At least she would weep for Dora.

CHAPTER 22

A spell of fine weather followed, and Ellie decided to tackle the garden. She went down through the orchard to the outbuildings by the back wall. The Bentley sat in the garage, and beside it there was a shed. It was locked with a large padlock. So this was where Nico kept his things! She would dearly have loved to see inside. But she found gardening tools at the back of the garage, and Bruno went to work clearing the former lawn of weeds. Ellie decided to start weeding the flowerbeds and trimming back plants that had run rampant. She searched for a water spigot to attach a hose, finally found one and turned it on. Nothing came out. She went to find Louis, who had come to install a new geyser over the bath, and found him sitting in the kitchen, talking to Mavis.

"I can't get any water out of the tap outside," she said.

Louis went to investigate. It took him most of the day, but in the end the news was not good. "You have a well that supplies the house water," he said. "It is a small well. Enough for you. But the outside water, that came from some sort of pipe higher up the hillside."

"Is the pipe broken, then? Does it come from another well?"

"I believe it comes from the viscount," Louis said. "That would be his property on the hillside above your driveway. You pass his gateway. We heard he put in a swimming pool recently. Maybe he has taken your water source."

"Damned cheek," Ellie muttered. Out loud she said, "Is he in residence now, do you know? How do I get to his house?"

"Not a house, madame." Louis smiled. "A small château is what I would call it. The viscount is very rich and lives very well. He does not buy his supplies from Saint-Benet, but rather has them delivered from Marseille or even from Paris. He brings his servants. But I am called up there occasionally when something does not work properly. He is rather spoiled. I don't think you will find him easy to deal with."

"I still intend to visit him," Ellie said. "Should I take the motor car?"

"That would be best. When he sees you are a woman of stature who drives a big motor car, he will think more kindly towards you."

"Right." Ellie gave a determined nod, then went up to her bedroom and changed into her smartest two-piece suit. She added a jaunty black velvet hat, and then, on impulse, she raided the opera singer's wardrobe and took out the mink stole. "Let him see who he is dealing with," she said to her reflection in the mirror.

She retrieved the Bentley, proceeded down the driveway and then along the road, until she found another driveway winding up the hill. She followed this until she came to impressive wrought iron gates. Through the gates she saw manicured grounds, a formal garden of flowerbeds and fountains, and beyond an impressive villa, whitewashed with dark-green shutters, a balcony running across the front and a turret at one side. She got out of the car, opened one side of the gates, drove into the property. She had only gone about halfway when a man came running towards her. He was dressed in a brown gardener's uniform and was carrying a shovel.

"Stop. You may not come here," he shouted, standing in front of the car, waving his arms. "This is private property. You are not allowed here."

Ellie wound down her window. "I have come to see monsieur le vicomte," she said.

"You have an appointment? No. He is not expecting you."

"And I was not expecting to find there is no water for my gardens," Ellie said. "I have rented the Villa Gloriosa just below this property, and it appears our water source has been blocked. Is your master at home?"

"He is, but . . ."

"Then please stand aside," Ellie said. She inched the motor car forward. The gardener stood, holding up his hand.

"Does your master teach you to be rude to important people?" she asked.

He took in the mink stole and her haughty expression.

"I hope you do not make me walk the rest of the way to the villa," she said.

He stood his ground for a moment, then stepped aside as she put her foot on the accelerator. As she drove on, she watched him running towards the house, trying to get there first. She parked under a portico at the side and marched up to the front door, trying to look more confident than she felt.

She pressed a bell and heard it jangle inside. An elderly man, a butler by the way he was dressed, opened the door, staring at her in surprise.

"Madame Endicott to see the viscount," she said. "I understand your master is at home. Please inform him that the English lady from the Villa Gloriosa wishes to speak to him."

"I will inform him, madame." The man gave a little bow and departed. Ellie noted she had not been invited in. After a few minutes, the man returned. "The master will see you. Please follow me," he said.

Ellie crossed an ornate entrance hall, decorated with classical statues, and was shown into a sitting room. It was an elegant, light room with floor-to-ceiling windows looking out over the village and the coastline. At the rear of the house there was a terrace and beyond it a sparkling swimming pool. Inside the room the furniture was modern with simple lines, chrome and glass, light fabrics and polished woods, and in one of the armchairs a man was sitting, or rather lounging, against the back of the chair, holding an ebony cigarette holder between his fingers. He did not attempt to sit up as Ellie came in. She stared at him with surprise. She had expected an old man, but this man was young, or youngish, maybe late thirties. He was chubby, with light-blond hair, a round, pink face and surprised blue eyes, like an overgrown cherub. He was dressed in a pale-blue shirt that matched the upholstery, a purple-and-gold cravat at his neck.

"Monsieur le vicomte, I am Madame Endicott," Ellie said. "I have rented the villa next to yours."

"The villa of the opera singer," he said. "We heard. We were surprised. We understood that it was a ruin, uninhabitable. But you are English ladies, no?" His voice was light and quite high.

"We are."

"You are here for the winter?"

"Perhaps," she said. "Perhaps longer. At this moment we have no plans. We stay as long as we enjoy this place."

"Your husbands do not miss you?" He sat up now, looking interested. "They do not expect you to return home to them quickly?"

"We have no husbands," Ellie said. "We are independent women, able to make our own decisions."

He tapped out the end of his cigarette into a glass ashtray. "Please do take a seat."

Ellie perched on an upright chair across from him.

"And this ruin that you now live in, it is suitable for ladies like yourselves?"

"It is not a ruin, and we have already made it quite pleasant," Ellie said. "You would be welcome to come and visit us. Do you live here alone?"

"Apart from my staff."

"You don't find it lonely?"

He shrugged. "I have plenty of company when I am in Paris. Then I come here to recuperate and to think. I write poetry, you know. And sometimes I have visitors, friends from Paris."

"As I said," Ellie went on, "you would be most welcome to come to take tea with us, or a glass of wine one day."

"Ah, the English tea," he said. "So strong." And he shuddered.

"You have been to England?"

"But of course. One travels. One has suits made in London." He paused. "Can I offer you refreshment? A tisane? A coffee? Or perhaps a citron pressé?"

"It's very kind of you. A coffee would be most agreeable."

He picked up a small brass bell from the side table and rang it. The butler appeared so quickly that Ellie suspected he had been listening outside the door.

The viscount merely said, "Coffee, Antoine," without turning around. He focused again on Ellie. "How is it you speak such good French?"

"When I was a child, my mother insisted I learn French. In those days it was the language of diplomacy and good breeding. She was preparing me to move in polite society and marry well."

"And did you?" There was a flicker of amusement in those light-blue eyes.

"In a material way, yes. In emotional satisfaction, no. We are now divorced."

"Ooh la." He waved a hand. "That was adventurous of you!"

"His idea, not mine," she said. "He found a younger woman."

"As so often happens when a man reaches a certain age," he said. "My father, too. But I think you are not too unhappy with this outcome?"

"Actually, no," she said.

"So you enjoy this new life here, no?"

"So far, yes. It's been a challenge to bring the villa back to life, but now the major work is done. Which is why I have come to you today. We are about to start work on the garden, to get the fountain running again, plant flowers and vegetables. But when we turn on the spigot, there is no water. My handyman tells me the pipe comes down from a spring or a well on the hillside above our property, but he thinks the water has now been diverted to your property instead. Maybe to your swimming pool?"

The viscount shrugged. "I know nothing of this. I am not interested in the construction, just the completion. It is quite possible that when I ordered this pool to be installed a few years ago the workmen saw that your villa was no longer occupied and thus helped themselves to your water. It was done when I was in Paris. I returned to find it ready for me, and quite delightful it is, too, in the summertime."

"So what do you suggest that we do about our water?" Ellie asked.

He waved a nonchalant hand again. "Have your man meet with my gardeners. They can determine what has gone wrong for you and hopefully put it right. It could also be that the well or spring you speak of has dried up years ago."

"It could also be that your men helped themselves to our water."

He shrugged again. "Why worry ourselves? We are approaching winter. The rainy season. Your plants will get all they need. And you will not wish to spend time on your lawns."

"This is a matter of principle," she said. "Besides, I wish to enjoy my fountain, the way you enjoy yours. So let's get this settled, shall we?"

"I do not wish to find that my pool has no water supply," he said, sounding testy now. "After all the trouble to get the permits and to build it."

"Then let's have our men see what the truth is, if this pipe is the only water from above or if your pool can use a supply of its own. Then we can discuss it further."

He gave a dramatic sigh. "I suppose so. If you wish. I hope this will not be inconvenient."

"Would you please speak with your gardeners and tell them to cooperate?" she said. "Your man that I met was most hostile."

"He is only doing his job," the viscount said. "I wish intruders to be kept at bay, especially the local people."

"I hardly think intruders drive a Bentley," she said. "It was quite obvious I was the right sort of visitor."

"Perhaps I don't wish any visitors. I like my solitude."

"You're too young to want solitude," she said. "It's not healthy."

"You are very forthright." He frowned. "No wonder your husband wanted a softer woman."

She hesitated, startled by his rudeness. "I was just being motherly. You can't be much older than my sons, and I wouldn't want them to live solitary lives."

"If you must know, I am lamenting a lost relationship," he said. "Nursing a broken heart. Handling a betrayal."

"I'm sorry," she said.

"It's no matter. I shall recover, no doubt. Usually I like to travel. Rome, Venice, Barcelona. But at this moment I wish to be alone and write poetry."

"Then I shouldn't wait for coffee. I should go and leave you to your solitude." She went to stand up.

He waved a hand at her again. "No, stay. Remain seated. I am interested to know more about you. You lived in London?"

"No, in Surrey, south of London, but my husband worked in the city."

"Ah. He worked. Not a man of leisure, then?"

"He's a banker. He likes making money."

"So he has made a generous settlement on you?"

"Not generous enough." She smiled. "But enough for me to live comfortably, especially here, where the cost of living is low."

"Unless you like champagne and foie gras as I do," he said. "Then they charge me a devil of a price to ship to me here."

Antoine came in, bearing a tray with a silver coffeepot and hot milk jug, two delicate little cups, sugar cubes and a plate of dainty biscuits. Without being asked, he poured and handed cups to both of them. The viscount took silver tongs and dropped in several sugar lumps.

"What brought you to Saint-Benet?" he asked after taking a sip. "Why not Saint-Tropez? Antibes? This is where the fashionable English go for the winter."

"As you can see from my dress, I am hardly fashionable," she said, smiling at him. "But in answer to your question, it was fate that brought us here. My motor car developed a problem. This was the first human habitation we came to. And once we were here, we liked the ambiance.

When we heard about the abandoned villa, I wanted to see it for myself. I saw it and fell in love with it instantly. It is hardly like this, but it's charming. And I felt . . . it may sound silly . . . I felt it wanted to be brought back to life."

"So you are a woman of sensibility?"

"Not before this. I was always efficient, practical, although I did enjoy playing romantic music on my piano." She glanced out of the window in the direction of her villa. "There was a grand piano in the window. I pictured the opera singer sitting there, singing and playing. I presume she was here before your time?"

"I don't think I ever met her. I was at home in Paris with my nursemaid in those days, but I remember my father speaking of her. I was told she was very beautiful. And of course my father was a good friend of her lover, the duke. Which was how they first came upon the property where you now reside. My father suggested it to his friend."

"Ah," Ellie said. "Then do you know what happened? Why she never came back here?"

"I suppose he grew tired of her, found another woman, and she did not like to be reminded of the happiness she knew here. Or . . . she found another protector, who bought her a bigger and better villa in a more fashionable resort."

That made sense. "I just thought she meant to come back," Ellie said. "Her belongings were all here. I just wondered if some kind of incident or tragedy had happened. The house felt sad."

"Sad?" he laughed. "I expect the tragedy was discovering another woman. It usually is."

Ellie finished her coffee. "I shouldn't keep you any longer," she said.

"Not at all. I have enjoyed your company, which I can't say for any of the other people in this place. I don't know why my father chose such a remote spot to build his villa. There are none of our kind of people to converse with. But you must come again. I have the most skilled chef. We will have lunch or dinner."

"That's most kind of you. I also share my villa with three other women. One is an elderly lady from a very good family. I am not sure the other two would feel comfortable at a house like yours."

"They are your servants? Why would I invite a servant?"

"Not exactly servants," Ellie said awkwardly, telling herself that neither Mavis nor Yvette would want to dine in such circumstances. "You should come to us first and meet them."

"Perhaps," he said. "But perhaps I shall return to Paris. It is always as the whim takes me. If I am invited to a good party, I pack up and go. If not, then I will come to visit you, but not the dreadful English tea, I beg of you."

"Luncheon, then," Ellie said, laughing.

"That is better."

"I look forward to it, and my ladies will also look forward to meeting you," Ellie said. "I take my leave, then, monsieur le vicomte."

He held out his hand to her. "My name is Roland," he said. "That is what my friends call me."

"Ellie," she replied. "My name is Eleanor. My friends call me Ellie."

He repeated the name. "Sometimes," he said, "it is good to have a friend."

She was smiling to herself as the butler let her out. He considered her a friend. She wasn't sure that she liked him. She could tell, as she had been told, that he was spoiled, but there was something of a little-boy-lost about him that finally charmed her.

As she drove away, she had a revelation: What if Roland was the actual heir to her villa? He did say his father had had something to do with choosing the site for the opera singer's villa. What if she had actually been his father's mistress, and his father had built the villa for her but never made her the owner? When he tired of her, she had to leave, and when he died, the villa came to Roland. Of course that made sense. Rumour had it that the aristocrat was a duke, but perhaps Roland was the younger son. Maybe there was an older son who had inherited the title, the château or Paris property, and Roland had been given this more humble place. The younger son of a duke would not inherit the dukedom but a lesser title.

Ellie was pleased with herself as she turned into her own driveway. She had solved the mystery, but she would keep Roland's secret if he didn't want anybody to know. Then her thoughts went one step further. Perhaps he was really the love child of the duke and his mistress, not the rightful heir. That was why he kept silent. Aha.

CHAPTER 23

Christmas was approaching. The water-pipe drama was sorted out satisfactorily for both sides, and Louis had finally managed to get the fountain running again. Bruno turned the soil at the back of the grounds for a future vegetable garden, and Louis promised to bring seedlings from his friend the local farmer. Ellie hesitated about sending a Christmas card to Lionel to let him know she was doing well. She sent greetings to both the boys, giving them her news and hoping she had the correct address for both of them. She had received a brief note from both boys expressing dismay at the way their father had behaved and hoping she had a good holiday in France. But they were the sort of notes you wrote to an acquaintance, written out of politeness. She took out the photograph album she had brought with her and turned back to the childhood pictures: Colin and Richard on the beach, Colin grinning and showing a missing front tooth, Richard clutching a teddy as Colin read to him. What sweet little boys they had been. And then boarding school, and it was as if they shut off all feelings. *I'll never forgive myself that I let Lionel do that to them,* she thought.

Mavis lamented that she couldn't get the right supplies for a Christmas pudding in the village shop and that it needed to be made on Stir-up Sunday. But then they received more than one invitation, meaning Mavis would not have to cook: Tommy and Clive invited them for Christmas lunch. They were going to kill a chicken, they said. And then Henri invited them for the late supper after Midnight

Mass. Ellie had not intended to go to Midnight Mass, but Father André stopped her in the street and said he hoped most sincerely that the ladies would be joining the rest of the inhabitants of Saint-Benet for the most solemn occasion. After that it would have been rude to refuse. So at eleven thirty they drove down the hill, dressed warmly as the night was chilly. Ellie wore Jeannette's fur stole again while Dora had one of her own. They had given the opera singer's long wool cape to Yvette, who had no warm clothing with her, and a smart wool jacket to Mavis. The sound of church bells floated towards them, echoing back from the valley sides in the still night air. The church was already filling up when they arrived. The smell of incense hung in the air, and the candlelight flickered from the altar and the window ledges. On one side was a large nativity scene with a thatched roof, and not just Mary and Joseph but shepherds and villagers of all sorts, local people as might have been seen in Saint-Benet.

The Mass began with a hymn the whole congregation knew and sang lustily so that the sound reverberated around the small building. The Mass itself was confusing to Ellie. She recognized the structure of it, the readings, the consecration of the host, the Communion, but there was a lot of murmuring in Latin, a lot of kneeling and rising, that she did not understand. It ended with another rousing carol, "Les anges de nos campagnes." The angels from our fields. And everyone hugging, kissing, wishing a happy Noël as they came out.

They joined the crowd, processing down the street until they came to Henri's bar. There tables awaited, covered in white cloths, decorated with candles and greenery. They were embraced like old friends and invited to sit with about twenty others. Ellie found herself sitting opposite Nico. Wine had already been poured, and he raised a glass to her.

"I wish you a 'appy Christmas," he said in English.

"And you too," she replied. "You still remember some English, then?"

He shrugged. "I learn in school, but it was many years ago. Now the words do not come easily. But then, your French is good. I do not need to try." He smiled. Then he introduced a tiny old woman as his mother. Ellie looked at her with interest. She was small, wizened, shrunken and nothing like her robust son, but she smiled politely when introduced. Ellie asked of his father and was told that he died years ago. A fisherman. Lost at sea. His mother spoke with a tiny, croaking voice that matched her appearance. She had been a widow for many years, but thanks to her wonderful son, she lacked nothing, and he took good care of her. Ellie wondered if his smuggling activities helped to fund the good life she led. He didn't seem to go out fishing with the other men too often. Anyway, it was none of her business.

They ate a wonderful meal—a bean soup, and then a large whole fish, roasted with herbs around it. So that was how they were supposed to cook the fish that Nico had left them! And last there was applause as Henri produced a chocolate log, decorated with berries. "The bûche de Noël," someone said, and Ellie realized it was their equivalent of the Christmas pudding. Only it was much richer—lots of cream and liquor in it. It was almost three o'clock in the morning when they retrieved the Bentley and Ellie drove them back to the villa. She noted that the viscount had not been amongst the churchgoers. Perhaps he had gone back to Paris for Christmas.

She fell into bed, exhausted, and was awoken by the sound of more church bells announcing the day. Light streamed in, and it was almost ten o'clock. They ate a light breakfast, knowing they were due at Tommy and Clive's house for lunch. Mavis had not managed to find mincemeat to make mince pies, but Ellie had made sausage rolls. They didn't taste exactly like English sausage meat, but close enough.

They had agreed not to give presents to each other, but Dora handed a little box to Ellie and one to Mavis. Ellie's contained a lovely square-cut emerald ring, Mavis's a blue enamel watch in the shape of a bluebird.

"Dora, I couldn't possibly," Ellie began. "I couldn't take one of your treasures."

Dora smiled. "I don't wear it anymore. It was my mother's, and I plan to leave you my jewellery when I die anyway. So enjoy them. It will give me pleasure to see them worn."

"I don't know what to say," Mavis said. "I ain't ever had anything as lovely. When I was young, I used to dream of owning a watch some day."

"You're very welcome, Mavis," Dora said. "And if you want to do something for me in return, then please stop saying 'ain't.' I'm going to work on your vocabulary so you sound like an educated woman." She paused. "I hope that doesn't offend you, but I want the best for your future."

"I think it's kind of you to care about me," Mavis said.

Dora turned to Yvette. "I have not forgotten you, Yvette," she said in French, "but I wanted to give you something practical. I have sent off for white knitting wool and patterns so that we can all knit outfits for the baby. And we have agreed to pay for a doctor to keep an eye on you and to deliver the child when the time comes."

"Merci, madame. You are good." Yvette's eyes were still on the emerald ring, and she did not sound thrilled.

"And I do have a little something for all of you," Mavis said. She retrieved three packages wrapped in brown paper. Dora's were two cushions to match the curtains in her room. "So that you can sit outside in the wicker chair when the weather is nice," Mavis said.

Yvette opened her parcel. "It's a proper maternity dress," Mavis said. "Hide the bump, eh?" And she chuckled. Ellie translated. Yvette nodded again. "Thank you."

Then Ellie opened hers and gasped. It was an elegant black dress with white panels at the side and a white collar. "But this is lovely, Mavis. How did you manage it?"

Mavis gave an embarrassed grin. "I used one of her dresses, the opera singer's, and I knew it was too small, so I used silk from one of her petticoats to make the panels."

"You're so talented," Ellie exclaimed. "You could be a dress designer."

"Go on with you!" Mavis giggled, blushing. "I'm used to doing alterations to keep old clothing going. I had to do it all the time when I was at home and my younger sisters grew out of things. I couldn't design nothing, though."

"Well, I think it's incredible," Ellie said. "And I feel terrible now because I thought we weren't giving presents."

"But you've given us the present," Dora said. "You brought us here. You fought to get this villa, and you've given us a new home. I am enjoying myself, something that hasn't happened in years."

Ellie turned away, tears in her eyes. "I feel the same way," she said. "You have all given me a new life, too. I can't tell you how abandoned and depressed I felt a few months ago, and now look at us. Dora is healthy. Mavis has turned into a dress designer, and I am friends with a viscount."

"You should work on that," Mavis said. "Maybe he's looking for a wife."

Ellie laughed. "Oh no, Mavis. I've no interest in finding a new husband at my age, and I'm certain he's not seeing me in that way."

"Go on, you're only as young as you feel," Mavis said. Then her face became pensive. "I wonder how Reggie's doing without me. Knowing him, I bet he's found someone to take my place. He always did have an eye for the ladies."

"Let's not think of anything unhappy today," Ellie said. "We're going for a lovely lunch, and look at the weather. It's perfect."

~~

At noon they made their way down the steps and across the village to Tommy and Clive's house.

Mavis had revealed that she had made silk cravats for Tommy and Clive from a silk evening gown, also a tie for Bruno.

"Mavis, you are a dark horse," Dora said. "You could make these and sell them, they are so good."

Mavis gave a sheepish grin. "I made one for Louis, too. Do you think he'll like it?"

"If it's from you, he will," Dora replied. "He's taken quite a shine to you, I've noticed."

Now Mavis blushed. "Not really. Just being friendly, like."

They stopped off at Bruno's mother's to deliver the gift, plus a Christmas bonus pay packet. He was as excited as a little boy. Bruno's mother begged them to stay for a meal, but they told her they were expected elsewhere.

The village was silent for once, as most people were recovering from last night's reverie. Henri's bar was shuttered. Even the cats were not in evidence. But Tommy and Clive's house smelled wonderfully of roasting fowl and stuffing. They were greeted warmly as Ellie handed them the cravats, a plate of sausage rolls, and a bottle of wine.

"Such treats," Tommy said, leading them through to a sitting room with a decorated Christmas tree in it. They were served sherry and cheese straws, then sat down for the luncheon. Ellie never remembered chicken tasting so good. It was followed by a peach pie and cream.

"I'm sorry we couldn't find crackers this year," Tommy said. "We should have ordered some from Harrods, but it seemed a little extravagant. Next year maybe Clive can make some for us."

"Just because I paint pictures doesn't mean I can design things that go bang," Clive said with mock severity.

They lingered over coffee, then rose to leave just before it became dark.

"What a wonderful day," Ellie said. "I don't remember enjoying Christmas so much for years."

"You've made our Christmas, too," Tommy said. "Usually it's just the two of us. Boring."

"Thanks a lot," Clive retorted. "But don't forget to tell them about their gift."

"Oh, of course. I nearly forgot. We have a gift for you," Tommy said. "Only we can't give it to you now. We're going to help you construct a chicken coop and give you some chicks when ours hatch. Then you can have your own fresh eggs."

"Oh, what a wonderful idea," Ellie said. "I was actually wondering if we could keep chickens, but it seemed a little too risky, not knowing how long we'd be staying here."

"If you decide to move on, we'll take them back," Clive said. "But we hope you won't."

I hope so, too, Ellie thought.

CHAPTER 24

Winter soon turned into spring. The breeze was scented and had a softness to it. The mimosa flowered with yellow puffy blossoms everywhere. Cyclamens bloomed. Birds sang. The chickens were installed in a new pen at the back of the garden. Vegetables were planted. Each of the women was busy with her own activities. Dora tried her hand at painting with Clive, although, as she confessed, she would never be a Van Gogh. Ellie went down the steps and took cooking lessons with Henri. Also, the viscount had returned from Paris in the new year, and Ellie found herself invited to his château. She felt awkward about this because the invitation did not include the others.

"For goodness' sakes go," Dora said. "He's a useful contact, at the very least, or you may find yourself a marchioness."

"Don't be silly. He would make a terrible husband. He's too young for me anyway," she replied.

~~

"I don't like coming without the other women," Ellie said to him when she visited the château. "It doesn't feel right."

Roland waved an imperious hand. "Just because I like you does not mean I have to embrace your nearest and dearest," he said. "Each person must live her own life, no?"

And so a weekly lunch became a standard practice. Ellie invited him to the villa, but he usually refused. He liked to be amongst his own things, he said. Ellie found him strange but endearing. He had a wicked sense of humour, a keen observation of life, but he never really opened up about himself. He was too young to be shut away and to be so set in his ways. Perhaps aristocrats were different, she thought. She remembered that her mother, also the child of an aristocrat of sorts, had had very set habits and opinions. She also kept her emotions firmly shut away.

Mavis, ever busy with her housework, cooking and sewing, also practiced her French. Only Yvette seemed restless and anxious. Ellie understood this. She was awaiting the birth of a baby she could probably not keep or care for. Ellie toyed with thoughts: Would Yvette want to stay with them once the baby was born? Would they want her indefinitely? She seemed grateful, but she had never gone out of her way to be friendly to any of them. She only spoke when spoken to. She often shut herself away in her room, and she rarely offered to help around the house unless asked to.

Mavis had always been suspicious of her, and Ellie thought this was because they couldn't communicate. But now Mavis was coming along well with her French and tried talking to the girl. Ellie found her up feeding the chickens one day.

"I thought Yvette was doing this," she said. "You shouldn't have to. You do far too much as it is, Mavis."

"Her!" Mavis pursed her lips. "She don't do nothing unless you're watching her." She threw the last of the corn down for the birds, then brushed her hands against her apron. "You know what I think," she said. "I don't believe that girl was ever on a farm. She didn't have much clue about what to do with chickens. What farm girl would not know about chickens? She was actually scared of them. And she didn't help much with the planting or weeding, did she?"

"So what are you saying, Mavis?" Ellie asked.

"I'm saying she ain't—isn't—what she says she is. I don't know who she is or what she's doing here, but I get a feeling she's up to no good."

Ellie shook her head. "I don't see how she could be up to no good here, Mavis. She's clearly expecting a baby soon, and she hasn't received any communication from the father as far as we know. We've taken her in, and where else would she have gone?"

Mavis shrugged. "I don't know. I just don't think she's telling us the truth. I think she's pulling the wool over our eyes somehow."

Ellie collected eggs, then walked back with Mavis. She found Yvette lying in her room. Yvette sat up guiltily when Ellie knocked. "Oh madame, you startled me," she said. "I was just resting. My back. It hurts me, you know. I carry much weight."

"I'm sorry you're not feeling well. I think your time will be quite soon now." She sat down on the bed beside Yvette. "Have you decided what you want to do when the baby comes? Obviously you don't have to make any decision in a hurry, but it is good to think through how you want your future to be. Do you plan to keep the child? I am sure we can help you find a good home for it so that you can get on with your life."

Yvette gave a big sigh. "I don't know what to think, madame," she said.

"You have still heard nothing from your young man? He doesn't know about the baby?"

"I have written to him," Yvette said. "I still have hope."

"You have heard from him?"

"Not exactly. But I still keep hoping . . ."

"Yvette," Ellie said, her voice solemn for once, "I don't understand you. You haven't seemed happy here with us. You don't want to help around the house or to work."

"Oh madame, I am grateful. Most truly I am." Yvette clutched Ellie's hand. "But everything has been so hard. And I worry so much."

"I understand that. It is hard for you. But now we must make plans for the future. You must tell me what your wishes are, and I will do my best for you."

"My wish is that Gaston returns and I marry him," she said. "But one cannot always have one's wishes."

"But Yvette, you say you have written to him, but he has not written back to you. Do you really think he will want to accept this child?"

"I hope so," she said. She looked away, averting her eyes from Ellie's scrutiny.

"Yvette," Ellie said, "Mavis has always been suspicious of you."

"She doesn't like me," Yvette said. "Because I am foreign."

"No, that's not true. She likes everyone else here."

"She likes that Louis," Yvette said, giving a sneaky smile. "I saw them together. He put his arm around her."

"I'm glad. She deserves to be happy," Ellie said. "But Mavis thinks you have not been telling us the truth. You were not from a farm, were you? You know nothing about chickens. You don't want to work hard. I don't even know if you have a young man in the army."

Yvette's face turned red.

"We have taken you in and fed you and looked after you," Ellie continued. "I think we have the right to know the truth. So who are you and where do you come from?"

Yvette went to reply angrily, then she seemed to deflate and sank back against the pillows. "Very well. I suppose you have a right to know. I am not from a farm. I'm from the city of Lyon. My lover is not Gaston. He is not in the army. He is Pierre Lupin, and he is in prison."

"In prison. What for?"

"A robbery. A stupid robbery," she said. "He wanted money for us to marry. When he was arrested, I ran away because I thought they would come for me, too."

"You were involved?"

"He hid things he stole at our apartment. I did not realize they were stolen."

"Then you are better off without him," Ellie said. "How long is his prison term?"

"They said five years." She turned away. "I didn't know what to do. I had no money to pay rent, and I feared they would arrest me."

"I'm very sorry for you," Ellie said. "You have found yourself in a difficult position. My advice would be to give up the baby to be adopted and then get yourself a good honest job, start a new life here on the Côte d'Azur."

"Yes," Yvette said. "Perhaps you are right. Perhaps it is the best thing to do." But she didn't sound convinced.

"Do you love him, this Pierre?"

"Oh yes," Yvette said. "And I'm sure he loves me, too. That is why he took such risks for us to be together."

Ellie's brain was racing. Could they keep Yvette and her child until Pierre was released and the little family could be together? That would be the kind thing to do, but five years . . . That was a long time. And Yvette hadn't exactly endeared herself to any of them. She didn't do her share of the work. She didn't make an effort to learn English or improve her own reading and writing skills. She was, in short, not an asset to their little community. But on the other hand, could they really turn her out with a young child?

Ellie confided these fears to Dora. "She's not our responsibility," Dora said. "You were kind enough to take her in, but you don't owe her anything more." And yet Ellie did feel responsible. But Yvette could not stay with them forever. She had to get on with her life, and that certainly meant giving up the baby. *When it's born I'll go into Marseille and find a convent that helps to adopt babies,* she thought.

In the meantime there was plenty to keep her busy. With the better weather English visitors had arrived to stay at the pension: a Colonel Rutherford, formerly of the army in India, two single ladies—Miss Barnes and Miss Furness, former schoolteachers—and a mother and daughter, the Cartwrights. They were all so stereotypical of what one would expect that Ellie tried not to smile when she met them. They talked about the threat of war, of Mr Chamberlain cleverly making peace with that monster Hitler.

"Of course he'd never have the gumption to tackle us," the colonel said. "He knows what a thumping they got in the last war."

They also complained about French food and lack of good tea—"We always bring our own, my dear, but they never boil the water properly"—and talked about the weather. The colonel seemed to take an instant shine to Ellie. At first she found this amusing, then, when he tried to seek out her company, annoying. The doctor's wife invited them all to musical evenings where Miss Cartwright sang badly while Ellie played the piano. As she observed them, she felt glad that she had left England behind. *So much pettiness,* she thought, and remembered so many similar and boring conversations.

The English visitors ate dinner at Henri's bar. Henri complained about them as Ellie practiced making a tarte tatin with him one day. "It's always no garlic. No onions. No spices. And couldn't we have a nice steak and kidney pie instead."

Ellie laughed. "I could return the favour and teach you how to make a nice steak and kidney pie," she said. "Or better still, I'll make one for you. You've been very kind to me."

"That would be something, wouldn't it?" He laughed. "I'd like to see their faces when we put it in front of them."

"All right," Ellie said. "You acquire the steak and kidneys, and I'll make it."

CHAPTER 25

The supplies came on the next delivery from Marseille. Ellie put on an apron and got to work. She was just putting the finishing touches to a big steak and kidney pie, her hands floury, when Henri came into the kitchen. "There is a man here who is looking for you," he said.

"A man?"

"English, I think."

"Not the colonel?" she asked warily.

"No. Not him. Young."

Ellie brushed off the worst of the flour and stepped outside, blinking in the bright sunlight.

"Mum?"

Ellie started at the word, squinted, and her son Colin came into focus. "Colin? Is it really you?"

She rushed forward, arms open to embrace him. He stood there, awkwardly, as she flung her arms around him. She stepped back laughing. "I'm sorry. I'm getting flour on you." She brushed his jacket front. "What on earth are you doing here? Why didn't you tell me you were coming?"

"I'm home on leave," he said. "Dad told me you'd gone on holiday to France, and he was rather worried that he hadn't heard from you in a long while."

"And why would he be worried?" Ellie asked. "I'm not his responsibility in any way. I'm no longer his wife."

"All the same, I think he still cares about you," Colin said. "He was concerned when you didn't come home. He's worried about a war starting and you being trapped in France."

Ellie looked around, noticing Henri watching them with interest. "Let's sit down and have a cup of coffee, shall we?" she said. She switched to French. "Henri, this is my son, visiting me from England."

"Your son? Welcome, monsieur."

"Do you think we could have coffee? And some of that delicious tart?" She asked Henri.

"But of course. Take a seat."

Ellie took off her apron and ushered Colin to an outside table. "I think it's warm enough to enjoy the sunshine, don't you?"

Colin sat, eyeing her critically as he sat opposite her. "Mum, what are you doing here? And look at you. Dad said he settled enough money on you. Are you in trouble? Why are you working in a café?"

Ellie laughed. "Oh Colin, it is lovely to see you," she said. "And as for what I'm doing here, I'm enjoying myself for the first time in years. I'm not working in a café. I've been taking cooking lessons from Monsieur Henri, and today I am returning the favour. I'm making a steak and kidney pie for him."

"But why are you here, of all places? I had a devil of a time even finding it. It's not even on all the maps."

"I'm here because the place chose me," Ellie said. "The car broke down right here. We had to stay here to have it mended, and we liked it. So we found a place to rent, and we are having a great time."

"'We'? Who is 'we'?"

"You remember Miss Smith-Humphries from the village?"

"The officious old biddy who runs everything? The one who told me not to ride my bike over the grass?"

"That's right. She has softened considerably; in fact I've become very fond of her."

"Good God."

"And you remember Mavis?"

"Mavis? The charwoman?"

Ellie nodded. "The former charwoman."

"You brought her to clean for you?"

"No. As a friend. I have to say she does more than her share of the cooking and cleaning, but I helped her to escape from an abusive husband. He was violent with her, and sadistic, Colin. She had to get away."

"Wait." Colin frowned. "Mavis's husband. Reg Moss? Was that his name?"

"That's right."

"I heard at the pub that he'd just died."

"Died?"

"Was killed, actually. Hit by a car on his way home from the pub. Staggered in front of it, blind drunk."

Ellie put her hand up to her face. "Oh no. I don't know what Mavis will say. She'll be relieved, of course, but she'll also feel guilty for leaving him."

"I don't see why if he hit her," Colin said.

"Because she's that sort of caring person. But what news of you, my darling?" Ellie reached out and put her hand over his. "It is so lovely to see you. I've missed both of you."

"Well, Richard's regiment has been posted to Aden," he said. "And my bank sent us home from Hong Kong until they see what's going to happen next in the Far East. You obviously read about Nanking and what the Japanese have been doing. Absolute monsters. They are bent on conquest of the entire region, you know. The bank isn't taking any chances. They pulled us out."

"So you're back in England now. How lovely. You can come and visit," she said. "Any chance of a young lady in your life?"

"There was one in Hong Kong," he said, averting his gaze. "You wouldn't have approved. She was Chinese."

"Of course I would have approved if you liked her," Ellie said. "Your father wouldn't."

"No." He smiled then.

"How is your father? Are he and what's-her-name married?"

"Oh yes. My new mummy is installed at the house."

"And the baby? When is it due? Soon?"

He frowned. "I don't know anything about a baby. She doesn't seem to be pregnant."

"Ah, so there never was a baby. Interesting." She paused as Henri put a tray of coffee in front of them. Ellie poured equal parts coffee and milk into cups and handed one to Colin before she asked, "And your father? Is he blissfully happy?"

"I'm not sure," he said. "You know how he hates change. She's changed everything in the house. New furniture. New curtains. All very modern. He's trying to be modern, too, but it's not working too well."

Ellie had to laugh. "Poor Lionel. He deserves everything he's getting." She slid a piece of apple tart on to a plate and handed it to Colin. "Henri's a wonderful baker."

"Oh, there you are, Mrs E." Colonel Rutherford spotted Ellie and came striding up to them. "I've just had a grand walk over to the Calanques. Perfect day. I feel fit as a fiddle. You must come with me next time. Splendid view from the top."

"Colonel, this is my son, Colin Endicott," she said. "He's just arrived from Hong Kong."

"Far East, eh? Bad things going on over there. The Japs have their eyes on bigger prizes, you mark my words. You're better safely out of it."

When it became clear that he wasn't invited to join them, he cleared his throat. "I better go and change for lunch, then. I'll be seeing you, my dear. Don't forget about the walk over to the Calanques. Splendid view. Absolutely splendid."

"He's one of the English contingent who come here every winter," Ellie muttered as the colonel walked off, humming to himself. "They stay at the pension."

"He seemed rather keen on you," Colin said, staring after the retreating figure. "I saw his expression when he noticed you. Rather keen."

"Yes. He is a little annoying," Ellie replied. "Lost his wife a while ago and looking for a replacement. Don't worry, I'm not interested. I better see if they have a room for you at the pension if you're planning to stay the night. We don't have a spare bedroom set up yet."

"Uh, no. I think I'd better push on," Colin said. "I'm actually on my way to see some friends in Nice, but I promised Dad I'd check on you."

"At least you have to come and see the villa," she said.

"You live in a villa? That sounds grand."

"It is, quite," she said. "It's perfect for us, anyway. How did you get here?"

"I drove. I've acquired a nice little runabout. Twin carbs. Splendid acceleration."

"You always were mad about cars," she said. "Speaking of which, has your father bought a new Bentley?"

"Oh, the Bentley. You took it, didn't you? He was absolutely livid, I gather. But he does have a new car. An Armstrong Siddeley, not quite as grand. He told me he'd had to cut back since he's giving you such a generous allowance."

"Generous, my foot!" she exclaimed. "If he'd had his way, I'd be living in one of the cottages in a row by the station. I fought hard and demanded my fair share. He was taken aback, shall we say." And she laughed.

"Good for you. It's about time you didn't let him walk all over you," Colin said. "I must say you're looking well. Healthy. Happy. I'm glad."

"So give me a few minutes to pop that pie I'm making in the oven, then I'll take you up to the villa," she said.

As she stood up, Nico was coming up from the port, carrying a basket of fish.

"Take a look at these," he called out to Ellie. "Not a bad day's haul, eh? You can take one, if you like. As long as you know how to cook it properly this time."

"How do you know I didn't cook it properly last time?" she asked, laughing.

"I have my spies."

"Well, I've improved," she said. "Henri has been instructing me. But I can't very well carry a big fish up the hill. I have no shopping bag."

"Henri!" Nico bellowed. The older man came running out.

"Where's the fire, Nico?" he asked.

"See what I have for you," Nico said. "Look at the size of them. How many do you want?"

"I'll take two," Henri said. "Madame here has created an English pie for the visitors' dinner tonight."

"An English pie?" Nico looked sceptical. "Do the English know how to bake pies?"

"Steak and kidney," Ellie replied. "You should try it."

"I'd rather try the fish you're going to cook," he said. "Aren't you going to invite me to sample it?"

"You've never shown any interest in coming to dinner at my house," she said.

"You've invited everyone else." He gave an imitation pout.

"I didn't think you'd want to come," she replied. "You stayed away from the party."

"I told you before I don't like parties."

"But now your curiosity has got the better of you," she said, grinning at him. "You want to see what we've done to the place."

"I've seen perfectly well most of what you've done," he said. "You didn't have any curtains until recently." And the way he looked at her made her think that he was referring to her bedroom. She blushed.

"Very well," she said. "Then you are welcome to come up tonight," she said. "Bring your mother."

"She can't make the steps," he said. "I'll come alone. You cook the fish. I will be the judge."

"All right, I will." She recoiled as he went to hand her a large fish. "But I still can't carry the fish," she said.

"Ah yes. Henri, do you have a basket for madame?"

Henri had been watching the interaction with amusement. "Of course," he said, "but first she has to instruct me how long to cook her pie. And we must wrap the fish in paper, or my basket will stink to high heaven."

"So how much do I owe you?" she asked.

Nico shook his head. "It's a gift. A gift from the sea gods."

"Well, thank you. I'll try to prepare it to your satisfaction."

"I look forward to it." He gave a little bow. "Until tonight, then."

Colin had been watching the rapid exchange of French.

Ellie turned to him. "This gentleman has brought me a fish," she said. "I have to go into the kitchen to show Henri how to cook a pie and get the fish wrapped up."

"All right." He looked a little stunned. Ellie went into the kitchen, then reappeared quickly, now carrying a basket with the fish wrapped in paper.

"Good," she said. "Now we have dinner. Can't I persuade you to join us?"

He looked uncomfortable. "I should be getting on my way."

"Are you sure? We eat quite well, you know, and the pension has spare rooms."

"No, really. The friends in Nice are expecting me."

"Fine." She put down the basket and resumed her place at the table, taking a swig of her coffee.

"Your French is bloody good, mum. And you don't seem to be lacking in male company," he said. "From colonels to fishermen. I'm impressed."

"Don't be silly," she said. "Although there's even a viscount, for your information. But Nico isn't exactly your average fisherman. He seems quite educated and he lives rather well. I think he might be an expert smuggler."

"And yet you're inviting him to dinner?"

"Even smugglers have to eat," she said.

～

They finished their coffee. Ellie went into the bar to let Henri know she was going, then she followed Colin to an MG roadster, bright red. "Do we walk to your villa?" he asked. "Should I leave the car here, or should we drive?"

"We'd better drive if you're heading out afterward, if you don't mind transporting a large fish."

"At least it's wrapped up and no longer flapping." Colin grinned as he opened the door for her and she sat. He jumped into the driver's seat, gunned the engine and they drove off. Several people waved as they passed. Mr Tommy was coming out of the bakery and stared in surprise, then gave her a thumbs up sign. Alphonse lifted a hand in salute from the police station.

"Do you know everyone here?" Colin shouted over the noise of the engine.

"Pretty much," she said. "It's a small place." She instructed him to take the driveway up the hill, then she got out to open the gate for them. They drove in.

"My word," he said, as they inched through the tall gates. "It really is a villa. How did you come by this?"

"It's a long story," she said. "It was a ruin. Nobody had lived in it for donkey's years. We restored it, or rather are still restoring it. There's still a lot to be done, but it's coming along. The previous owner was a famous opera singer, and she left all her belongings behind."

"Gracious. Why did she do that?"

"We've no idea. There is an absentee owner who apparently has no interest in the place. We're now paying him rent via the local notaire. Stop here." They got out and walked up the avenue of palm trees.

"But this garden is glorious," Colin said.

"It will be when we've got it all restored again," she replied. "We're working on it. I've had our helper Bruno dig out all the weeds and the things that have run riot, and we've ordered new plants from a nursery in Marseille. But wait until you see the view at the other side. It still takes my breath away every single time."

She led him around the house to the terrace, where Dora was sitting. She had been reading but had fallen asleep. Ellie woke her gently. "We've got company," she said. "This is my son Colin. Perhaps you remember him."

Dora squinted in the bright sunlight. "Of course I remember him. Used to be a choirboy, though rather a naughty one."

"How do you do, Miss Smith-Humphries?" He held out his hand to shake hers. "I'm afraid my voice is no longer soprano."

"So you've come to visit your mama at last," Dora said. "Or have you been sent by your father to check on her?" She squinted as she eyed him.

Colin grinned. "The latter, actually. Dad's instructions were to tell you you'd better return to England sooner rather than later. He's convinced there's going to be a war. He doesn't think Hitler is going to stop, and we can't just let him walk into one country after another."

"If there is a war, I rather feel I'd be safer here," Ellie said. "Nobody will want to invade Saint-Benet."

"Mum, it's no joke," Colin said. "Maybe Mr Chamberlain can smooth things over again, but if not . . ." He took a deep breath. "If not, you wouldn't be able to return home if you wanted to."

"I'm touched that your father is concerned for my welfare," Ellie said. "But do tell him that I'm running my own life now and actually enjoying myself for the first time in years. Now let me give you a tour of the villa."

217

She led him inside and found Mavis in the kitchen.

"I'm just making Dora a cup of tea," she said. "Do you want one?" Then her eyes grew wide. "It's Master Colin," she said. "Well, I never. What a surprise."

"Just come to check on me on his way through to Nice," Ellie said. "And we've had coffee, so we don't want tea."

"Right you are, then," Mavis said. "It's good to see you again, Mr Colin. Are you back in England now?"

"For a while, yes," he said. "And you're looking well, Mavis."

"Ah well, yes," she said. "I'm enjoying myself. We all are."

Colin glanced at his mother, went to say something, but she shook her head. "Not now," she mouthed. She knew Mavis would hate to show any emotion in front of a stranger. Better to wait until they were alone.

"Come on, then. Show me your mansion," he said.

Ellie took him around the villa.

"I must say you've landed on your feet," he said. "This place is bloody impressive."

"Make sure you tell your father," she said. "And Michelle."

CHAPTER 26

Colin did not stay long, turned down the offer of a glass of wine and
went to depart in the little red sports car. Ellie walked him down the
avenue of palm trees to where he had parked.

"This is quite lovely," he said. "I can see why you want to
stay, but I do think you should listen to Dad and plan to come
home soon."

"I don't have a home any more, remember?" she said, making
him stare at her. He was clearly surprised at the anger in her speech.
"My home was taken from me. Everything I had worked for—my
furniture, my garden, my lifestyle—all taken from me. Why on
earth should I come back when people like me here, and I feel as if
I belong?"

He nodded, not quite sure what to say next. He cleared his throat,
something his father did when nervous. "Well, I wish you luck then,
Mum. Let's hope there is no war and you continue to have a good life
here." He gave her an awkward hug.

"You are welcome to come and visit any time," she said. "We eat
very well—which reminds me, I've a fish to prepare for tonight. I expect
Nico will be quite critical."

"He's another one who fancies you," Colin said.

"Nico, I suspect, is a flirt, and a little bit dangerous," Ellie said,
although she felt her cheeks turning pink.

"Which makes a change from Dad." Colin grinned. "I'll make sure I tell him about your retinue of men."

"Oh, don't be silly." She gave him a playful slap.

She waved as he drove away, then stood there, thinking. She had to admit she did find it flattering that men showed interest in her. At home she had felt like part of the furniture, a nebulous object in the background who put food on the table and laughed dutifully at her husband's jokes. How long since she had felt desirable? There had been a man at the golf club once with whom there had been a spark, but he had gone off to fight during the Great War and not returned. Since then she had been boring housewife Mrs Endicott, pillar of the community, launderer of altar cloths. And now . . . "Heavens," she said, stirring from her thoughts, "I've a fish to put in the oven."

She hurried back to the kitchen. "Mavis, help," she said. "The fisherman Nico is coming to dinner. He's given us a large sea bream, and it has to be cooked perfectly."

"Nico? The bad-tempered one? What's he coming for?"

"I expect he's curious about what we've done with the place," she said. "I could hardly say no if he gave us the fish and wouldn't let me pay for it."

"Well, you better show me what we have to do," Mavis said. "I don't know nothing about garlic and that sort of thing."

As Mavis prepared the fish in a big poaching dish and Ellie cut up the herbs with which to stuff it, Mavis said, "Well, that was nice to see your son, wasn't it?"

"However briefly," Ellie replied. "It feels rather like having a conversation with a stranger. They were such lovely little boys, weren't they? So full of fun. And now two men I really don't know."

Mavis nodded. "They take after that husband of yours."

"Oh." Ellie paused. "Speaking of husbands, Colin had a piece of news for us."

"Good or bad?"

"I'm not sure which. I didn't want to tell you while Colin was here. Perhaps you'd better sit down. It's your husband, Reg."

"He's found himself another woman?"

"No, Mavis. I'm afraid he's dead."

"Dead?" Mavis froze, the spatula still in her hand. "My Reg? He's dead? Are you sure?"

"Colin heard it at the pub," Ellie said. "It seems he was run over by a car. He was very drunk, apparently, and stepped out in front of it."

"Blimey," Mavis said. She sank on to the kitchen chair. "I don't know what to say. I suppose I'm relieved, but now I'm going to worry that he drank so much because I'd left him."

"He drank so much before," Ellie said. "And he came home and he hit you and pushed you around, Mavis. You're free of him. You don't have to worry any more."

"You're right," she said, pondering this, frowning. "I am free, aren't I?" And she turned bright red. "Well, that changes things, doesn't it? It would mean that . . ." She broke off and wouldn't say any more. Ellie did not press her.

"I'll get you a glass of brandy," Ellie said. "You've had a big shock."

Mavis was staring in front of her. Ellie took down the brandy bottle and poured a little into a glass. "Get that down you."

"I don't normally drink, as you very well know," she said. "But on this occasion . . . well, blow me down. That's the last piece of news I expected. Reg dead? I'm a widow." She took a big swig of brandy, coughed, then finished the glass. Of course it would take Mavis time to process such a life-changing event, but Ellie was glad for her. She was now able to make a new life for herself and would not have to worry if they went back to England.

Went back to England . . . Ellie toyed with this. If there was a war, would they be stupid and reckless to stay here? But then she pictured England. Dora could go back to her cottage, but she and Mavis, where would they go? What would they do? She imagined grey, rainy days, plodding to the local shop, nodding politely at people she knew. Yes, the weather has been frightful, hasn't it? But yes, it is good for the runner beans.

She shook her head. No. That was not what she wanted. She was not going back.

~~

Nico came about seven thirty, almost unrecognizable in a dark suit and striped tie, his unruly dark curls smoothed into place. Ellie had a desire to laugh but was actually charmed. She just nodded instead.

"You got dressed up for the occasion, I see," she said.

"How often do I have a chance to wear a suit?" he said. "Only for funerals, and nobody dies here. Luckily the moths have not found it yet."

They sat in the drawing room drinking Campari and eating cheese straws.

"I've always loved this view from your terrace," Nico said. "The best thing about this place, in my opinion."

She was about to ask how he knew about the view, but then she remembered that he crossed this terrace at night when he came up from his boat.

"Yes. It still takes my breath away," Ellie replied. "It was when I saw the view that I knew I had to live here."

"You had a nice house in England? A castle?"

Ellie laughed. "Nothing like a castle. But a nice house. Big garden. Five bedrooms. The sort of house a prosperous banker owns, close enough to London to take the train up every day."

"And your husband still lives there?"

"He does. With his new wife."

Nico made a small snort of derision. "I am sorry," he said.

"Oh, don't be. This is the best thing that ever happened to me," she said. "I find myself truly happy."

"You do not miss a man in your life?"

"No. I am content. I do not have to wait on anyone." She paused, looking at him. "And you. You do not have a wife?"

"Not any more," he said. "I married as a young man. She was beautiful. Perfect in every way." He paused. "And then she died in the Spanish flu epidemic in 1920. And then my father died and my mother needed me, so I came home. And since then . . . well, there was nobody to compare to Claudine."

"Dinner's ready." Mavis appeared in the doorway.

"Shall we go through?" Ellie led him to the dining room, glad that the conversation had been interrupted. It had been a little too intimate. The long table had been covered in a white cloth, and they had managed to salvage enough chairs for the five of them to sit at one end. Yvette had declined to join them. "I don't feel too well," she said. "And I do not like fish."

The fish was produced on its long platter, crisp on the outside but stuffed with herbed butter and plenty of garlic. Nico nodded at his first bite, impressed. "Ah, I see you have learned to prepare the fish à la provençale. I congratulate you. You are Cordon Bleu. Perfect."

The fish was accompanied with scalloped potatoes and spinach and followed by chocolate mousse and cream.

"I must come and eat here more often," he said.

"Stop for a snack on your way to the shed," Ellie said before she had time to consider if this was wise.

"Ah yes. The shed." He gave a little grin. "I hope you don't mind that I use it."

"If the owner has given you permission, I can't really object, can I?" Ellie said.

"True." He nodded but didn't elaborate. "I find it convenient to keep my things there, especially if I dock my boat at the little harbour below the villa. That way, I don't need to go all the way into the harbour."

Of course, Ellie thought. He could bring smuggled goods in and out without anyone seeing. So that was why he wanted to make sure he stayed in her good books. She had almost forgotten that she suspected him. *Tread carefully here,* a voice whispered.

"Oh, by the way," he said as they finished the meal with coffee. "I have bought a new motorboat. It's lovely. Sleek. Made of polished teakwood. And fast. A proper speedboat."

"Goodness," Ellie said. "You can hardly go fishing in that."

He laughed. "Not for fishing. For the tourists. Probably not the English. They are too timid and proper. When the French come in the summer, I will take them out for rides, or they can pay to rent it by the hour. A good investment, I think."

"Oh, definitely." Ellie was thinking that a speedboat could outrun any coast guard if necessary.

"So would you like to come out for a trial run?" he asked. He looked around the table. "All of you ladies?" he added politely.

"Oh, not me," Mavis said. "I get seasick."

"And I am too old to be bumped around on a speedboat," Dora added.

Nico looked at Ellie. "How about you? Are you ready for an adventure?"

"Absolutely," Ellie said.

∿

They went out in the boat the next day. It was as attractive as Nico had described it, and a crowd had gathered at the harbour to watch them.

"Where did you get the money for that, Nico?" one of the men shouted. "Did you rob a bank?"

Nico looked up, laughing. "It was a steal," he said. "Jewish banker from Germany fleeing to South America before Hitler confiscates his property. Couldn't wait to hand me the key."

Ellie tried not to glance at him as they eased out of the dock. Just how did a fisherman from tiny Saint-Benet meet a Jewish banker from Germany? As they left the harbour walls, Nico gunned the motor and the boat took off with a roar of power, flinging her back in her seat and leaving a white trail. Ellie felt pure exhilaration. She glanced at Nico and saw that he, too, was half excited, half scared, but the warning voice in her head told her not to get too friendly. She had taken in Yvette, and now it transpired that Yvette's lover was a robber and in prison. Did she want to find herself accused of accepting and storing Nico's ill-gotten goods?

~~

When they were out to sea, Nico slowed to a crawl and turned to her. "Your turn," he said. "Do you want to know how to drive it?"

"Oh, I don't think—" she began, but he cut her off.

"Be brave. Try. You may not get this chance again."

"All right," she said. He stood up, and she slid into the driver's seat. He explained patiently the throttle, the steering. "It's so easy a child could do it," he said. "But one thing. If we ever encounter a big wave, you make sure you face it head on. If we are sideways, it can flip the boat, and that would be most unpleasant."

Ellie nodded, her heart now beating fast. She pulled back on the throttle, and the boat picked up speed. "Faster," Nico shouted. She obeyed. White spray flew around them. She felt her heart pounding. Nico watched her, her mouth and eyes wide open, a silent laugh coming from her. Then she slowed it again. "We're getting close to the islands," she said. "I'd better hand it back to you."

"Not at all," he said. "Let's see you take it back into port. If you can do that without a mishap, then you can take out the boat whenever you want."

"Really? Oh, I don't think I dare."

"Dare," he said.

She brought the boat back towards the harbour, conscious of the stone walls and narrow entrance, but she slowed to a crawl and managed to reverse the throttle, cut the motor and drift into the docking space without a scratch.

"See, I knew you could." He gave her shoulder a friendly shake. It was the first time he had touched her, and it felt as if a new level of intimacy had been reached. *Watch out,* a voice whispered again.

CHAPTER 27

Ellie climbed the steps to the house, the sun and salt stinging on her skin. It was the first thing she had done in her whole life that had felt dangerous, but exciting. And Nico had told her she could take the boat out if nobody was renting it. The thought of taking it out alone was terrifying, but she knew she was going to do it.

Opening the front door, she called out, "The pirate woman returns. You won't believe what I've just done . . ."

Silence met her. "Dora? Mavis?"

Then from upstairs came a scream. Ellie stumbled as she rushed up the stairs. The scream came again, from Yvette's room. She opened the door. Yvette was lying on the bed, while Dora and Mavis stood beside her.

"The baby's coming," Mavis said. "I'm so glad you're back. We don't know what to do."

Yvette let out a little moan. "The pain, the pain," she whimpered.

"Mavis, is Bruno working today?" she asked. "Tell him to go and fetch the doctor. Tell him the baby is coming. I'll wash my hands and do what I can."

Ellie washed, then assembled towels and a bowl of hot water. She had given birth twice, but the midwife had given her instructions, and frankly the pain was so overwhelming that the whole thing was a blur. She wasn't sure what she was supposed to do to help Yvette.

"Don't worry," she said, putting a comforting hand on Yvette's arm. "It will all be over soon."

"Make it go away," the girl shouted. "I don't want this. I don't want a baby. I want to go home."

Mavis burst back into the room, panting, having run. "Bruno's nowhere around," she said. "I'd better go down to get the doctor."

"Yes, thank you, Mavis," Ellie said. "I'm afraid you better. I'm no expert at this. I don't know what's normal."

The last part of her sentence was cut off by Yvette screaming again, imploring the Madonna and all the saints. Since she had shown no interest in religion before, Ellie assumed she must be in great distress. She stared down at Yvette's swollen body, at blood that was now escaping on to the towel. What if the child was stuck and needed to be pulled out? And what if the child died, or Yvette died because she didn't do what she had to?

Time passed as an eternity. Yvette screamed, tossed, sweated, then grew calm again. Dora stood on the other side of the bed, shooting worried glances at Ellie.

"Is it supposed to take this long?" she asked in English.

"One of mine was over twelve hours," Ellie said.

"I don't think I can stand it that long," Dora said. "Can she really be in that much pain? Do you think she's dramatizing?"

"Oh no," Ellie said. "I'm sure she is in pain. I was, but being British, I didn't scream."

Dora smiled.

At last they heard footsteps coming up the stairs. Mavis came in. "I found the doctor. He was about to drive to a farm, but luckily I stopped him."

The doctor came into the room, carrying his black bag. "Now, young lady," he said firmly. "Stop that noise. I am here. There is nothing to concern yourself about. This is all quite normal. Let's take a look at you."

He washed his hands in the basin on the wall, dried them, then examined Yvette.

"Good," he said. "The head is coming down nicely. It should not take too long now."

"Make it stop," Yvette begged, tears streaming down her cheeks.

"It will soon be over. What you have to do is to push when I tell you. Not yet, but soon. Understand me?"

"Yes, monsieur le docteur," she replied in a small voice.

After that, everything calmed down. Yvette stopped screaming and only made small grunting noises of desperation as she pushed. And then, all of a sudden, there was a rush of fluids, and the baby came shooting out. "Congratulations, young lady," he said. "You have a lovely baby girl."

"Oh," Yvette said. "A baby girl."

The doctor tied off the cord, cut it, wrapped the child in a towel and handed her to Ellie. "You can get her cleaned up," he said, turning to Ellie, "then give her to the mother to let her nurse. That encourages the milk to come in. And make sure the afterbirth is delivered properly. I must be on my way. I'm needed elsewhere."

Then he was gone, and Ellie was left literally holding the baby. When she finally handed her to Yvette, the girl stared down at the tiny bundle, the dark eyes staring in wonderment at her face.

"She is so perfect," Yvette said.

"What would you like to call her?" Dora asked.

Yvette kept on staring. "Josephine, I think. After the empress. She was very beautiful, wasn't she?"

"Josephine. Very nice," Dora said.

"She can be Jojo," Yvette said. "N'est-ce pas?"

Ellie encouraged her to put the baby to her breast. Josephine immediately latched on and began sucking. This made Yvette laugh. "How does she know?" she asked. "This feels so strange."

"Well," Dora said after they had left Yvette to sleep with the baby beside her, "that's that, then. I hope she doesn't become too attached to that child, because she'll surely have to give it up. There's no way she can keep it."

"I suppose not," Ellie said hesitantly. Dora frowned, watching Ellie's face.

"Now don't you dare say that she can go on living here with us and we'll help take care of the child," she said firmly.

"At least until she's got her strength back, Dora. And then it's up to her what she wants to do. Maybe she can write to her young man in prison and make a plan for their future."

"I don't see how, if he's got five years to serve," Dora said. "They are not going to release him on compassionate grounds because he's fathered a child."

"No, I suppose not."

"And frankly, I don't want to be uncharitable, but I'd prefer to have my last moments on earth without her mooching around. She's not exactly the most lovable of creatures at the best of times."

"I know," Ellie said. "But let's not discuss this now. I'll go and see Father André and learn where she can safely hand over the child."

But she put this off, returning to the doorway and watching the tiny human asleep in Yvette's arms. *What if she does want to keep it?* a voice whispered. *Couldn't we make it possible for her?*

∿

And then it was decided for them. One morning two weeks later they woke up to find that Yvette had gone. No note. No message. Just her clothing taken from the wardrobe and the baby lying in its bed, howling to be fed.

"Well, at least that settles it," Dora said as Ellie picked up the baby and attempted to quieten it. "We take the child to the nearest nuns and drop it off there."

Ellie looked down at Jojo's tiny face. "I can't do that," she said. "What if Yvette has only gone off to think, to make up her mind? What if she's gone in an attempt to see Pierre? Or to find a situation that will let her keep her child?"

Dora shrugged. "She hasn't shown much initiative before," she said. "So you're suggesting we keep this child?"

"For now, Dora. Just for now."

"And how do we feed her?"

Ellie sighed. "I presume there are plenty of mothers who can't breastfeed for some reason or other."

"They employ a wet nurse, and neither of us is equipped to perform such a task," Dora said icily.

"I think wet nurses went out of fashion long ago," Ellie said. "I'll ask the doctor. He'll know." She reached out and put a tentative hand on Dora's shoulder. "It's only for now, Dora. We have to give Yvette a chance."

"I'd say you've given her more than a fair chance, Ellie. We've handed everything to her on a plate. We're paying her doctor bills. We've fed and housed her. And now she has left us in the lurch. Gone without a word, without a single thank you. She has played us for fools, Ellie. That's what she's done. I guarantee she's off on the Riviera at this moment."

"How can she be? She's no money, has she?" She paused. "I'd better check my jewellery box. So should you."

They returned almost immediately. "One or two of my good pieces are gone," Dora said.

"And the emerald ring you gave me," Ellie said. "Oh Dora, I'm so sorry. You were right. She was using us. Not the least grateful."

"So do we tell the police? Have her arrested for theft?"

"I hate to do that," Ellie said. "For all her faults, I did become fond of her. And she could have taken all our jewellery, but she took just enough to get by for now. Let's give her a chance to make amends."

"Hmph," Dora said.

Mavis agreed with Dora. "I never did trust her," she said. "And where I grew up, you got a pretty good feel for who was up to no good. I've always felt that. Maybe she was scared and we rescued her from a bad situation, but then she saw how soft-hearted you were, and she realized she was not only on to a good thing, but she could hide out with us, if they were looking for her." She met Ellie's gaze. "What's to say she wasn't part of a robbery ring with her young man? And we helped her hide out until the heat died down."

"Oh Mavis," Ellie said. "You may well be right. I wish I knew what the best thing to do was."

"I'd say we are well rid of her," Mavis said.

"If we have her arrested, then this child has no chance of ever returning to her mother. She'll go straight into an orphanage and maybe a loving family will never be found for her."

"So you're thinking that we could be that loving family?" Mavis asked.

"For now, anyway. Poor little innocent babe. At least we can love her." Ellie picked up the baby and nuzzled her against her cheek, smelling that sweet smell of talcum powder and baby softness.

～～

Ellie visited the doctor and learned to make a formula from evaporated milk, sugar and boiled water. She drove into Marseille and purchased baby bottles and a good supply of cans of milk. Jojo seemed to tolerate it well, but it didn't take Ellie long to realize that motherhood is for the young. Jojo woke every three hours, demanding to be fed. Her loud protests echoed through the house, disturbing the sleep of all three women.

"You need a rest," Dora said over breakfast one morning. "Let me get up in the night to her. You look quite ragged."

"Oh Dora, you have your own health problems. You need your rest, and I'm afraid this is disturbing you. I try to wake to anticipate Jojo's needs, but then I doze off."

"As for my health problems, my doctor told me I only had a few months before my heart gave out. I should point out that it's been six months, and I'm still going strong. So maybe he was wrong, or maybe this climate has worked miracles. Or maybe just being with you, where I feel cherished and wanted, has made all the difference."

Ellie put a tentative arm around her, as Dora was not one who had demonstrated physical contact before. "Dora, I've been so glad to have you here with me. You've made all the difference to such a difficult time. Instead of feeling lost and worthless I've never felt more alive and hopeful. Let's hope the miracle has happened and you live another twenty years."

Dora gave a snort. "I don't see that happening, but I am making the most of the present. And I suppose that child will grow out of her nightly wailing soon enough."

"Let's hope so," Ellie said. "She is putting on weight nicely."

"But in the meantime take a day to yourself. You've been washing nappies, making formula and running yourself ragged." She gave Ellie a little push. "Go on. We can cope. Go and buy yourself a magazine and a pastry and sit on a rock somewhere."

"Like the Lorelei on the Rhine?" Ellie laughed.

"Singing for your fisherman, no doubt."

Ellie gave her a withering glance. "Just because I went out in a boat with him once does not make him my fisherman. If you want to know, I find him quite intriguing. He is certainly not your average peasant."

"Of course not. He's a smuggler. We've all said so. Maybe you should confront him about it."

"Dora, if he brings in cigarettes or brandy from Italy via Corsica, is that such a terrible thing?"

"Or guns? Or drugs?"

"Oh no. I'm sure he wouldn't do that," Ellie said, but she hesitated. *How can I be sure?* she wondered. And yet she didn't want to ask him, because at that moment any trust would be broken. He'd no longer use the shed, or ever take her out in a boat again.

CHAPTER 28

Ellie walked down the steps into Saint-Benet. It was a perfect spring day, birds chirping, seagulls whirling, the air full of the scent of blossoms. She did as Dora had suggested and bought herself a pain au chocolat from the bakery.

"And how are mother and baby faring?" Madame Blanchet, the baker's wife, asked. Nothing escaped the notice of the residents of the village.

"The baby is thriving," Ellie said. "The mother has gone off and abandoned her. We're taking care of the child until she comes back for her."

"If she comes back for her," the baker's wife said with a knowing look. "I know these young girls. All they want is a good time. No responsibility. My own younger one is the same—my Giselle. Head in the clouds about bright lights and city life. Wants to go off and be a fashion model for Chanel. Have you ever heard of anything so stupid? I tell her, 'Be happy like your sister Gabi. Look at her, settled with that nice Luc and already two babies.' But she doesn't listen to me or my husband. I don't know what will happen when she leaves school . . ." She paused, wiping down her apron. "I'd say you're stuck with the child. But there's an orphanage in Marseille you could think about."

"Oh no," Ellie said. "I couldn't put Jojo in an orphanage. We'll raise her if we have to."

"Then I wish you good luck," the baker's wife said. "It's not easy raising a child these days, especially at your age."

Ellie came out with her croissant and headed towards the harbour. *At my age,* she thought angrily. Did she really look old now? Did she feel old? Then she had a brilliant thought: Nico had told her she could take the boat out if it was not being used. She knew where he hid the key. It was a beautiful, calm day. She would do it! Feeling self-conscious and a little silly, Ellie climbed down into the boat, retrieved the key from its secret hiding place, and started the motor. It sprang to life right away with a satisfying *pop pop pop.* Holding her breath she eased it out of its berth, managed to turn it to face the exit and crept forwards until the harbour walls were passed. Then she pushed the throttle, feeling the boat pick up speed. She had no intention of the type of speed that Nico had used but kept going until Saint-Benet was far behind. The chain of small islands grew closer, and she steered for the first one, interested to get a better view. From her terrace at the villa, they all looked like inhospitable lumps of cream-coloured rock. Now she saw that the biggest one showed patches of green. Surely nobody lived there, because she had never seen a boat going to and from the shore. She slowed the boat to a crawl as she approached the first island. It was indeed a rocky crag with limestone cliffs rising steeply and a colony of seabirds wheeling above it. Nowhere to land here. Not coming too close to shore, she eased slowly around it, wary of unseen rocks.

It was the change in wind direction that made her look back. The shore seemed remarkably far away, and black clouds had now gathered over the mainland mountains, rapidly swallowing up the sky. Within minutes a chill wind was blowing directly at her. Waves slapped against the boat. She remembered Nico's admonition to keep the boat facing the waves, so she steered it towards that distant shore. How was she going to make it back? Then she looked towards the biggest island and saw, miraculously, a jetty. So it was inhabited, or at least people came over for picnics. As she came nearer, she saw that it might well be some kind of park. There were steps going up, a trellis, a bench and flowering shrubs. Giving a silent prayer of thanks, she managed to tie up the boat and climb out and was mounting the steps when the first harsh drops of rain fell.

Within minutes the sky opened. There was a rumble of thunder, then hail began bouncing around her like ping-pong balls. Ellie looked around for shelter. Ahead of her were cultivated gardens, an orchard, and in the background some kind of rambling grey stone building. Thunder crashed overhead, and there was a flash of lightning. No use trying to find shelter amongst the trees of the orchard, then. Covering her head with her hands in a futile attempt to keep off stinging hail, she ran up the gravel pathway. There was an archway halfway down the side of the building, and Ellie staggered into it, gasping for breath, freezing cold and drenched. At least she was out of the rain here, but someone had to live in this building and would offer her a chance to shelter and dry off. As she stood there, she heard the sound of chanting . . . sweet, melodic tones that cut through the fury of the storm.

For a moment Ellie considered the fact that she might have died and that this was some kind of transition to the afterlife. Then she laughed at the absurdity of her own mind. She came through the archway and found herself in a courtyard with arched cloisters along one side. The chanting came from behind the tall doors at the far end. She started towards it but had only gone a few steps when a hooded figure stepped out in front of her. She gasped, took an involuntary step back and sat down heavily on a bench against the wall. The figure loomed over her. Before she had time to consider whether it was a ghost, it said, in a deep man's voice, "What are you doing here? You must not be here. Leave immediately."

"I'm sorry," she stammered. "I was on a boat. Caught in the storm. I couldn't make it back to land, so I saw the jetty and came here. I won't bother you long . . . I only needed to—"

"No," the voice interrupted. "I just told you. You cannot stay. This is a place of men. No women allowed. Now go. Go."

Ellie stood up, hesitated. She was loath to go out into the storm but had a feeling this man would hound her until she did. At that moment a door opened nearby, and another man came out.

"What's happening, brother?" he asked. "I heard a cry, raised voices."

"I found this woman, Father Abbot," the first man said. "A woman. Wandering around. Here."

"I'm so sorry," Ellie said. "I was on a boat and was caught in the storm. I just came to seek shelter until the storm passed. I had no idea this was a monastery. I didn't even know anyone lived here."

"Not a monastery, an abbey," the newcomer said.

He had a soft, gentle voice. Ellie looked up into the face of the most handsome man she had ever seen. It was hard to tell his age. He had a square jaw, and his blond hair was trimmed very short, making him look like a Roman general, and—Ellie had read of piercing blue eyes in novels but had never experienced them until now—his eyes were an alarming blue. They observed her now, with a hint of amusement.

"Brother Michel," he now addressed the younger man. "You mean well, but rules must give way to charity. Didn't our Lord say we must welcome the stranger? And I'm sure this lady has not come with the object of bringing us temptation." Now the humour spread to his lips, and he smiled. "Go back to your task."

"Yes, Father Abbot," the man mumbled and shuffled away.

The abbot turned to Ellie. "My dear, you are soaked and shivering. Come into my study to get warm."

He held open a door for her, and she stepped into a simple room, one wall lined with books, the others whitewashed and bearing only a crucifix. There was a big desk with neatly stacked papers on it. At the far end, two well-worn armchairs faced a fire.

"Just a minute," he said. Ellie waited. He disappeared, then came back, handing her a towel. "You'll want to dry yourself a little, then you can wrap yourself in this." He put a rug down on the arm of the chair. Ellie dried her face and hair, conscious of the man standing a few feet away, then wrapped herself in the rug as she sat down.

"I'll fetch you a tisane," he said. "Ginger, I think, is warming," he told her when she returned, handing her a cup.

Ellie sat, feeling the warmth of the fire on her legs and the hot liquid spreading through her body. "I had no idea this place existed," she said. "Nobody in the village ever mentioned it."

"We do keep ourselves apart," the abbot said. "We are a contemplative order. We pray, we grow our own produce and of course we make the liqueur for which we are famous and which keeps our abbey going."

"Oh yes," she said. "I did hear once about the liqueur from the abbey, but they never said where it was."

He came to sit in the other armchair, regarding her with interest. "You are not French, I think, although you speak it remarkably well."

"I'm English."

"You are visiting Saint-Benet?" he asked.

"I'm living there now, at least for the present. I've rented a villa."

"Villa? That sounds impressive."

She smiled. "It was a ruin, abandoned. We have been restoring it."

"We? You and your husband?"

"No. I'm not married any longer."

"Ah. A widow. A merry widow?"

Ellie shook her head. "Not widowed. Cast aside. He chose a younger woman."

"Clearly a man of bad taste," he said. "So who has been restoring the villa with you?"

"Two other Englishwomen . . . an old lady who has been told she didn't have long to live and wished to see the blue Mediterranean again, and my former housekeeper, who escaped from an abusive husband."

"And you? Why here?"

"I remembered it from my youth. I, too, wanted to escape and start afresh, and I wanted beauty around me."

He nodded, his eyes still focused on her face. "So you brought these women with you because you needed to be needed."

"I brought them because they needed help, yes. Because I could do something to make their lives better at that point."

"And in doing so, you have restored your own sense of worth, I think?"

"I suppose I have," she said. "I didn't do it for that reason, I want you to know."

"Of course not. You did it because you are a naturally kind person, but in doing so, I suspect you have begun to heal yourself."

"Yes," she said. "I feel that I have a purpose, that I belong, which is what I needed." She considered this, then added, "Actually, I have too much of a purpose at the moment." And she told him the story of Yvette and baby Jojo.

He listened, saying nothing. "And how do you feel about being left with this child?"

"I want to do what is best for the baby," she said. "I cannot let her be put into an orphanage. If Yvette does not return, maybe we will find a kind family for her. Otherwise we will raise her. I wanted grandchildren. I wanted a daughter after I had two sons, but that did not happen. She seems a little bit like a gift."

"Then I'm sure she will be a very lucky young lady, growing up spoiled with three aunties around her."

"Yes. She will," Ellie said.

Outside a bell rang, solemn, melodious. The abbot looked up. "Ah. Sext has ended. My brothers will be preparing for the midday meal. I wish I could invite you to join us, but I think that would cause great alarm." He chuckled now.

"You remain completely cut off from the rest of the world?" Ellie asked. "No visitors? No family ever?"

"Not quite," he said. "In the summer months we hold an open house on the first Sunday of the month. A boat brings visitors over from the mainland, and we welcome them. We give tours of our workshop, our distillery, our art. It is good for our men not to forget what they left behind. You must come over when the tours start in May and see what we accomplish here. We have a happy life, I assure you, and I like to think that our constant prayers do some good, too."

"Do you think that your prayers can prevent a war from happening?" she asked. "Everyone is worried. Can you ask God to remove Hitler and Mussolini?"

He laughed at that. "I don't think God works in that way," he said. "In fact, I wish I knew how he works. But I know one thing. He works through us. That's why we are here—to be his hands and voice."

"Have you always been so . . . set on monastic life?" she asked.

"Not always," he said. "I grew up in very privileged surroundings. A rich family. A small château. I was sent to the Sorbonne. I travelled. Visited America and Africa. Then I met a beggar. He was sitting hunched in an alleyway in the cold in Paris. He looked up at me and held out his hand. I was about to walk past when I found that I couldn't. I lifted him up and took him for a meal. Then I gave him my coat and scarf and all the money I carried on me. And I went home deciding there and then that I would enter the priesthood and do some good, because, you see, that beggar I had just met was Jesus."

Ellie felt tears prick in her eyes. She nodded. "But you decided on a monastic life instead?"

"No. I entered the seminary, but frankly I was not comfortable. I did not like what they were saying to us. It was very much holier than thou. 'We are advising you on how to live your lives,' not 'We are trying to become better men.' But I stuck it out until I was ordained. When the Great War broke out, I volunteered to be a chaplain on the battlefield. I held men who had had their legs blown off, or were hopelessly entangled in barbed wire, and I gave them the last rites as they died in my arms. I saw the worst of human suffering. After it was all over, I was assigned to a parish in Marseille. A tough parish. Lots of suffering made worse by the Spanish flu. I did what I could, but the darkness began to overtake me. Why was God allowing all this? I had a crisis of faith. What I was doing couldn't make a difference. I was stupid. I should go and have a good life and forget about it."

"But you didn't."

"My superiors told me I was burned out, spent from what I had been doing. They sent me on a retreat to this place. I found tranquillity and peace here. I took to the Benedictine lifestyle, the Rule. And I applied to join. I've never regretted it for a moment."

"I'm sorry," she said. "I must be keeping you from your duties."

"One of the good things about being the abbot is that nobody can tell me what to do," he said, with a boyish grin. "The bell will summon me to our midday meal, but you . . . feel free to remain here until the rain has stopped. In fact, let me get you a bowl of soup from our refectory. You will need sustenance for the return journey." Without waiting for a response, he went out. Ellie took the opportunity to rub herself dry and squeeze moisture from her wet clothes into the towel. Also to smooth down her hair. "I must look a fright," she thought and then decided that this man didn't care. He returned soon after with a large earthenware bowl of soup on a tray with a big hunk of coarse bread.

"I'll leave you to eat it because I am required to say the blessing over our meal," he said. "Also I have placed a bucket outside, as I am sure you will need to bail out your boat. What sort of boat is it? I hope you didn't row over here."

"Oh no," she said. "It is a friend's speedboat."

"That's good. So I wish you a safe return. I am Abbot Gerard, by the way, and you are?"

"Ellie Endicott," she said. "Or used to be Endicott. Now I'm not sure. My maiden name was Harkington."

"It's up to you to choose who you want to be," he said. "Well, Ellie, I will bless your safe return journey and your new life here." He made the sign of the cross. Awkwardly Ellie crossed herself and watched him depart. She ate the soup, a hearty vegetable stew with bread that was still warm. Then she placed the tray outside the door, picked up the bucket and hurried to the archway. From an open door on the opposite side of the courtyard came the sound of someone reading aloud. The rain had stopped as suddenly as it started, and blue sky was already reappearing. The boat, as Abbot Gerard had predicted, did need a lot of bailing out, but she did the best job she could and was relieved when the motor restarted. Half an hour later she was back in the harbour at Saint-Benet, and the abbey felt like some kind of ethereal vision.

CHAPTER 29

Spring melted into summer with plenty of work to occupy their days. Ellie enjoyed the garden, planting vegetables, reviving fruit trees and coaxing flowers to spill out of pots and beds. Jojo began sleeping through the night, which made things easier. Tommy came over with goat's milk that he said was better for a baby's stomach than the evaporated stuff from a can. Roland, the viscount, returned from his latest visit to Paris and invited Ellie to coffee. She brought Jojo with her. She had become a smiley, adorable baby, and he was entranced with her. Ellie watched him as he dangled his pocket watch over her basket.

"Are you not supposed to marry and produce the heir?" she asked, amazed at her own boldness.

"Fortunately, I have an older brother who is doing his duty in that department," Roland said. "I'm afraid my interests lie elsewhere, much to the disgust of my pious mother. But she need no longer worry. I have had my heart broken, and I doubt that I shall fall in love again."

He bent to tickle Jojo, who gave a delightful laugh.

French summer visitors started to arrive, some staying in the pension, others in rooms the villagers let, or camping in the meadow behind the police station. Nico and his speedboat were much in demand. Henri was constantly busy at the bistro, and Tommy helped out, waitering or washing dishes with his usual good humour. Mavis had become quite pally with Mrs Adams and helped her when the pension was full, thus making a bit of money for herself.

"I don't like accepting charity," she said to Ellie as she tried to press the money on her. "You've been too good to me for too long."

"Mavis." Ellie gave an exasperated smile. "You've done more than your share of work. You cook for us. You've made us curtains and pillows and lovely clothes. Please keep the money for a rainy day. You never know when you might need it."

"Some new clothes might be a good idea," Mavis said. "It's about time I tarted myself up a bit. I don't like looking frumpy all the time." And she went red. *She wants to impress Louis,* Ellie thought. It had been obvious that Louis came up to do small jobs around the house more often than he needed to. He seemed like a kind man, and Ellie was glad for them.

Dora no longer left the property unless it was in the motor car. The steps had become too much for her. She was growing weaker, Ellie noted, but she still insisted on doing her share of chores, taking painting lessons from Clive and writing in her journal. One day she announced that the weather was finally warm enough and she wanted to go swimming. Would Ellie please drive her down to the water.

"Oh Dora, dear, I don't think that's wise," Ellie said. "The water will still be cold. And with your heart condition . . ."

"I've set that heart on a swim in the Mediterranean, and I intend to do it," Dora said firmly. She went to change into her bathing suit and bathrobe. Reluctantly Ellie put on her own swimsuit in case she had to go into the water to rescue Dora. Mavis stayed with Jojo.

"You ain't getting me going in that water," she said. "You'll both catch your death of cold."

"Nonsense," Dora said. "It will be bracing."

They drove down and parked at the harbour, then took the little path around the headland to the beach. It was quite deserted, for which Ellie was grateful when she took off her robe. Dora put on a rubber swimming cap, then waded in fearlessly, gasped a little as the first wave hit her thighs, but then stepped in deeper and began swimming, striking out with confident strokes. Ellie stood at the edge, reluctant to go any deeper. The water was indeed cold, but the sun, warm on her shoulders, made it bearable.

"Coward," she whispered to herself and forced herself to wade in deeper. Before she had to make the decision to actually start swimming, Dora came towards her and stood up.

"There," she said. "I did it. Wonderful. But that's enough for one day. It actually isn't quite warm enough yet." She had a big smile on her face as they drove home. *She really is a remarkable woman,* Ellie thought.

Soon after this, she received a letter from England and drew Ellie aside.

"I've just heard from my solicitor," she said. "I've drawn up a new will, making you my heir. There's not a lot: the cottage, a small bank account, my jewellery, but I want you to be provided for when I go."

"That's very generous," Ellie said. "Are you sure? You wouldn't rather leave it to a favourite charity?"

"Nonsense," Dora replied. "Charity begins at home, don't they say, and you have given me a home and a reason to want to go on living."

"Dear Dora." Ellie put a gentle hand on her arm. "I hope you won't go for a long time yet."

"I have certainly proved that idiot doctor wrong so far," she said with a satisfied nod. "It's amazing what sunshine and good food can do. Oh, and good friends."

Ellie gazed at her, realizing how fond she had become of the old woman.

∿∿

On the first Sunday of May, Ellie had taken the ferry across to the island for the abbey's first open house of the season. It was filled with picnickers, the curious and family members of the brothers. They were shown around the gardens, the process of liqueur making was demonstrated, with samples, and there was an organ concert in the abbey. Ellie had not hoped to spend any time alone with Abbot Gerard, but he sought her out and walked in the gardens with her, apparently interested in her latest news. After that he made time for her each month, sharing a dish of fruit with her or sitting on a bench overlooking the sea. *If only I'd married a man like this,* Ellie thought. *A man I can really talk to, who listens, doesn't judge, is wise and yet can laugh at the absurdity of our human frailty.* She found herself counting off the days to the next ferry. *I mustn't be selfish and take up more than my share of his attention,* she told herself, but she sensed that he also enjoyed talking and walking with her.

"You're becoming rather holy," Nico commented when she met him on the quayside. "Are you thinking of joining an order?"

"No, of course not," she retorted. "There is just something about that place—you can feel the tranquillity and the holiness. And with a baby screaming at six in the morning, it's good to get away once in a while."

"That girl won't ever come back, will she?" he said. "Ungrateful little . . ." He corrected what he was about to say. "Mademoiselle."

"We did the right thing, whether she was grateful or not," Ellie said. "If we hadn't rescued her, she would have come to no good."

"Saint Ellie the righteous," he said, giving her a wicked grin. "I'm waiting for you to come and save my soul."

"Does your soul need saving?"

He considered this. "Probably not," he said. "But I'd like to see you try."

He was incorrigible, she thought. And yet there was something about him . . .

〜

The summer passed with the small town crowded with visitors. The beach was no longer deserted when Ellie took Dora to swim. The water became delightfully warm, and Ellie enjoyed swimming, too, although Mavis still refused to join them for more than a paddle. They brought Jojo, who lay in the shade in her basket, giving a toothless smile whenever they looked at her. *Such a delightful child,* Ellie thought. *How could anyone abandon her?* She pictured the little girl crawling soon, then toddling. Mavis would sew her pretty dresses, and then later, they'd have to think about school . . .

Then, on September 1, just when all the summer visitors had gone back, the news came that German troops were amassing on the Polish border. There was a stern warning from the Allied nations, but Hitler paid no attention. His troops swarmed over the border, and on September 3, 1939, war was declared. Ellie and Dora had acquired a radio earlier in the year and now listened to grim announcements both from Paris and the BBC.

"Do you think we should go home?" Ellie asked, the worry showing on her face. "But then I couldn't take Jojo back to England, could I? She's not mine to take. So I suppose that means we're trapped here."

"I suspect that we shall be safer here than in England," Dora said. "Obviously Hitler will set his sights on London. I'm sure there will be bombings, but who will show any interest in a remote corner of the French coast with little strategic use? Anyway, let us be optimists and believe that even now peace will be negotiated. They must remember the toll of the last war. Neither side can want that again."

"Let us hope so," Ellie said.

"All the same, it might be good to be prepared," Dora said. "Let's go into Marseille and stock up on provisions—things like sugar and coffee that might become scarce. Also, let's buy enough jars so that we can preserve our produce."

They made the trip into Marseille. In that city life went on as it always had. The pavement cafés were full; there was laughter and music. No hint of panic or approaching war.

"We have the Maginot Line," one shopkeeper was saying. "The Germans will never breach that, however hard they try. They'll give up and turn on easier targets in Eastern Europe, you'll see."

This prediction seemed to be true. Hitler aimed for the Balkans, then Norway. Life went on as usual in Saint-Benet. Dora and Ellie worked at preserving fruits and vegetables. They made sure they had enough chickens and even acquired a young nanny goat, named Babette, from the nearby farm for future milk supplies. Nobody in Saint-Benet mentioned that the women were aliens. They were, after all, on the same side. Britain and France prepared to fight against the might of the Nazi regime.

At the end of September, Ellie received a letter from her son Colin. *Dad begged me to write to you to tell you to come home while you still can,* he said. *You may find yourself trapped in France. If you need money, he'll cable it to you. I've just received my call-up papers and will be reporting. As I have been to university, I gather I can go enlist as an officer, which should be a damned sight better than sleeping in a barracks with a hundred other men. I'm trying to think whether I want army, navy or naval air arm. I think flying might be quite a lark.*

Ellie stared down at the letter. Quite a lark. Being shot at by enemy aeroplanes. How could the young be so stupid? And yet she knew it was no good writing back to tell him to take a safe desk job. She remembered young men in the last war who couldn't wait to join up and get to the battlefield—and so many of those young men didn't come back or came back horribly damaged: maimed, gassed, mentally disturbed. And then there was Richard, already in the army, his regiment presumably being sent to an arena of conflict. *My boys,* she thought, and stared down at the village. How many young men from the village families would go and not return?

Bruno's mother came to see her with consternation. Bruno had received a summons to join the French army. "He can't go and fight," Bruno's mother said. "He's just like a child. He won't understand."

Ellie had a word with the doctor, who wrote a stern letter exempting him on account of mental incompetency. Bruno's mother hugged Ellie and kissed her when she found out. So Bruno was to be spared, but not the baker's son, or Luc, married to the baker's daughter, or the two sons of François the fisherman. They all went out, proudly wearing uniforms, boasting how they were going to stop Hitler.

September became October. They had been in Saint-Benet for a year, but it seemed inappropriate to have a party. Instead they dined at Henri's with Tommy and Clive, thus giving him business after the visitors had departed. Henri produced a beautiful beef bourguignon for them. "I don't know how long we'll be able to get good supplies," he said. "So make the most of it while we can. Frankly, I don't know if I'll be able to stay open if no visitors come or if they start implementing rationing. Damn that Hitler—that's what I say."

But nothing dire happened. Ellie took care of Jojo, went out in the motorboat, sometimes alone, sometimes with Nico, with whom she had developed an easy camaraderie. Dora continued swimming for a while, although she had given up her painting lessons. "One realizes when one has no talent," she said. With the wintery weather she read, painted and slept a lot. Ellie watched the palm trees bending and swaying crazily as rain battered the windows. Roland had gone back to Paris, saying he was sure the Maginot Line would keep the Germans at bay and there was good theatre and opera to see. They went to Midnight Mass on Christmas Eve, where Father André offered prayers for their safety and the safety of France. Their presents were meaningful ones, given the situation: a bottle of good cognac for Dora, a pair of shoes for Mavis, a box of English Black Magic chocolates for Tommy and Clive. "Who knows when we'll see these things again?" Ellie said.

But 1940 dawned, and still Saint-Benet slumbered peacefully, hearing news of distant battles, German invasions of French colonies, but nothing that impacted France. The chickens laid eggs, the young nanny goat produced milk and Ellie learned to milk her without getting kicked or butted. Spring vegetables appeared. Everyone in Saint-Benet began to feel hopeful that this was a war that, while terrible, affected other people.

On March 12, Jojo turned one year old. She had grown into a pretty little girl with dark curls and dark eyes, already toddling around, chasing the cat, saying her first words in a mixture of French and English. Ellie was adamant that she learned both. She called Ellie "Maman" and Dora and Mavis "Tante" or "Auntie." Ellie would watch her with pride and love as she practiced walking in the garden, chasing birds, holding out her hand to be splashed by the fountain and then squealing with delight. And she relived those happy first years with her boys. Where were they now? she worried. She hadn't heard anything since a Christmas card from Colin saying he was still in training in Surrey but Richard had been moved to the Far East. She continued to write to them, hoping the letters would finally reach them, sending them love and prayers for safety.

On Easter Sunday they went to church, and Henri roasted a whole lamb for the inhabitants of Saint-Benet. Ellie's thought was that it would soon be May. Would the boat take people across to the island this year? She looked forward to seeing the abbot.

"I should go into Marseille while we can," she said to Dora. "Jojo is outgrowing everything. If I buy some fabrics, we can make her new outfits for the summer. Do you want to come?"

"I think not, my dear," Dora said. "I find it tiring enough going upstairs to bed these days. But perhaps you could look for English books for me to read. I've got through everything we have, and one can only read P. G. Wodehouse so many times."

"Of course." Ellie kissed her forehead. She paused, looking back at the older woman. It was true that Dora was fading. She had taken on an ethereal look, her skin like parchment. Only her eyes still had life in them. She saw Dora watching her in her turn and smiled as she walked away. As she went down the garden path towards the motor car, she saw the gate opening and someone coming towards her. It took a moment to recognize it was Yvette.

CHAPTER 30

Yvette took one look at Jojo and ran towards her, arms open. "My little child," she called. "My precious little child. Look at you. How beautiful you are. How you've grown. Come to maman, ma chérie."

And she swept up the little girl into her arms, covering her with kisses.

"I've come to take you home," she went on.

Jojo tried to squirm out of her embrace and let out a loud wail, holding out her hands to Ellie. "Maman!" she cried.

"This lady is not your maman," Yvette said, swinging her away. "I am Maman. She was just looking after you until I came back."

"What were you doing, Yvette?" Ellie demanded, her voice taut. "A whole year and we hear nothing from you. Then you show up as if nothing has happened and want to take your child back?"

"Of course," Yvette said. "Before, I could not look after her. Now I can." She glanced back, and Ellie saw that a man had entered the garden behind her. He was lean and dark skinned, and he moved with an animal stealth. He stared at Ellie with utter contempt as he came towards them.

"Is this Pierre?" Ellie asked.

"No," Yvette said. "I tired of waiting for Pierre. This is Ali. He will take good care of us."

"No!" Ellie said loudly. "I can't let you take her. You've shown yourself to be irresponsible before. What's to say you won't decide a baby is an annoyance and leave her? Abandon her somewhere? She has a good home here. Everything she needs."

"But I am her mother. You can't keep her. By law she is mine, and I can prove it," Yvette said. "The doctor signed the birth certificate with my name on it. You can't stop me from taking her."

"I can go to the police and prove that you are not a good mother," Ellie said.

"They will laugh in your face." The lean man joined Yvette. "She is the rightful mother. It is her child. You were just the nursemaid. There is no more to be said."

"Absolutely not," Ellie said. "I will fight for her."

The lean man moved forwards until he was a few inches from Ellie's face. "It is not wise to cross those you don't know and who might be more powerful than you. Bad things can happen. So go back to your house and do your knitting with the other old women."

Ellie was afraid, but she wasn't about to back down. "Very well," she said. "But then you owe me for all the money I have spent taking care of this child for a year—nappies, formula, clothing, bedding. And the jewellery you stole from us. I expect to be compensated. I can take you to court."

He stared at her, an insolent smirk on his face. Then he reached into his pocket, took out some banknotes and flung them at her feet. "There," he said. "And you should go back where you came from before it's too late. You are not wanted in France." He turned to Yvette. "Come. Let us go."

"Don't you even want any of her things? Her toy dog? Her nappies?"

"We came on a motorbike," Ali said. "We can't carry unnecessary items. She will have new ones."

"Do you even know how to feed her? How to bathe her?" Jojo was still squirming in Yvette's arms, holding out her little hands to Ellie.

"Maman," she cried piteously.

"Do you think my family has never raised a child before?" Ali said. "She will lack for nothing. Let's go." He put an arm on Yvette's back and steered her towards the gate. Ellie wanted to run after them, to snatch the child from her arms, but she was all too aware that this man was dangerous and probably violent. She stood like a statue as she heard a motorbike roar to life and then the sound fade as it went down the long driveway.

Tears were running down her cheeks as she went back to the house. Dora and Mavis were standing there, having witnessed the whole thing.

"It's what you wanted, my dear." Dora put a hand on her shoulder. "You always hoped that her mother would come for her again."

"But not like this. Not with that man. I feel so helpless, Dora. There's nothing I can do. She is the mother. She does have the birth certificate. I'm afraid that man was right. We were just the nursemaids."

"Come on in and have a cup of tea." Mavis reached out for her. Ellie shrugged her off.

"Just leave me for a moment," Ellie said. "I need to be alone."

She rushed out into the garden. There was a bench against one wall, with wisteria spilling around it. She collapsed on to this, and putting her hands up to her face, she sobbed. She was not conscious of someone standing over her until a voice said, "What is wrong?"

She looked up to see Nico standing there. He sank to the bench beside her. "What has upset you so?"

"The girl came back—Yvette. She took Jojo, and I couldn't stop her." The words came out in gasps between sobs.

"But didn't you want her to come back? Now you don't have responsibility for the child."

"But she's with an awful man. And I'm afraid Yvette will find Jojo a nuisance and just abandon her again. And I loved her so much. She was the little girl I never had . . ."

"There now." He took her into his arms, and she continued to sob against his rough jacket front. He stroked her hair. "You did your best. You gave the child a good start. She would have wound up in an orphanage if you hadn't cared for her."

She looked up, realizing now who he was and how they were sitting together so closely. She straightened up instantly. "I'm so sorry. I've made your jacket wet."

He laughed. "I'm a fisherman. I'm used to wet jackets."

"But what are you doing here during daylight hours? Isn't your activity normally in the nighttime?"

"If you want to know, I am stocking up on oil and petrol for my boat. In case there are shortages. I may store some of the oil cans in the garage here. I am going to put in a big tank down by the dock and keep it full of petrol. It is well hidden down there, I think."

"Does the dock actually belong to this house?" she asked. "Does the owner know?"

"He does. And fully approves," Nico said. "You need not worry about me or what I do. For now it is all legitimate. If things get worse later, who can say?"

"Do you think they will?"

"Oh yes," he said. "I think there is no way that France can come through this unscathed."

Ellie stood up, now horribly self-conscious at the intimacy. "I shouldn't keep you," she said. "You've been most kind. Thank you."

"What else are friends for?" he said, rising, too. "You are my friend, aren't you?"

"I hope so," Ellie replied.

"Then that is good." He put his hands on her shoulders, pulled her towards him and kissed her forehead. "Go back to your ladies. All will be well."

He watched as she walked back to the house, then went on his way.

Inside Ellie found that Mavis had made tea.

"Come and sit down, love," she said. "I expect it's all for the best. If there's going to be rationing, and that's what they are saying, we couldn't get a ration card for her, could we?"

"Or for ourselves," Dora said. "Maybe this is the time to reconsider and go home while we can still cross the Channel."

"Maybe it is," Ellie said. She looked around her. *I love this place,* she thought, *but now every day will remind me what I have lost.*

"Oh." Mavis stared, shook her head. "You really want to go back there? Where would we go?"

"I have my cottage still," Dora said.

"Oh Dora, I wouldn't want to live in the same village as Lionel and that woman," Ellie said. "I do have a flat in London. It's rented now, but we could always . . ."

"London would be the worst place to go," Mavis said. "It's bound to be bombed, isn't it? If you want my opinion, I don't want to go back there. In England I was nothing. The charwoman. Mop your floors and get treated like dirt."

"I hope I never treated you that way, Mavis," Ellie said.

"Of course not. You were lovely. But here it's different. People treat me as one of them. I feel like I belong more than I ever did in England. And then there's Louis . . ."

"You're fond of him, aren't you?" Dora asked.

Mavis went pink. "He's a lovely man. Kind. Gentle. All the things Reg wasn't."

"I don't really want to go home, either," Dora said. "I want to die here, looking out at this view, not in some grim English hospital."

"I agree. I'm not keen to go back there," Ellie said. "This feels like home to me now. Should we look into applying for French nationality, just in case?"

"Give up being British, you mean? I don't think I'm prepared to do that," Dora said. "Besides, I believe that Mr Tommy said you had to have been a resident here for five years before you could apply. So that's not going to work."

"I'm just worried what might happen when rationing starts. There is already a mention of it in the newspapers."

"The newspaper!" Mavis said out loud. "That's it! That's where I saw that bloke before."

They both turned to her as if she had gone crazy. She was waving excitedly. "Remember when we were first staying at the pension, and we were looking at a newspaper, and it had the picture of a gang of bank robbers? One of them looked just like him."

"Like whom?" Ellie asked.

"The bloke that came with Yvette just now. I'd swear it was him."

"Oh Mavis," Dora said. "I'm sure most Arabic men would look similar to you."

"But no, listen," Mavis went on excitedly. "Remember when we were at the pension and Yvette came into the room and acted startled? She claimed it was because she had never seen the sea before. Well, what if it was because she saw their picture? Those blokes were her mates? One of them was that Pierre, and another was that bloke. And she was part of the gang. And when we picked her up, she was on the run, so she played up to us so that we'd hide her and keep her out of sight until everything blew over."

Ellie and Dora stared at her, digesting this.

"So her lover wasn't an innocent young man who only stole to allow them to be married. He was a crook, a gangster," Dora said. "That makes sense. That's why she always hid away when we had guests. In case she was recognized."

"You mean we've let Jojo go off with criminals?" Ellie said.

"We had no choice, and frankly, my dear, we are well rid of them," Dora replied. "What if Yvette had stayed and they had decided this villa would be a perfect hideout? We could have done nothing. They might have conveniently killed all of us and taken over. Frankly I think we might have dodged a bullet here, both for ourselves and for Saint-Benet."

CHAPTER 31

Even though she told herself it was all for the best, grief continued to consume Ellie by day and plague her dreams at night. Memories of holding Jojo on her lap, having her nestle against her shoulder, felt like a physical wound. Mavis and Dora were concerned for her. They quietly packed up all of Jojo's things and stored them in a trunk where Ellie wouldn't see them. But Ellie kept the stuffed dog and slept with it, hugging it to her. Tiger, the cat, also sensed her mood and curled up beside her on the bed or on the lounge chair. The loss was like a hole in her heart, and she dreamed, night after night, of the little girl being hit or abandoned by the roadside. It was awful to feel so powerless. As she lay, unable to fall asleep, she'd go over and over the scene in her mind, wondering what she could have done to have reached a different outcome. If she had offered them money to go away? But then they'd know she had money available and might come after her. And Yvette was the child's mother, she told herself. Maybe she would love Jojo and treat her well. She tried to believe this.

On the first Sunday of May, the ferry boat showed up as usual to take visitors to the abbey. When Ellie went to board, she found the quayside crowded—some trippers newly arrived from the north and curious to see the abbey, others to check on sons and brothers and yet others to buy what produce they could from the monks to preserve for a potentially barren winter ahead. Ellie found herself holding her breath as the boat neared the island. She so wanted to see Abbot Gerard again.

She wanted to hear his comforting voice and was sure he'd have words that would help sooth away the hurt she was carrying. But apart from a brief nod and how-are-you pleasantries, she never got a chance to speak to him. It seemed that someone was claiming his attention every second, and she boarded the boat back angry and frustrated.

Then there were bigger things to worry about. On May 10 the Germans swept around the north of the Maginot Line and poured into France from the north. The French army was unable to resist them. Gradually they moved further and further into France, pushing the Allied troops west until they were trapped on the beaches of Dunkirk. Ellie and the women listened, horrified, on the radio as the evacuation was reported and, miraculously, almost all the soldiers were brought across to England in small boats.

"Well, there goes our escape route," Dora said as she turned off the radio. "The Germans now hold the Channel ports. If we wanted to leave here, it would have to be Spain or Portugal."

"I don't speak Spanish," Ellie said, "And I don't agree at all with how Franco has behaved against his fellow countrymen. And I don't want to start all over again. I think we have to hope that we live in a small village and nobody would be interested in us."

It seemed this might be true. Visitors arrived from the rest of France, earlier than usual, some fleeing from Paris and the North, hoping they'd be safely far away from conflict, as they were in the last war. Henri and the Adamses were happy they had more than enough customers. Ellie sat at the piano, trying to remember pieces she had known by heart, her fingers stumbling with lack of practice. She'd have to see if the doctor's wife had music she could borrow. She had hoped that the music would soothe her but found that the tunes she remembered were loaded with indescribable longing. She threw herself into work, tending to the chickens and goat, which she continued to milk even though she and Dora did not care for the taste of goat's milk. She planted as many vegetables as possible, coaxing the tomatoes and lemon tree back into production. One day Mavis came out to help her, finding her putting up strings against the trellis for the beans and peas. They were quiet for a while, then Mavis said, "I've been waiting to tell you this, but there never seems to be a good time."

Those echoed Lionel's words when he announced his intention to divorce Ellie. She looked up sharply. "What?"

Mavis gave a little smile. "Louis has asked me to marry him. He wants to make sure I'll be taken care of if it comes to being a French citizen."

"Oh Mavis," Ellie said. "I suppose I'm happy for you."

Mavis had gone pink. "He asked me quite a while ago, but I didn't like to leave you in the lurch. But now you don't have all that extra work with the baby I thought it was the right time. I'll come over and help you with the house and the chickens . . ."

"Mavis, you don't have to. You don't owe me anything."

"Of course I do," Mavis said. "You've given me a whole new life. You've let me be happy for the first time ever. I can never repay you for that. And I wouldn't want to just walk away, but Louis is a good man, and I think I could be happy with him."

"I think you could, too," Ellie said. "Well, God bless you. When are you planning to do this?"

"As soon as possible now," Mavis said. "I thought you and I might go into Marseille and see if I can find some fabric to make a wedding outfit. Oh, nothing daft like a long white dress, but something special. Something to celebrate when everything around us is gloom."

"Yes," Ellie said. "Good idea."

Dora gave her blessing right away. "I am delighted for you, my dear," she said. "If any of us deserves happiness, it's you. You've spent your life taking care of other people. Now it's your turn." And she gave Mavis a nice amount of cash—"for your trousseau, if people still have trousseaus in wartime."

So Ellie drove Mavis into Marseille, and they picked up some pale-blue silk dotted with flowers for the dress and some white silk for undergarments, because, as Mavis said, "I wouldn't want to show him my flannel bloomers." And some heavier fabric for a smart suit. Then they added shoes and a handbag. Mavis stared at it all in wonder. "I ain't never seen such lovely things in my whole life. I don't know what I've done to deserve them."

She went to work, sewing feverishly. The result was most satisfying, and she stared at herself in the mirror. "Blimey. If Reg could see me now," she said. "He'd realize what he lost, poor bugger. I suppose I can feel more charitable towards him now. He was a soldier in the trenches. He must have seen plenty of things that unsettled him and made him how he was."

Ellie also bought herself a new dress and hat, plus a hat for Dora, because she feared there might be no new clothes for a long time. On June 14, the German tanks rolled into Paris. Everyone in Saint-Benet listened to the news in stunned silence, then wept and embraced.

"Those English soldiers let us down," one of the men said. "They ran for the coast with their tails between their legs and abandoned us to the Germans."

"At least they lived to fight another day," Ellie replied. "Better than all being killed or taken as German captives. Everyone expected the Maginot Line to hold."

"Those Nazis had been planning this for years," someone else added. "They've been rearming secretly while we were caught unprepared—both of us. France and England."

"Well, there's nothing we can do now," the doctor's wife said. "Let's just hope that they are only interested in the industrial north, and we have nothing for them down here."

~~

It seemed this was going to be true. France was to be divided into the occupied zone in the north and the free zone in the south. Everyone listening on the radio heaved a sigh of relief. The free zone was to be governed by the new French government—puppets put in place by the

Germans. Nobody approved of this, of course. "But they will have the interests of the French people at heart," was the common sentiment. "They'll do their best for us."

Mavis's wedding happened a few days later at the village church. Mavis not being Catholic had presented a problem, but she had to swear that she would raise any offspring in the Catholic faith. She thought this hilarious. "At my age," she said. "That would be another miracle."

Dora and Ellie were her attendants. The church was packed, as Louis was a popular figure and everyone wanted a chance to celebrate. Henri managed to get his hands on a young goat and it was roasted on a spit outside the bar. Everyone brought items for the feast—fruits, cheese, bread and wine. One of the men brought his accordion. There were toasts, ribald comments, much laughter, then singing and dancing. Ellie sat silently, observing as the celebration went on around her. Mavis, her face alight with joy as she danced with Louis, then with one of the fishermen after another. Dora, her eyes sparkling as she clapped to the music. Ellie's eyes moved to Nico, sitting with his mother in the shade, smiling. As if he sensed his eyes on her, he turned to look. Their eyes met. He winked. For a moment she thought he was going to come over and ask her to dance, but he didn't. She felt absurdly disappointed.

Ellie saw Dora flagging about ten o'clock and drove her home, but she stood out on the terrace listening to the music and laughter. Dora came out beside her.

"Who would have thought it was our little Mavis who made the whole village forget the tragedy of war?" Dora said.

Ellie continued to stare out into the darkness. "I hope we're doing the right thing, Dora," she said. "I hope we won't regret not going back to England."

"I think we're going to be all right," Dora said. "We're in the free zone, and if anyone invades us, it will be the Italians. They are so easygoing that I can't think they'd be brutal invaders. We'd offer them some wine and cheese and be their friends for life."

Ellie had to laugh. "Oh Dora," she said. "I hope you are right." She put a hand on the old woman's shoulder. "I am glad you're here."

Dora placed her own hand over Ellie's. "You have been a great blessing to me," she said. "I want you to know that this has been the happiest time of my life for many, many years."

They remained there, as the gentle breeze blew in from the sea, tinged with salt and seaweed, and the sounds of the wedding floated up towards them.

～

Mavis and Louis went on honeymoon up to a nearby hill town where a cousin owned an auberge. Ellie lent Louis the Bentley for the occasion. He was embarrassingly grateful. Ellie had no qualms about this—if anyone could mend the car if it broke down, it was Louis. And it was really no inconvenience. She rarely had to drive anywhere, except for taking Dora down to the village now that she couldn't manage the steps. This didn't happen often any more. Dora was content to sit in the sun, feasting her eyes on the view, watching passing ships or observing the activities of the village below.

The day after the wedding Ellie received a note, hand-delivered, from the viscount. He had returned. Would she like to come to lunch? She found Dora, already in her favourite chair on the patio, her journal and a book on her lap, unopened.

"You'll be all right, will you?" she asked Dora. "I've put out some pâté and salad for you in the kitchen."

"I really am quite content, my dear. All is well. Go and enjoy yourself. Give my best wishes to the viscount," Dora said.

Ellie bent to give her a little kiss on the cheek, then gave herself a final check in the hallway mirror. She realized she didn't have the convenience of the motor car but decided there must be a shortcut between properties by following the water pipes. She arrived, a little out of breath, and stood in the shade of a large pine tree to collect herself before she came around the swimming pool to the house. Roland was sitting on the terrace facing the swimming pool and looked up, startled to see her coming from the wrong direction.

"Mon Dieu, how did you get here?" he asked. "I did not hear the automobile."

"I've lent it to a friend," Ellie said. "I came over the hill from my property. It's more of a hike than I expected."

"My dear, sit down, please. We'll have Antoine bring you a citron pressé to revive you." He rang a bell. His butler appeared almost as if by magic, and the drink was ordered. Ellie sat.

"You've come back," she said. "I'm so glad. I was worried about you when we heard that Paris fell."

"I was fortunately at my family home in the Loire Valley," he said. "My mother was dying. The prodigal son went to make his peace."

"I'm so sorry. Did she die?"

"She did, before the invasion. That would have broken her heart. She was fiercely French and hated the Germans." He gave a sigh. "I left as soon as I heard they had invaded. And fortunate for me that I did, as our home is now in the occupied zone. I told my father to come with me to my villa, but he is a stubborn fool and insisted on remaining on his property so the Germans don't take it over. As it is I've had to abandon my lovely Paris house. Le Bon Dieu knows what will happen to that. Trashed by the enemy, I suppose. Looted at the very least. I have some fine artwork. I sent a telegram to my notaire before I departed, asking him to go to the house and put my most valuable things in the wine cellar, where there is a big storeroom. They should be safe there, unless the house is ever bombed."

"But you got away safely," Ellie said. "I do not imagine it will be easy to leave the occupied zone after this."

"Of course not. One hears that the place is crawling with Nazis. Tanks everywhere. Brutes with jackboots. And I'm sure they'd love to beat up men like me. But I hope we can remain safe down here. They've put a puppet government in place, as no doubt you've heard. Men who are willing to lick the boots of the invaders in return for a little bit of power. I'm sure there are plenty of sadists and homophobes amongst them, so I will lie low here until the situation is resolved."

"You think the war will end that easily?" Ellie asked. "Look at the last one. We all thought it would be over in weeks, and yet they were dug into those stupid trenches for four years, with all those men dying every day."

He shrugged. "I don't think it will be the same sort of war this time. Those old cavalry generals are long dead. Hitler is bent on conquest, that is obvious. I think we will see a repeat of Napoleon—swallowing up Europe and then ultimately meeting his doom—unless someone assassinates him first, which is always a possibility."

"Napoleon lasted a long while before Waterloo," Ellie said.

"We'll ride it out here," he replied. "My wine cellar is well stocked. That's all that matters." He paused, regarding her. "But you—why have you not returned to your homeland? Do you fear that England, too, will be invaded?"

"Oh Roland," she said. "I have nothing to return to. No family, except my sons, who will both be fighting to protect us. I have no home. This is my home now. I have people like you, like the rest of the inhabitants of Saint-Benet, and I have Dora. She's certainly not up to travelling in arduous circumstances. Like you, I'm prepared to ride it out."

A delicious lunch was served on the terrace—a seafood terrine, veal cutlet with a mushroom sauce and then petit fours and cognac.

"I should get back." Ellie stood up. "Thank you for a lovely lunch. It almost makes one forget there is war raging in the rest of the world."

"I intend to keep my own little corner of paradise for as long as I can," Roland said. "I suppose the only good thing one can say about the damned Germans is that they are rounding up their Jews. If they insist on race purity, at least you and I are quite safe." He laughed, then reached for a cigarette, placing it into his long ebony holder.

Ellie went to express disapproval at this sentiment, but Roland had already moved on easily to the next topic.

She found the return trip more arduous than the way there, with the effects of the wine and the heat of the sun later in the day. She let herself quietly into the house as Dora usually took an afternoon sleep in her bedroom. The house slumbered in delightful coolness. Ellie tiptoed up the stairs and peeped into Dora's bedroom. The bed was empty. She went downstairs again, into the sitting room, and saw that Dora was still on the terrace, still looking out on to the view.

"Oh, there you are," she said, opening the French doors and going out. "I hope you've had lunch."

Dora did not reply. Ellie saw that she was asleep. She touched Dora's arm gently and recoiled in surprise. The arm was cold. It took her a moment to realize that Dora was dead. Ellie dropped to her knees beside the old woman, stroking the veined hand. "I'm so sorry," she said. "I should have been here." Then she understood, with utter clarity, that Dora had chosen her moment to die when Ellie did not have to witness it. She had slipped away without causing a fuss. So typical of her.

"Oh Dora." She picked up the dead hand and held it against her cheek. "What am I going to do without you?" she whispered.

CHAPTER 32

Dora was buried in the small cemetery behind the church, beside fishermen who had drowned a hundred years ago, all surnames that Ellie recognized. Father André was kind enough to admit her to a Catholic burial ground because, as he said, "The good Lord loves us all." He said a simple blessing over her. Tommy and Clive, the doctor and his wife, Henri and Monsieur Danton stood as witnesses as flowers were dropped on to her coffin. Mavis and Louis were still on their honeymoon, and Ellie didn't want it spoiled by this news. Instead she watched as if she were observing a film, something not real. She couldn't imagine life without the old lady. But she stood, stoic and proud, in her black dress and her black cotton gloves. Afterwards they had a drink and a simple snack at Henri's, and she went home to an empty house.

How big it seemed. How echoing and empty. Ellie walked from room to room, finding traces of Dora in each of them. Tiger followed her, occasionally giving a plaintive meow as if he shared her mourning.

"I know," she said. "She's gone, Tiger. She's not here."

She went into Dora's meticulously neat bedroom. Her journal lay on her bedside table, where Ellie had placed it. Feeling uneasy she opened it, looking at page after page of Dora's perfect, copperplate handwriting. She saw a lot of the pages were poems, and the latest one:

I see the way ahead quite clear.
I take those steps. I have no fear.
For all ahead is good and gold,
And all my story has been told . . .

Tears welled in Ellie's eyes. She clutched the journal to her, carried it to her bedroom and placed it on her bedside table. She would read it when she felt she could handle it without breaking down.

"I'm all alone," she said. No Mavis, no Jojo and now no Dora. Nobody. Bruno no longer came up so often, preferring to stay home with his mother, still fearful about news he didn't really understand. Besides, Bruno, while sweet and lovable, would not understand her hopelessness. She could, of course, go to see Tommy and Clive. They'd ply her with food and drink and make her smile, but she wasn't ready for that. She wasn't really ready to talk to anybody. Tiger jumped on to the bed and rubbed up against her, purring. She stroked him and he climbed on to her lap.

"At least I've got you," she said. "You're all I've got now."

After a few days of silence and emptiness, she felt as if she had to talk to someone, and the face that swam into her consciousness was the abbot's. But the next ferry was two weeks away, and last time she had not been able to get anywhere near him. She stood up, making a decision. She would take Nico's boat if he wasn't using it. She grabbed a headscarf and a jacket and marched down the steps. Nico was sitting on the waterfront, talking with some people she didn't recognize. Her heart lurched—what if he was about to take them out in the boat? Ellie hung back, unwilling to interrupt a private conversation, but Nico saw her, waved.

"Where have you been?" he asked. "I haven't seen you in a while."

"Miss Smith-Humphries died," she said. "I didn't feel like being sociable."

"And now you do?"

"Not really," she said. "I was wondering if you need your boat this morning."

"Not so far," he said.

"I wanted to go over to the abbey."

"The abbey? You are about to become a nun now that your friend is dead?" He gave one of his cheeky smiles.

"That would hardly be the place since they are all men," she replied, giving him a stern look for making a joke. "But no. There is something I wanted to discuss with the abbot."

"It must be important since it is not their usual visiting day."

"It is," she said. "So do you think I could have the boat? It shouldn't take much more than an hour."

"I'll drive you if you like," he said. "I wouldn't mind taking a look at the place for myself."

Her immediate thought was that he wanted to find a good site to hide smuggled goods, or maybe black market goods, and what better than a holy island. She shook her head. "Thank you, but I'd rather be alone if you don't mind."

"Suit yourself." He frowned, and she saw he was disappointed. Was it being denied her company or denied seeing the island that had produced that look?

"I'm not good company at the moment," she added. "I'll be back quickly."

And without waiting for him to say any more, she hurried down the steps to the harbour and climbed into the boat, finding the key and then setting the ropes free. As she emerged from the harbour, she relished the breeze in her face. She pushed the throttle and felt the power as the boat shot forward. The sea was a pure dark blue and smooth as glass, and suddenly she was conscious of shapes in the water beside her. Two dolphins broke the surface, keeping up with her as if enjoying the fun.

"Oh," she gasped, entranced. It was almost as if it was a sign. Maybe one of those dolphins was Dora, as she had loved to swim and had regretted that she wouldn't be able to make it over the rocks to the beach any longer. The dolphins kept up with the boat for a minute or two, and then they vanished again, leaving only miles of smooth blue sea. As the boat approached the island, she saw monks working in the gardens, black figures, some with cowls over their heads. That was good. She wouldn't have to intrude too far. She eased the boat to the dock, tied it up and was halfway up the flight of steps when one of the monks loomed over her.

"No, madame. You cannot come here," he called out. "This is a monastery. A holy place."

"I know," she called back. "I came to see your abbot. If he could spare me a few minutes of his time, it's quite important."

"He knows about this?"

"Not this visit, but he knows me. Please tell him that Ellie Endicott needs to see him." As she spoke she came up the rest of the steps. The monk had his cowl back, and she saw he was very young—younger than her boys. She gave him an encouraging, motherly smile. He nodded, put down the hoe he had been using and walked away. Ellie sat on the bench close to the steps. Other monks kept at their tasks and did not look up. It was a pleasant place to wait. Roses climbed a trellis behind her, and the air hummed with the buzz of bees. The scent of flowers mixed with the smell of the sea below, and she listened to the gentle slap and hiss of waves on the rocks. As she sat there a bell tolled, the sound echoing out over the stillness. The monks put down their tools and headed back to the monastery. Ellie was afraid that this would mean the abbot, too, would be required at some form of service. But then she heard the slap of sandals on the sandy path, looked around and saw him coming towards her.

"I came as soon as I could," he said. "You wanted to see me? There is an emergency?"

"Not an emergency," Ellie said, feeling foolish now. "I'm sorry. Perhaps I shouldn't have come, but I just needed words of wisdom, and you are the only person I know I could talk to."

"You are in distress. I see it in your face," he said. He sat beside her on the bench. "Are you frightened because you are now trapped here by the war?"

"I suppose I am," she said. "Now I question my decision to remain here."

"And now you think it is too late to depart?"

She nodded. "It is. The route north through France is now closed to me. I suppose I could make for Portugal through Spain, but what would be the point of a country where I don't speak the language?"

"Would you rather be back in England? You miss it?"

She thought about this. "Not really. My life was comfortable there, but boring. And I had no true friends."

"So why would you wish to go back? Because it is safer? I do not think this will be true. Hitler will want Britain more than he wants the South of France."

Ellie nodded. "I think I know this. It was fine when I had my friends with me, but now I find myself alone," Ellie said. And she told him about Jojo, and Dora and Mavis. "I had everything I desired, people I loved and who loved me. And one by one they have been taken away. I have this lovely big house and beautiful view but nobody to share it with. I sit down to my supper in silence. I'm afraid, I wonder what's going to happen to me, what I'm doing here, and if I made a terrible mistake."

He nodded. "Grief is a powerful emotion," he said. "It consumes one. It saps the ability to see joy. And you add this to the terrible news we hear, so much suffering, the defeat of good people . . . No wonder you feel lost. Even we, who have the peace and safety of the abbey, feel the great disturbance in the fabric of humanity. So what would you want me to tell you?"

"How to keep going," she said. "No, it's more than that. How to believe. I told you before that I've only gone through the motions of Christianity. I've never really prayed, and I'm afraid at this moment I seriously wonder if there is a God."

"I can only tell you from my own experience, but I have to say that yes, there definitely is a power behind this universe. Call him what you will. I personally believe that he sent down his son to save us, and his son gave us the mandate to save those around us. So I think if you want to heal, you should start by doing that: reach out to others, do what you can to make their lives better. And reach out to God, too. Prayers don't have to be elaborate things. Why don't you start with three things you're blessed with, three things you're afraid of and finally three things you ask of him? And don't forget to listen, too."

"Listen? He talks back to you?"

"Oh yes. Not always a great voice in the silence, but sometimes I get up from my knees absolutely sure of what I have to do. Sometimes I just feel a comforting presence, that invisible hand on my shoulder saying, 'Don't worry, my son. I'm here with you, whatever happens.'"

"I wish I had that belief," she said. "How I envy you."

"Belief has to be worked at the same as any other skill," he said. "Try practicing it. Go to church every Sunday. Let God see that you're trying hard." And he smiled, his eyes crinkling at the sides.

"Would it be possible to come out here and see you from time to time?" she asked.

"It depends why you wish to come," he said. "Your real motive."

"My motive?" She was confused.

He nodded. "I wonder. Am I a male figure you can fall in love with, but who is quite safe from your having to get more intimate with?"

"Oh." It felt like a slap in the face. "No. Not at all." She shook her head vehemently.

"You are still a young woman," he went on.

Ellie had to smile. "I'm almost fifty-two."

"Young at heart. You have been betrayed by one man, and so you make sure you don't get too close to any other man, in case it happens again. But I am unreachable, therefore safe."

"Oh no," she said again, but then added quietly, "You may be right."

"You might also consider that this is a temptation for me. You saw how quickly we established a rapport. We definitely felt a spark of shall I say attraction . . . between us."

"So you are telling me you don't want me to come again."

"Not at all. I'm just saying we have to make sure we understand that we must tread lightly, analyse our feelings. Be honest about this with each other."

"Yes," she said. "I would not want to cause you any embarrassment or discomfort."

"Then I would suggest an occasional visit. Come with the ferry, and I will make time for you, but don't rely on me and my comfort as your main support. Find that elsewhere. My words for you are that being alone is not healthy. That is why we men live in a community as we strive for holiness. Make sure you reach out to others. Believe me when I say that we are all going to need the support of those around us very soon. The war has not touched us yet, but it will. There will be sorrow and suffering and need, and we all must make sure that we do our part to bring a little light into that darkness."

He got up then, took her hands, holding them for a long minute before he released her and gave a blessing. "Go with God," he said.

Ellie walked away, her hands warm from his touch. She realized that everything he had said was true. She would have to be careful. She was already more than a little in love with him.

CHAPTER 33

Mavis returned from her honeymoon looking radiant. That pinched, hollow, sallow face had bloomed into a happy one. "We had the best time, Mrs E.," she said as she arrived at the villa one morning. "It was this pretty little village with smashing views all over the countryside—lots of vineyards and olive groves, and Louis knew everybody, so we were being invited to people's houses for one meal after another. They were amazed how quickly I learned French. Of course I didn't like to tell them that the way they nattered on so quickly I could only pick up one word in a sentence. I did a lot of nodding and saying, 'Oui, oui.'"

"I'm so glad for you, Mavis," Ellie said. "I can't tell you how glad I am."

Mavis paused, looked around. "What's up?" she said. "Something ain't right, is it?"

"It's Dora," Ellie said. "She died last week."

"Oh no. Poor Dora. Why didn't you send a telegram? I'd have come home."

"As if I'd disturb your honeymoon, Mavis."

"But you were all on your own. You had to cope with her funeral yourself. I'm so sorry. I feel terrible."

"You've nothing to feel sorry about. Everyone was very kind. She's buried in the cemetery here. And she died quite content, I'm sure. She said this was the happiest time of her life."

"But what are you going to do now? You're all alone in this big place. Don't worry. I'll come and help you clean and manage the gardens and the chickens. And you've still got Bruno."

"Mavis, you have your own life now," Ellie said. "I'd certainly appreciate a little help now and then, and of course I welcome your company, but I don't want you to feel torn between helping me and looking after your husband."

"Oh, Louis won't mind." Mavis laughed. "He's been on his own for so long now he's good at taking care of himself. He's quite a good cook, and his taste in food is really simple. If you give him bread, cheese and wine, he's quite happy. You must come down to our house for a meal. If only it were a bit bigger, I'd invite you to come and live with us, but . . ."

"Mavis, I wouldn't dream of barging in on newlyweds," Ellie said. "I love this house, as you know. And I've got Tiger, who has become quite affectionate. And Babette the goat. And the viscount has returned. I've been for lunch with him."

"You want to work on him, ducks," Mavis said, giving her a nudge. "Maybe he needs a wife."

"Oh goodness, no," Ellie laughed. "He absolutely does not want a wife. His great love was another man. Besides, he's much younger than I am, and I think he'd be impossible to live with. He's rather a spoiled little boy. Quite delightful to chat with, but I think one could take him only in small doses." She paused, considering. "Besides, I can't see myself getting married again. I had one selfish and annoying husband, and that was enough."

"But what will you do once this new government starts throwing their weight around? Louis says they'll do what the Germans tell them, even though we're in the free zone. They might think that you're the enemy."

"I have to take that risk," Ellie said. "I can't go back to England, and I've nowhere else to go. Besides, I feel safe here. I think everyone will look after me."

"I hope you're right. You never know who your friends are until they are tested."

～

Ellie thought about this after Mavis had gone that afternoon. Did she have any real friends here? She enjoyed Roland's company, and Tommy and Clive. She found Nico fascinating but was wary of him. The doctor and his wife gave civilized little soirées. But which of them would turn on her if they had to? She had no idea. The long, light evenings stretched out in silence, unless she listened to the radio or played the piano. She was improving at the latter, her fingers relearning old, familiar pieces. Occasionally, as she prepared for bed, she would watch Nico moving through the garden. *Should I stop him from coming?* she wondered. *I could appeal to the owner through Monsieur Danton. Are his activities going to put me at risk?* But somehow it was comforting to know that he was close by, if she needed him. She remembered his arms around her when Jojo was taken and how easily she had lain against his chest.

I should find out the truth from him, she thought. *Demand that he tell me, to make sure I'm not harbouring stolen goods.* But she didn't think she would have the nerve to do so.

～

July was not that different from any other summer in Saint-Benet. French holidaymakers came to stay and went to the beach with their sand toys like any other year. Some of them looked into renting rooms on a longer basis. "This place feels as if it will be safe," one of them said. Ellie took the ferry across to the island, again crowded with the curious. She and Abbot Gerard sat together in his office and shared a glass of wine. He told her he was worried about the enemy coming for his monks. Hitler was no great fan of the church, he said. What if his monks were conscripted and sent to work in German factories or even into the German army?

"We haven't seen any sign yet that the Germans are actually interested in what goes on down here," Ellie said.

"So far," he agreed. "I'm sure they'll come for Marseille—the most important port in the Mediterranean. And Toulon. They'll want to take over the French navy ships or disable them. But the Italians . . . Mussolini has had his eye on Nice and Monte Carlo for a long time. Very prosperous places. I can see him trying to invade, to sneak into bits of territory."

"The Italians wouldn't be so bad, would they?" Ellie said. "They've always appeared so easy-going to me."

"Better than Germans, I agree, but when you see newsreels of the Fascist black-shirted bullies, you'll know there are some in every country who enjoy throwing their weight around. But I think we might be safe here. The Germans won't want them to hold Marseille. They might draw a line, and we'll be in no-man's land."

He asked her about coming to terms with her grief.

"I don't think it was grief as much as self-pity at my loneliness," she said. "And fear."

He nodded approval. "So you are already making progress when you can analyse your own feelings," he said. "But of course you mourn your friend. You mourn the child you raised. It's only natural. But grief fades after time. Time is a great healer."

They were interrupted by one of the monks, saying that a government official from Vichy wanted a word with the abbot.

"So now it starts," he said, standing up. "Go with God, my dear."

～

July turned to August with a trickle of summer visitors and hot, humid air. Ellie was glad of the high ceilings and marble floors of the villa. She sat on the back terrace, relishing the breeze from the sea, sipping lemonade from her own lemons. Sometimes she went down the steps into the village and bathed at the beach. On one occasion she was coming back with a robe loosely over her bathing suit when she came across Nico and a group of men at the harbour.

One of the men gave a wolf whistle, then joked: "So the bathing beauties of the Riviera are coming to Saint-Benet now."

Nico scowled at him. "That is not called for," he said. "Madame is still mourning the loss of her friend." He made eye contact with Ellie. "I'm glad to see you out and about, and swimming. Good, healthy activity is what you need."

"Walking up and down those steps is enough activity for anybody to stay fit," Ellie replied. "But then you must know that."

And she walked on, again confused by him. He had stood up for her, rebuked the man who had made an inappropriate comment, but had his own words had a double meaning? She had seen that flash of sparkle in his eyes. She never knew with Nico. That was so infuriating.

～

At the end of August the last of the visitors disappeared and Saint-Benet resumed its sleepy quiet. The news from the outside world was more and more alarming. The Nazis had bombed airfields and factories in England. Battles were raging in the skies over southern England, but so far the Royal Air Force was holding off the might of the Luftwaffe. Then, at the beginning of September, the first bombing raids hit London.

"Aren't you glad you stayed here now?" Mavis asked. She had been coming up to the villa most days to check on Ellie, as she put it, but always found work to do when she was there.

"It looks like the Germans are about to invade England, doesn't it? I certainly wouldn't have wanted Jerries on my doorstep, thank you very much."

"Perhaps they won't succeed," Ellie said.

Mavis shook her head. "I don't think we have the means to keep them out."

"I hope you're wrong," Ellie said. "We English do have a strong sense of pride and fighting spirit, but the retreat at Dunkirk was embarrassing, wasn't it? Especially because they left all their equipment behind. Let's hope they can keep the Nazis at bay for a while."

"We'd still have been worrying about getting bombed all the time."

"I don't suppose they'd bomb us if we lived in a village in the countryside," Ellie said. "All the same, I suppose we are better off here. You are, anyway. You have Louis to love and support you now. That's a great blessing."

As she said it, a voice in her head said that the last ferry to the abbey of the season had made its final trip. She would not see Abbot Gerard again until next May. The thought felt like a small dagger through her heart. *I mustn't think about him,* she told herself. *It's not right.* She could take the speedboat, of course, but then she would be compromising him in his position as abbot. The monks would talk. Make suppositions. And she couldn't risk that.

There had been little interest in Saint-Benet from the new puppet government. Perhaps they didn't even know it existed. Perhaps they didn't care. Ellie and Mavis with help from Bruno harvested a bumper crop of fruits and vegetables and used every available jar to preserve them.

"Let's hope they don't decide to ration sugar," Mavis said.

"I had a hard time getting any when I put in my last order to the delivery lorry," Ellie said. "I suppose it's to be expected, isn't it? Sugar has to be imported from the colonies, and merchant ships are being sunk all the time."

"Well, these jars will keep you going for a while," Mavis said.

"Keep us going," Ellie replied. "I want you to come and help yourself whenever you like."

The news got worse. Bombing against England had intensified. It seemed inevitable that the invasion would start soon and that Britain would be unable to resist. The radio had become less reliable as a source of news. It wasn't always easy to pick up the BBC, and French radio now played patriotic music and propaganda. It felt as if everyone in Saint-Benet was walking around holding their breath for what might happen next.

And in October they found out. Every person over the age of sixteen was instructed to register at the local town hall for an identification card and a book of coupons. Rationing had begun. Most food items were now on ration, if they were available. Ellie's worst fears were realized.

"So what will you do?" Roland asked her when she was lunching with him. He had spent a quiet summer in Saint-Benet, as most of his usual guests were now prisoners in the occupied zone, and he welcomed her company.

"I don't really know," Ellie said. "I won't get an identity card or a ration book. I suppose I'm an enemy alien. If they come for me, they could take me to one of the camps they are setting up. If I lie low here, maybe I can escape notice, but I won't be able to buy any staples. I suppose I'll be all right. I've milk and eggs and plenty of produce from the garden. I could go down to the dock and do some fishing, but I will need flour and fats, and sugar would be nice."

He sat there looking at her. "I am concerned for you," he said. "You may think you are safe here, but someone will betray you."

"Not here in Saint-Benet, surely?"

"Even here in Saint-Benet there are Nazi sympathizers, I am sure. And those who might do something immoral for an extra handout of food or petrol. No, chère Ellie, I do not think you are safe here."

"Then what do you suggest?" she asked. "That I try to make my way to Spain? We've no guarantee that they'd admit me. They might be happy to hand me over to the Germans."

Roland was sitting in one of the silk-upholstered armchairs. He leaned back, took a long draw on his cigarette in its ebony holder, then said, "I suppose I could always offer to marry you, if that's what it takes."

Ellie looked at him in utter surprise, then laughed. "Oh Roland, you don't have to be that noble. I know you have absolutely no interest in marrying me. I'm almost old enough to be your mother."

"You would not have to worry," Roland said. "I assure you that I would not want any so-called marital rights. It would be purely a marriage of convenience."

Ellie reached out and touched his hand. "It is very, very sweet of you to think of such a thing, and I am touched. But I could not put you at risk, and I would not want you to be responsible for me in any way." She paused. "Besides, I'm sure your family would have a fit if they learned of it. Fifty-one years old and divorced? I would not be the daughter-in-law they had chosen."

He had to smile at this. "No, you would raise some eyebrows, I assure you. But it need not be a permanent thing. When this cursed war is over we get a quiet divorce and go our ways, yes?"

Ellie shook her head. "No, dear Roland. I suppose I'm romantic and old-fashioned, but I'd like to marry someone I loved."

He looked relieved. "Alors, I made the offer. It still stands if you change your mind."

As she walked back to the villa, she wondered if she was mad not to have taken him up on it. She had to admit that it would solve a lot of problems. She'd get a ration card, an identity card, and be a respectable French citizen. She'd also be a viscountess. That was a heady thought. For a second she pictured her mother's face. So you finally managed to marry well. Tempting. But she suspected that it was an offer made spur of the moment and one he'd soon regret. So would his family if he died first and she inherited a fortune and a château.

Mavis thought she was quite barmy. "You could have been one of them aristocrats," she said. "I'd have had to curtsy to you. And you could have lived in that bloody great château and had servants to wait on you."

"I don't think Roland went as far as suggesting that I move in with him," Ellie said.

"That would be some kind of weird marriage if you kept separate houses," Mavis said.

"I suspect Roland enjoys his isolation. I'm sure he'd be difficult to live with. He does like everything just so and his own way. And he is prejudiced and opinionated."

"Even so . . ." Mavis shook her head. "Now what will you do?"

"I've no idea, Mavis," Ellie said. "Wait and see what happens next, I suppose."

CHAPTER 34

What happened next was quite unexpected. Ellie was down at the bakery buying bread, as Bruno had not been up to the villa for several days. Ever since his escape from being called up into the army, he had become fearful. So had his mother, and he only left the house when absolutely necessary.

"We'll be lucky if I can even bake ten loaves a day the way things are going," Madame Blanchet said. "I've tried to store up some flour, but it won't last that long. And then what? Are we supposed to eat grass like the goats? Curse these damned Nazis and curse the so-called Frenchmen who gave in to them."

"I don't think they had much choice," Ellie said. "They are probably doing their best to prevent French people from being killed or sent off to work camps."

Madame Blanchet looked as if she didn't believe this. "And I don't know how I'm going to make it fair for my regular customers with the ration coupons if I don't have enough to go around. Does everyone get half a loaf? Do you only get a quarter because you're alone?" She shook her head. Then she frowned. "But you're not a citizen, are you? How are you going to manage?"

"I haven't figured that out yet," Ellie said.

The baker's wife leaned closer. "My dear, you should try to go to Switzerland. You'd be safe there."

Ellie gave a sad smile. "That was my first thought, but I made some enquiries. I heard that the Swiss are adamant about not taking sides. They wouldn't let me in, unless I had a fortune in Swiss banks."

As she walked away, she heard her name being called and saw Mr Tommy hurrying down the steep alley from his house, waving to her.

"There you are!" he said, beaming at her. "We haven't seen anything of you for days. Clive was getting worried. 'We should go and see if she's all right,' he said. But here you are looking hale and hearty."

"Not exactly hale and hearty, but doing all right," she said.

"Come up and have a bite to eat," Tommy said. "We've been dying for a good natter. I won't take no for an answer. I'll be a brute and drag you there if necessary."

"I'd like to see that." Ellie had to laugh.

He took her arm and steered her towards his house.

"Look who I've found," he called as he came in.

Clive poked his head around the kitchen door. "Finally. We were a bit concerned," Clive said. "Now that Mavis has gone swanning off to live happily with Louis, we knew you'd be all alone up there. Come and sit down. Tommy has made a goat cheese tart. Quite delicious. And we got our hands on a crate of really good rosé."

Ellie let herself be swept into the kitchen, let them pour a glass of wine for her and place a slice of tart in front of her. "You must teach me to make goat cheese," she said. "I've got Babette producing milk every day, and I really don't drink much of it. I'm not a fan of the taste."

"My dear, we'll be grateful for it when they ration cow's milk," Tommy said. "I'm betting all the milk will go to the big places like Marseille, and we'll be forgotten. I know M. LeClerc at the farm up the road has two cows, but what good is that for a whole village?"

"I'm sure there are a lot of things we'll have to do without," Ellie said. "Especially me, since I'll not get a ration book."

"Ah, well, we've been discussing that, haven't we, Clive?" Tommy looked at the other man for affirmation.

"We have." Clive nodded. "We may have come up with a solution."

"Really?" She tried not to sound hopeful.

Tommy glanced at Clive again. Clive nodded. "I'm going to suggest that you and I get married."

"Oh, not again!" Ellie burst out laughing. "Why does the whole world suddenly want to marry me? I'm sure you don't."

"The whole world wants to marry you?" Tommy said. "Then, my dear woman, why haven't you accepted one of the proposals? Look at Mavis. She's happy and safe now. You could be, too."

"The whole world was a slight exaggeration. It was the viscount who suggested it."

"Oh la la," Clive said. "You could be a viscountess, my dear. We'd have to bow. And he does come with a château."

"Be serious, Clive," Ellie said. "You know he was only trying to help me out, which was good of him. It was a spur of the moment thing. I don't think he meant it seriously anyway."

"Well, our offer is quite serious," Tommy said. "You don't have an identity card, and you won't get one. There's a chance you'll be rounded up and sent off to a camp as an enemy alien. I presume you've weighed your options?"

"Spain and then Portugal seem like the only ones," Ellie said. "And I don't fancy that journey. Switzerland has made it quite clear that they won't accept refugees from German-controlled territories."

"Of course not," Clive said. "The one thing they don't want to do is to give the Germans an excuse to invade them. They couldn't stop an army that size. So they have to remain totally neutral."

"Which brings us back to our offer," Tommy said. "First of all, it would be good to pool resources. You're all alone in that big house with lots of land. We could bring our chickens and goats up there, and we'd have three ration books . . ."

"How is that?" Ellie asked.

"If you married me," Tommy said. "Listen, my dear, this idea is not entirely unselfish on our part. You must know what happens to men like us in Germany. We've heard about it from friends in England. Off to a work camp, and the more brutal the better. It could well happen here. So if you and I were a couple, and Clive was our nephew . . ."

Ellie nodded, paying attention now. "But when the war is over . . . if that's soon, please God . . . what about then? We get a divorce and go our ways?"

"The beauty about our little idea is that we don't even have to do that," Tommy said. "You see, Clive here trained as a draftsman before the last war. He does meticulous work. He'd make an excellent forger. He'll make us a fake British marriage certificate that should hold up to scrutiny. I have my parents' old marriage certificate. He'll copy that. If the war ends and we're still in one piece, we burn it in a celebration bonfire."

Ellie looked from Tommy to Clive and gave a nervous giggle. "But everyone knows we were not married in England."

"Everyone here. They won't say anything. They like us."

"Not Mrs Adams," I said. "She'd turn you over in a heartbeat."

"No, she wouldn't," Clive said, "because I happen to know that her husband is Jewish."

"He's Jewish?"

Both men nodded. "So it's in their interests to lie low and shut up now," Clive added.

Ellie looked around the bright kitchen and out to the sea below. It was a lot to take in. "So when are we supposed to have married? Am I your long-lost wife come in search of you?"

"Not at all," Tommy said. "We thought that out, too. You are an old and dear friend from my childhood. Last year we learned that your husband had died. I went over to console you, and we found the spark was still there. We got married, and you came over here, where we now live happily ever after."

"It sounds so simple," Ellie said. "Surely if the Germans come, they will be meticulous in inspecting papers."

"Maybe not a really elaborate English marriage certificate from Saint Andrew's Church in Chiddingfold?" Tommy smiled.

There was a long pause. Ellie was aware of a clock ticking on the shelf and the gentle clucking of chickens outside the open window.

"So what do you think?" Tommy said at last. "Are you willing to give it a try?"

Ellie laughed again. "Well, it's certainly the most ridiculous thing I've done in my life. Dora always wished she had done more, lived a more adventurous life. Perhaps it's time for me to take a risk. At this stage, what do we have to lose?"

"What indeed," Tommy said, laughing with her.

CHAPTER 35

It didn't take long for the whole of Saint-Benet to know that Mr Tommy and Clive were moving into the villa with Ellie. Makes sense, was the general opinion. It's good to pool resources. But then Ellie risked using up precious petrol to drive into Marseille, and the rumour was spread that she and Tommy had gone to be married. Most of Saint-Benet scoffed at this idea but agreed it made sense for Ellie, or she'd get no rations.

"Good luck to them, that's what I say," Mr Adams said. "In wartime, you do what you have to."

"Yes, but not to that man," Mrs Adams replied with a sniff of disgust. "You know what sort he is."

"Perhaps he's seen the error of his ways," Mr Adams suggested.

"A likely story."

Possessions were carried, bit by bit, down from Tommy and Clive's house and up the steps to Ellie's. She used more valuable petrol to pack her motor car with heavier things they'd need, including a crate of chickens on the back seat, while the goats were led across by hand. Clive brought their cat across and introduced her to Tiger. Tiger, being the most easy-going of cats, was prepared to make instant friends, but Clive's cat retreated under a table and hissed.

"I expect they'll soon sort it out," Clive said.

The major furniture was left in place as a tenant had been found to rent the house—a couple who had decided that Lyon was too close to the border of the occupied zone for comfort.

"My husband's Jewish," the wife said. "We can't take any risks."

As Ellie was crossing the harbour with baskets of provisions from the house, Nico came up to her and grabbed her fiercely by the arm, swinging her around. Ellie gave a small cry of alarm.

"Is it true what they say?" he asked, frowning at her. "It can't be true. They say that you've married that man. Mr Tommy. It's not true, is it?"

"I'm afraid it is," she said.

"But he's . . ." He tried to frame the sentence.

She smiled then. "Nico, don't worry. If ever there was a marriage of convenience, this is one. I couldn't get an identity card and could have been arrested and sent to a camp. Now I'll be safe. It makes sense to only use one house, and it helps Tommy and Clive, too. Now he's a respectable married man if the Germans ever come here and start probing."

"Yes, but . . ." Nico still looked angry. "There must have been other options."

"I should have thought that Mr Tommy was the safest option ever," she replied. "I shall not have to worry about him, especially with Clive in the same house. Besides," she added, "I notice you didn't make me an offer."

"No," he said, looking startled at this accusation. "If I'd made you an offer . . ." He broke off, then said quickly, "Anyway, I couldn't. I have my mother to take care of. I have to think of her first."

"Yes, of course," Ellie said.

"You have your landlord's permission, I assume?" he said, his eyes now challenging hers.

"No, but I have no written lease that spells out whether I'm allowed visitors. Besides, the owner will be glad that I have two very handy men making sure the property is in tiptop condition."

He nodded at this.

"So I won't mention what you are storing on his property if you don't mention this," she said.

"Touché." He went to say more but turned and walked away abruptly.

~~

By the end of October, when identity cards were required of all adults, they were fully moved in, a bigger coop had been constructed for the chickens and the two goats had made friends with Babette. Clive had produced an impressive marriage certificate. He showed Ellie the original he had copied from.

"It's really good, Clive," she said. "It looks quite authentic."

"Yes, I did do a pretty good job, didn't I?" He gave a satisfied smile. "Maybe there is work for me as a forger as this war progresses. People will need fake ID cards."

"If you could do that, you could have made one for me," she said. "Simpler than getting married."

"Ah, but ID cards are more of a challenge. They require the official stamp on them, and they are registered with the town hall in Marseille," he said. "They could easily check on you. But they can't check on a parish church in England right now."

So they went into Marseille, registered and collected identity and ration cards. It all seemed ridiculously simple, and nobody commented on the marriage certificate, except the clerk, a serious-looking woman with black hair in a severe bun, who remarked, "So there is hope for all of us widowed women to find a new happiness in life."

Ellie felt a twinge of guilt as the clerk shook hands and wished them well. A new phase of life started. Ellie wasn't at all sure what it would be like living with two men, but she soon saw the advantages. They were constantly busy. Tommy loved to cook. Clive enjoyed working in the garden and tending to the livestock. At the end of the first week they had a celebration dinner, and after they had drunk coffee, savouring it since coffee might not be available much longer, Ellie was led outside.

"We've managed to find a wedding present for you," Clive said. "For us, really."

And he pointed to a beehive. "We got it from the man who owns the vineyard close to the main road. With any luck we'll have honey when there is no more sugar. And the bees will fertilize our crops."

"Oh, how lovely." Ellie looked from one face to the other. "I really haven't thanked you properly for taking care of me. You've saved me. Well, done more than saved me. You've given me interest in life again. I want you to feel that this house is your home and to do what you like with it."

"I'm so glad you said that," Tommy replied, "because Clive has some great ideas for redecorating." Then he burst out laughing. "Your face! Just joking, my dear. We are quite content the way it is."

∾

Also soon after they had moved in, Ellie received a letter. This was quite a shock as no post had come from England for a long while and she was not used to finding anything in her post office box. The postmistress hailed her as she went for the weekly ration of flour and margarine.

"You know there's a letter sitting there for you?"

Ellie hurried to retrieve it, expecting news from England or at least another lecture from Lionel. Her heart was beating fast in case it was bad news about one of her sons. Instead, the letter had a local French stamp. She opened the envelope.

My dear Ellie, the letter began in beautiful sloping handwriting. *I have been worried about you, so I am writing to see if you are safe and sound.*

She skimmed to the bottom of the page. It was signed, *With God's blessing, Gerard.*

Her face flushed, and she clutched the letter a little tighter. He had been worrying about her. She read the rest of the letter. Only pleasantries about the monastery, nothing intimate or too friendly. But it ended, *We should all enjoy this moment of calm and peace here, because I fear it won't be too long before the enemy sees Marseille and Toulon as strategic ports for their Mediterranean fleet.*

Ellie finished the letter and folded it back into the envelope.

"Good news?" The postmistress had been observing her.

"Neither good nor bad," she said. "Just a friend concerned about me. But all is well."

She hadn't realized before that mail was taken out to the island, but the postmistress said that one of the fishermen would drop any letters off when needed. So Ellie sat at her desk and wrote back to the abbot, telling him of the fake marriage and that Tommy and Clive were now living at the villa with her. She expressed her relief that she no longer had to worry about being caught. She wrote of the chickens and goats and a good crop of apples that Clive was now drying on trays to preserve them.

It felt good to know that she could write to him, that he was in touch with her, even if she couldn't go out to the island. She saw nothing of Nico, even though she had warned Tommy and Clive that he might be seen sneaking through the garden at night.

"I've often wondered about him," Tommy said. "He always seems to have enough money, but he doesn't actually go out fishing much. I know he has that speedboat he takes people out in, but there haven't been many visitors this year." He gave Ellie a questioning glance. "So do you think he's a smuggler? A black marketeer?"

"I don't know what to think," she said. "I only know he keeps things in the locked shed, and apparently this is all right with the owner."

"But we've never met this owner, have we?" Tommy asked.

"I understood he lived in Paris and his affairs are handled by Monsieur Danton," she said. "But maybe it's just his attorney who lives in Paris. Who knows where the actual owner lives. I've often wondered . . ." She paused.

"About the viscount. Could it be that he is the son of the duke who bought this villa for his mistress? I didn't like to ask him, and he didn't offer the information. But it would make sense—his father bought this whole piece of land on the hillside and built two properties, side by side."

"I suppose it would," Tommy agreed. "He's a funny chap, isn't he? One never knows when he's here. He never mixes with us at all. Brings his own servants. Has his provisions shipped in from outside, and yet one understands that he's quite young."

"He is," Ellie said. "I would think maybe late thirties, early forties?"

"You'd expect his family to want him to marry," Tommy said. "And produce the heir."

"He did clarify that for me. He's the second son, and there already is a satisfactory heir from his brother. He has interests elsewhere, so I gather."

"Really?" Tommy looked amused. "Well, I never. So is he here for the duration of the war, do you think?"

"I really don't know. Possibly. He does have a house in Paris he can't go to now."

"You'd think he'd want company, wouldn't you?"

"I have lunch with him quite often," Ellie said. "For some reason he has taken to me."

"Of course he would," Tommy said. "You are the least judgemental person in the universe. He'd feel comfortable with you."

Ellie considered this comment later. It was nice of him to say that, and she had to admit that it was probably true. She had brought Dora here, even though for all she knew Dora could have been a demanding and critical old woman. She had brought her cleaning lady, treating her as an equal, which most of her peers would not have done. And she had embraced Tommy and Clive, and the viscount.

So I do have a few good qualities, she thought. *I must tell Gerard when I write to him again.*

CHAPTER 36

Life in Saint-Benet continued unchanged and untouched throughout the winter of 1941. Ellie felt as if she was in a sort of no-man's land, safe enough for now, with good conversation with kind and witty men, and yet holding her breath as if waiting for doom to fall. England was still being pounded. She had received no word about her sons since France was invaded. At night she lay awake worrying about them, worrying about Jojo, missing Dora.

"I'm so glad she died before any of this happened," she said to Mavis, who came up to visit once or twice a week. She no longer volunteered to help with housework, as the two men kept everything immaculate.

Mavis nodded in agreement. "I reckon you gave her a lot of happiness those last years of her life," she said.

"We gave her. You too, Mavis. She became very fond of you."

"God rest her soul," Mavis muttered. "Louis has me going to church every Sunday now. He's determined to make a good Catholic of me. I must say I like the idea of praying to saints. Louis says God is often too busy, so you can put the call through to one of his workers instead. It turns out there is a saint for everything—lost items or even headaches."

"Is there one to take care of my boys?" Ellie asked. "I worry about them all the time."

"I reckon you could ask the Virgin Mary herself about that," Mavis said. "She was a mother who worried, after all."

"It didn't stop her son from being killed, did it?" Ellie said.

When Mavis got up to leave, Ellie made up a basket of produce, eggs and cheese. Mavis shook her head. "I won't take this for myself, if you don't mind. Or I'll take it for others that need it more. The Belfonts' child is not doing well. He had scarlet fever, and now he needs building up again. So I'll take them the eggs and maybe some of your goat's milk?" She paused, thinking. "You know, I was thinking, maybe we could set up a little food exchange. I'll handle it . . . see who needs food in the village and who has extra to spare."

"I'm happy to contribute," Ellie said.

"Well, Louis is already doing this sort of thing—lending tools, fixing things in return for some onions or a bottle of wine."

"Mavis, you never cease to surprise me," Ellie said. "If those people at home could see you, the life and soul of Saint-Benet, they'd never believe it."

Mavis gave a shy smile. "Sometimes I can't believe it myself," she said. "It's having Louis beside me. It makes all the difference."

And so the village food bank was set up. Ellie took down cheese and honey and got fish, onions and wine in return. She wrote to the abbot, not too frequently, and received friendly replies. There were plenty of storms that battered the front windows and made the palm trees dance, but also plenty of rain that produced good spring crops. It seemed almost embarrassing to be in this beautiful haven with enough to eat. From the snippets of news, they gleaned Britain was being heavily bombed and the invasion could happen any day. Ellie worried about her sons, wished she had some way of writing to them or getting news of them. Were they even still alive? Colin flying for the RAF? Would he still think it was quite a lark? And where was Richard now? She hadn't heard from either of them in ages since the Germans occupied France. She also wondered about Lionel. If the Germans came to his part of the world, she was pretty sure he'd cooperate, welcome them, just as long as they left him and his bank alone.

~~

Spring brought blossoms and balmy weather. The first visitors came, including German officers and their wives or mistresses. One of these overheard Tommy and Ellie speaking English.

"You people," he said in clipped English. "What are you doing here? How did you get out of England? Do you not know you are in enemy territory?"

"But we are French," Tommy said. "We've been naturalized French citizens for almost twenty years."

"Let me see your papers," the officer said. Tommy and Ellie produced their identity cards. The officer nodded. "All good," he said. "You made a good decision to leave that little island. It will soon be a German colony."

Tommy shot Ellie a warning look that she should say nothing.

"Enjoy your time here," Ellie said. "The food at the bar is very good."

~~

In May the first boat came to take visitors to the island, and Ellie was amongst the handful of people who went across. Abbot Gerard looked pleased to see her and embraced her warmly.

"So how is married life treating you?" he asked with a twinkle in his eye.

"I'm sure you don't approve," she said.

"On the contrary. I have seen enough of the ways of the world before I entered the priesthood to know that love comes in many forms. I am glad to know you can stay safe."

"I am enjoying being taken care of," she said. "We have our first honey, and I've been taught to make goat cheese. I've brought you some. And the beans and peas are going to be wonderful. So no complaints."

"But really—you are comfortable with this arrangement?" He looked concerned now. "It is working out for you?"

"Absolutely. They are two very dear men. They treat me well, absolutely spoil me, and they are witty and like to laugh, so very good for me."

"Then I am glad for you," he said. "But we mustn't forget to pray for your countrymen who are getting so badly bombed. Such inhumanity. There was a time when wars at least had rules. It was trained army against trained army in a strategic battle. A certain nobility to it. But to target innocent civilians—we have all become barbarians."

Ellie left with a bottle of liqueur, a basket of strawberries and the knowledge that she could come again, once a month, all summer. Life seemed to be more promising.

Also in May came another surprise that made them more hopeful. The tide was beginning to turn in North Africa where British forces were repelling General Rommel. And in a surprise move, Hitler had withdrawn his forces from the English coast and had decided instead to attack his former ally, the Soviet Union. The war was now in the East. Everyone heaved a sigh of relief. Hitler now had no more interest in France. Perhaps the occupied zone might soon be opened up again.

Viscount Roland was of this opinion. "I shall be able to go back to Paris soon, I am sure of it," he said. "Oh, how I have missed the theatre, the clubs, the Bois de Boulogne. And the food, of course. I hope those brutish Huns have not taken all the good food." He looked at Ellie. "You should come and visit once I'm settled. I have a charming house in the first arrondissement. Close to everything. Let's just pray it's still intact."

Then in December 1941, the Japanese bombed Pearl Harbor and the United States entered the war on the side of the Allies. This produced renewed hope in Saint-Benet.

"Remember when they joined the fight in 1917," one of the men said as they sat around at Henri's bar. "It made all the difference. They have money for new weaponry, which Britain desperately needs. You'll see—that fiend Hitler will soon be on the run with his tail between his legs."

In spite of the first victories in North Africa, the German army in France showed no signs of withdrawing from the North. The Allies were fighting in Crete, the Americans were now conducting bombing raids over Germany, but there was no indication of victory in sight. Still Ellie felt they were safely hidden in Saint-Benet, until May of 1942. Then an edict came from the French puppet government that all Jews were now to wear a yellow star.

Ellie sought out Mrs Adams.

"Aren't you terribly worried?" she asked her.

Mrs Adams shrugged. "I don't think most people even know that Abe is Jewish, and those that do won't say anything. He's not about to wear any ridiculous yellow star. The indignity of it. Who do they think they are?"

"I'm afraid they are in power," Ellie said. "We hear reports of terrible things being done to Jewish people in the rest of Europe."

"Not here," Mrs Adams said. "There are plenty of French Jews, and those Nazis haven't touched them. We're in the free zone, you know."

Ellie said no more, and Abe Adams did not wear a yellow star. But Ellie noticed that he became less sociable. She felt he was running a terrible risk, as German soldiers came to stay at the pension during that summer. Perhaps his being English prevented the Germans from being suspicious of him. He didn't look different from any other Englishman.

"Could you make him a false ID card, just in case?" Ellie asked Clive. The identity cards had to list race as well as occupation.

"I could try," Clive said. "But nobody seems to have noticed he's not wearing a yellow star, have they?"

The summer passed. The visitors stopped coming, and Ellie let out a sigh of relief. Abe Adams had passed scrutiny, just as she had. There were more Allied victories and it really seemed hopeful that ultimately Hitler might soon be defeated.

Then in November German warships arrived in Marseille. The announcement was given that the free zone no longer existed. German tanks rolled down the route nationale to occupy most of the South while the Italian army came into Provence from the east. Clive was quite cheered by this. "I don't mind being occupied by Italians," he said. "Pour them a glass of good wine, and they'll be happy."

But it was not to be. The Italians stopped short, in the town of Toulon, while the Germans swarmed into Marseille and trickled into Saint-Benet.

The first sign was a German staff car that pulled up at the harbour. An officer in highly polished black knee boots got out and looked around, nodding with pleasure at what he saw.

"You!" he beckoned Henri. "Are there hotels in this place? I wish to billet my men."

"There's only the one small pension," Henri said. "Very simple. Very primitive. We are a fishing village, not a tourist destination."

"So the only properties here are the ones I can see?"

"That's correct," Henri said.

"Too bad. It's a pretty little place. My men would like to relax after a taxing time in the North." Henri was about to let out a sigh of relief when the officer added, "Perhaps I will just take a look at the pension . . ." And he strode over to it. Apparently it was not too primitive, and the next day twelve German soldiers were billeted there. Mrs Adams didn't seem as worried as Ellie was for her husband.

"They won't make trouble as long as we take good care of them," she said to Ellie. "They are simple foot soldiers, happy to be at the seaside. They asked me about bathing and whether it was too cold at this time of year."

Immediately after they had moved in, they got to work putting in barricades and barbed wire around the harbour, making it hard for the fishermen to reach their boats. They blocked off the path to the little beach.

Tommy and Clive sprang into action the moment they received the news.

"We need to hide the chickens and the goats," Tommy said. "Those Huns will take them without a second thought." So they set to work constructing a new chicken coop behind an arbour of wisteria and staked out the goats during the day outside the property on a section of hillside where they could not be seen from any footpath. "Just as long as the chickens don't make too much noise," Tommy said. "Thank God the last rooster died and we never got a new one from the farmer."

"And the motor car," Clive added. "We should hide the motor car so that they don't take it."

"But if we need it to get away?" Ellie asked.

"There's nowhere to go, is there?" Tommy said. "We're sitting ducks here. And no way to get petrol."

Ellie thought that Nico could probably find some for them, but she did realize that a British motor car, spotted on any road, would be too obvious. They went down to the garage. Ellie drove out the Bentley, and together they managed to manoeuvre it into the space behind the garage and shed, covering it with a tarpaulin and letting the bougainvillea spill over it. Then Clive and Tommy placed old rubbish bins and pieces of trash around it. The result was satisfying.

Ellie wrote to Abbot Gerard, warning him that Germans were now in occupation. He wrote back that he had assurances that the abbey would be safe and allowed to continue but warned her to be very careful. It didn't seem that the Germans were going to make life difficult, apart from establishing a curfew at ten p.m. This upset the fishermen. "We often go out at night or in the very early morning," they said, appealing to the officer in charge. "That's when the best fishing is. So if you'd like a good fish supper, you have to let us fish."

"You will now fish during the daytime when your boats can be inspected," the officer told them. "We cannot risk any kind of smuggling of goods."

Ellie's thoughts went instantly to Nico. She hadn't seen much of him in recent weeks. If he had come to the villa, it must have been in the middle of the night. Then one night Ellie had just gotten into bed when there was a rattle of something at her window. She opened it, looked out and saw a dark shape of a man below.

"It's me, Nico," he called up to her in a whisper.

"I'll come down." Ellie hurriedly put on her robe and came down the stairs. She opened the front door, and he slipped inside, glancing around before he closed it behind him.

"I have to ask a favour," Nico said. He was breathing heavily, as if he had run up the steps.

"Yes?" She looked at him uncertainly.

"I had to make a dash for your little harbour," he said. "Luckily my speedboat can outrun them, but I can't get back into the town. There are Germans everywhere," he said. "Guarding the harbour. Can I perhaps stay here tonight?"

"Of course," she said.

He smiled then, and she realized how harried he had looked.

"Come into the kitchen," she said. "I have cognac."

He nodded. "That's good. I am really cold."

She led him through and poured him a glass from the decanter. He took a sip, then gave a sigh of satisfaction. "Thank you," he said. "And thank you for taking me in."

Ellie nodded, not sure what to say.

"I may need to make this request more often," he said. "Would that be all right? That I could spend the night here when I need to?"

Ellie hesitated. "Look, Nico," she said. "I have other people in the house I can't put in harm's way. I have to know if you are doing something illegal—something that could get us all into trouble."

He stared at her. "Yes," he said. "I suppose I am, in a way. And you are right. I should not put you in harm's way. I'll stay here now, but . . ."

She took a deep breath. "I've wanted to ask this question for ages. Nico, are you a smuggler? Are you bringing in black market goods?"

She was surprised that he smiled then. "I have been known, at times, to import an occasional bottle of wine or spirit without paying the taxes," he said, "but the answer is no. But it is dangerous. I will be taking messages. I may be bringing items up to store in the shed . . . items that could be useful, like guns."

Suddenly she understood. "You're helping the Resistance?"

"The less you know, the better," he said. "If you see me at night, crossing the garden, then pull the blinds and look away. Then if you are questioned, you can genuinely say that you know nothing."

"Nico—" She reached out and touched his arm. "Please be careful."

"You sound concerned," he said. "I'm touched. I thought you despised me."

"Of course I'm concerned," she said. "And I never despised you."

"To start with you did. I saw your expression when you caught me crossing the garden that night." He laughed.

"I thought you were up to no good. Hiding stolen goods in someone else's shed."

He put hands on both her shoulders. "My dear Ellie, I am going to tell you something that is strictly between us, and only because I might not make it out of this war alive. But I want you to know the truth about me . . . I was born in this house. In the room where you are now sleeping."

She stared at him, trying to digest this. She saw the twinkle in his eyes. "You're joking," she said.

He shook his head. "Not this time. My mother was Jeannette Hétreau."

"The opera singer? Your mother was the opera singer?" She fought not to raise her voice. "But that's ridiculous. I've met your mother, a sweet little old lady called Madame Barbou."

"My adoptive mother," he said. "When Jeannette became pregnant, Marcel, the very rich duke, decided he couldn't allow a baby. His wife was the jealous sort and would make a fuss in Paris society. He insisted Jeannette find a good home for it, like a puppy, if she still wanted to be his mistress. Of course she liked the perks of the job, so to speak, so she obeyed. She found a childless couple in the village, and they agreed to say it was the child of a cousin who had died in childbirth."

"I saw your photograph," Ellie blurted out. "It was in Jeannette's drawer, hidden amongst her underclothes. A beautiful baby. I often wondered . . ."

"It's more than I've ever seen," he said. "I don't remember her at all."

"You never met your mother?"

He gave a little sigh. "Apparently she did come to see me a few times when I was very young. But then the relationship with my father came to an end, and she never returned to the villa."

"She just walked away. Abandoned you?"

"She preferred money and fame, I suppose. And she wasn't the motherly type. Oh, she did provide for me financially. Paid for me to go to a good school and then to the Sorbonne. But she never wanted to meet me."

"But then she died and left you this villa?"

He nodded. "The villa and a good amount of money. That's why I don't need to work hard, which is nice."

"Why didn't you take over the villa?"

"Two reasons. Because the truth would come out and it would upset my mother, the woman who raised me, and second because Jeannette never wanted me in her lifetime. I bore a grudge against her and wanted nothing to do with her. Let the villa crumble into dust."

She examined his face. "So you're really the son of a duke," she said. "That's why there was always something different about you. Did you never try to contact him?"

Nico shook his head. "Once," he said. "I was in Paris at the Sorbonne, and I had the absurd notion that I should present myself to my true father. I was sure he would acknowledge me, welcome me with open arms and afford me all the privileges of a duke's son. I found his house in the eighth arrondissement, near the Seine, and I was getting up courage to approach the front door when it opened and he came out. He stalked past me as if were a speck of dust on the pavement, shouted some command to his chauffeur, got in and drove away. That look of absolute arrogance. I decided he would not want to know me."

"I'm sorry, Nico. It must have been hard for you."

"On the contrary. I grew up in a loving home. My father taught me everything about fishing. I went out with him on the boat. Much better than being raised by servants or dragged around by an opera singer."

Ellie stood up, realizing how late it was. "I'll make up a bed for you."

"No need. I'll sleep on a sofa. I'm easy to please." He smiled then. "But if I do have to come again . . ."

"I'll have the spare room ready," she said. "And I'll leave the front door unlocked."

He stood up, too. "So what will your husband say?" he asked, his eyes teasing hers. "Will he beat you for inviting a strange man into your house?"

"My husband is currently asleep in his room with someone other than me," she said. "I should go back to bed."

He put his hands on her shoulders. "You asked me earlier why I didn't make you an offer," he said. "You accepted Tommy's because you knew he would make no demands of you. I should have wanted to make demands."

For a moment she thought he was going to kiss her. Then he released her and went through to the sitting room, leaving her feeling a little shaken.

CHAPTER 37

Ellie sat on the side of her bed, staring out into the blackness of the garden, trying to digest all that she had learned and felt. That Nico was Jeannette's son was almost too much to believe, and yet it explained his behaviour, and she had sensed he wasn't lying to her. That he was now working with the Resistance was a worry, both on his behalf and on hers. If he stayed at this house, he would put them in danger, too, and yet she couldn't say no if he needed help. And there was the other matter, the fact that he desired her, that she had definitely felt something for him.

I'm too old for such nonsense, she told herself, but there had been a shiver of excitement when he looked at her that way and told her he wanted her. After so many years of not being desired, of being taken for granted, of occasional passionless sex after Lionel had drunk a good deal of wine with dinner, it felt strangely exciting to realize that she might not, after all, be too old.

When Ellie got up in the morning, Nico was gone. Over breakfast she told Tommy and Clive about the nighttime visit and warned them that he might have to spend the night on occasion if he couldn't get back into the village.

"So he's working with the Resistance, is he?" Tommy said. "I must talk to him about that."

"Oh, I don't think he'd like to talk about it," Ellie said hastily. "The less we know the better. That's what he said."

"No, I mean I'd like to find out how we can help," Tommy said. "I feel that I'd like to be doing something useful, and Clive can offer his forger's talents."

"Oh no. Please don't get involved," Ellie said. "These are brutal men. Look how many Resistance workers have been executed in the North."

"But we only have a chance of defeating those brutes if we all help out," Tommy said. "Don't worry. I can't see myself blowing up any railway lines or shooting generals. But I'm sure there's a small job I could do."

Apparently he had a conversation with Nico, and the small job turned out to be a radio positioned under the floorboards of Tommy's bedroom. Nico came up to instruct him how to use it, and he started leaving messages he had received in the big stone urn on the terrace for Nico to pick up at night.

"Italy has occupied Corsica," he said at dinner one night. "That is good news. It gives us more chance of an escape route, if anyone needs it. The Italian guards won't be as strict, and that coastline is so mountainous and rocky that they can't put guards everywhere."

Ellie felt a shiver of fear. Tommy was enjoying being part of the action, but now, for the first time, they were in the midst of danger and the war had become real. Rations were cut severely, and they heard that local farms had had their livestock taken. But still the chickens and goats survived at Villa Gloriosa. Ellie and Mavis took down the extra eggs and milk to be shared with those who needed them most. It seems the Germans had not yet discovered the villa. Perhaps they thought those steep steps merely led up to hiking trails to the Calanques.

~~

After the Germans had been in evidence for a few weeks, Ellie came home to find they had a visitor. The viscount was in their sitting room, sipping a cup of herb tea. He looked less like his sophisticated and polished self than usual; in fact he looked positively unkempt, as if he had dressed in a hurry.

"Thank God you have returned safely," he said as Ellie walked in. "None of us is safe any longer. They came to my villa today—German officers. Horrible, rude men. They pushed my servants out of the way, looked around the house and told me to get out, as they would now be occupying it. And keeping my servants to look after them."

"How awful, Roland. What did you say?"

"I asked where I was supposed to go, and they said there was a pension in the village that would probably have room for me if I had no relatives nearby. They stood there while I packed a couple of suitcases into my motor car. Luckily they didn't requisition that. I got out quickly before they could change their minds. So I came here. I couldn't think where else to go."

"Of course you can stay here," Ellie said. She turned to the other men. "If that's all right with you?"

"The more the merrier," Tommy said. "But don't expect the Ritz. We live very simply."

"Don't we all these days?" Roland said. "Do you know there is no coffee to be had? And those ruffians will now get their hands on my wine cellar. I muttered to my butler that he should close it and hide the key, but I bet they'll force it open."

Ellie went upstairs and made up the bed in the last of the bedrooms. She was tempted to offer her own room to Roland and to take the room that was clearly designed for a servant, but she had become comfortable in that room with no wish to move, and besides it was where Nico knew to find her if he ever needed to in the middle of the night. He had not stayed at the villa again, but she had seen him cross the garden and knew that he was coming and going at night. She told Tommy to mention nothing of this to Roland. She feared he would give in all too quickly to Nazi interrogation. She wondered about herself. Of course she would not betray Nico. But what if the Gestapo came, or the Abwehr? So far it had only been regular soldiers who stayed in the village, but if she were ever taken for questioning, could she hold out? If they tortured her?

I know nothing, she told herself. *I would genuinely have nothing to tell them. They'd have to believe that.*

"That Nico," one of the fishermen said, when she was down in the village and casually asked after him. "He's finally decided to work for a living. He goes out in his boat almost every day now. Makes a good catch, too."

Ellie wondered if there was a double meaning in those words. Did the man know he was also running supplies for the Resistance as well as catching fish? It appeared the Germans didn't, so far. Nor had they yet discovered the villa. The officers held loud parties at Roland's château. The sound of their late-night singing and laughter drifted from over the hill. Roland was proving to be not the easiest of guests. Tommy and Clive, usually so easy-going, were clearly finding him a strain.

"Do you know—he took two eggs this morning," Clive said. "Two eggs. And he put all that sugar in his coffee. Doesn't he know we are on rations?" He rolled his eyes. "And yesterday he asked Tommy to polish his shoes."

"And did Tommy do it?"

Clive gave a little grin. "Tommy said there were no servants in this house, and anything he wanted done he'd have to do for himself. He went away in a huff, but he did later come down to ask for the shoe polish."

It was going to be a big adjustment for Roland, Ellie thought. He'd probably never had to do a thing for himself his whole life. He was lucky to be with three such patient people. After a few admonitions, he seemed to realize that they were being kind to him because he started to offer to help set the table, do the weeding. However, he declined at being asked to collect the eggs.

"Horrible birds, chickens. Absolutely murderous eyes. They'd peck you to death if they could."

A month went by with nothing terrible happening. At the villa they were still surviving quite well with enough eggs, cheese, vegetables plus the occasional fish that could be bought from the dockside. Christmas was approaching, but there was no sense of excitement or anticipation in the village. The boulangerie was now barely given enough flour to make small loaves—one each per family.

"There will be no bûche de Noël, no special patisseries, no holiday at all," Madame Blanchet said. "And one of those cursed Germans had the nerve to ask me why I do not bake pain au chocolat. I told him we have not seen chocolate for two years now. If he'd like to produce some for me, along with the necessary butter, I will most certainly bake him a pain au chocolat."

Ellie came out of the shop with her small loaf and had started towards the steps when she heard a scream. Bruno's mother was running towards her, her hands waving in panic.

"You must help me, madame," she screamed. "My boy. They've taken my boy."

"The Germans have taken Bruno? Why?"

"The officer saw him, asked why he wasn't working in a factory and then realized he was not as other men. So they came in a big black lorry and took him away. They said there is no food for those who are not useful to society. And nobody did anything to help me. They let it happen. They just watched and let him be taken. Where can those devils have taken him?"

"I really don't know," Ellie said. She felt sick. She had heard that within Germany they had removed those with disabilities, sending them to the notorious labour camps, or perhaps to their deaths.

"He won't be able to cope without me," Bruno's mother said, clutching at Ellie's sleeve. "You know what he's like. How easily he gets frightened, and then he starts talking gibberish."

"I wish I could do something for you," Ellie said. "Have you spoken to Father André? To Monsieur Danton? They could perhaps enquire officially to see where he might have been taken."

Tears were streaming down the woman's face. She shook her head fiercely, causing tears to fly out. "What good are they? They believe we should not make a fuss and thus keep the village safe. But it's my son. My poor Bruno."

"I'll do what I can," Ellie said, although she had no idea what this might be. She thought she might have a word with Father André, just in case the word of a priest might help, and she was on her way to the church when she saw Nico. She ran over to him, grabbing his arm. "You have to help," she said, breathless. "They've taken Bruno."

He looked down at her with concern. "That poor boy. I feared this might happen. But I'm afraid it's too late to do anything. If they've already taken him, there is little we can do."

"We can stop them," Ellie said. "You could stop them. You must be able to send a message to somebody, someone who can help."

He was frowning. "I'll come up with you and try to contact someone on the radio. It depends how long ago it was and where they are taking him." He put an arm around her shoulder. "Come on, then, let's hurry. Did you bring your motor car?"

"Of course not. There's no petrol," she said. "I always use the steps."

He didn't say any more, but together they climbed the steps, pausing, panting at the top before going into the house. Clive opened his mouth to say something when he saw Nico, but Ellie shot him a warning look and shook her head as Nico ran up the stairs. A little later he came down again.

"They will try to intercept the lorry before it reaches the train station, assuming he is to be deported to a camp or even to Germany," he said. "But they are not hopeful."

"At least we tried," Ellie said. "That's the main thing. That poor woman. She dotes on that boy."

Nico looked at her with concern. "I fear it is getting worse," he said. "The Germans are suffering defeats. They fear the Allies will come up through Italy. There are already reprisals. So for God's sake, stay up here out of the way."

Ellie walked with him out of the front door. "Listen," he said. "We should have a sign if you need me." He paused, looking around. "The property can't be seen from the village, which is lucky for you, but useless for me." He walked around to the terrace overlooking the sea. "But from my boat or even from the end of the harbour, I could see these palm trees. If you erected a washing line, maybe between the trees? Hang out your laundry regularly on it, but if you need me, hang out something . . ." He paused, thinking. "Something blue, the colour of France, eh? And I'll come right away."

"Something blue," she agreed.

"I made up a room for you," she said, "but you haven't needed to stay the night."

He shook his head. "I didn't want to disturb you. I have managed to slip down into the village without the sentry seeing me."

She realized that he did not want to involve her, to let her run any risk. She reached out to touch his sleeve. "Nico, don't take chances," she said.

He looked at her tenderly now. "I have to take plenty of chances, I'm afraid, but I want to involve you as little as possible." He put his hand gently against her cheek. "I wish things were different," he said. "I wish I could protect you better."

"I'm fine up here, really," she said. "It's you I worry about. If they catch you carrying weapons or even messages, they'll shoot you."

He patted her cheek now. "Luckily I know this coast better than they do. There are plenty of little coves where I can hide out if I spot an enemy ship. And my speedboat can outrun most of them." He paused, thinking. "I want to ask a favour of you."

"Go on." Ellie wasn't sure what was coming next.

"My mother. If anything happens to me, will you take care of her? Take her in? Look after her? I'm all she has."

"Of course."

"You promise?"

"I promise. But let's not think about such possibilities. I want you to stay safe."

"So do I, actually." He smiled. Then his lips brushed her forehead, and he hurried off.

It was the next day that Tommy received a message. Resistance fighters had indeed intercepted the lorry in Marseille. They had created a roadblock and opened the back door for the prisoners to escape. Most ran away but Bruno just stood there, unable to decide what to do next. The Germans shot him. Ellie had to give this news to his mother and let the woman cry on her shoulder. "My Bruno," she kept saying. "My little boy. All I had in the world."

Ellie felt a profound sense of failure, even though she had done all she could . . . They had all done all they could. Sometimes the odds were just too great.

CHAPTER 38

A funeral was held for Bruno, which the whole village of Saint-Benet attended. Everyone wept. Even Ellie, raised to show no emotion in public, sobbed. That such a sweet and gentle soul could have been taken so brutally seemed the ultimate inhumanity. Bruno's mother sat with a stunned look on her face, as if she still could not believe that her son was gone.

"Don't worry, madame, we'll take care of you," Mavis said to her. "Everyone in Saint-Benet. We all loved your son."

As she walked back up the steps, Ellie realized how much she was going to miss him. He had become part of her life, appearing in the mornings with a big smile on his face and bringing the loaf of bread in better times, still nodding and smiling when she'd given him a task to do. "I can do that, madame, don't you worry," he'd say and set to work right away.

"Maybe a swift death was better than one of those camps we're hearing about," Tommy said as he walked beside her. "For him that would be the ultimate horror."

Ellie tried to agree. "I keep thinking this is just the beginning. Who will be next? Which person I love will be taken from us?"

Christmas came and went, with a Midnight Mass in a packed church. There was no Christmas feast at Henri's bar, and the people who filed out of church after Mass wished each other a simple joyeux Noël, then went silently on their way home. Tommy and Clive went out of their way to make the house look festive with draped greenery, a pine sapling as a Christmas tree and cutout paper decorations. Mavis and Louis came to join them for a Christmas lunch. For the celebration, they killed one of the hens that had stopped laying. Tommy, sentimental as usual, said a eulogy over it before putting it in the pan, and served it with roast potatoes, parsnips and cabbage, followed by stewed apples and goat milk cream. They accompanied it with one of the last bottles of good wine. Roland toasted them. "To the magnificent chefs and the dear people who have made me so welcome," he said. "You are my dearest friends."

Ellie realized this was the wine talking but was glad that he no longer seemed discontent and surly and had accepted his lot.

"If only we were at my château, I could have showered you with gifts," he went on. "But here I have nothing except the clothes I stand up in. I am a pauper, an outcast, homeless . . ." And he started to weep.

"What a treat to have chicken," Mavis said to Ellie as they washed up after the meal. "We've been living on turnips and beans mostly, unless Louis traps a rabbit. Things have been hard for Louis, you know. Those bloody Germans come and take his tools, bring things to be mended and then never pay. I can tell you, I'm half tempted to hit one of them over the head with a big shovel." She laughed. "But it looks like you're still doing all right up here?"

"So far. You know you're welcome to share any of our produce. You don't come often enough."

"It's all right. You've got four mouths to feed now," Mavis said. She glanced back into the sitting room, where the four men were now drinking the latest excuse for coffee. "Who would have thought it when we left England that we'd both be living with strange men. Your Lionel would have a fit. So would my Reggie, God rest his poor soul."

Ellie had to smile. "Not my choice of 'strange men,' as you put it. But you're obviously happy with yours."

Mavis nodded. "He's a good bloke. Kind. And not a bad kisser, either."

Ellie hoped to see Nico, at least to wish him a joyeux Noël, but he wasn't at church, and she had no idea where he was or what he was doing. She found it hard not to worry. And at night she lay there, worrying about her two sons. She had no idea where Richard's regiment was now, no idea if Colin was now an airman, if he was even still alive. And she had no way of finding out. At the Christmas Mass, she had prayed for both of them, to the Virgin Mary as Mavis had suggested, but with so much death and destruction it was hard to believe that her one small prayer would make any difference or that any God would single out her sons to keep safe.

The new year came with no celebrations, except for those German officers, who had clearly found a way to access the wine cellar at Roland's château, judging by their raucous songs. Then, in the middle of January, Tommy came downstairs with a grim look on his face. "They have started rounding up French Jews," he said. "In Paris now, but I'm sure it will include the rest of the country soon enough. Taking them on trains into Germany."

"We should let the Adamses know," she said.

"You'd better tell them," Tommy said. "She despises us."

So Ellie went down to the village. It was a cold and stormy day. Rain swept in off the sea, making the steps slippery, and the wind snatched at her breath. She held her scarf tightly around her head. At least the weather had kept people off the street. There was no sign of German sentries guarding the port. As she slipped into the pension, she knew why. The sound of animated German conversation came from the parlour, and a pall of cigarette smoke drifted into the lobby. From the kitchen came the delicious smell of real coffee brewing. Ellie stood for a moment, looking around for Mrs Adams. Then she rang the bell on the counter. Mrs Adams appeared, but one of the Germans poked his head around the parlour door.

"Hello, my dear," Ellie said, in warmest tones and in English. "I haven't seen you in ages, and I miss our little chats. How have you been keeping?"

Mrs Adams looked at her strangely but then caught on. "Not so bad," she said. "Yourself? Why don't you come into the kitchen and have a cup of tea?" She turned back to the German soldier who was observing them. "An old friend from our days in England," she said to him in French.

Ellie followed her through the dining room and then into the kitchen. An old-fashioned stove gave a comforting warmth. There seemed to be a big pot of some kind of stew cooking on the stove. "Now then, what's up?" Mrs Adams asked Ellie.

Ellie lowered her voice. "They are rounding up Jews further north. Taking them away by train to camps. I thought Mr Adams should know. He may want to try and escape before it's too late."

Mrs Adams's expression did not change. "Oh, don't worry about us, dearie," she said. "I think we're quite safe here. Nobody knows or cares he's Jewish. He doesn't wear the star, so how would those Germans even find out? Besides, we're getting along quite nicely with them. They bring me the occasional coffee or bit of meat. I think they like the way we treat them here, and they're quite content."

"But if men come in from the outside, Gestapo, Abwehr?"

Mrs Adams shook her head with a patronizing smile. "As if anyone would know or care about Saint-Benet. No, dearie, they'll want the big prizes—Marseille and Toulon. That's where they'll go looking." She paused. "Besides, where would he escape to? If they are checking papers, he'd not get two yards on a train. And I can't see him hiking over the mountains into Switzerland." She gave a little chuckle. "But it was kind of you to think of us. How did you hear about this, anyway?" There was something in the tone of her voice that made Ellie wary. She suspected that Mrs Adams wouldn't hesitate to turn herself and Tommy in to the Germans if it got her an extra ration of something.

"We can sometimes pick up the BBC on our radio," she said. "Being so high up, we get a good signal. Of course, it's still crackling and going in and out, but I'm sure that's what we heard."

"You'd better not let these Germans know you're listening to the BBC," Mrs Adams said.

"Of course not," Ellie said. "But it's good to be informed, isn't it? Make plans just in case the worst happens?"

"I'd rather not know, personally," Mrs Adams said. "They pay good money to stay here. I treat them well, and we'll ride out this stupid war until it's over."

There was nothing more to say. As Ellie walked through the lobby, one of the Germans stuck his head out again. "Hey, Frau . . . madame. Come and keep us company," he called in bad French. "We're lonely boys far from home."

"We'd be very happy if you went home to your loved ones," Ellie said. "But I must go back to my husband. He wouldn't like me chatting with soldiers."

As she glanced into the parlour, she noticed a girl sitting on the knee of one of the soldiers and was shocked to see it was Madame Blanchet's daughter—the younger one her mother had described as flighty. Giselle Blanchet caught her eye and gave a defiant stare back before she puffed on a cigarette and blew out smoke. Should she warn Madame Blanchet, she wondered? Then she realized that the girl still lived at home. Her mother surely knew, but perhaps she also benefited from the occasional gift of coffee or sugar.

Ellie bade a polite goodbye to Mrs Adams, then went back up the steps, as always a little shaken at any encounter with the German soldiers. They could be genial now, but rumours indicated that they wouldn't think twice about shooting someone who annoyed them in any way. Or grabbing any woman they wanted. *Thank heavens I look middle-aged and not at all desirable,* she thought.

The storms continued, the wind rattling shutters, moaning through the roof and hurling rain at the windows. The palm trees swayed and bent until Ellie thought they had to snap. The chickens huddled miserably in their coop and wouldn't lay. The goats were fretful in their pen. Ellie had just gone to milk them one morning and was returning when she heard someone hammering on the gate. She went to open it, and Mr Adams half fell into the garden.

"Mr Adams, what is it?" she asked.

She noticed then that he was carrying a small bag with him. His expression was of terror. "There's a German lorry in the village, and they're going house to house looking at papers," he said. "I don't know what to do. They'll take me away, won't they? My ID card gives my race."

"Come in before you get soaked," Ellie said. "Then we'll think."

"I don't want to put you in any danger," he said.

"Don't be silly. Nobody checks up here." She went ahead of him into the house, put the milk on the kitchen table and told him to sit down. She gave him a cup of mint tea.

"We have to get you away," she said. "But I'm not sure how. Just lie low here for now."

Then she went out to the clothesline and, in spite of the rain and wind, she hung a blue shirt on it. She didn't think it was likely that Nico would notice it on a day like this, but if he came through the garden at night he would see it hanging there. The day passed. Tommy tried contacting the Resistance operator on the radio, but without success. Ellie made up a bed on a sofa for Mr Adams. Then, as she was getting ready for bed herself, filling a hot water bottle, there was a tap at the front door and Nico stood there, the rain running off his oilskin.

"What's wrong?" he asked, shaking off the worst of the drips before he stepped inside.

"Oh, you came. Thank God," Ellie said. She led him inside and pointed to Mr Adams. "The Nazis were in the village, checking identity cards. They'd see he was Jewish."

Nico sighed. "Yes. They've already started taking Jews from Marseille. We have to get him away."

"But where? How?"

"Corsica is now in Italian hands," he said. "If we can get him that far, he shouldn't be in too much danger, and we can work out what to do next."

"Corsica? You don't have a boat that can go that far, especially not in this weather."

"True," he said. "But I could take him out to the island. That abbot is a good fellow. I'm sure he wouldn't mind hiding Mr Adams until we could work out the next step."

"Yes, that's a good idea," Ellie said. "Nobody would notice an extra monk, would they?"

Nico smiled. "Right," he said. "Have him get ready. I'll take him down to the speedboat."

"Now? In the dark? In this weather?"

"More chance of making it in the dark and in this weather," he said. "The German navy won't bother to patrol as much when they think everyone stays home."

A spasm of worry crossed her face. "But Nico. Your little boat can't handle this rough sea, surely?"

Again he grinned. "We'll have to see, won't we?"

"Wait until the storm dies down. He'll be safe enough here," Ellie said.

Nico shook his head. "I don't want the Germans to find Adams here," he said. "They shoot people for harbouring Jews. The sooner we get him away, the better. Don't worry. The worst thing that can happen is that he'll be seasick."

They went through into the sitting room, where Mr Adams was getting ready for bed. He listened in silence, nodded, then put his shoes on again. "If it must be done this way, it must," he said. "Better than a train trip to Germany, anyway."

Ellie followed them to the front door. "Take care, won't you," she said. "Good luck, both of you."

Then she watched them cross the terrace and disappear down the steps. The wind was making too much noise to hear the speedboat start up. She sat up for several hours, hoping that Nico would report back, then hoping he'd decide to stay on the island until the storm died down. At last she fell into a restless sleep.

When she awoke the first streaks of a red dawn were in the eastern sky. She put on her dressing gown and went downstairs. She half hoped she'd find Nico asleep on her sofa, but there was no sign of him.

CHAPTER 39

Ellie dressed and went down to the village, hoping to use the excuse of a fresh baguette for breakfast to find out if Nico had made it safely back. His fishing boat lay at its usual moorings. There was no sign of the speedboat. If he had returned, he would have left it docked below the villa, she told herself. But then he would have come up through the garden and surely given her some sign that he was safely back. She debated whether she could go to his house, but if he hadn't returned, she didn't want to worry his mother. So she lingered in the town, buying a newspaper, or what passed for a newspaper these days, passing the time of day with those she met, before going back up the steps, glancing around first to make sure she was not noticed.

The day seemed to go on forever. On several occasions she went out on to the terrace, and once went down the narrow steps in the cliff to the little dock. It was empty. Fear overtook worry. She had heard the sort of things Germans did to those they captured, especially if they were with the Resistance. She hadn't realized until this moment how very fond she had become of Nico. And, of course, of the abbot, too. If the Germans had followed Nico's boat to the island, found Mr Adams and taken both Nico and the abbot away . . . It was too awful to think about.

"Don't worry," Tommy said, putting a comforting hand on her shoulders. "That bloke lives a charmed life. He'll turn up, I'm sure."

They ate dinner. Ellie went to bed and was just closing the shutters when she heard the tap at the front door. She rushed down. Nico was standing there.

"You made it. You're safe." She flung herself into his arms. He embraced her tightly, and they stood there for a moment, her cheek against his rough jumper.

"You didn't have to worry," he said at last. "It was simplicity itself. We made it to the island . . . A little choppy, I have to agree. Mr Adams had to keep bailing, or we would have filled with water." He laughed at the memory. "He was scared silly, I can tell you. But we found the abbot. He agreed this was a good plan, gave Mr Adams a habit to wear, and all was well."

"I'm so glad." She heaved a big sigh of relief. "So he can stay there until someone can pick him up in a bigger boat?"

"That's right," Nico replied. "I spent the night there. The sea really had become too wild to risk it home. But since then I've had a busy day. I've been talking to people in Marseille. We now see this could be a perfect solution for what to do with Jewish men who are trying to escape. Not with women, unfortunately. We are trying to find places for women and children in hilltop villages and out-of-the-way farms. But we can set up a system to take some men to the island. Especially the most valuable men—professors and scientists." As Ellie went to say something, he added, "Obviously we can't save them all. That is the problem."

Ellie nodded, trying to process this.

"The abbot reckons a few men could stay there for quite a while without being detected. He says that since the Germans invaded he's made sure that all his monks are never in the same place at the same time—some working in the fields, others at chapel, others in their cells, so that it would be hard to establish the number of monks on the island."

"Oh, that's clever," she said.

"And then, when we can, a boat will come for them and take them across to Corsica. Or if we can get a big enough boat, then over to Majorca, which is part of Spain. Either way, they'll be safer than here."

She nodded, sensing he wanted to say more. "But I'm not sure about this next part, because it would put you in danger."

"You want the men to come here?"

"That would be ideal." He paused, looking directly at her. "If someone takes them from the city, directs them to a point on the other side of the hill, where they would be out of sight of the village, then we'll alert by radio. Maybe one of the men in your house can lead the Jewish man down to you, you'll put out the signal for me and at night I'll come for him in the boat. But it would mean you'd be harbouring the Jewish man until nightfall. Always a risk."

"So far they don't seem to know about us," Ellie said.

"So far. Look, you can tell me now if you don't want any part of this. I understand."

"Of course I want to help," she said. "Rounding up Jewish people like cattle. Taking them off to God-knows-where. It's not human. And if I can help get a few of them to safety, then count me in."

"I always knew you were a wonderful person," he said.

"No, you didn't. You thought I was an annoying, spoiled Englishwoman." She laughed.

"Well, I've changed my mind."

"Look, Nico," she said, still considering this, "I can only agree for myself. It's possible the others will not want to put themselves in danger. You'd have to ask them."

"Are they already in bed?"

"They went up some time ago," Ellie said.

"Then I'll come back in the morning and explain it to them," he said.

Ellie sensed he was about to leave. "You must be hungry, and thirsty."

"I've managed to grab a bite here and there," he replied. "But I wouldn't say no to a glass of wine, if you still have any."

"We have a few bottles still," she said. "Come through to the kitchen."

Nico paused, looking up the stairs. "That man you have staying here, the viscount. Is he safe, do you think?"

"Certainly not a fan of the Germans," she replied. "The officers have taken over his château and turned him out with only the clothes on his back. They also kept his servants and have helped themselves to his wine cellar. So no, I don't think he'd want to report us to them."

"Good. But I think the less he knows about our little operation the better."

"That's all right," Ellie replied. "The viscount has no contact at all with the village. If he sees a strange man having a drink with us, we can tell him it's a neighbour who has come to visit."

"Just watch what you say in front of him."

"Yes. Definitely." Ellie took down a bottle of wine from the shelf and poured Nico a glass. Then she put out bread and goat cheese. He ate and drank with relish. "That was just what I needed," he said, getting up to go. "Now what I need is a good night's sleep. I don't think I've had one in a while."

"You're welcome to stay here," she said. "You know I made up a bed for you."

"Tempting." His eyes held hers. "But I feel responsible for my mother. She worries. I need to go home. I'll be back in the morning. Perhaps you could brief the Englishmen before I come, so they are not too surprised."

"Yes. I'll do that." She walked with him to the front door. "Good night, then. Go carefully."

He paused. "I have an absurd desire to kiss you, but that would not be wise. Then I should not want to go home." He blew her a kiss and hurried off, leaving her heart beating a little faster.

Ellie used the pretext of asking Tommy and Clive to help with the goats to get them out of the house. Roland was still sitting at breakfast and did not volunteer to help. When they were suitably far away, she told them the plan.

"It's entirely up to you," she said. "I don't want to put either of you at risk unless you fully agree to it."

"Of course we must do it," Tommy said. "We can't have human beings rounded up and sent off to God knows what fate." He looked at Clive. "What do you think? I won't agree if you don't."

Ellie looked at Clive. He seemed less certain, but then he shrugged. "I've a personal vendetta against Germans since they lobbed a grenade at me in the last war, so I think we should do it." He took a deep breath, as if not completely sure of what he was saying. "I've been trying to work on fake identity cards. It's proving not to be that easy, given the limited equipment I have. I suppose I can probably do a job that will pass scrutiny. Cards that give race as Aryan in case they are needed."

"Oh, I'm sure they'll be needed," she said. "The more you can make of those the better."

"But what about you?" Clive said. "This will be dangerous for all of us, including you, if they find out."

"I know. But I think we have to do it." Ellie stared out to the blue sea below them, wind-whipped with white-capped waves. "It can't be too many, just in case the Germans visit the island. So it won't put us in harm's way too often, I hope."

They looked up as they heard footsteps coming towards them. It was Nico.

"I've told them," she said. "And they agree."

"Good men." Nico slapped Clive on the back. "Now let me fill you in on the details. Come with me. We'll decide on the path they will take and the meeting point."

The men went off with Nico. Ellie returned to the house.

"Where are your friends?" Roland asked.

"I've put them to work, mending part of the fence," she said. "If the goats get out, they'll eat all our plants."

He seemed to accept this.

"I keep wondering if I should go back to Paris," he said. "I am good for nothing here, except eating your food."

"Oh, surely not Paris," Ellie replied. "They don't have enough food, and the Germans are everywhere."

"I'm sure I could arrange for food through the black market," he said. "Money is a useful commodity. I just feel so useless here."

It did occur to Ellie that it would be much easier for their future plans if he did go. "But how could you travel?"

"I do have my motor car."

"You'd need enough petrol."

"True. But I expect the black market might provide that."

"And there will be checkpoints all along the way."

"I shall tell them my aged mother is sick. I am returning as the dutiful son. I don't think they would stop me."

"They could commandeer your car, the way they took your house."

He considered this. "That's true. Maybe I should wait for the weather to improve. It may be hard to find coal for heating in Paris."

Tommy and Clive returned much later, chatting and laughing as if they hadn't a care in the world.

"We went for a little stroll up the hillside," Tommy said. "What a fine view there is from the top. But it's steep coming down. Clive sat on his bottom at one point."

"It's not polite to mention such an indignity," Clive replied. "I shall go to my room and work on my calligraphy."

What have we got ourselves into? Ellie thought. *Will we be able to bluff our way through if the Germans find out?*

CHAPTER 40

The first of the men arrived two days later. He came, bundled in a great overcoat and scarf. It seemed he was wearing a jacket and jumper underneath since he could not carry a suitcase with his clothing. Instead he carried a small bag. He was sweating profusely, as much from fear it seemed as from the overabundance of clothing he was wearing. His eyes darted nervously as he looked around the room.

"Don't worry," Ellie said. "You're safe here for the moment. We'll give the signal for your transport to pick you up tonight. In the meantime you can take off your overcoat and sit down. I'll get you a glass of water."

"Most kind. Most kind," he muttered. He had a deep, rumbling voice. He removed his hat and had a shock of grey curly hair.

"If anyone asks, you are a friend, visiting us," Ellie muttered before she went through to the kitchen to pour the water. The man was sitting, perched on the edge of a chair, when she returned. Tommy had disappeared, and the man was staring out at the view below.

"You have a lovely view here," he said.

"Yes. It's a beautiful spot." Ellie handed him the glass.

"I should introduce myself," he began, but she cut him off.

"No, don't. The less we know about each other the better. Just in case."

"You're right. Just in case." He took a gulp of the water. "That was quite a walk. Rather steep. I'm afraid I'm not incredibly fit." Then a spasm of pain crossed his face. "I still can't believe it," he said. "I never thought it would happen to me. I thought I was a respected member of the community. I'm the conductor of the Marseille symphony orchestra, you know. I've held the position for years. I have so many friends . . . so when they said all Jews have to report I didn't think for a moment that I would be involved. But then one of my violists got a tip that they were coming for me. I left in the middle of a rehearsal." He shook his head as if he was still trying to make sense of it. "So many of my musicians are Jewish, too. How can they do this to us? We are valuable members of the community." His voice cracked, and he took another drink of water to swallow back the emotion.

"I'm so sorry," Ellie said. "But with any luck you'll be safe. The Italians are in control of Corsica, and they value music, don't they?"

"Who knows anymore," he said. "The world has gone mad. We are all being ruled by a madman."

"What about your wife?" Ellie asked because she noticed the wedding band on his finger. "What will happen to her?"

"She is not Jewish, thank God," he said. "But she has gone up to a friend in the countryside, just in case they come to question her. Who knows if I'll ever see her again." And a tear trickled down his cheek. He wiped it away hastily.

Tommy returned and sat keeping him company while Ellie went out to the terrace, and with hands that trembled a little she pegged the blue shirt on to the line, raising it high enough to be seen. It fluttered bravely in the breeze. Would Nico see it? she wondered. How often did he check her line? Anyway, the man was safe for the moment. She fed him vegetable soup for lunch. Roland was delighted to find a guest and chatted to him about music.

"How I have missed artistic company," he said. "I keep thinking I must go back to Paris, where I can attend the opera again."

"Is the opera still performing, I wonder?" the man said. "I heard they have shut down so much, and of course there is the curfew after dark."

"But the Germans love music," Roland said.

"You would have thought so, wouldn't you," the man replied.

Ellie made a big show of inviting their guest to stay the night. Clive and Tommy went up to bed. Roland lingered. At last Ellie said, pointedly, "You must be tired, my dear," to the man. "Let me show you to your room. You don't have to stay awake and be polite any longer."

She led him upstairs. Roland also came up and went into his room. After a suitable while, Ellie tapped on the spare room door and led the man down again.

"Get ready," she said. "We don't know when the boat will come, but I should take you down, just in case."

She put on her overcoat. He put on his, and she led him out into the night. It was fortunate that the moon was almost full. She had brought a torch and picked out the steep and winding steps as they went down the cliff.

"Go very carefully," she said. They took the steps one by one. At the bottom they came to the small harbour—a little dock protected by an outcropping of rocks. Any boat moored there would be invisible from passing ships. Ellie stood looking and listening, every fibre in her being tense and alert. She heard the slap of waves against the rocks, the rustle of wind in the pine trees above. Apart from that, silence.

"You should sit down here, out of the wind," she said, indicating a flat area of rock. "It may be some time. He'll have to wait until he can slip away without being noticed. There are German sentries in the village now."

The man brushed off the rock surface before sitting on it. "I don't know why you people risk your lives for someone you don't know," he said. "In my culture you would be called a righteous person."

"We have to do what we can," Ellie said. "We can't let evil swallow the world."

"No. We can't."

They sat in silence. Then Ellie stood up. "What was that?"

She heard it then. The low *pop pop* of a motor, and the boat came into sight. Nico flashed a signal from his torch, then cut the motor and the boat drifted to them. He stood up, leapt out before it could hit the dock.

"I've picked up some oars," he said. "Better to row silently until I'm well clear of the village." He turned to the stranger. "Good evening, sir. A fine night for a sea voyage, I think."

He helped the man into the boat, then pushed off, waved and started the motor. Once they were out to sea, she heard it rev up to full power and they were gone.

~~

In the morning there was a note from Nico outside the front door: *All went smoothly. This is a great idea.*

Ellie herself was amazed how smoothly it had gone. More Jewish men followed. They were always men of consequence: professors, scientists, artists, writers. It seemed unfair to Ellie that some lives were considered more valuable than others—how could anyone determine that a professor had more worth than a baker or a shoemaker?—but she understood that not all could be saved. Also these men usually had non-Jewish wives. Those whose families were also Jewish had refused to leave them. The men were all movingly grateful, and some even hugged her when she took them down the cliff to meet Nico's boat.

Because it was working so well, Ellie had stopped worrying so much. But with the warmer spring weather and calmer seas, the German navy was more in evidence, guarding the strategic port of Marseille. It was now not unusual to see a naval vessel or even a convoy passing out at sea from where they sat on the terrace. They never came near the coast, which was a relief. Then one night Ellie had gone to bed. There had been no Jewish guest that day. They had enjoyed a good meal, a big chicken stew with lots of vegetables, thanks to one of the chickens that had died of old age. They had played a few rounds of bridge, and Ellie had felt quite content as she pulled the covers over her. She had just dozed off when she heard the rattle of pebbles at her shutters. She jumped up, opening the shutters. In the dark she could just make out Nico standing there.

"I'll come down," she whispered, then hurriedly slipped on her robe and tiptoed down the stairs. He had come around to the front door and slipped inside the moment she opened it. He was breathing heavily, as if he had been running.

"What's wrong?" she asked.

"They almost got me," he said. "I was delivering some supplies to the cell further down the coast when this German patrol boat appeared out of nowhere. They shone a searchlight on me and told me to come alongside. I had ammunition in the boat. Of course I wasn't going to do that, so I put the throttle on full and got out of there. But they fired at me. I managed to outrun them, and naturally I know this stretch of coast better than they do, so I was able to hide out in a hidden cove and then, when they had gone past, make my way back here."

Ellie noticed he was wincing. "You said they fired at you. Did they hit you?"

"I'm not sure. Probably yes. I felt something, but there was so much adrenalin coursing through me that I hardly noticed."

"Take off your coat," she said. "Let's see."

As he took off the heavy jacket, she saw the blood. "Oh God, Nico. You're bleeding. Come into the kitchen. Let me get a cloth."

He followed her and sat on a stool while she put a pan of water on the stove, then grabbed a clean cloth and moistened it with water. "We need to find where it's coming from," she said. "Here. Let me help you off with your jumper."

He held up his arms like a small child as she pulled it over his head. Blood was running down his front. "It's your neck," she said. "Oh God." She started to wipe the blood away, dreading what she was going to find. Did one have to remove a bullet? How would she do that? Then she heaved a sigh of relief.

"You're a lucky man," she said. "It just grazed the side of your neck. A centimetre to the left and it would have struck your jugular vein and you'd be gone. You must lead a charmed life."

"The devil doesn't want me yet," he said, giving a nervous chuckle.

The water was heating up. She dipped the cloth in it and cleaned up all traces of blood. All that was left was a long scratch along one side of his neck. "It seems the bleeding has stopped," she said. "Let me put a bandage over it. I'll get some Dettol to make sure it's not infected."

"Ow, that hurts," he said as she dabbed at it with a cotton swab.

"Don't be a baby. I always did this for my boys when they skinned their knees. They didn't make a fuss."

He grinned, then he said, "Tell me about your boys. You never mention them."

"No, but I think about them a lot," she said. "One was in the army before the war even started. The other was going to join the RAF. I haven't heard any news from either of them for a long while. I don't know if they are still alive or not. It's hard not to worry."

"You were close to them?"

"Not really. When they were little, we were close. They snuggled with me when I read them a bedtime story. Such darling little boys. And then my husband insisted that we send them to boarding school when they were seven, because that was what the best families did. I tried arguing, but Lionel always got his own way, so off they went. And they were never the same again. They never dared to show their emotions after that. It was as if they shut off from any affection." She gave a little sigh. "Oh, they were always polite and nice enough to me, but there was never that spark of connection anymore."

"Not like we have," he said. When she looked up he smiled. "'That spark of connection,' you said. We have that, don't we?"

"Yes, I think we do."

He was looking at her steadily. "I can't go home tonight," he said. "They may be looking for me. They'll want to find out who the boat belongs to. It does look rather distinctive."

"Then leave it hidden down below for a while. Until the heat has died down," she said.

"There are still more Jewish men coming. I have to take them. It's my duty," he said. "But tonight, you don't mind if I stay here? I don't think they can trace me, but you never know."

"Of course you can stay," she said. "I told you I made up a room already for you."

He put an arm around her shoulder. "I want to be with you," he said. "I want to remember what it feels like to be close to someone, to fall asleep in someone's arms. It's been so long . . ."

He was looking at her steadily. "All right," she said unsteadily.

"Just all right? You don't want it, too? You'd just be doing me a favour?"

Ellie's eyes held his. "Don't be silly," she said. "I do want it, too."

He held her close to him as they walked up the stairs together.

CHAPTER 41

Ellie was just aware of Nico slipping away at the first streaks of dawn. He bent to kiss her forehead, then he was gone. She lay there, savouring the long-dormant feelings he had awoken in her, the utter joy of being loved and wanted by someone. *He had a bad scare and he needed reassurance,* she told herself. *And I was available.* And yet she was sure it was more than that. He did love her. The incident was not repeated in the following days. More Jewish men came and were picked up by the speedboat, but Nico stayed suitably far away from her, as if he didn't want to put her in any danger. Ellie tried to keep their presence from Roland, hiding them in the kitchen, or occasionally introducing them as friends visiting up from the village.

One day Tommy had gone up the path, ready to meet the next person to be transported. Ellie was making lunch. Clive was in his studio working, and Roland was lounging on the terrace in the sun when Tommy came in. "Yoo-hoo! Hello, my darling, I've come home," he called, in English. "I hope you've prepared something delicious for lunch because I've brought a visitor."

Ellie came out, surprised by the strange and hearty greeting. It was Tommy being funny, she decided, if different from his usual understated humour. She stepped into the foyer, prepared to see another Jewish man carrying a small bag. Instead a German soldier stood behind Tommy, a gun pointed at his back.

"What's this?" Ellie asked, not having to feign horrified surprise. "What's happening?"

"You wish to speak English. We speak English, then." A German officer stepped into the hallway. He was immaculately dressed in highly polished knee boots and a uniform that identified him as no ordinary soldier. "You are the wife of this man?"

"Yes, I am," she said. "What do you want with him? We are good people. We've done nothing wrong."

"We have reason to believe that this man is working with the Resistance," the officer said.

"Don't be silly. He doesn't even speak French very well," Ellie said. "I told you, we live in our own little world up here."

"Then what was he doing waiting for a Jew on the path from the road?"

"I told you," Tommy said. "I go up on the hill to try and snare rabbits. We need food these days. I put out snares."

"Of course you do," the German sneered. "You must think we are very naïve. We know all about your little scheme."

"We have no scheme," Tommy said quickly. "And please do not upset my wife. She is a simple woman. She keeps house for me and feeds whatever guests I bring in."

"Of course she does." Again the German smiled. "And who else lives in this house?"

"Our nephew from England," Ellie said. "He is a well-known painter. He came to visit us out here and liked it, so he stayed. He's up in his room painting right now."

"Call him."

Ellie went halfway up the stairs. "Clive, sweetheart. It's Auntie Ellie. Stop your painting and come down here," Ellie called. "There is a German officer who wants to speak to us."

"I told you, we are all innocent," Tommy said. "Please just let us get on with our lives."

"Don't they pay you for your ferrying of the Jews? These people have money, don't they? You could have made them pay up."

Clive appeared at the top of the stairs, his face ashen when he saw the gun in Tommy's back.

"Why are you pointing a gun at him?" he asked. "He is the most peaceful person you'll ever meet. He is not causing you any trouble, I promise you."

"You promise us." The man shook his head. "Every Jew that escapes is an insult to the Führer."

"I don't know what you're talking about," Clive said. "You have the wrong people."

"Oh no. We have exactly the people we want," he said. "And later we will round up the bigger fish." He turned back to the open door and barked a command. "They will now search your house," he said. "And let us see how innocent you are." He pulled out his own revolver, nodded to the man with the gun, and another soldier came in to join them. They went from room to room while Tommy, Clive and Ellie stood like statues. Ellie's brain was racing. She had to warn Nico, but their flag on the terrace would bring him to them, not keep him away. Would they be taken? Shot immediately? It was surely only a matter of time before these men found the radio. She heard the sounds of furniture being moved, heavy boots crossing the floor above. It felt as if time stood still. Ellie found it hard to breathe. She did not dare look at anyone, staring instead through the open door to the windows of the sitting room and that tantalizing blue sea beyond. Suddenly it dawned on her that Roland was still out there, probably engrossed in his book and with no idea that the Germans were here. If she said nothing, at least he might escape their notice.

At last the men came down the stairs. "Nothing up here," one of them muttered in German, and they proceeded to go through the downstairs rooms. Apparently they hadn't noticed Roland, his back to them on the wicker chaise, because they came back to the officer.

"Nothing irregular," Ellie thought she understood one of them to say. "A lot of messy paint in that artist's room."

Ellie saw Clive's mouth twitch. So they hadn't found any false ID cards. She suspected Clive had poured paint over anything incriminating. And they had not located the radio. Whoever had hidden it had done a good job.

"Have the outbuildings searched as well," the officer said. "They could be hiding Jews, or weapons."

"There is nothing in our outbuildings," Ellie said as the officer turned to head towards the shed with one of the soldiers. She followed them. "The garage is empty since I no longer have a motor car, and the shed is used by a local fisherman to store his tackle."

"Is that so?" The officer came up to the shed and saw the padlock. "In which case why the need to lock it?" He took out his pistol, aimed at the lock and fired. The shot reverberated around the hillside. Ellie was holding her breath and hardly dared to look.

"Gott im Himmel." The officer recoiled at the smell of fish that came out. Ellie looked and saw buckets, fish scales on the floor, fishing nets hanging across the back on hooks. "It seems your local fisherman does what he says. What a filthy stink." And he turned away again. Ellie tried not to let out a sigh of relief.

"Very well," the officer said as he walked towards the house, where Tommy was still standing with a gun in his back. "That will be all for now. One of my men will be waiting to intercept the Jew when he comes. And we will proceed to take care of the rest of your little operation—the man with the boat, and the so-called churchman on the island." He laughed again. "Don't look so surprised. You know all about this, I am sure. And now so do we. But for the moment we just take this man." He prodded Tommy in the side. "You will tell us all we need to know, and I think we will be back soon. Come. Move." He jabbed the gun again. Ellie ran over to him, flinging herself at him with a little cry of grief. "Don't take my husband. He's a good man. What will I do without him?"

"Don't worry, my darling," Tommy said, holding her in his arms and looking down at her tenderly. "I'm sure all will be well. They'll accept that we know nothing. We are innocent. Be brave. Be strong. I'll be home in time for dinner." He looked over her head at Clive. "Be strong, my nephew. Take good care of your aunt."

It felt as if she was part of a play with a really bad script. Tommy released her and walked ahead of the officer out of the front door. Clive had his hand pressed to his mouth so that he didn't cry out, and Ellie put a restraining hand on his shoulder. "It will be all right," she said, although she was sure that it wouldn't.

"I won't ever see him again," Clive muttered, blinking back tears. "What will they do to him? I didn't even get to say goodbye."

"We must hope for the best," Ellie said. "They didn't find the radio. That's good. Perhaps they'll believe Tommy that he was out snaring rabbits."

"I poured black paint over the card I was working on," Clive said. "Thank you for warning me. I heard how different your voice sounded."

She nodded. "Yes. Tommy tried to warn me when he came in by saying silly things. If I'd been quicker on the uptake, I could have slipped away then and maybe got down to the village to warn Nico. Now I don't know how I can."

She looked out of the window. There was a German guard standing at the far end next to their garage. Another one at the gate above the steps down to the village.

"I don't suppose they'd let me go to buy food."

Clive shook his head. "No way. We're prisoners here. They'll be back for us."

Ellie fought back nausea. They would torture Tommy, and he would tell them everything. It would only be a matter of time before they came for her, for Clive and for Nico. Someone had betrayed them, she thought. Maybe someone working with the Resistance in Marseille, because nobody in Saint-Benet knew what they were doing. *Except Mrs Adams,* a little voice whispered. But surely she wouldn't betray them when they had saved her own husband, would she? Ellie was sure that Mrs Adams disliked her, was jealous of her. But it didn't matter who. They were living on borrowed time.

How can I possibly warn Nico? She looked around desperately. "We could try the radio," she said. "Perhaps someone in the Resistance cell can get a message to him. Do you know how to use it?"

"I've watched Tommy," Clive said. "I think I could, but I would rather not use the radio right now. It's quite possible that they've found us because they've cracked a Resistance cell in Marseille. They may well be eavesdropping on anything we say, so we'd only invite Nico to walk into a trap."

"Oh gosh. You may be right," she said. "But I'm going to get a message to him somehow. I'm not going to let those brutes take him and the abbot. It's just possible he left the speedboat at the dock. They don't seem to have noticed the steps down the cliff. I can go down there without being seen."

"You're rather fond of him, aren't you?" Clive asked.

"Yes," she said. "Rather fond. Very fond."

"You plan to take the boat and go looking for him?"

"If I have to," she said.

"That's running an awful risk."

"What choice do we have?" She heard her voice rising.

"I should come with you."

She could tell he was trying to do the right thing. "Absolutely not. You have to stay here and bluff it out if they come back before me. Tell them I always go for my walk over to the Calanques at this time of day."

He nodded. "I'd better go and clear up the studio. Make sure there are no traces of anything incriminating."

As he was about to walk away, the French doors opened and Roland came in. "I've just had the most delightful snooze," he said. "I was reading, and I fell asleep in the sun. Now I'll get a lovely tan. Is it lunchtime yet?"

"The German military were here," Clive said. "They've taken Tommy."

"What on earth for?" Roland looked amused. "If there is anyone who obviously doesn't pose a threat to the might of the Führer, it's dear Tommy."

"Let's hope they see it the same way," Clive said. "Come on, Roland, you can help me pick some vegetables for lunch. Let's see what's ripe. Grab a basket." He glanced back at Ellie and nodded.

As they went towards the vegetable garden, past one of the guards, she slipped away in the other direction, out of the French doors at the back of the house, across the terrace and down the steps cut into the cliff. She half expected to see German sentries waiting for her at the bottom, but the little harbour stood there, quiet and deserted. No sign of any boat, or of Nico. If he had spotted German soldiers at the villa, then he would have moved off again, and hopefully gone to warn the abbot. That would be the best thing that could have happened. But in case he had no idea that they had been discovered, Ellie still felt she had to warn him. She stared at the coastline, rocks and tide pools jutting out at the headland before it curved around into the harbour of Saint-Benet. *Can I do it?* she asked herself. It was worth a try. At least she didn't have to cross any beach that could have been mined. She started clambering over rocks. Some were taller, dry and with good footholds. At other points the surface dipped lower so that they were submerged at high tide and covered in seaweed and slime.

She pressed bravely on, slithering and going on all fours at times, feeling the weight of time on her shoulders. She rounded the headland and saw the village before her, nestled in its narrow valley. How pretty it looked with its pastel houses glowing in the midday sun and the water sparkling in the harbour. Such a perfect setting of peace and security. But at least there was no German gunboat to be seen. She continued until after several minutes she picked up a proper path. She ran along this, conscious of her wet legs and skirt, hearing her shoes squelch. As she came to the harbour, she spotted two of the fishermen at their boats.

"Help. Over here!" She called to them. They came around the harbour to her.

"What is it, madame? Has there been an accident? You are hurt."

She saw him looking at her legs and realized that she had skinned her knees on the rocks. Blood was running down. "No, it's not me," she said. "It's Nico. Do you know where he is? We must find him right away."

One fisherman looked at the other. "He went out in his boat," he said. "Not the fishing boat of his father, but that little toy of his."

"Do you know which direction?"

"Towards the city, I think. Who knows why? Better not to ask these days. There are certainly no visitors to escort."

"We have to find him." Ellie was still gasping for breath. "The Germans came to my house. I don't know if the officer was part of the Abwehr or what, but they have taken Mr Tommy away. They may well be back for Clive and me, so there is not much time."

"Taken Mr Tommy?" The man looked incredulous.

She wasn't going to explain any more.

"But they want Nico."

"Ah, so Nico has been doing more than fishing," one of them said, nodding to the other. "We wondered what he was doing out in that little boat of his with no tourists around."

"Is it black market? Is that it?" the other asked.

"Of course not," Ellie snapped, her nerves at breaking point. "He's aiding . . . you know."

Her brain was racing, wondering what she could say that would not give too much away. "If you find him, just tell him they've taken Mr Tommy. Tell him they know everything, and he must not come to the villa."

The man seemed to understand. "All right."

Ellie grabbed his arm. "So can you try to find him? That boat of his is easy to spot, isn't it?"

The man still looked doubtful. "If he's gone all the way into Marseille? I prefer to stay away myself. That port is crawling with Germans."

"But we can't let them take him, can we? They'll shoot him."

The fisherman nodded, as if he realized this was probably true. "Very well," he said. "I was about to take my boat out anyway. I'll do what I can. And Jacquot here, he's working on his torn net, so he'll be in the harbour if Nico returns."

"Thank you," she said. "Thank you. Tell him not to come up to the villa. There are German guards."

"So how did you get out?"

"Down the steps and around the cliff," she said. "Not the easiest route. And now I must go back so that I am not missed. I don't want to put anyone in more danger."

"You're a brave woman," the fisherman said. "But if you've managed to get away from German guards, why go back? You could make your way down the coast to where the Italians are. They'd take pity on you, I'm sure."

"I left the others," she said. "And I may need to vouch for Mr Tommy. We have to get him away from those monsters."

"Well, I wish you luck," he said. "God be with you."

She nodded, tears stinging at the backs of her eyes, and retraced her steps, returning to the house without any guards having noticed her absence.

CHAPTER 42

They waited for Tommy's return, for the German officer's return. The guards stayed in their positions, guarding both exits to the property, but there was no other sign of German activity. Ellie wondered whether they had intercepted the Jewish man who was supposed to come to them; she worried that the fisherman would not be able to locate Nico, that the Nazis would take the abbot and even shoot all the monks. She paced the terrace, staring out to sea. Clive warmed her some soup, but she couldn't eat. He was equally upset, and the two of them sat staring at full plates while Roland ate his with gusto.

"Delicious," he said, putting down his spoon. "Now if this was only the first course and there was venison to follow, or veal maybe . . ."

"Don't you understand?" Ellie blurted out. "They've taken Tommy. We're all in danger here. They could come back for the rest of us at any moment."

"I'm sure you're overreacting," Roland said. "They'll deliver Tommy back, and all will be well . . . unless there is something going on here that I don't know about."

"Better that you don't," Clive said.

"The men who come to visit sometimes," Roland said, looking directly at Ellie. "They are escaping, are they not? Are they Jews? Is that why?"

"As Clive said, better that you know nothing," Ellie said.

"As you wish." Roland shrugged. "My God. I wish I were not out of my favourite cigarettes. One does need a smoke to calm the nerves."

He got up and left the room.

"I don't like that man," Clive said. "Never have. You don't think that he could have alerted the Huns, do you?"

"What, and risk his own life? He also lives here in the house. If they decide we've harboured Jewish people, he'll be equally guilty."

"If they catch today's Jewish man, we'll definitely be in for it," Clive said. "If they hadn't taken Tommy away, I'd try to get out of here, pay one of the fishermen to take us to Corsica or wherever. But I'm not going to leave Tommy."

"Neither am I," Ellie said. "Let's just hope."

At last they went to bed, but Ellie couldn't sleep. She lay awake, remembering Nico's arms around her, the warmth of his body against hers. A new day dawned with mist hanging over the sea and the jutting cliffs along the coast receding in indistinct outlines. A seagull's cry echoed eerily through the mist. Ellie drank a cup of herb tea and wondered if she'd be allowed down to the village to buy bread. That way she might get news of Nico. She had decided to go and ask the sentry, to use any kind of feminine flattery to appeal to his gentler side, and was halfway down the garden path when the gate opened and a German staff car drove in. The same officer got out. She waited for Tommy to appear, but he did not. The officer strode towards her.

"You are thinking of going somewhere?" he asked.

"We have to buy bread from the village before it sells out every day."

"Of course you do." That self-satisfied, mocking smile made Ellie want to slap him.

"Where is my husband?" she asked. "Why have you not returned him to us?"

He was still smiling. "Your husband told us many things, just as I knew he would. I have to think he is a simple man who didn't quite understand what he was doing in offering shelter to Jews. You English are too soft-hearted."

"So you've let him go?" She breathed a sigh of relief.

"Let him go?" The officer now laughed. "Oh no, dear lady. He has committed a crime. He is on his way to a camp, maybe in Germany." When she gasped, he added, "You should consider yourselves lucky. I could have had you all shot here and now. As it was, your husband kept insisting that he was the only one involved in the stupid scheme and you and his nephew were completely innocent. So you can thank him. I've decided to give you the benefit of the doubt, for now. Since your little operation is no more . . ."

He paused, observing her face, savouring the moment. "Oh, didn't I tell you about your other friends? The so-called churchman and the fisherman? How remiss of me. Our navy met up with them, trying to flee to Corsica. Their boat was sunk, and both of them were shot in the water."

"You monster." She spat out the words. "Those were two good men. The best." She glared at him. "How can you live with yourself?"

His expression did not change. "Everything I do is for the Fatherland," he said. "And for the Führer. My orders are to eradicate all Jews and traitors. And I should warn you to watch your mouth, madame. I could shoot you at this moment for daring to speak to me in that way. Now go back to your house and stay there if you know what is good for you."

She wanted to say more but noticed his fingers toying with the revolver at his hip.

She stumbled back to the house, not aware of putting one foot in front of the other. Clive took one look at her face. "Ellie. Is it bad news?"

She nodded, unable to speak. He took her hand and led her over to the nearest chair. Then she took a deep breath, and the words tumbled out. "They've shot Nico and the abbot. They sunk their boat and then shot them both in the water."

"And Tommy?" He shouted the word.

"He's on a train, going to a prison camp in Germany."

"No!" The word came out an anguished cry. "Then where is that German bastard? I want to strangle him with my bare hands."

"He'd shoot you first."

"Then I want to go with Tommy. I'll tell them I was also involved."

"Don't be silly. No good could come of turning yourself in."

"But I want to be with Tommy, wherever he is. You know he's not strong. He'll get sick in one of those camps, or they might put him to hard labour . . ."

"Clive, my dear." Ellie put her hands on his shoulders. "I know how you must be feeling. I feel the same way, utterly lost. But Tommy is still alive. He may be released and come back to us. We have to keep on hoping."

Clive stared at her, his face bleak. "But how shall I go on?"

"I'm asking myself the same thing. We will go on, because if we gave in and ended it all, then those murderers would have won. We have to stay alive until they are out of here for good."

Clive nodded. "I suppose you're right. Although there seems no point, does there?"

"No point at all."

Ellie turned around as Roland came into the room. "I saw a German car. Is Mr Tommy back with us?"

"No," Ellie said. "He's probably been tortured, and he's now on a train bound for a German prison camp."

"No, that can't be right." Roland sounded perplexed. "He promised . . ." He broke off.

"Who promised what, Roland?" Clive asked, taking a step towards him.

"That we wouldn't be touched. They only wanted the ringleaders. He promised. That officer. Gentleman to gentleman."

"That Nazi is no gentleman, Roland," Ellie said. She glared at him, her face set in stone. "You told the Germans about our little operation here? You betrayed us? Why? We've taken you in and made you welcome. How could you do this?"

"I don't like Jews," he said simply. "I never have. They don't belong in my country. And I thought if I told them, they might let me come back to my house . . . maybe live in one portion of it and have my servants back again."

"They shot Nico and the abbot from the island," Ellie said, fighting back the desire to strike him. "You had two wonderful men killed."

"I didn't mean to." He sounded like a little boy. "I just thought it would stop the Jews coming here, and I didn't realize it was your lover, Nico, who was involved."

"I want you out of here," Ellie said. "Pack up your things and go."

"Go where?"

Ellie shrugged. "I don't care. I'm sure they'll find you a room at the pension with your pals the German soldiers."

"But you can't mean it. We've been friends . . ."

"I thought we were friends," Ellie said. "But friends don't betray each other. Now go."

"Very well," he said, now giving her an arrogant stare. "I'll go back to Paris to my family. I have plenty of places to stay there if my own house has no servants at the moment. I will be just fine."

Ellie did not reply. She turned her back on him and did not see him go.

CHAPTER 43

As Ellie stood alone on the back terrace, the pain overwhelmed her. No Nico, no Abbot Gerard. Two men she had truly loved and respected. She tried to picture life without them and saw only a dark tunnel with no light at the end. She had been brave and defiant for Clive, but now she wondered if her words really meant anything. Did she want to go on? Completely alone, unloved? But the one feeling that still drove her was her anger, her desire for revenge. She was not going to give that Nazi monster the satisfaction of knowing he had killed her, too.

As soon as Ellie had processed her loss, she thought of Nico's mother. She would have to give her the news. And she remembered that she had promised Nico to take care of the old lady. She went down to the village and was heading for Nico's house when she remembered Mavis. Mavis was still here, a true friend, a kind woman. Ellie hesitated. Did she want to take her grief to someone who was happy, settled, loved? Then she thought tomorrow it could be Louis who was taken. None of them was safe. So she kept walking until she came to the house behind the toolshed. There was no sign of Louis working as she walked past, for which she was grateful. She had no wish for polite conversation today.

Mavis was out in the back garden, hanging up washing.

"At last a fine day," she called when she saw Ellie. "I thought these bloody sheets would never dry." Then she saw Ellie's face. "What's happened, love? Bad news?"

Ellie nodded, unable to speak. Then when she spoke the words came out in a torrent: "Took Tommy, killed Nico, killed the abbot . . ." She fought back great sobs as Mavis took her into her arms.

"Killed them? Why?"

"Because they were helping Jewish men to escape from France," Ellie said. "They knew they were risking their lives, and they still did it . . . for strangers, Mavis."

"And I always thought that Nico was a crook," Mavis said. "You know, black market smuggling. That kind of thing. And all the time he was doing this?"

Ellie nodded. "He always did like to live dangerously, but—" She couldn't finish.

"Oh my love, I'm so sorry," Mavis said. "The bastards. The absolute monsters. If only we could give them what's coming to them." She paused. "What you need is a good cup of tea. I can't give you that, on account of no proper tea any more, but I can make you a cup of chamomile. Supposed to be restorative."

Ellie shook her head. "I don't want anything. I was actually on my way to Nico's mother. She doesn't know yet. And I promised him I'd take his mother in if anything happened to him."

Mavis regarded her. "You were very fond of him, weren't you?"

"More than fond. We loved each other," Ellie said. "How strange it is to say that, but it's true. I don't know why it took me so long to realize that I loved him. I suppose I was scared of getting hurt again. And now he's gone, Mavis. I won't ever see him again."

She turned away. "First Jojo, then Dora and now this. It's too much, Mavis. I can't take any more. Why did I ever come to this horrible place? I could have stayed in England and done the sensible thing, acted as I'd always acted all my life: sane, sensible, reasonable. I'd have made jam and knitted socks for the Women's Institute. Accepted my fate as a rejected woman . . . and not had to feel . . ."

Mavis put her hands on Ellie's shoulders. "Would you, really? Never have played with Jojo and listened to her laugh? Never have learned to love Dora or Nico? Never have looked out at your view? At least you experienced those once, didn't you? At least you were loved by a good man. How many people can say that?"

Ellie nodded. Then she said, "I don't know how I can keep going, Mavis. I've been strong all my life, but now I feel broken."

Mavis slipped an arm around her. "Look, come and stay with us for a while. Louis and me, we'll take care of you."

"I can't. I've got Clive. He's broken, too. He needs me. And Nico's mother. I have to keep going for them." She pulled away. "I should go and tell her the news right now. I can't put it off any longer."

"Well, you know where I am if you need me," Mavis said. "I'll come up and visit as much as I can. Help you take care of the house."

"You're such a good friend, Mavis." Ellie reached out to touch her hand. "I'm so glad I've got you. Please take care of yourself. I couldn't bear it if anything happened to you."

"Don't you worry, love. Those Germans need to keep Louis around to help fix their stupid motor cars. They even gave him some coffee the other day. So I'll be here, I promise."

She walked with Ellie to the road.

"I'd better get it over with," Ellie said. She gave Mavis a quick hug, then set off resolutely, heading straight for Nico's house. It seemed strange that she had never been in there before when she had become so comfortable with his presence at her own home.

"Come in, my dear," Nico's mother said and led her to a tiny, immaculate kitchen. Rows of pots hung above the stove. There was a marble-topped table. Madame Barbou invited her to sit, but Ellie shook her head.

"I'm afraid I've come with bad news," she said and told her the whole story.

The old woman didn't weep but shook her head. "I knew he was doing something brave. That was my boy. Always wanting to take a risk, and I knew he'd want to be involved against these invaders. At least he died doing something good. But I'm not sure how I'll go on without him."

"I feel the same way," Ellie said.

The old woman looked up at her. "He spoke about you all the time," she said. "He loved you."

"And I loved him," Ellie replied. "He asked me to take care of you if anything happened to him, and I want to do that. Will you come and live up at the villa with me and Clive? We've chickens and goats, vegetables and fruit. You won't starve, and you'll have company."

The old woman paused, looking around her kitchen. "I'd like that, my dear," she said. "This house feels very empty without him and my late husband. Two big men seemed to take up all the space. Now it's just me."

Ellie enlisted Clive to help carry Madame Barbou's possessions up the hill. She was most impressed with the villa. "I was here once, all those years ago," she said, nodding with approval. "Jeannette invited us, me and my husband. She was with child at the time and didn't want anyone to know. We were sworn to secrecy. She said she had consulted the priest, and he knew we wanted a child but God had not provided. So she offered us hers. We went up again to collect Nico after he was born. She wanted him called Nicolas, so we obliged. I don't know why that name was special to her. She did not elaborate. Poor woman. She did not want to give up her child, I could tell, but she didn't want to lose all that she had, either. But her loss was our blessing."

She was settled into Nico's room and taken around the garden to be introduced to the animals.

"I want to do my share," she said. "I'm not afraid of hard work."

Having something positive to do, being able to help someone else, made a small difference for Ellie. Now she'd have to be brave for Nico's mother's sake.

However, they were not to be left ignored. The next day German soldiers came back and took away the chickens and one of the goats as well as any spring vegetables that could be grabbed.

"We'll have a feast tonight, boys." Ellie thought she understood the German. "Good meat at last."

The goat they took was Hortense, Clive's favourite, and it hurt him almost as much as the loss of Tommy.

"Not Hortense," he kept saying. "How could they? They are devils. I'm praying they'll use her for milk, not meat, but I'm sure they'll roast her, the brutes. I hope she chokes them."

"We must hide the other two," Ellie said. "Take them up on the hill, out of sight, and tether them well away from the paths. We'll move the goats every day."

"Just let them take the others. Starving to death wouldn't be the worst way to go."

She put her hands on his shoulders. "You mustn't think like that. I am not going to give them the satisfaction of killing me. I will survive no matter what, and you must, too. You're an artist, Clive. Paint your feelings. I wish I could write poetry like Dora." She paused. "But I'm glad Dora isn't here right now. I hope she's looking down on us."

Clive gave a sad smile. "I'm glad you have such naïve beliefs," he said. "I can't believe there is anything after this. If you saw what I did in the trenches, when you hear what is happening now, how can you believe there is a God?"

"The abbot did," Ellie said. "He was quite confident. I hope he's looking down on us at this moment."

~~

Everyone in the village had learned of the death of Nico and the abbot. A Mass of the Resurrection was held for Nico. The church was packed. Ellie felt that she had to attend, as Nico's mother was deeply religious and insisted on going. "It's my son's soul we are praying for," she said. It was almost more than Ellie could bear to sit amongst the whole village and listen to a eulogy in which the priest praised Nico for his kindness and generosity. *I'll never see him again.* The words kept repeating in her head. It felt as if there were a great hole where her heart had once been. As they came out after Mass, Monsieur Danton drew Ellie aside.

"Nicolas came to me a while ago," he said. "He made a will. He's left everything to you on the condition that you look after his mother for the rest of her life. You're quite a rich woman."

Ellie stared at him. "As if that matters," she said. "What good is money any more when you lose the people you love?"

"That's true," he said. "But I wanted you to know that you don't have to worry about paying for the villa. It's yours now."

~

Life went on. The summer arrived with blistering heat that fried the most delicate plants. The goats survived on the hillside, in the shade of big pines. The villa remained delightfully cool with all the windows open for the breeze off the water. Ellie went down to the village most days. There was usually a small loaf of bread to be had, and the fishermen brought in their catch. The Germans oversaw the harbour and took the best of everything, but the local inhabitants were allowed to buy the rest. Ellie and Clive took to going down to the dock and fishing for themselves. They found shrimp and mussels in the rock pools and occasionally something bigger. The two cats, as if sensing that life had become harder and that meat no longer appeared on the table, took to catching things, depositing a mouse or a bird on the doorsteps in the mornings. Ellie found it touching, and didn't have the heart to tell them to stop.

The war news was encouraging. The Allies had landed in the south of Italy and were making progress northward. Then, in September 1943, the Italians surrendered. Germany poured soldiers into Italy to occupy it and stop the Allies' advance. There were bloody battles, but it seemed that small gains were being made on all fronts. Finally Germany was losing. News trickled in about death camps in the east of Europe, also about death and destruction nearer to home. The Nazi forces had rounded up hundreds of citizens of Marseille, mostly Jewish, and had destroyed the old town. Ellie and Clive worried constantly about Tommy. They had heard nothing and had no way of asking.

Just when Ellie was hopeful, the Allied advances seemed to have stalled. It was taking so long to inch forwards through Italy, as the Germans had dug in with lines of great bunkers. Whatever was happening, it made little difference to Saint-Benet. Everyone shared what little food they had. Those with smallholdings brought in extra crops and traded for fish. Clive's goat cheese and honey were traded for grapes and beans. This way, they kept going into the spring of 1944.

On June 6, the Allies landed on the Normandy beaches. Although news was hard to come by, it seemed as if the beginning of the end had come. A beautiful summer followed, with abundant crops, as if the earth itself were trying to make up for the suffering they were enduring.

And on August 15, the biggest feast day in the French calendar—the Feast of the Assumption of Mary—the American Seventh Army landed along the south coast of France. The German soldiers were pulled away from Saint-Benet, and everyone held their breath, waiting for good news. A week later the Free French army, with the help of the Americans, landed in Marseille. A fierce battle ensued that lasted several days. From Saint-Benet they could see smoke and hear distant explosions. But after three days of fighting, the Germans withdrew. Marseille was free. There was a great celebration in Saint-Benet as French troops came into the village. People brought out hidden bottles of wine, and there was music and dancing. Ellie, Clive and Madame Barbou sat off to one side, watching the joy but unable to join in and share it.

Will I ever be happy again? she asked herself. *Will I ever laugh? Have hope?* It still seemed impossible. But at least her neighbours were feeling their freedom. At least they could bring down the goats, who had survived remarkably well.

∽

It was September 29, the feast day of Saint Michael, reminding Ellie of that first celebration when they arrived in France. How different and foreign it had seemed, the women in their local dress and the dancing and laughing, the obvious enjoyment of life. So not British. All the things she now took for granted. She was sitting on the harbour wall, watching the revelry, when she looked up, froze. A naval vessel was approaching. Silence fell as everyone saw it coming. Then there was a collective sigh of relief when the American flag was spotted on it. It tied up at the harbour, and several American sailors stepped ashore.

"We've come at the right time, Joe," one called to the other. "There's a party going on. Come on. Let's join in."

More sailors followed. They were greeted warmly, hugged by the women, slapped on the back by the men and offered glasses of wine. Ellie had turned away from the boat to watch, but it was hard to take such revelry, so she stared back, out to sea. A lone man had left the boat and was coming towards her along the harbour. He walked with a slight limp, and his unruly hair was grey. She stared. Blinked. Stared again. Then she climbed over the harbour wall, not minding who saw her petticoat or her thighs, and she began to run. He spotted her and started to run, too. They fell into each other's arms.

"I don't believe it," she gasped. "Is it really you? Am I imagining it? Are you real?"

"Does this feel real?" he asked, and he kissed her.

They remained locked together, not noticing the other people who swarmed up to them. "It's Nico. Nico come back from the grave." The words echoed around the harbour.

"They said you were dead," she said, blinking back tears, when they finally broke apart. "That German officer said they shot you and the abbot in the water after they sank your boat."

"They did," he said. "A German gunboat fired a shell at the boat and blew up the petrol tank, hurling us both into the water. Then they circled back and shot both of us." He gave that cheeky, long-remembered grin. "A bullet went into my shoulder. Another into the abbot's chest. I decided to play dead. I floated face down until they had gone away. Then I went to see if there was anything I could do to save the abbot." He paused. Ellie steeled herself for bad news. "I located him nearby. He was still alive, but he was in a bad way, bleeding a lot. We were probably a couple of miles from the coast of Corsica. I could see it in the distance. So I started to swim with him. I didn't give us much chance, as I couldn't use one arm. I was bleeding, I wasn't sure exactly from where, but he was bleeding badly. But I kept going, and I suppose it was having the abbot with me, divine providence, you know, but at nightfall a fishing boat came out from Calvi and spotted us. Picked us up. Took us to a little village down the coast where they said we'd be safe from the Italian troops. There were members of the Resistance nearby, and they got the abbot up to a hospital. They patched me up, too. Turns out the bullet had gone clean through my shoulder, missed my heart by a centimetre. I'd also damaged my leg when they blew up our boat and I was thrown clear." Ellie squeezed his hand. He smiled at her. "God knows how I even managed to swim. Again it must have been the abbot, calling down divine assistance. We were hours in the water, both bleeding, but no sharks came near us."

He stopped, looking around at the crowd that had now gathered and spotting his mother.

"Maman." He ran to her with open arms and hugged her fiercely.

"My son! We thought we'd lost you," she sobbed.

"I tried to send a message," he said. "But the German navy patrolled this area so well it was impossible to get a boat through. The local Resistance tried sending radio messages to Marseille, but they must have broken up that cell and we got no answer. So I just had to wait it out and recover. It did take me several months."

"What of the abbot?" Ellie asked. "Did he survive? Do you know?"

"He did. They removed the bullet, and he was sent to a monastery up in the mountains to recover. He's still there until he can contact his motherhouse and come home."

"It's a double miracle," Nico's mother said. "Praise God. We must make a big donation to Saint Jude, because you were surely a lost cause."

"So go on with your story," someone called from the crowd.

Nico nodded. "And then the Italians surrendered, and all was good. They were hugging us and sharing their wine with us. I don't think any of them had wanted to fight in the first place. Then at last the Americans came, and here I am."

"Here you are," Ellie said.

"Come and join the feast, Nico." One of the fishermen put an arm around his shoulder.

"Thank you, but right now I'd just like to go home," he said.

"Your mother is living with me up at the villa," Ellie said. "Can you make it up the steps?"

"I'll give it a damned good try," he said.

He put one arm around Ellie and the other around his mother, and together they walked away from the harbour.

CHAPTER 44

Nico and Ellie climbed the hill to the villa together with his mother.

"What will your husband say about my coming here to live?" he asked.

"Poor Mr Tommy was taken away by the Germans and is probably in a prison camp," she said. "The viscount betrayed all of us, I'm afraid. You, the abbot and Mr Tommy."

"The nasty little rat," Nico said. "Where is he? I'll knock his head off."

"He went back to Paris when I threw him out. He did it because he hates Jews, and he thought he could parlay his way back into his château. So naïve."

"Let's hope that destiny meets up with him in Paris," Nico said. "So they took Mr Tommy. How lucky they didn't take you, too."

She nodded. "Tommy kept insisting that Clive and I were innocent and knew nothing. He probably did this under torture. He saved us, Nico. We don't even know where he is or if he's still alive."

"Poor man." Nico paused on the steps, looking down at the village. "So much suffering."

"But you're here. And the Germans have retreated. That's all that matters at this moment," Ellie said.

Nico stepped through the gate into the garden and stared at the villa. "I never thought I'd be happy to return to this place," he said. "I was so bitter, all those years. But I had a lot of time to think, and I understand now that I had the best childhood possible, running around barefoot, swimming, helping my dad on the boat. If I'd stayed with my real mother, I would have been dragged around from place to place while she performed or left somewhere with a nanny. And who would have wanted to be part of that world?"

He looked across at his mother. "And I had the best parents a boy could have. Taught me everything. Cared about me." He put an arm around his mother and hugged her to him.

Clive had not attended the feast. He told Ellie he couldn't be present where other people were happy. Ellie quite understood. She had felt the same way. He came out of the house, hearing voices, then stopped and stared in amazement. "Nico? How is this possible? So there are miracles after all. I can go on hoping that Tommy will come back to us."

That night, after dinner, when Nico headed for Ellie's bedroom with her, his mother stopped him. "Where do you think you are going? That's not the right thing to do, my son. You might be fond of her, but you are not married to her."

Nico looked at Ellie and winked. She blushed.

"But Mama, officially she's still married to Mr Tommy," he said. "Even if it was just a marriage on paper to give her an identity card. We have to hope he is still alive."

"But it's a sin," Madame Barbou insisted. "What would Father André say?"

"He'd say it was a miracle that I returned to you. And I'll go to confession if you like, but tonight I am going to be with the woman I love." He took Ellie's hand, led her into the bedroom and closed the door firmly behind them.

∼∽

Now that Marseille was in the hands of the Free French army, Ellie went with Clive and managed to speak to the Red Cross, asking for news about Tommy. They were able to find out that he was at a camp called Natzweiler-Struthof, in the Vosges Mountains in the annexed territory of Alsace. Not one of the worst, according to the Red Cross. Not known as a death camp, and mainly for French civilians. So there was hope. They immediately made a package of nourishing foods for him and asked for the Red Cross to deliver it. Over a month later they received a letter from Tommy, heavily censored. They read it and cried. He was alive. Able to write.

Nico settled back into life at home. One day he walked through the grounds with Ellie and noticed the lock on his shed was broken.

"Did the Germans search my shed?" he asked.

"They did," she replied. "At least they opened it. I told them a local fisherman kept his tackle there. They smelled the fishy stink, saw the nets and lines and went away again."

"You were lucky they didn't search more." He went into the shed and pulled aside the pile of fishing nets. Underneath he unearthed a box of rifles and another of grenades.

Ellie recoiled in horror. "We might have been blown to kingdom come," she said.

"Worse still, you'd surely have been carted off to the Gestapo and deemed to be with the Resistance if they'd found these. I worried about this a lot when I lay there in Corsica. And your car?"

"Is now back in the garage, thank you. They never found it. We hid it well."

The sound of loud bleating made him look over at the pen. He smiled. "And what's this? Baby goats? That's good. All is well again."

All seemed to be getting better by the day. The Allies had landed in Normandy the previous June and pushed up through Italy. The south coast of France returned to its previous peaceful state. But all was not well. Further attempts to send Tommy a package through the Red Cross were not successful. And then the news trickled through: the occupants of that camp in the Vosges had been moved to a camp in Eastern Europe as the Allies approached. A camp called Auschwitz. It was much later that they found that Tommy had not survived the transport there. Clive gave a great wail of anguish.

"I think I knew all the time that I'd never see him again. Oh my poor sweet, kind Tommy. How could they do this to him?"

"I'm so sorry, dearest Clive." Ellie attempted to hug him, but he pushed her away.

"Where will I go?" he asked. "What will I do?" He looked around him. "I can't stay here. There is nothing for me now." In spite of Ellie's entreaties, he went back to the house he had shared with Tommy. He wanted to be in the place where they had been happy together. Ellie urged him to take his goat and some chickens with him, but he refused.

"You can't give up now, Clive," Ellie said. "Not when we've endured so much. Tommy wouldn't have wanted you to. Keep painting. You have great talent. Paint a memorial to a brave man whom I loved, too."

He held her then, and they cried in each other's arms. He did take the cat Minou with him, and Tiger walked around the house complaining bitterly.

After Tommy's death was confirmed, Ellie and Nico waited a while before they were married. "It's not the right moment," she said. "We are in mourning for a wonderful man. Such a brave man. I will treasure him forever."

"I agree," Nico said, "but I have grown tired of my mother making me go to confession because we are sharing a sinful bed."

Ellie looked at him tenderly. "After what the world has just been through, do you think the fact that we love each other counts as sin?"

"Of course not, but you know my mother. Old-school Catholic. Confession every time you have an impure thought."

"I bet you had to go to confession a lot when you were younger, then," she teased.

He wrapped his arms around her. "I love you so much," he said. "I never believed I could be happy again, and now I am."

"So am I," she said. "All right, then. I'll marry you as soon as you want. But shouldn't we wait until the war is officially over? I know the end is in sight and the Germans are gone from here, but we have to remember that there are still people in camps as Tommy was, still waiting to be liberated, and so many people displaced from their homes."

Nico nodded, considering this. "You're right. We'll get married, but it should only be a small ceremony, as we are still in mourning for Mr Tommy, and Hitler has not yet surrendered."

She went down to tell Mavis the news and ask if she and Louis would stand as witnesses for them.

Mavis looked at her in disbelief. "A small ceremony with just two witnesses? Are you barmy? What we all need now is a chance to celebrate something. Look how many people in the village have lost a relative or friend. We should learn to be happy again—" She broke off. "I've been happy. I've got the best man you could want. And now you have, too, even though I thought he was a pirate to start with."

Ellie laughed. "So you think we should have a proper wedding, then? Invite everybody?"

Mavis nodded. "I do."

"But shouldn't we wait until the Germans have surrendered and the war is officially over?"

"Who knows how long that will take? They are stubborn and proud, those Germans. They might keep fighting even though they can't win. I say let's be happy now." She frowned. "Too bad there won't be any fabric in the stores. I'd like to make you a wedding dress."

"We can raid Jeannette's wardrobe again," she said. *My mother-in-law,* she thought, toying with the words and the ridiculousness of this. Maybe one day she'd tell Mavis.

"Righty-oh, then," Mavis said. "Let's come up and have a look."

They went through the ballgowns, and Mavis decided on a pale-blue silk.

"There's enough in that skirt to make you a simple dress," she said. "They are wearing everything short these days, aren't they?"

"Help yourself to anything you can use for yourself," Ellie said.

"Me? I've got my own wedding outfit that I haven't had a chance to wear since," Mavis said.

∼∽

The invitations went out. The dress was made, and Ellie and Nico were married in a simple ceremony. Somehow enough wine was found for everyone, and Madame Blanchet managed to make a cake, although she complained about the lack of butter and eggs. As the toasts were raised, Nico stood up. "I would like everyone to raise your glasses to a brave man who gave his life for my wife and me. To Mr Tommy."

Glasses were raised. To Mr Tommy. The words echoed in the clear air. Clive brushed away a tear. Ellie knew how hard it must have been for him to attend any celebration and that he had only come because of his fondness for her.

"I'm so glad to see you happy at last," Mavis said. "Who'd have thought, when we set off all those years ago, that we'd find the place where we belonged right here?"

∼∽

The Germans surrendered. The war was officially over, and Saint-Benet held a party. The street was decorated with bunting and balloons and flowers. Flags flew from all the boats in the harbour. A band played. People hugged each other. Then, as everyone sat at long tables, Monsieur Danton called for silence and got up to speak.

"I was about to raise a toast to the citizens of Saint-Benet, for their courage and endurance and the part they played in defeating the enemy, but I have received a communication from the new government, asking us to name and shame those who collaborated with the enemy."

"Madame Adams." One of the women stood up, pointing a finger at her. "She was one. She was friendly with those Germans."

"They were forced upon me." Mrs Adams spat out the words, her face bright red. "I had no choice. I was told to house and feed them. What could I do? A woman alone with no man to protect her?"

"Yes, and you didn't do badly from it, did you?" the woman snapped. "We could smell the coffee and the meat that you cooked for them."

"So they gave me coffee and meat to cook for them," Mrs Adams retorted. "I couldn't refuse to cook it, could I? They could have shot me."

"My brothers and sisters, calm yourselves." Father André stepped in front of them, raising his hands. "I think we must agree that Madame Adams had no choice in the matter. We all saw how the soldiers threw their weight around, how they robbed us of all our foodstuffs and tools. And this poor woman had to survive alone, with her husband gone and presumably dead. She did what she could to survive, as we all did. Now is a time for forgiveness, as our Lord would want us to forgive."

"But what about Giselle Blanchet?" one of the young men shouted out. "She collaborated. She went with German soldiers."

Giselle screamed as hands grabbed her and dragged her forwards to stand in front of Monsieur Danton. "Here she is, the slut, the whore. What should we do with her? Hang her from the flagpole?" Voices echoed around the square.

"No," Giselle screamed. "It wasn't like that. I really loved Wolfgang. He was a nice person. He didn't want to fight. He wanted to marry me."

Monsieur Danton hesitated. "This girl doesn't deserve to die," he said.

"She's a sinner if ever there was one, Father. She needs to be punished, taught a lesson," someone shouted from the crowd.

Then a woman screeched, "Shave her head. Let the world see her for the traitor and whore she is."

And in spite of Father André's pleas, someone rushed away and returned with clippers. Madame Blanchet shouted in protest. Giselle struggled as they attempted to hold her down. Ellie glanced at Nico and nudged him.

"Make them stop," she said.

Nico stood up, roaring, "Enough! Stop this nonsense."

He stepped out, grabbed a man by the collar and jerked him away from the girl. "We are civilized people. We will not behave as our oppressors behaved. You should be ashamed of yourselves. She's a young girl who was attracted to a young man. What is so wrong with that? There was only one traitor in Saint-Benet, and that was the viscount who betrayed us and is responsible for the death of our beloved Mr Tommy. He better not show his face here again, or I will be the first to press charges or to strangle him with my bare hands."

"The viscount." The words echoed around the square.

"And now, enough drama," Nico shouted. "Let us get on with celebrating."

There were cheers, and glasses were raised in a toast. Madame Blanchet came over to Ellie and Nico. "I can't thank you enough for saving my daughter," she said. "I warned her. I tried to talk to her, but she wouldn't listen. She was flattered that a German boy liked her. Now let us hope she will settle down and get some sense into her head."

The party went on until the first streaks of dawn appeared in the sky.

"Now perhaps we can finally go back to enjoying life," Nico said as they walked home.

～

Visitors started to return, as did Mr Adams. He had spent the war in Gibraltar, having been taken from Corsica to the coast of Spain and then making his way south. But he said he had not suffered as they had. Life in the British enclave had not been unpleasant. There were plays and Gilbert and Sullivan, bangers and mash and English beer. Mrs Adams did not seem overly pleased to see him back, especially as this was a new and confident Mr Adams who was clearly going to be the boss. Ellie thought about Mrs Adams. She had never warmed to her or really understood her from the first day they had met. The sort of woman who is a survivor, she realized. She did not consider right and wrong, just what was best for her at a particular moment. Ellie realized how easily Mrs Adams could have turned them in if they hadn't helped her own husband.

The viscount did not return. A little later they learned that the château had been sold to a film director. There was excitement about this and the hope of seeing movie stars in Saint-Benet.

As soon as postal contact had been restored with England, Ellie wrote to Lionel asking about their sons. She wrote a brief, factual note saying that she had survived the war and life was returning to normal. A brief, impersonal letter arrived back saying that Richard was still stationed out in the Far East but was well and had been promoted to major. Colin had been demobbed from the RAF and returned to his bank. Here were the latest addresses for both of them. Before Ellie could write to her sons, she received a letter from each of them. Richard hoped she was well and looked forward to visiting when he returned from the Far East. Colin wrote a longer letter. He had survived flying four years of Spitfires before being put on to training new recruits. He had also met a young lady and hoped to bring her out to meet his mother when travel was reestablished. *She's from a good family, you'll be pleased to know. Her father is a vicar, so quite holy! And she was jolly brave in the WRAF.* Ellie treasured the letter, looking forward to a future wedding, grandchildren, hope for the future.

Thinking of grandchildren made Ellie's thoughts turn to Jojo. Recently the little girl hadn't plagued Ellie's dreams so often, with so many other worries. But now she felt she had to know. She talked to Nico about it. "Do you think we have any way of finding out whether she's all right? I've worried about her so much."

"I suppose we can make enquiries," he said, "although everything is still so chaotic that I doubt records are up to date. What was the mother's name?"

"Yvette," Ellie started to say, then shook her head. "It's probably useless. I don't even think she gave us her real name. All I know is that the man she was with was called Ali, and he was a bad lot. Someone in the police somewhere in France will know about him."

"Someone, somewhere in France. And he's called Ali. That gives me a lot to go on," Nico said with a wry smile.

Ellie sighed. "I know. It's hopeless. But I'd just like to know Jojo is safe and well."

"We'll do our best," Nico said. "But she is with her mother. And not all mothers are perfect, as I can attest. But the mother has her rights."

"I know," Ellie said. "I just want to know, that's all."

They spoke to the police in Marseille, but they were not helpful, saying, "If you don't know a last name, really we have no chance. And we have so many missing persons to trace right now."

Then, when Ellie had given up hope, she received a letter:

Dear Madame Ellie,

I'm sure you are surprised to hear from me, but I felt I had to write to you. It took a long while for me to realize how very kind you were to me, how you took me in, a complete stranger, and believed in me when I was lying to you all the time and using you for my own ends. Now I feel so bad. When you met me I was not running away from home. I was fleeing from the police. They rounded up our gang, but I managed to escape. I saw your face at that garage, and you looked kind. Without your help, I don't know what would have happened to me. I would have had my baby in prison, and she would have been taken from me. So you saved both of us.

It has taken me all this time to see what a fool I was. I met Pierre. He was handsome, and he flashed money around. I was from a poor home with a dismal future ahead and was immediately seduced by him. When I found out that he was in with a group of bad men, it was too late. Ali came for me to make sure I did not talk to the police or give anyone away.

He was very evil. At last the police caught up with him, and he is now in jail for many years. So I had a chance to take Jojo and go to an aunt, where we live today. Jojo is a lovely little girl, so pretty, so clever. You would be proud of her. And I am working hard to give her a good life.

I said once that you were an angel, and it's true. You were.

A thousand thanks,

Your Jeanne-Marie (not Yvette)

CHAPTER 45

Nico started fishing again. He told Ellie he wasn't good at doing nothing and missed the sea. He also bought a new speedboat, expecting the return of summer visitors, and demonstrated it to Ellie. "What do you think? Better than the last one?"

"Do you think we could go over to the island?" she asked. "I wonder if the abbot is back there yet? Don't you think he would have written to us? I do hope he survived and regained his strength."

"At least the monks will know," Nico said. He turned the boat towards the island, and they sped forward. As they came up the steps, a monk threw down his gardening rake and hurried towards them.

"What do you want here?" he called. "No visitors except on the first Sunday of the month."

"We've come to see the abbot," Ellie said. "Abbot Gerard?"

The monk shook his head. "It is now Abbot Bernard," he said.

"What happened to your last abbot?" Nico asked.

"We heard he almost died and was very sick. Abbot Bernard will know more. Was Abbot Gerard a relative?"

"A dear friend," Ellie said.

"Ah. I see. Please follow me."

He hadn't gone far when they saw a large man striding towards them. He had a round, bald head and an impressive paunch under his black habit. "What is this, Brother Matthieu? Who are these people?"

"Visitors asking about Abbot Gerard, Father Abbot."

The big man reached them, staring at them with such dislike that Ellie shrank closer to Nico.

"We were good friends of Abbot Gerard," she said. "My husband and Abbot Gerard were part of a team that transported Jewish men to safety. Nicolas and the abbot were both shot and left for dead, but Nicolas managed to bring them both to shore in Corsica, as I'm sure you've heard."

"I did hear and do not approve. His reckless acts put the whole abbey at risk," he said.

Ellie wanted to say that his acts saved some good men and she was sure Jesus would have approved, but she swallowed back the words. "Do you know where he is now?" Ellie asked. "We should like to write to him."

"When I last heard, he had been transported to the motherhouse. They will know. Now, it is almost time for Compline. I bid you good day. Show these people back to their boat, brother, and please do not disturb our peace again."

"I hope the monks appreciate what they have now," Nico said as he helped Ellie back into the boat. Ellie looked back at the island as they sped away. She would now never need to go there again.

They returned home and Ellie wrote to the motherhouse. She received a reply almost immediately:

> My dear Ellie,
> I can't tell you what a joy it was to receive your letter and to know that you and Nico are well and happy. He talked of you so frequently when we lay in hospital. I could see how fond he was of you. I, too, thought of you often and prayed for you daily. I have finally recovered enough to return to my order, although not to my former position. It is thought that I would lack the stamina to run the show, as they say. Instead they want me to stay on here as librarian, a

quiet and peaceful existence until one day I am back to full strength.

However . . . that is not what I want. I have shut myself away from the world for long enough. I began to see, when I lay in the hospital bed, that I had been called to the priesthood not to make liqueurs and minister to pious young men but to make the world a better place. So at the end of the month I am leaving the order and volunteering as a priest at a refugee camp in Germany. It's in a former concentration camp. Other volunteers are already planting flowers and trees, painting the buildings, to make it a welcoming place for those who have nowhere to go.

I hope you might visit us sometime. I will continue to pray for you both.

Your friend,

Gerard

Ellie held the letter to her and fought back tears.

"You cared about him, didn't you?" Nico asked.

"Very much. I always thought he was the sort of man I'd like to have married. Gentle, studious, good sense of humour . . ."

"Instead you married a loud fisherman." Nico laughed.

"And I have no regrets," she said.

~~

Mr Tommy was finally honoured in a ceremony in Marseille along with Nico and other freedom fighters and posthumously given a Croix de Guerre by the French government. The ceremony was held on a brisk and breezy day in March on the waterfront. A bell was rung as each name was called and flowers were placed on the memorial. Clive went up to lay flowers for Tommy, a proud, defiant look on his face. He told Ellie he had started painting again—big, dark, swirling canvases that were getting a lot of attention. One of his canvases was chosen to be hung in the newly renovated cathedral. After the ceremony, at which he received Tommy's medals, he moved away to join an artist's colony down the coast. "I'll miss you," he said as he hugged Ellie. "You've been a sister to me. But I have to be brave enough to start a new life."

Ellie hugged him, promising to come and visit soon.

Madame Barbou had gone down to the village to visit friends, and Ellie was alone in the house one day when she was alerted by a motor horn. She went outside to see the gate being opened and a taxi there. The driver poked his head out of the window.

"Visitor for Villa Gloriosa," he said. "This is it?"

"It is." Ellie waited. A man got out of the taxi. He was bald, with sagging cheeks, and walked with a stooping gait.

"Lionel?" Ellie called as she recognized him. "What a surprise. What are you doing here? You hate abroad, remember?"

"I came to see how you were, if you were all right," he said. He looked around him. "I was concerned about you, Ellie."

"I'm doing very well, thank you," Ellie replied, watching him walk towards her.

He looked around. "Colin said you lived in an impressive house, and you certainly do."

"Come inside," she said. "Are you planning to stay nearby or just passing through?"

"I'm not sure yet," he said. "I took the train to Marseille. Horrible place. Dirty. Full of foreigners."

Ellie tried not to smile. They reached the villa, and she opened the door for him to enter the foyer.

"I must say you're looking awfully well, Ellie," he said. "Obviously, you had it much better than we did in England. Bombed night and day."

"I hardly think the Germans would have wasted their bombs on Surrey," Ellie said.

"Well, not as bad as London, obviously, but the occasional one fell not too far away. And rationing, of course. We're still rationed, you know. Tiny portion of meat for a week. Haven't seen a banana in years. Can't get my decent Scotch. It's been hell. But I suppose you were nicely out of it down here."

"We had our share," she said.

She installed him in the sitting room and went to make him a glass of fresh lemonade. When she came back, she found him out on the terrace, looking out across the bay.

"This view is magnificent. How can you afford to rent something like this? Your monthly allowance wasn't that big."

"No, it wasn't," she said. "Luckily I don't need to pay rent any more because I own it."

"How can that be?" he asked. "Did you sell the London flat?"

"I didn't need to," she said. "I just heard from my solicitor in England, and the rent has been accumulating nicely during the war years. I'm going to use it to buy a couple of properties here. There will be more need for tourism now."

"Ellie." He said the word firmly, making her stop and look at him. "Are you really happy here? In this place? With these people? How can you want to live amongst foreigners?" He took a deep breath. "Ellie, I really came to bring you home. I want you back. I miss you. Goddammit, it's never been the same since you went away. Nothing was ever right."

"What about Michelle?" she asked.

"There is no more Michelle," he said. "She got bored with me quite quickly, I think. Anyway, she met a Yank and she's gone off to America with him. It never really worked. She was useless as a housekeeper, didn't know how to cook properly. Lots of foreign muck like spaghetti. The place was a mess, and I was always in a bad mood because I could never find anything. I realize now that I made a big mistake in marrying her. I suppose I was flattered that such a bright young thing could be interested in me."

"There was supposed to be a baby," Ellie said.

Rhys Bowen

"Ah yes. The baby. She made a mistake. She never was very regular, she said, so she jumped to conclusions."

"She jumped at the chance to marry someone rich, Lionel," Ellie replied.

"Anyway, it was a mistake, and I let you down. I don't think I can forgive myself. So what do you say, Ellie? Shall we give it another chance? You could keep on this place for summer holidays if you like. I wouldn't mind if you went away for a month."

Ellie gave him a sweet smile. "I'm sorry, Lionel. But I like it here. I'm happy here. And besides, I'm already married."

"You married a Frenchman?"

"I did," she said.

"This is his villa, then?"

"It is."

"Ah. So he's an aristocrat. Not a local person."

"He's both. He's the son of a duke but was raised by a fisherman. His father is dead, but his mother lives here with us. And before you ask, we are very happy." She looked up as she heard steps coming up from the dock. "Ah. Here he is now."

Nico emerged from the steps on to the terrace. His hair was windswept, he was wearing old blue denims, and he was carrying a large ray. "Look what I caught," he called out. "We'll be feasting tonight." He stopped when he saw the visitor.

"This is my former husband," she said in French, then added in English. "Lionel, I'd like you to meet Nicolas Barbou, my husband."

Nico went to shake hands, then realized he was still holding a fish. "How do you do?" he said in English. "Welcome to our home."

"Well, thank you," Lionel replied in a clipped voice. "Nice place you have here."

"That is because my wife made it beautiful like this," Nico replied, giving Ellie a beaming smile. "She made this house into what you see."

"I did," Ellie agreed. "It was a ruin when I took it over. It's been a labour of love."

382

"You always did have the knack of making a place beautiful," Lionel said. "Our home always looked just perfect."

"So will you stay the night, Lionel?" Ellie asked. "I can make up a bed for you in the guest room."

"No, thank you," he replied stiffly. "I should be getting back, then. Damn. I let that taxi go. Do you have a way of calling another?"

"We can drive you into Marseille," Ellie said, "Or better still, Nico can take you in the speedboat. It's a lovely ride." She switched to French in case he hadn't understood.

He nodded. "D'accord."

"Well, that's jolly kind of you," Lionel said.

"Are you sure you don't want to stay in the village?" Ellie asked. "There's a nice little pension run by English people, and the bar cooks good food."

"Presumably laden with garlic," Lionel said. "No, I think I'll be going back, then. It was foolish of me to come. I should have realized an attractive woman like you would be snapped up. My mistake. I'll be regretting it for the rest of my life."

"Look, at least stay and have a meal with us," Ellie said. "Lunch on the terrace. I'll make sure there's no garlic."

"No. I ought to go. Too painful," he said. "I suppose it's gradually dawning on me what lies ahead. It was bad enough during the war, but now that Michelle has gone, I'm rattling around in that big house. You can't get household help for love or money. Nobody wants that sort of job since the war. I eat in the club most of the time, but I'm sixty-two. Going to retire soon. And then what? What on earth will I do with myself?"

"I've got a nice little flat in Knightsbridge," Ellie said. "If my tenant moves out, you can use that. It's only one bedroom, but you won't be entertaining much, will you? And it's quite convenient for Harrods."

She saw him wince as he remembered the wording he had used for her, and immediately felt bad. "Come on, Lionel. I'll walk with you down to the boat. Nico has a lovely new speedboat at our dock."

He followed her gingerly down the steps to the little harbour below. The new boat bobbed at its mooring, its polished teak gleaming in the sunlight. Nico helped him climb in.

"Are you coming, too?" Lionel asked.

"No, I think I'll leave you men to it," Ellie said.

"Why don't you take him instead?" Nico asked her in French, pausing on the quayside, giving her a knowing grin. "Show him how well it handles."

"All right." Ellie returned the smile, accepted the challenge and clambered aboard.

Lionel looked at her, then at Nico on the dock, as the latter started to unwind the ropes. "Your husband is not coming?"

"No. He thinks it's better that I drive you."

"You? You know how to handle a speedboat like this? Are you sure? Are you qualified to do it?"

"Oh yes, Lionel," she replied. "You'd be amazed at the things I can do now. So hold on tight." She steered the boat away from its mooring into open sea, then she pulled back to full throttle. The boat surged forwards with a roar, flinging Lionel against his seat. Ellie allowed herself a big smile.

EPILOGUE

Ellie and Mavis sat together on the terrace outside the Villa Gloriosa. It was the anniversary of Dora's death, and Ellie had opened a bottle of champagne to toast her.

"I never thought I'd take to her," Mavis said. "Bossy old cow back in England, wasn't she?"

"She softened up a lot, when she got here and she knew we cared about her," Ellie replied.

"She certainly did. She loved every minute of it here, didn't she? Remember how she went swimming? She was fearless." She paused. "Unlike me. I've never learned to like the water. Luckily, Louis doesn't, either." She looked at Ellie. "I'd say we've done quite well for ourselves, wouldn't you? Who would have thought, when we set out in Lionel's Bentley all those years ago, that we'd find a whole new life here, good men and happiness?"

"I know," Ellie said. "Sometimes I still can't quite believe it myself. We dared to take the first step, Mavis, and that's why it worked out for us. How easy it would have been to retreat to a dismal cottage in England and feel sorry for ourselves for the rest of our lives. Instead we've had a great adventure."

"We certainly have," Mavis agreed.

Ellie poured champagne and handed Mavis a glass. "To Dora," she said.

Mavis raised her glass. "And to us."

AUTHOR'S NOTE

Saint-Benet is a fictional town, but anyone who knows the south coast of France might recognize it as Cassis, as it might have been before WWII—a simple fishing village.

ABOUT THE AUTHOR

Photo © Douglas Sonders

Rhys Bowen is the *New York Times* bestselling author of more than sixty novels, including *The Rose Arbor, The Paris Assignment, Where the Sky Begins, The Venice Sketchbook, Above the Bay of Angels, The Victory Garden, The Tuscan Child,* and *In Farleigh Field,* the winner of the Lefty Award for Best Historical Mystery Novel and the Agatha Award for Best Historical Novel. She is also the author of the Royal Spyness mysteries and several other series. Bowen's work has been translated into many languages and has won sixteen honors to date, including multiple Agatha, Anthony, and Macavity Awards. A transplanted Brit, Bowen divides her time between California and Arizona. For more information, visit www.rhysbowen.com.